SOLDIERS THREE and IN BLACK AND WHITE

Rudyard Joseph Kipling was born in Bombay in 1865. His father, John Lockwood Kipling, was the author and illustrator of *Beast and Man in India*, and his mother, Alice, was the sister of Lady Burne-Jones. In 1871 Kipling was brought home from India and spent five unhappy years with a foster family in Southsea, an experience he later drew on in *The Light That Failed* (1890). The years he spent at the United Services College, a school for officers' children, are depicted in *Stalky and Co.* (1899) and the character of Beetle is something of a self-portrait. It was during his time at the college that he began writing poetry and *Schoolboy Lyrics* was published privately in 1881. In the following year he started work as a journalist in India, and while there produced a body of work, stories, sketches and poems – notably *Plain Tales from the Hills* (1888) – which made him an instant literary celebrity when he returned to England in 1889. *Barrack-Room Ballads* (1892) contains some of his most popular pieces, including 'Mandalay', 'Gunga Din' and 'Danny Deever'. In this collection Kipling experimented with form and dialect, notably the cockney accent of the soldier poems, but the influence of hymns, music-hall songs, ballads and public poetry can be found throughout his verse.

In 1892 he married an American, Caroline Balestier, and from 1892 to 1896 they lived in Vermont, where Kipling wrote *The Jungle Book*, published in 1894. In 1901 came *Kim* and in 1902 the *Just So Stories*. Tales of every kind – including historical and science fiction – continued to flow from his pen, but *Kim* is generally thought to be his greatest long work, putting him high among the chroniclers of British expansion.

From 1902 Kipling made his home in Sussex, but he continued to travel widely and caught his first glimpse of warfare in South Africa, where he wrote some excellent reportage on the Boer War. However, many of the views he expresed were rejected by anti-imperialists who accused him of jingoism and love of violence. Though rich and successful, he never again enjoyed the literary esteem of his early years. With the onset of the Great War his work became a great deal more sombre. The stories he subsequently wrote, *A Diversity of Creatures* (1917), *Debits and Credits* (1926) and *Limits and Renewals* (1932), are now thoug[illegible] death of his only son in 1915 also contributed to a new inwardness of vision.

Kipling refused to accept the role of Poet Laureate and other civil honours, but he was the first English writer to be awarded the Nobel Prize, in 1907. He died in 1936 and his autobiographical fragment *Something of Myself* was published the following year.

Salman Rushdie is author of the novels *Grimus*, *Midnight's Children* (winner of the 1981 Booker Prize, the James Tait Black Memorial Prize and the English-Speaking Union Literary Award), *Shame* (winner of the Prix du Meilleur Livre Etranger) and *The Satanic Verses* (winner of the 1988 Whitbread Award for Best Novel); of *Haroun and the Sea of Stories* (winner of the 1991 Writers' Guild Best Children's Book Award); *The Jaguar Smile: A Nicaraguan Journey*; and of the television films *The Riddle of Midnight* and *The Painter and the Pest*. His books have been translated into twenty languages.

Rudyard Kipling

SOLDIERS THREE
and
IN BLACK AND WHITE

PENGUIN BOOKS

PENGUIN BOOKS

Published by the Penguin Group
Penguin Books Ltd, 27 Wrights Lane, London W8 5TZ, England
Penguin Books USA Inc., 375 Hudson Street, New York, New York 10014, USA
Penguin Books Australia Ltd, Ringwood, Victoria, Australia
Penguin Books Canada Ltd, 10 Alcorn Avenue, Toronto, Ontario, Canada M4V 3B2
Penguin Books (NZ) Ltd, 182–190 Wairau Road, Auckland 10, New Zealand

Penguin Books Ltd, Registered Offices: Harmondsworth, Middlesex, England

This edition first published 1993
1 3 5 7 9 10 8 6 4 2

Set in 10/12 pt Monophoto Ehrhardt
Typeset by Datix International Limited, Bungay, Suffolk
Printed in England by Clays Ltd, St Ives plc

Contents

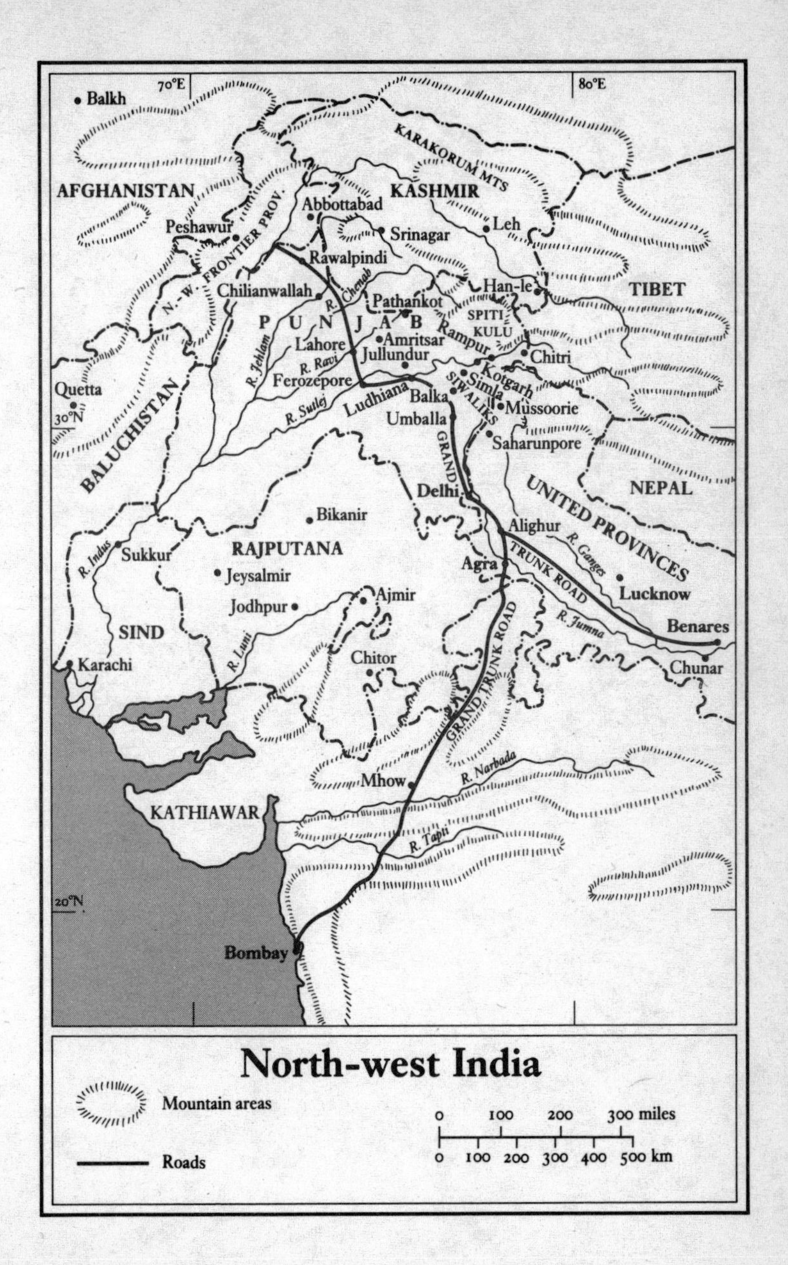

North-west India

Introduction by Salman Rushdie

In Luis Buñuel's last film, *Cet obscur objet de désir*, the heroine was played by two actresses, one cool and poised, the other fiery and sensual. The two women looked utterly dissimilar, yet it was not uncommon for people to watch the entire movie without noticing the device. Their need to believe in the homogeneity of personality was so deeply rooted as to make them discount the evidence of their own eyes.

I once thought of borrowing Buñuel's idea for a TV programme about Rudyard Kipling. I wanted him to be played by an Indian actor as well as an English one, to speak Hindi in some scenes and English in others. After all, when the child Rudyard was admitted to his parents' presence, the servants would have to remind him to 'speak English now to Mama and Papa'. The influence of India on Kipling – on his picture of the world as well as his language – resulted in what has always struck me as a personality in conflict with itself, part bazaar-boy, part sahib. In the early Indian stories, such as the ones in this volume, that conflict is to be found everywhere, and Kipling does not always seem fully conscious of it. (By the time he wrote *Kim*, twelve years later, his control had grown. But Kim's torn loyalties have never seemed as interesting to me as the ambiguous, shifting relationships between the Indians and the English in, for example, the story collected here entitled 'On the City Wall'.)

The early Kipling is a writer with a storm inside him, and he creates a mirror-storm of contradictory responses in the reader, particularly, I think, if the reader is Indian. I have never been able to read Kipling calmly. Anger and delight are incompatible emotions, yet the stories in this volume do indeed have the power simultaneously to infuriate and to entrance.

Kipling's racial bigotry is often excused on the grounds that he merely reflected in his writing the attitudes of his age. It's hard for members of the allegedly inferior race to accept such an excuse.

Ought we to exculpate anti-Semites in Nazi Germany on the same grounds? If Kipling had maintained any sort of distance between himself and the attitudes he recorded, it would be a different matter. But, as story after story in this volume makes plain, the author's attitudes – the attitudes, that is, of Kipling as played by the English actor – are identical with those of his white characters. The Indians he portrays are wife-killers ('Dray Wara Yow Dee'), 'scamps' ('At Howli Thana'), betrayers of their own brothers ('Gemini'), unfaithful wives ('At Twenty-Two') and the like. Even the Eurasian Mrs DeSussa in 'Private Learoyd's Story' is a fat figure of fun. Indians bribe witnesses, desert their political leaders, and are gullible, too: 'Overmuch tenderness . . . has bred a strong belief among many natives that the native is capable of administering the country'. Mr Kipling knows better. 'It [India] will never stand alone' (p. 155).

But there is the Indian actor, too; Ruddy Baba as well as Kipling Sahib. And it is on account of this fellow that Kipling remains so popular in India. This popularity looks like, and indeed is, an extraordinary piece of cultural generosity. But it is real. No other Western writer has ever known India as Kipling knew it, and it is this knowledge of place, and procedure, and detail that gives his stories their undeniable authority. The plot of 'Black Jack' turns on the operational differences between two different kinds of rifle; while the story 'In Flood Time' owes its quality to Kipling's precise and magnificent description of a swollen river in the monsoon rains. Nor could he have created the salon of the courtesan Lalun in 'On the City Wall' had he not been a regular visitor to such establishments himself.

Not all the stories in this collection have stood the test of time – 'The Sending of Dana Da' seems particularly flimsy – but all of them are packed with information about a lost world. It used to be said that one read in order to learn something, and nobody can teach you British India better than Rudyard Kipling.

These stories are, above all, experiments in voice. In *Soldiers Three*, Kipling has sought to give voice to the ordinary British soldier whom he admired so much. (The original version of the first story, 'The God from the Machine', was published in the Indian Railway Library edition with a dedication to 'that very strong man,

T. ATKINS . . . in all admiration and goodfellowship'.) How well he has succeeded is open to dispute.

There can be no doubt that he knew his characters inside out, and that, by abandoning the world of the officer classes in favour of the view from the ranks, he opened up a unique subculture that would otherwise have been very largely lost to literature; nor that many of these stories are very good indeed. 'The Big Drunk Draf'', in which a company of men on their way to board the ship for England nearly turns upon its young officer, but is thwarted by the wiles of Terence Mulvaney and the courage of the officer himself, is one such splendid tale; while 'Black Jack', which tells of a murder plot, and owes something – as Kipling admitted in the the Railway Library edition – to Robert Louis Stevenson's story 'The Suicide Club', is my own favourite yarn.

But the surface of the text is made strangely impenetrable by Kipling's determination to render the speech of his 'Three Musketeers' in thick Oirish (Mulvaney), broad Cockney (Ortheris) and ee-ba-goom Northern (Learoyd). Mulvaney's 'menowdherin', and minandherin', an' blandandherin'' (p. 13) soon grows tiresome, and Ortheris drops so many initial H's and final G's and D's that the apostrophes begin to swim before our eyes. George Orwell suggested, of Kipling's verse, that such mimicry of lower-class speech actually made the poems worse than they would be in standard English, and 'restored' some of the lines to prove his point. I must confess to feeling something similar about these stories. There is something condescending about Kipling's mimicry:

'Ah doan't care. Ah would not care, but ma heart is plaayin' tivvy-tivvy on ma ribs. Let ma die! Oh, leave ma die!' (p. 46)

Learoyd's suffering is curiously diminished by the music-hall orthography. Kipling's affection for the 'soldiers three' can often seem *de haut en bas*.

The other main point of linguistic interest in the *Soldiers Three* stories is the incorporation of a number of Hindi words and phrases. This is kept at a pidgin, Hobson-Jobson level: 'Take him away, an' av you iver say wan wurrud about fwhat you've *dekkoed*, I'll *marrow* you till your own wife won't *sumjao* who you are!' (p. 17). The Indian critic S.S. Azfar Hussain has pointed out that, of the eleven

Hindi sentences which appear in *Soldiers Three* (and these are the only complete Hindi sentences to be found in the whole of Kipling's *œuvre*), ten are imperative sentences; and nine of these are orders from English masters to their servants. It is important, then, not to overstate the extent to which Kipling's Indian childhood influenced his work. It seems certain that Kipling did not remain literate in Hindi or Urdu. Dr Hussain reports that 'Kipling's manuscripts in the British Museum . . . show that he tried several times to write his name in Urdu, but oddly enough did not succeed even once. It reads "Kinling", "Kiplig" and "Kipenling".'

In the *Soldiers Three* stories the Hindi/Urdu words are simply sprinkled over the text, like curry powder. The *In Black and White* stories attempt something altogether more ambitious. Here it is the Indians who have been given voice, and since, in many cases, they would not actually be speaking in English, a whole idiolect has had to be invented.

Much of this invented Indiaspeak is so exclamatory, so full of 'Ahoo! Ahoo!' and 'Ahi! Ahi!' and even 'Auggrh!' as to suggest that Indians are a people incapable of anything but outbursts. Some of it sounds very like the salaaming exoticism of the pantomime: 'The mind of an old man is like the *numah*-tree. Fruit, bud, blossom, and the dead leaves of all the years of the past flourish together' (p. 136). Sometimes Kipling's own convictions place impossible sentences in Indian mouths: 'Great is the mercy of these fools of English' (p. 173) is one such contorted utterance. But much of it is brilliantly *right*. The device of literal translations of metaphors is certainly exotic, but it does also lend a kind of authenticity to the dialogue: '. . . it is the Sahib himself! My heart is made fat and my eye glad' (p. 95). And the Indian *bunnias*, policemen, miners and whores sound Indian in a way that – for example – Forster's never do. This is because they think like Indians, or at least they do when Kipling lets them. For the problem of condescension remains. Kipling could never have dedicated a story to the 'natives' as he did to 'T. Atkins', after all. And if the tone of *Soldiers Three* seems patronizing at times, *In Black and White* can sound far, far worse.

Kipling's Indian women, in particular, are (at best) the cause of trouble and danger for men – the Hindu heroine of 'In Flood Time' is the cause of a deadly rivalry between a Muslim and a Sikh –

while, at worst, they cheat on their old, blind husbands as Unda does in 'At Twenty-Two', or on their ferocious Pathan husbands, as the 'woman of the Abazai' does, with unhappy results, in 'Dray Wara Yow Dee':

> And she bowed her head, and I smote it off at the neck-bone so that it leaped between my feet. Thereafter the rage of our people came upon me, and I hacked off the breasts, that the men of Little Malikand might know the crime . . . (p. 99)

And yet, and yet. It is impossible not to admire Kipling's skill at creating convincing portraits of horse-thieves, or rural policemen, or Punjabi moneylenders. The story of how the blind miner Janki Meah finds the way out of a collapsed mine may feature a flighty female, but the world, and the psychology, and the language of the men is superlatively created.

The most remarkable story in this collection is unquestionably 'On the City Wall'. In it, the two Kiplings are openly at war with one another; and in the end, it seems to me, the Indian Kipling manages to subvert what the English Kipling takes to be the meaning of the tale.

'On the City Wall' is not narrated by an Indian voice, but by an English journalist who, in common with 'all the City', is fond of visiting Lalun's brothel on the Lahore city wall to smoke and to talk. The brothel is presented as an oasis of peace in the turbulence of India; here Muslims, Hindus, Sikhs and Europeans mingle without conflict. Only one group is excluded: 'Lalun admits no Jews here' (p. 157). One of the most vocal figures at Lalun's is Wali Dad, the Westernized young man who calls himself 'a Product – a Demnition Product. *That* also I owe to you and yours: that I cannot make an end to my sentence without quoting from your authors' (p. 158). The deracinated – or seemingly deracinated – Wali Dad is one of the story's main actors. Another is the imprisoned revolutionary Khem Singh, who is kept locked in Fort Amara. The third major 'character' is the crowd of Shia Muslims thronging the city streets, for it is the time of the Mohurrum processions, and violence is in the air.

Kipling's treatment of Wali Dad is, by any standards, pretty appalling. He builds him up purely in order to knock him down, and when the young man, seeing the frenzy of the Mohurrum processions, is transformed into a sort of savage – 'His nostrils were distended, his eyes were fixed, and he was smiting himself softly on the breast' (p. 168), Kipling tells us, and makes Wali Dad say things like 'These swine of Hindus! We shall be killing kine in their temples to-night!' (p. 167) – the meaning is clear: Western civilization has been no more than a veneer; a native remains a native beneath his European jackets and ties. Blood will out. Wali Dad's regression is not only unbelievable; it also shows us that Kipling had failed to appreciate that it was among these very people, these Wali Dads, Jawaharlal Nehrus and M.K. Gandhis, that the Indian revolution would be made; that they would assimilate Western culture without being deracinated by it, and then turn their knowledge against the British, and gain the victory.

In the story's other main narrative strand, Lalun tricks the narrator into assisting in the escape of the revolutionary, Khem Singh. Kipling suggests that the old leader's followers have lost their appetite for revolution, so that Khem Singh has no option but to return voluntarily into captivity. But his narrator understands the meaning of the story rather better than that: 'I was thinking,' he concludes, 'how I had become Lalun's Vizier after all' (p. 173). Louis Cornell, in his study of this story, suggests rather oddly that 'the ostensible climax . . . where the reporter discovers that he has unwittingly helped a revolutionary to escape from the police, is too minor an incident, placed too close to the end of the tale, to seem in proportion with the rest of the story'. It seems to me not at all unusual for a climax to be placed near a story's end; and, far from being a minor incident, Khem Singh's escape seems central to the story's significance. India, Lalun-India, bewitches and tricks the English, in the character of the reporter; the master is made the servant, the Vizier. So that the conclusion of the very text in which Kipling states most emphatically his belief that India can never stand alone, without British leadership, and in which he ridicules Indian attempts to acquire the superior culture of England, leaves us with an image of the inability of the sahibs to comprehend what they pretend to rule. Lalun deceived the narrator; Wali Dad deceived the author. 'On the City Wall' is Ruddy Baba's victory over Kipling Sahib. And now that the 'great idol called *Pax Britannica*, which, as the newspapers say, lives between Peshawar and Cape Comorin' (p.

155), has been broken, the story stands, along with the others in this volume, as a testament to the old quarrel of colonizer and colonized. There will always be plenty in Kipling that I will find difficult to forgive; but there is also enough truth in these stories to make them impossible to ignore.

Selected Further Reading

Charles Carrington, *Rudyard Kipling: His Life and Work*, London: Macmillan, 1955; reprinted Penguin Books, 1970, 1986.

Louis L. Cornell, *Kipling in India*, London: Macmillan, 1966.

Roger Lancelyn Green (ed.), *Kipling: The Critical Heritage*, London: Routledge & Kegan Paul, 1971.

John A. McClure, *Kipling and Conrad: The Colonial Fiction*, Cambridge, Mass.: Harvard University Press, 1981.

Harold Orel (ed.), *Kipling: Interviews and Recollections* (2 vols.), London: Macmillan, 1983.

Thomas Pinney (ed.), *Kipling's India: Uncollected Sketches 1884–1888*, London: Macmillan, 1986.

Alan Sandison, *The Wheel of Empire*, London: Macmillan, 1967.

Angus Wilson, *The Strange Ride of Rudyard Kipling*, London: Secker & Warburg, 1977.

Note on the Text

In 1887 Kipling moved from Lahore to Allahabad to work on the *Pioneer*. He was given the job of editing the *Pioneer*'s weekly supplement, *The Week's News*, and he wrote for it no less than one story a week. All the stories in *Soldiers Three* (except 'Black Jack') and all the stories in *In Black and White* (except 'On the City Wall') were first published there. The stories subsequently published in both *Soldiers Three* and *In Black and White* all appeared between January and August 1888. ('Black Jack' and 'On the City Wall' had no magazine publication: they first appeared in these two collections.)

In 1888, the publisher of the *Pioneer*, A.H. Wheeler & Co., who had had the idea of producing cheap reprints for railway reading, issued the first six volumes of the Indian Railway Library: Kipling's *Soldiers Three*, *The Story of the Gadsbys*, *In Black and White*, *Under the Deodars*, *Wee Willie Winkie* and *The Phantom Rickshaw*. *Soldiers Three* and *In Black and White* went through three Indian Railway Library editions between 1888 and 1890, and many editions subsequently. The third Indian edition was also the first English edition (published in Allahabad by A.H. Wheeler & Co. and in London by Sampson Low, Marston, Searle & Rivington). For this wider readership, Kipling carefully revised his text: in particular, he removed italics that he had used for emphasis, and he replaced most of the Hindi with English equivalents. These two collections, together with *The Story of the Gadsbys*, were published in a two-volume edition by Sampson Low in 1892, and in a one-volume edition by Macmillan in 1895, which was the basis for all subsequent Macmillan editions.

The text reprinted here follows Macmillan's Sussex Edition of 1937, the last Collected Edition in Kipling's lifetime, containing his final revisions. (The present volume excludes *The Story of the Gadsbys*.) The dedication and Preface to *Soldiers Three* and the Introduction and dedication to *In Black and White* have, however, been reinstated for this Penguin edition: these appeared in the Indian Railway Library editions and in the 1890 Sampson Low edition but were omitted from the 1895 Macmillan edition (and subsequent Macmillan editions).

SOLDIERS THREE

A Collection of Stories

SETTING FORTH CERTAIN PASSAGES IN THE LIVES AND ADVENTURES OF PRIVATES TERENCE MULVANEY, STANLEY ORTHERIS, AND JOHN LEAROYD

We be Soldiers Three –
Pardonnez-moi, je vous en prie.

TO

THAT VERY STRONG MAN,

T. ATKINS,

PRIVATE OF THE LINE,

THIS BOOK IS DEDICATED

IN ALL ADMIRATION AND GOODFELLOWSHIP.

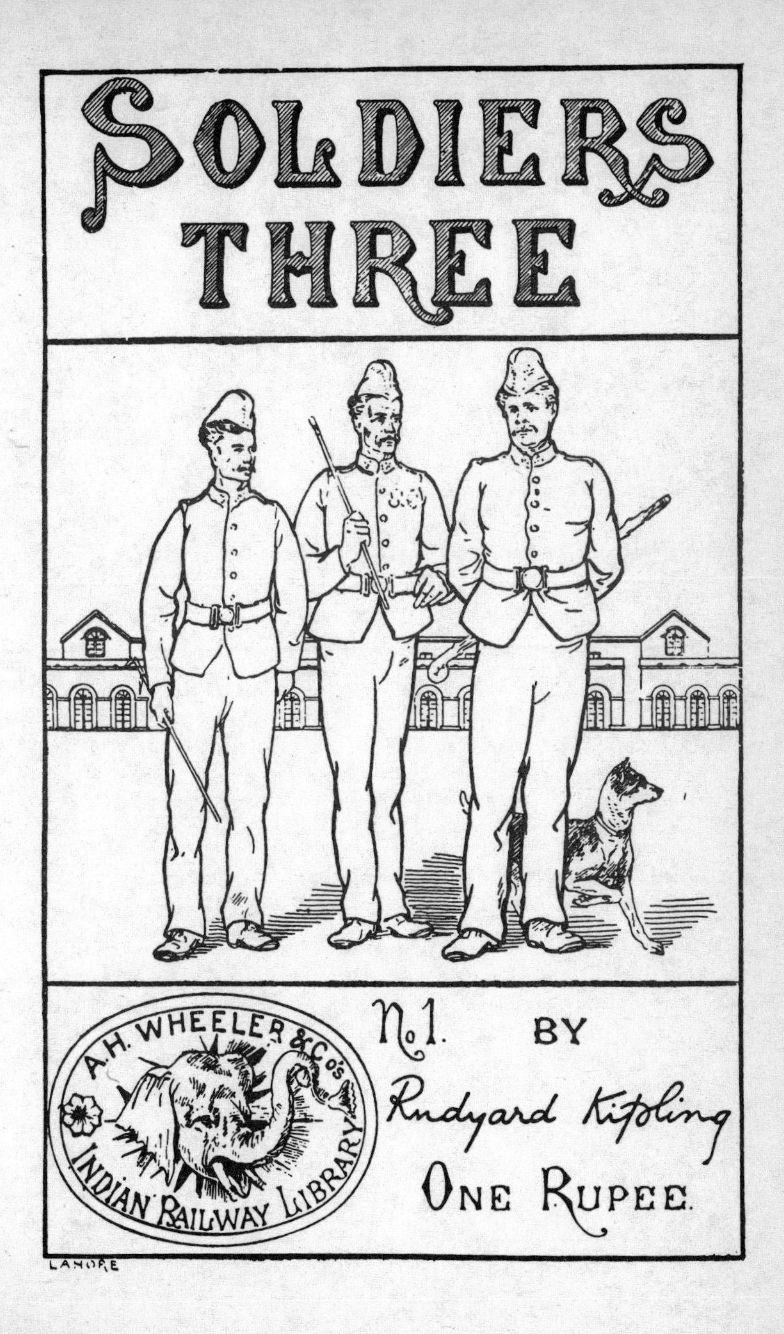
SOLDIERS
THREE
A.H. WHEELER & Co's
INDIAN RAILWAY LIBRARY
No.1. BY
Rudyard Kipling
ONE RUPEE.
LAHORE

Contents

Preface

This small book contains, for the most part, the further adventures of my esteemed friends and sometime allies, Privates Mulvaney, Ortheris, and Learoyd, who have already been introduced to the public. Those anxious to know how the three most cruelly maltreated a Member of Parliament; how Ortheris went mad for a space; how Mulvaney and some friends took the town of Lungtungpen; and how little Jhansi McKenna helped the regiment when it was smitten with cholera, must refer to a book called *Plain Tales from the Hills.* I would have reprinted the four stories in this place, but Dinah Shadd says that 'tearin' the tripes out av a book wid a pictur' on the back, all to make Terence proud past reasonin',' is wasteful, and Mulvaney himself says that he prefers to have his fame 'dishpersed most notoriously in sev'ril volumes'. I can only hope that his desire will be gratified.

RUDYARD KIPLING

The God from the Machine

Hit a man an' help a woman, an' ye can't be far wrong anyways. – *Maxims of Private Mulvaney.*

The Inexpressibles[1] gave a ball. They borrowed a seven-pounder[2] from the Gunners, and wreathed it with laurels, and made the dancing-floor plate-glass, and provided a supper, the like of which had never been eaten before, and set two sentries at the door of the room to hold the trays of programme-cards. My friend, Private Mulvaney,[3] was one of the sentries, because he was the tallest man in the Regiment. When the dance was fairly started the sentries were released, and Private Mulvaney went to curry favour with the Mess-Sergeant in charge of the supper. Whether the Mess-Sergeant gave or Mulvaney took, I cannot say. All that I am certain of is that, at supper-time, I found Mulvaney with Private Ortheris, two-thirds of a ham, a loaf of bread, half a *pâté-de-foie-gras*, and two magnums of champagne, sitting on the roof of my carriage. As I came up I heard him saying: –

'Praise be, a danst doesn't come as often as Ord'ly-Room,[4] or, by this an' that, Orth'ris, me son, I wud be the dishgrace av the Rig'mint instid av the brightest jool in uts crown.'

'*Hand* the Colonel's pet noosance,' said Ortheris. 'But wot makes you curse your rations? This 'ere fizzy stuff's good enough.'

'Stuff, ye oncivilized pagin! 'Tis champagne we're dhrinkin' now. 'Tisn't that I am set agin'. 'Tis this quare stuff wid the little bits av black leather in ut. I misdoubt I will be disthressin'ly sick wid ut in the mornin'. Fwhat is ut?'

'Goose liver,' I said, climbing on the top of the carriage, for I knew that it was better to sit out with Mulvaney than to dance many dances.

'Goose liver is ut?' said Mulvaney. 'Faith, I'm thinkin' thim that makes ut wud do betther to cut up the Colonel. He carries a power av liver undher his right arrum whin the days are warm an' the nights chill. He wud give thim tons an' tons av liver. 'Tis he sez so. "I'm all liver to-day," sez he; an' wid that he ordhers me ten days' C.B.[5] for as moild a dhrink as iver a good sodger tuk betune his teeth.'

'That was when 'e wanted for to wash 'isself in the Fort Ditch,"[6] Ortheris explained. 'Said there was too much beer in the barrick water-butts for a God-fearin' man. You was lucky in gettin' orf with wot you did, Mulvaney.'

'Say you so? Now I'm pershuaded I was cruel hard treated, seein' fwhat I've done for the likes av him in the days whin me eyes were wider opin than they are now. Man alive, for the Colonel to whip *me* on the peg[7] in that way! Me that have saved the repitation av a ten times betther man than him. 'Twas ne-farious – an' that manes a power av evil!'

'Never mind the nefariousness,' I said. 'Whose reputation did you save?'

'More's the pity, 'twasn't my own, but I tuk more throuble wid ut than av ut was. 'Twas just my way, messin' wid fwhat was no business av mine. Hear now!' He settled himself at ease on the top of the carriage. 'I'll tell you all about ut. Av coorse I will name no names, for there's wan that's an orf'cer's lady now, that was in ut, and no more will I name places, for a man is thracked[8] by a place.'

'Eyah!' said Ortheris lazily, 'but this is a mixed story wot's comin'.'

'Wanst upon a time, as the childher-books say, I was a recruity.'

'Was you though?' said Ortheris. 'Now that's extryordinary!'

'Orth'ris,' said Mulvaney, 'av you opin thim lips av yours agin, I will, savin' your presince, sorr, take you by the slack av your trousers an' heave you.'

'I'm mum,' said Ortheris. 'Wot 'appened when you was a recruity?'

'I was a betther recruity than you iver was or will be, but that's neither here nor there. Thin I became a man, an' the divil of a man I was fifteen years ago.[9] They called me Buck Mulvaney in thim days, an', begad, I tuk a woman's eye. I did that! Orth'ris, ye scrub, fwhat are ye sniggerin' at? Do you misdoubt me?'

'Devil a doubt!' said Ortheris; 'but I've 'eard summat like that before!'

Mulvaney dismissed the impertinence with a lofty wave of his hand and continued: –

'An' the orf'cers av the Rig'mint[10] I was in in thim days *was* orf'cers – gran' men, wid a manner on 'em, an' a way wid 'em such as is not made these days – all but wan – wan o' the capt'ns. A bad dhrill,[11] a wake voice, an' a limp leg – thim three things are the signs av a bad man. You bear that in your mind, Orth'ris, me son.

'An' the Colonel av the Rig'mint had a daughther – wan av thim lamblike, bleatin', pick-me-up-an'-carry-me-or-I'll-die gurls such as was made for the natural prey av men like the Capt'n, who was iverlastin' payin' coort to her, though the Colonel he said time an' over, "Kape out av the brute's way, me dear." But he niver had the heart for to send her away from the throuble, bein' a widower an' she their wan child.'

'Stop a minute, Mulvaney,' said I; 'how in the world did you come to know these things?'

'How did I come?' said Mulvaney, with a scornful grunt. 'Bekaze I'm turned durin' the Quane's pleasure to a lump av wood, lookin' out straight forninst me, wid a – a – candelabbrum in me hand, for you to pick your kyards out av, must I not see nor feel? Av coorse I du! Up me back, an' in me boots, an' in the short hair av the neck – that's where I kape me eyes whin I'm on jooty an' the reg'lar wans are fixed. Know! Take my word for it, sorr, ivrything an' a great dale more is known in a rig'mint; or fwhat wud be the use av a Mess-Sargint, or a Sargint's wife doin' wet-nurse to the Major's baby! To reshume. He was a bad dhrill was this Capt'n – a rotten bad dhrill – an' whin first I ran me eye over him, I sez to mesilf: "Me Militia bantam!" I sez. "Me cock av a Gosport[12] dunghill" – 'twas from Portsmouth he came to us – "there's combs to be cut,"[13] sez I, "an' by the grace av God, 'tis Terence Mulvaney will cut thim."

'So he wint menowdherin', and minandherin', an' blandandherin'[14] roun' an' about the Colonel's daughther, an' she, poor innocint, lookin' at him like a Comm'ssariat bullock[15] looks at the Comp'ny cook. He'd a dhirty little scrub av a black moustache, an' he twisted an' turned ivry wurrud he used as av he found ut too sweet for to spit out. Eyah! He was a tricky man an' a liar by natur'. Some are born so. He was wan. I knew he was over his belt in money borrowed from natives; besides a lot av other matthers which, in regard for your presince, sorr, I will oblitherate. A little av fwhat I knew, the Colonel knew, for he wud have none av him, an' *that*, I'm thinkin', by fwhat happened aftherwards, the Capt'n knew.

'Wan day, bein' mortial idle, or they wud niver ha' thried ut, the Rig'mint gave amshure theatricals – orf'cers an' orf'cers' ladies. You've seen the likes time an' agin, sorr, an' poor fun 'tis for thim that sit in the back row an' stamp wid their boots [16] for the honour av the Rig'mint. I was told off for to shif' the scenes, haulin' up this an' draggin' down that. Light work ut was, wid lashin's av beer and the gurl that dhressed the orf'cers' ladies – but she died in Aggra [17] twelve years gone, an' me tongue's gettin' the betther av me. They was actin' a play thing called *Sweethearts*,[18] which you may ha' heard av, an' the Colonel's daughther she was a lady's maid. The Capt'n was a bhoy called Broom – Spread Broom [19] was his name in the play. Thin I saw – ut come out in the actin' – fwhat I niver saw before, an' that was that he was no gentleman. They was too much together, thim two, a-whishperin' behind the scenes I shifted, an' some av what they said I heard; for I was death [20] – blue death an' ivy – on the comb-cuttin'. He was iverlastin'ly oppressin' her to fall in wid some sneakin' schame av his, an' she was thryin' to stand out agin' him, but not as though she was set in her will. I wonder now in thim days that me ears did not grow a yard on me head wid list'nin'. But I looked straight forninst me an' hauled up this an' dragged down that, such as was me jooty, an' the orf'cers' ladies sez one to another, thinkin' I was out av listen-reach: "Fwhat an obligin' young man is this Corp'ril Mulvaney!" I was a Corp'ril then. I was rejuced aftherwards, but, no matther, I was a Corp'ril wanst.

'Well, this *Sweethearts* business wint on like most amshure theatricals, an' barrin' fwhat I suspicioned, 'twasn't till the dhress-rehearsal that I saw for certain that thim two – he the blayguard, an' she no wiser than she shud ha' been – had put up an e-vasion.'

'A what?' said I.

'E-vasion! Fwhat you call an elopemint. E-vasion I calls it, bekaze, exceptin' whin 'tis right an' natural an' proper, 'tis wrong an' dhirty to steal a man's wan child, she not knowin' her own mind. There was a Sargint in the Comm'ssariat who set my face upon e-vasions. I'll tell you about that –'

'Stick to your bloomin' Captains, Mulvaney,' said Ortheris; 'Comm'ssariat Sargints is low.'

Mulvaney accepted the amendment and went on: –

'Now I knew that the Colonel was no fool, any more than me, for I was hild the smartest man in the Rig'mint, an' the Colonel was the best orf'cer commandin' in Asia; so fwhat he said an' *I* said was mortial truth. We knew that the Capt'n was bad, but, for reasons which I have already oblitherated, I knew more than me Colonel. I wud ha' rolled out his face wid the butt av me rifle before permittin' av him to steal the gurl. Saints knew av he wud ha' married her, and av he didn't she wud be in great tormint, an' the divil av a "scandal". But I niver sthruck, niver raised me hand on me shuperior orf'cer; an' that was a merricle now I come to considher ut.'

'Mulvaney, the dawn's risin',' said Ortheris, 'an' we're no nearer 'ome than we was at the beginnin'. Lend me your pouch. Mine's all dust.'

Mulvaney pitched his pouch over, and Ortheris filled his pipe afresh.

'So the dhress-rehearsal came to an end, an', bekaze I was curious, I stayed behind whin the scene-shiftin' was ended, an' I shud ha' been in barricks, lyin' as flat as a toad under a painted cottage thing. They was talkin' in whishpers, an' she was shiverin' an' gaspin' like a fresh-hukked fish. "Are you sure you've got the hang av the manewvers?" sez he, or wurruds to that effec', as the coort-martial sez. "Sure as death," sez she, "but I misdoubt 'tis crool hard on my father." "Damn your father!" sez he, or anyways 'twas fwhat he thought. "The arrangemint is as clear as mud. Jungi will drive the carr'ge afther all's over, an' you come to the station, cool an' aisy, in time for the two o'clock thrain, where I'll be wid your kit." "Faith," thinks I to mesilf, "thin there's a *ayah*[21] in the business tu!"

'A powerful bad thing is a *ayah*. Don't you niver have any thruck wid wan. Thin he began sootherin'[22] her, an' all the orf'cers an' orf'cers' ladies left, an' they put out the lights. To explain the theory av the flight,[23] as they say at Musk'thry,[24] you must ondhersthand that afther this *Sweethearts* nonsinse was ended, there was another little bit av a play called *Couples*[25] – some kind av couple or another. The gurl was actin' in this, but not the man. I suspicioned he'd go to the station wid the gurl's kit at the end av the first piece. 'Twas the kit that flusthered me, for I knew for a Capt'n to go trapesin' about the Impire wid the Lord knew fwhat av a *truso* on his arrum was nefarious, an' wud be worse than easin' the flag,[26] so far as the talk aftherwards wint.'

''Old on, Mulvaney. Wot's *truso*?' said Ortheris.

'You're an oncivilized man, me son. Whin a gurl's married, all her kit an' 'coutrements are *truso*, which manes weddin'-portion. An' 'tis the same whin she's runnin' away, even wid the biggest blayguard on the Arrmy List.[27]

'So I made me plan av campaign. The Colonel's house was a good two miles away. "Dennis," sez I to my Colour-Sargint, "av you love me lend me your kyart, for me heart is bruk an' me feet is sore wid trampin' to and from this foolishness at the Gaff."[28] An' Dennis lent ut, wid a rampin',[29] stampin' red stallion in the shafts. Whin they was all settled down to their *Sweethearts* for the first scene, which was a long wan, I slips outside and into the kyart. Mother av Hivin! but I made that horse walk, an' we came into the Colonel's compound as the Divil wint through Athlone[30] – in standin' leps. There was no one there excipt the servints, an' I wint round to the back an' found the gurl's *ayah*.

'"Ye black brazen Jezebel,"[31] sez I, "sellin' your masther's honour for five rupees – pack up all the Miss Sahib's kit an' look slippy! Capt'n Sahib's order," sez I. "Going to the station we are," I sez, an' wid that I laid me finger to me nose an' looked the schamin' sinner I was.

'"*Bote acchy*,"[32] sez she; so I knew she was in the business, an' I piled up all the sweet talk I'd iver learnt in the bazars on to this she-bullock, an' prayed av her to put all the quick she knew into the thing. While she packed, I stud outside an' sweated, for I was wanted for to shif' the second scene. I tell you, a young gurl's e-vasion manes as much baggage as a rig'mint on the line av march! "Saints help Dennis's springs," thinks I, as I bundled the stuff into the thrap, "for I'll have no mercy!"

'"I'm comin' too," sez the *ayah*.

'"No, you don't," sez I. "Later – *pechy*![33] You *baito*[34] where you are. I'll *pechy* come an' bring you *sart*,[35] along with me, you maraudhin'" – niver mind fwhat I called her.

'Thin I wint for the Gaff, an' by the special ordhers av Providence, for I was doin' a good work, ye will ondersthand, Dennis's springs hild toight. "Now, whin the Capt'n goes for that kit," thinks I, "he'll be throubled." At the ind av *Sweethearts* off the Capt'n runs in his kyart to the Colonel's house, an' I sits down on the steps an' laughs. Wanst an' agin I slipped in to see how the little piece was goin', an' whin ut was near endin' I stepped out all among the carr'ges an' sings out very softly, "Jungi!" Wid that a carr'ge began to move, an' I waved to the dhriver. "*Hitherao!*"[36] sez I, an' he *hitheraoed* till I judged he was at proper distance, an' thin I tuk him, fair an' square betune the eyes, all I knew for good or bad, an' he dhropped wid a guggle like the Canteen beer-engine whin ut's runnin' low. Thin I ran to the kyart an' tuk out all the gurl's kit an' piled it into the carr'ge, the sweat runnin' down me face in dhrops. "Go home," sez I, to Dennis's *sais*.[37] "Ye'll find a man close here. Very sick he is. Take him away, an' av you iver say wan wurrud about fwhat you've *dekkoed*, I'll *marrow* you till your own wife won't *sumjao*[38] who you are!" Thin I heard the stampin' av feet at the ind av the play, an' I ran in to let down the curtain. Whin they all came out the gurl thried to hide herself behind wan av the pillars, an' sez "Jungi" in a voice that wudn't ha' scared a hare. I run over to Jungi's carr'ge an' tuk up the lousy old horse-blanket on the box, wrapped me head an' the rest av me in ut, an' dhruv up to where she was.

'"Miss Sahib," sez I. "Going to the station? Captain Sahib's order!" an' widout a sign she jumped in all among her own kit.

'I laid to an' dhruv like steam to the Colonel's house before the Colonel was there, an' she screamed an' I thought she was goin' off. Out comes the *ayah*, saying all sorts av things about the Capt'n havin' come for the kit an' gone to the station.

'"Take out the luggage, you divil," sez I, "or I'll murther you!"

'The lights av the thraps wid people comin' from the Gaff was showin' across the p'rade-ground, an', by this an' that, the way thim two wimmen worked at the bundles an' thrunks was a caution![39] I was dyin' to help, but, seein' I didn't want to be known, I sat wid the blanket roun' me an' coughed an' thanked the Saints there was no moon that night.

'Whin all was in the house again, I niver asked for *bukshish*[40] but dhruv tremenjus in the opp'site way from the other carr'ges an' put out my lights. Prisintly I saw a naygur-man wallowin' in the road. I slipped down before I got to him, for I suspicioned Providence was wid me all through that night. 'Twas Jungi, his nose smashed in flat, all dumb sick as ye plaze. Dennis's man must have tilted him out av the thrap. Whin he came to, "*Hutt!*"[41] sez I, but he began to howl.

'"You black lump av dhirt," I sez, "is this the way you dhrive your *gharri*?[42] That *tikka*[43] has been *owin'* an' *fere-owin'*[44] all over the bloomin' country this whole bloomin' night, an' you as *mut-walla*[45] as Davey's Sow. Get up, you hog!" sez I, louder, for I heard the wheels av a thrap in the dhark. "Get up an' light your lamps, or you'll be run into!" This was on the road to the railway station.

'"Fwhat the divil's this?" sez the Capt'n's voice in the dhark, an' I cud judge he was in a latherin' rage.

'"*Gharri* dhriver here, dhrunk, sorr," sez I. "I've found his *gharri* sthrayin' about cantonmints,[46] an' now I've found him."

'"Oh!" sez the Capt'n; "fwhat's his name?" I stooped down an' pretended to listen.

'"He sez his name's Jungi, sorr," sez I.

'"Hould my harse," sez the Capt'n to his man, an' wid that he gets down wid the whip an' lays into Jungi, just mad wid rage an' swearin' like the scutt[47] he was.

'I thought, afther a while, he wud kill the man, so I sez, "Stop, sorr, or you'll murther him!" That dhrew all his fire on me, an' he cursed me into Blazes an' out again. I stud to attenshin an' saluted: – "Sorr," sez I, "av ivry man in this wurruld had his rights, I'm thinkin' that more than wan wud be beaten to a jelly for this night's work – that niver came off at all, sorr, as you see!" "Now," thinks I to mesilf, "Terence Mulvaney, you've cut your own throat, for he'll sthrike, an' you'll knock him down for the good av his sowl an' your own iverlastin' dishgrace!"

'But the Capt'n niver said a single wurrud. He choked where he stud, an' thin he went into his thrap widout sayin' good-night, an' I wint back to barricks.'

'And then?' said Ortheris and I together.

'That was all,' said Mulvaney; 'niver another wurrud did I hear av the whole thing. All I know was that there was no e-vasion, an' that was fwhat I wanted. Now, I put ut to you, sorr, is ten days' C.B. a fit an' a proper tratemint for a man that has behaved as me?'

'Well, any'ow,' said Ortheris, ''tweren't *this* 'ere Colonel's daughter, an' you *was* blazin' copped[48] when you tried to wash in the Fort Ditch.'

'That,' said Mulvaney, finishing the champagne, 'is a shuparfluous an' impart'nint observashin.'

Private Learoyd's Story

And he told a tale. – *Chronicles of Gautama Buddha.* –

Far from the haunts of Company Officers who insist upon kit-inspections, far from keen-nosed Sergeants who sniff the pipe stuffed into the bedding-roll, two miles from the tumult of the barracks, lies the Trap. It is an old dry well, shadowed by a twisted *pipal*[1] tree and fenced with high grass. Here, in the years gone by, did Private Ortheris establish his depôt and menagerie for such possessions, dead and living, as could not safely be introduced to the barrack-room. Here were gathered Houdin pullets,[2] and fox-terriers of undoubted pedigree and more than doubtful ownership, for Ortheris was an inveterate poacher and pre-eminent among a regiment of neat-handed dog-stealers.[3]

Never again will the long lazy evenings return wherein Ortheris, whistling softly, moved surgeon-wise among the captives of his craft at the bottom of the well; when Learoyd sat in the niche,[4] giving sage counsel on the management of 'tykes,'[5] and Mulvaney, from the crook of the overhanging *pipal*, waved his enormous boots in benediction above our heads, delighting us with tales of Love and War, and strange experiences of cities and men.

Ortheris – landed at last in the 'little stuff' bird-shop[6] for which your soul longed; Learoyd – back again in the smoky, stone-ribbed North, amid the clang of the Bradford looms; Mulvaney – grizzled, tender, and very wise Ulysses, sweltering on the earthworks of a Central India line[7] – judge if I have forgotten old days in the Trap! . . .

Orth'ris, as allus thinks he knaws more than other foaks, said she wasn't a real laady, but nobbut a Hewrasian.[8] Ah don't gainsay as her culler was a bit doosky like. But she *was* a laady. Why, she rode iv a carriage, an' good 'osses, too, an' her 'air was that oiled as you could see your faice in it, an' she wore di'mond rings an' a goold chain, an' silk an' satin dresses as mun ha' cost a deal, for it isn't a cheap shop as keeps enough o' one pattern to fit a figure like hers. Her naame was Mrs DeSussa, an' t' waay I coom to be acquainted wi' her was along iv our Colonel's Laady's dog Rip.

Ah've seen a vast o' dogs, but Rip was t' prettiest picter iv a cliver fox-tarrier 'at iver I set eyes on. He cud do owt yo' like but speeak, an' t' Colonel's Laady set more store by him than if he hed been a Christian. She hed bairns iv her awn, but they was i' England, and Rip seemed to get all t' coodlin' an' pettin' as belonged to a bairn by good rights.

But Rip wor a bit on a rover, an' hed a habit o' breakin' out o' barricks like, and trottin' round t' plaice as if he were t' Cantonment Magistrate[9] coom round inspectin'. The Colonel leathers him once or twice, but Rip didn't care an' kept on gooin' his rounds, wi' his taail a-waggin' as if he were flag-signallin' to t' world at large 'at he was 'gettin' on nicely, thank yo', and how's yo'sen?' An' then t' Colonel, as was noa sort iv a hand wi' a dog, tees him oop. A real clipper iv a dog, an' it's noa wonder yon laady, Mrs DeSussa, should tek a fancy tiv him. Theer's one o' t' Ten Commandments[10] says yo' maun't cuvvet your neebor's ox nor his jackass, but it doesn't say nowt about his tarrier dogs, an' happen thot's t' reason why Mrs DeSussa cuvveted Rip, tho' she went to church reg'lar along wi' her husband, who was soa mich darker 'at if he hedn't such a good coaat tiv his back yo' might ha' called him a black man and nut tell a lee nawther. They said he addled his brass i' jute;[11] an' he'd a rare lot on it.

Well, yo' see, when they teed Rip oop, t' poor awd lad didn't enjoy very good 'ealth. Soa t' Colonel's Laady sends for me as 'ad a naame for bein' knowledgeable about a dog, an' axes what's ailin' wi' him.

'Why,' says I, 'he's getten t' mopes, an' what he wants is his libbaty an' coompany like t' rest on us; wal happen a rat or two 'ud liven him oop. It's low, mum,' says I, 'is rats, but it's t' nature iv a dog. An' soa's coottin' round an' meetin' another dog or two an' passin' t' time o' day, an' hevvin' a bit on a turn-up wi' him like a Christian.'

Soa she says *her* dog maun't niver fight an' noa Christians iver fought.

'Then what's a soldier for?' says I; an' I explains to her t' contrairy qualities iv a dog, 'at, when yo' coom to think on't, is one o' t' curusest things as is. For they larn to behave theirsens like gentlemen born, fit for t' fost o' coompany – they tell me t' Widdy[12] hersen is fond iv a good dog and knaws one when she sees it as well as onnybody: then on t' other hand a-tewin'[13] round after cats an' gettin' mixed oop i' all manners o' blackguardly street-rows, an' killin' rats, an' fightin' like divils.

T' Colonel's Laady says: 'Well, Learoyd, I doan't agree wi' yo', but yo're right in a way o' speeakin', an' Ah should like yo' to tek Rip out a-walkin' wi' yo' sometimes; but yo' maun't let him fight, nor chaase cats, nor do nowt 'orrid.' An' them was her very wods.

Soa Rip an' me gooes out a-walkin' o' evenin's, he bein' a dog as did credit tiv a man, an' I catches a lot o' rats an' we hed a bit iv a match on in an awd dry swimmin'-bath[14] at back o' t' cantonments, an' it was none so long afore he was as bright as a button again. He hed a waay o' flyin' at them big yaller pariah dogs[15] as if he was a harrow offan a bow, an' though his weight were nowt, he tuk 'em so suddint-like they rolled ovver like skittles in a halley, an' when they coot he stretched after 'em as if he were rabbit-runnin'. Saame wi' cats when he cud get t' cat agaate[16] o' runnin'.

One evenin', him an' me was trespassin' ovver a compound wall after one of them mongooses 'at he'd started, an' we was busy grubbin' round a prickle-bush, an' when we looks oop there was Mrs DeSussa wi' a parasel ovver her shoulder, a-watchin' us. 'Oh my!' she sings out. 'There's that lovelee dog! Would he let me stroke him, Mister Soldier?'

'Ay, he would, mum,' says I, 'for he's fond o' laadies' coompany. Coom here, Rip, an' speeak to this kind laady.' An' Rip, seein' 'at t' mongoose hed getten clean awaay, cooms oop like t' gentleman he was, niver a hauporth shy nor okkord.

'Oh, you beautiful – you prettee dog!' she says, clippin' an' chantin' her speech in a waay them sooart has o' their awn; 'I would like a dog like you. You are so verree lovelee – so awfullee prettee,' an' all thot sort o' talk, 'at a dog o' sense mebbe thinks nowt on, tho' he'll bide it by reason o' his breedin'.

An' then I meks him joomp ovver my swagger-cane,[17] an' shek hands, an' beg, an' lie dead, an' a lot o' them tricks as laadies teeaches dogs, though I doan't haud wi' it mysen, for it's mekkin' a fool o' a good dog to do such-like.

An' at lung length it cooms out 'at she'd been thrawin' sheep's eyes,[18] as t' sayin' is, at Rip for many a daay. Yo' see, her childer was grown up, an' she'd nowt mich to do, an' wor allus fond iv a dog. Soa she axes me if I'd tek somethin' to drink. An' we gooes into t' drawn-room wheer her 'usband was a-settin'. They meks a gurt fuss ovver t' dog an' I has a bottle o' aale an' he gev me a handful o' cigars.

Soa Ah coomed awaay, but t' awd lass sings out: 'Oh, Mister Soldier, please coom again and bring that prettee dog.'

Ah didn't let on to t' Colonel's Laady about Mrs DeSussa, an' Rip he says nowt nawther; an' I gooes again, an' ivry time there was a good drink an' a handful o' good smooakes. An' Ah telled t' awd lass a heeap more about Rip than Ah'd ever heeard. How he tuk t' fost prize at Lunnon dog-show an' cost thotty-three pounds fower shillin' from t' man as bred him; 'at his own brother was t' propputty o' t' Prince o' Wailes, an' 'at he had a pedigree as long as a Dook's. An' she lapped it all oop an' wor niver tired o' admirin' him. But when t' awd lass took to givin' me money an' Ah seed 'at she wor gettin' fair fond about t' dog, Ah began to suspicion summat. Onnybody may give a soldier t' price iv a pint in a friendly waay an' theer's no 'arm done, but when it cooms to five rupees slipt into your hand, sly like, why, it's what t' 'lectioneerin' fellows calls bribery an' corruption. Specially when Mrs DeSussa thrawed hints how t' cold weather would soon be ovver, an' she wor gooin' to Munsoorie Pahar[19] an' we wor gooin' to Rawalpindi, an' she would niver see Rip onny more onless somebody she knawed on would be kind tiv her.

Soa I tells Mulvaaney an' Orth'ris all t' taale thro', beginnin' to end.

''Tis larceny that wicked ould laady manes,' says t' Irishman. ''Tis felony she is sejucin' ye into, my frind Learoyd, but I'll purtect your innocince. I'll save ye from the wicked wiles av that wealthy ould woman, an' I'll go wid ye this evenin' an' spake to her the wurruds av truth an' honesty. But, Jock,' says he, waggin' his heead, ''twas not like ye to kape all that good dhrink an' thim fine cigars to yo'sen, while Orth'ris here an' me have been prowlin' round wid throats as dry as lime-kilns, and nothin' to smoke but Canteen plug.[20] 'Twas a dhirty thrick to play on a comrade, for why should you, Learoyd, be balancin' yo'sen on the butt av a satin chair, as if Terence Mulvaney was not the aquil av anybody who thrades in jute!'

'Let alone me,' sticks in Orth'ris, 'but that's like life. Them wot's really fitted to decorate society get no show, while a blunderin' Yorkshireman like you –'

'Nay,' says I, 'it's none o' t' blunderin' Yorkshireman she wants; it's Rip. He's t' gentleman this journey.'

Soa t' next daay, Mulvaaney an' Rip an' me gooes to Mrs DeSussa's, an' t' Irishman bein' a strainger she wor a bit shy at fost. But yo've heeard Mulvaaney talk, an' yo' may believe as he fairly bewitched t' awd lass wal she let out 'at she wanted to tek Rip awaay wi' her to Munsoorie Pahar. Then Mulvaaney changes his tune an' axes her solemn-like if she'd thowt o' t' consequences o' gettin' two poor but honest soldiers sent t' Andamning Islands.[21] Mrs DeSussa began to cry, so Mulvaaney turns round oppen t' other tack and smooths her down, allowin' 'at Rip 'ud be a vast better off in t' Hills than down i' Bengal, an' 'twor a pity he shouldn't go wheer he was so well beliked. And soa he went on, backin' an' fillin' an' workin' up t' awd lass wal she felt as if her life worn't worth nowt if she didn't hev t' dog.

Then of a suddint he says: 'But ye *shall* have him, marm, for I've a feelin' heart, not like this could-blooded Yorkshireman. But 'twill cost ye not a penny less than three hundher rupees.'

'Don't yo' believe him, mum,' says I. 'T' Colonel's Laady wouldn't tek five hundred for him.'

'Who said she would?' says Mulvaaney. ''Tis not buyin' him I mane, but for the sake o' this kind, good laady, I'll do what I never dreamt to do in my life. I'll stale him!'

'Don't saay steeal,' says Mrs DeSussa; 'he shall hev the happiest home. Dogs often get lost, yo' know, and then they stray, an' he likes me an' I like him as I niver liked a dog yet, an' I *must* hev him. If I got him at t' last minute I cud carry him off to Munsoorie Pahar and nobody would niver knaw.'

Now an' again Mulvaaney looked acrost at me, an' tho' I could mek nowt o' what he was after, I concluded to tek his leead.

'Well, mum,' I says, 'I never thowt to coom down to dog-steealin', but if my comraade sees how it cud be done to oblige a laady like yo'sen, I'm nut t' man to hod back, tho' it's a bad business I'm thinkin', an' three hundred rupees is a poor set-off again t' chance iv them Damning Islands as Mulvaaney talks on.'

'I'll mek it three-fifty,' says Mrs DeSussa. 'Only let me hev t' dog!'

So we let her persuade us, an' she teks Rip's measure theer an' then, an' sent to Hamilton's[22] to order a silver collar again' t' time when he was to be her verree awn, which was to be t' daay she set off for Munsoorie Pahar.

'Sitha,[23] Mulvaaney,' says I, when we was outside, 'yo're niver goin' to let her hev Rip!'

'An' wud ye disappoint a poor old woman?' says he. 'She shall have *a* Rip.'

'An' wheer's he to come thro'?' says I.

'Learoyd, my man,' he sings out, 'you're a pretty man av your inches an' a good comrade, but your head is made av duff.[24] Isn't our frind Orth'ris a Taxidermist, an' a rale artist wid his cliver white fingers? An' fwhat's a Taxidermist but a man who can thrate shkins? Do ye mind the white dog that belongs to the Canteen Sargint, bad cess to him[25] – he that's lost half his time an' snarlin' the rest? He shall be lost for *good* now; an' do ye mind that he's the very spit in shape an' size av the Colonel's, barrin' that his tail is an inch too long, an' he has none av the colour that divarsifies the rale Rip, an' his timper is that av his masther *an'* worse? But fwhat is an inch on a dog's tail? An' fwhat to a professional like Orth'ris is a few ring-straked[26] shpots av black, brown, an' white? Nothin' at all, at all.'

Then we meets Orth'ris, an' that little man, bein' sharp as a needle, seed his waay through t' business in a minute. An' he went to work a-practisin' 'air-dyes the very next daay, beginnin' on some white rabbits he hed, an' then he drored all Rip's markin's on t' back of a white Commissariat bullock, so as to get his 'and in an' be sure of his cullers; shadin' off brown into black as nateral as life. If Rip *hed* a fault it was too mich markin', but it was straingely reg'lar, an' Orth'ris settled himsen to make a fost-rate job on it when he got haud o' t' Canteen Sargint's dog. Theer niver was sich a dog as thot for bad timper, an' it did nut get noa better when his tail hed to be fettled a inch an' a haalf shorter. But they may talk o' theer Royal Academies[27] as they like. *I* niver seed a bit o' animal paintin' to beat t' copy as Orth'ris made iv Rip's marks, wal t' picter itself was snarlin' all t' time an' tryin' to get at Rip standin' theer to be copied as good as goold.

Orth'ris allus hed as much conceit on himsen as would lift a balloon, an' he wor so pleeased wi' his sham Rip he wor for tekkin' him to Mrs DeSussa before she went awaay. But Mulvaaney an' me stopped thot, knowin' Orth'ris's work, though niver so cliver, was nobbut skin-deep.

An' at last Mrs DeSussa fixed t' daay for startin' to Munsoorie Pahar. We was to tek Rip to t' staashun i' a basket an' hand him ovver just when they was ready to start, an' then she'd give us t' brass – as wor 'greed upon.

An' my wod! It wor high time she wor off, for them 'air-dyes upon t' cur's back took a vast iv paintin' to keep t' reet culler, tho' Orth'ris spent a matter o' seven rupees six annas i' t' best drooggist shops i' Calcutta.

An' t' Canteen Sargint was lookin' for 'is dog everywheer; an', wi' bein' teed oop, t' beast's timper got waur nor ever.

It wor i' t' evenin' when t' train started thro' Howrah,[28] an' we 'elped Mrs DeSussa wi' about sixty boxes, an' then we gev her t' basket. Orth'ris, for pride iv his work, axed us to let him coom along wi' us, an' he cudn't help liftin' t' lid an' showin' t' cur as he lay coiled oop.

'Oh!' says t' awd lass; 'the beautee! How sweet he looks!' An' just then t' beauty snarled an' showed his teeth, so Mulvaaney shuts down t' lid an' says: 'Ye'll be careful, marm, whin ye tek him out. He's disaccustomed to travellin' by t' railway, an' he'll be sure to want his rale mistress an' his frind Learoyd, so ye'll make allowance for his feelin's at fost.'

She would do all thot an' more for the dear, good Rip, an' she would nut oppen t' basket till they were miles awaay, for fear onnybody should recognize him, an' we wor real good an' kind soldier-men, we wor, an' she honds me a bundle o' notes, an' then cooms oop a few of her relations an' friends to say goodbye – nut more than seventy-five there wasn't – an' we coots awaay . . .

What coom to t' three hundred an' fifty rupees? Thot's what I can scarcelins tell yo', but we melted[29] it – we melted it. It was share an' share alike, for Mulvaaney said: 'If Learoyd got hoult av Mrs DeSussa first, sure 'twas I that remimbered the Sargint's dog just in the nick av time, an' Orth'ris was the artist av janius that made a work av art out av that ugly piece av ill-natur'. Yet, by way av a thank-offerin' that I was not led into felony by that wicked ould woman, I'll send a thrifle to Father Victor[30] for the poor people he's always beggin' for.'

But me an' Orth'ris, he bein' Cockney an' I bein' pretty far north, did nut see it i' t' saame waay. We'd getten t' brass, an' we meaned to keep it. An' soa we did – for a short time.

Noa, noa, we niver heeard a wod more o' t' awd lass. Our Rig'mint went to Pindi,[31] an' t' Canteen Sargint he got himself another tyke insteead o' t' one 'at got lost so reg'lar, an' wor lost for good at last.

The Big Drunk Draf'

We're goin' 'ome, we're goin' 'ome –
  Our ship is *at* the shore,
An' you mus' pack your 'aversack,
  For we won't come back no more.
Ho, don't you grieve for me,
  My lovely Mary Ann,
For I'll marry you yet on a fourp'ny bit,
  As a time-expired ma-a-an!
Barrack-Room Ballad.

An awful thing has happened! My friend, Private Mulvaney, who went home in the *Serapis*,[1] time-expired,[2] not very long ago, has come back to India as a civilian! It was all Dinah Shadd's fault. She could not stand the poky little lodgings, and she missed her servant Abdullah more than words could tell. The fact was that the Mulvaneys had been out here too long, and had lost touch with England.

Mulvaney knew a contractor on one of the new Central India lines, and wrote to him for some sort of work. The contractor said that if Mulvaney could pay the passage he would give him command of a gang of coolies for old sake's sake. The pay was eighty-five rupees a month,[3] and Dinah Shadd said that if Terence did not accept she would make his life a 'basted purgathory'. Therefore the Mulvaneys came out as 'civilians', which was a great and terrible fall; though Mulvaney tried to disguise it, by saying that he was 'Colonel on the railway line, an' a consequinshal man'.

He wrote me an invitation, on a tool-indent form, to visit him; and I came down to the funny little 'construction' bungalow at the side of the line. Dinah Shadd had planted peas about and about, and nature had spread all manner of green stuff round the place. There was no change in Mulvaney except the change of clothing, which was deplorable, but could not be helped. He was standing upon his trolley, haranguing a gangman, and his shoulders were as well drilled, and his big, thick chin was as clean-shaven as ever.

'I'm a civilian now,' said Mulvaney. 'Cud you tell that I was iver a martial man? Don't answer, sorr, av you're strainin' betune a complimint an' a lie. There's no houldin' Dinah Shadd now she's got a house av her own. Go inside, an' dhrink tay out av chiny in the drrrawin'-room, an' thin we'll dhrink like Christians undher the tree here. Scutt, ye naygur-folk! There's a Sahib[4] come to call on me, an' that's more than he'll iver do for you onless you run! Get out, an' go on pilin' up the earth, quick, till sundown.'

When we three were comfortably settled under the big *sisham*[5] in front of the bungalow, and the first rush of questions and answers about Privates Ortheris and Learoyd and old times and places had died away, Mulvaney said, reflectively: 'Glory be, there's no p'rade to-morrow, an' no bun-headed Corp'ril-bhoy to give you his lip. An' yit I don't know. 'Tis harrd to be something ye niver were an' niver meant to be, an' all the ould days shut up along wid your papers. Eyah! I'm growin' rusty, an' 'tis the will av God that a man mustn't serve his Quane for time an' all.'

He helped himself to a fresh peg,[6] and sighed furiously.

'Let your beard grow, Mulvaney,' said I, 'and then you won't be troubled with those notions. You'll be a real civilian.'

Dinah Shadd had told me in the drawing-room of her desire to coax Mulvaney into letting his beard grow. ''Twas so civilian-like,' said poor Dinah, who hated her husband's hankering for his old life.

'Dinah Shadd, you're a dishgrace to an honust, clane-scraped man!' said Mulvaney, without replying to me. 'Grow a beard on your own chin, darlint, and lave my razors alone. They're all that stand betune me and dis-ris-pect-ability. Av I didn't shave, I wud be tormented wid an outrajis thurrst; for there's nothin' so dhryin' to the throat as a big billy-goat beard waggin' undher the chin. Ye wudn't have me dhrink *always*, Dinah Shadd? By the same token, you're kapin' me crool dhry now. Let me look at that whisky.'

The whisky was lent and returned, but Dinah Shadd, who had been just as eager as her husband in asking after old friends, rent me with: –

'I take shame for you, sorr, comin' down here – though the Saints know you're as welkim as the daylight whin you *do* come – an' upsettin' Terence's head wid your nonsense about – about fwhat's much better forgotten. He bein' a civilian now, an' you niver was aught else. Can you not let the Arrmy rest? 'Tis not good for Terence.'

I took refuge by Mulvaney, for Dinah Shadd has a temper of her own.

'Let be – let be,' said Mulvaney. ''Tis only wanst in a way I can talk about the ould days.' Then to me: – 'Ye say Dhrumshticks is well, an' his lady tu? I niver knew how I liked the grey garron[7] till I was shut av him an' Asia' – 'Dhrumshticks' was the nickname of the Colonel commanding Mulvaney's old Regiment. – 'Will you be seein' him again? You will. Thin tell him' – Mulvaney's eyes began to twinkle – 'tell him wid Privit –'

'*Mister*, Terence,' interrupted Dinah Shadd.

'Now the Divil an' all his angils an' the Firmament av Hiven fly away wid the "Mister", an' the sin av makin' me swear be on your confession, Dinah Shadd! *Privit*, I tell ye. Wid *Privit* Mulvaney's best obedience, that but for me the last time-expired wud be still pullin' hair on their way to the sea.'

He threw himself back in the chair, chuckled, and was silent.

'Mrs Mulvaney,' I said, 'please take up the whisky, and don't let him have it until he has told the story.'

Dinah Shadd dexterously whipped the bottle away, saying at the same time, ''Tis nothing to be proud av,' and thus captured by the enemy, Mulvaney spake: –

''Twas on Chuseday week. I was bahadherin'[8] round wid the gangs on the 'bankmint – I've taught the hoppers[9] how to kape step an' stop screechin' – whin a head-gangman comes up to me, wid about two inches av shirt-tail hangin' round his neck an' a disthressful light in his eye. "Sahib," sez he, "there's a rig'mint an' a half av sodgers up at the junction, knockin' red cindhers out av ivrything an' ivrybody! They thried to hang me in my cloth," he sez, "an' there will be murther an' ruin an' rape in the place before nightfall! They say they're comin' down here to wake us up. What will we do wid our wimmen-folk?"

'"Fetch me throlley!" sez I. "Me heart's sick in my ribs for a wink at anything wid the Quane's uniform on ut. Fetch my throlley, an' six av the jildiest[10] men, and run me up in shtyle."'

'He tuk his best coat,' said Dinah Shadd reproachfully.

''Twas to do honour to the Widdy. I cud ha' done no less, Dinah Shadd. You and your digresshins interfere wid the coorse av the narrative. Have you iver considhered fwhat I wud look like wid me *head* shaved as well as me chin? You bear that in your mind, Dinah darlin'.

'I was throlleyed up six miles, all to get a shquint at that draf'. I *knew* 'twas a spring draf' goin' Home, for there's no rig'mint hereabouts, more's the pity.'

'Praise the Virgin!' murmured Dinah Shadd. But Mulvaney did not hear.

'Whin I was about three-quarters av a mile off the rest-camp, powtherin'[11] along fit to burrst, I heard the noise av the men, an', on my sowl, sorr, I cud catch the voice av Peg Barney bellowin' like a bison wid the belly-ache. You remimber Peg Barney that was in D Comp'ny – a red, hairy scraun, wid a scar on his jaw? Peg Barney that cleared out the Blue Lights'[12] Jubilee meeting wid the cook-room mop last year?

'Thin I knew ut was a draf' of the Ould Rig'mint, an' I was conshumed wid sorrow for the bhoy that was in charge. We was harrd scrapin's at any time. Did I iver tell you how Horker Kelley went into Clink nakid as Phoebus Apollonius,[13] wid the shirts av the Corp'ril an' file undher his arrum? An' *he* was a moild man! But I'm digresshin'. 'Tis a shame both to the rig'mints and the Arrmy sendin' down little orf'cer bhoys wid a draf' av strong men mad wid liquor an' the chanst av gettin' shut av India, an' *niver a punishmint that's fit to be given right down an' away from cantonmints to the docks*! 'Tis this nonsinse. Whin I am servin' my time, I'm undher the Articles av War,[14] an' can be whipped on the peg for *thim*. But whin I've *served* my time, I'm a Reserve man, an' the Articles av War haven't any hould on me. An orf'cer *can't* do anythin' to a time-expired savin' confinin' him to barricks. 'Tis a wise rig'lation bekaze a time-expired does *not* have any barricks; bein' on the move all the time. 'Tis a Solomon[15] av a rig'lation, is that. I wud like to be inthrojuced to the man that made ut. 'Tis aisier to get colts from a Kibbereen horse-fair[16] into Galway than to take a bad draf' over ten miles av country. Consiquintly that rig'lation – for fear that the men wud be hurt by the little orf'cer bhoy. No matther. The nearer my throlley came to the rest-camp, the woilder was the shine, an' the louder was the voice av Peg Barney. "'Tis good I am here," thinks I to mesilf, "for Peg alone is employmint for two or three." He bein', I well knew, as copped[17] as a dhrover.

'Faith, that rest-camp was a sight! The tint-ropes was all skew-nosed, an' the pegs looked as dhrunk as the men – fifty av thim – the scourin's, an' rinsin's, an' Divil's lavin's av the Ould Rig'mint. I tell you, sorr, they were dhrunker than any men you've iver seen in your mortial life. *How* does a draf' get dhrunk? How does a frog get fat? They suck ut in through their shkins.

'There was Peg Barney sittin' on the groun' in his shirt – wan shoe off an' wan shoe on – whackin' a tint-peg over the head wid his boot, an' singin' fit to wake the dead. 'Twas no clane song that he sung, though. 'Twas the Divil's Mass.'

'What's that?' I asked.

'Whin a bad egg is shut av the Arrmy, he sings the Divil's Mass for a good riddance; an' that manes swearin' at ivrything from the Commandher-in-Chief down to the Room-Corp'ril, such as you niver in your days heard. Some men can swear so as to make green turf crack! Have you iver heard the Curse in an Orange Lodge?[18] The Divil's Mass is ten times worse, an' Peg Barney was singin' ut, whackin' the tint-peg on the head wid his boot for each man that he cursed. A powerful big voice had Peg Barney, an' a hard swearer he was whin sober. I stood forninst him, an' 'twas not me eye alone cud tell Peg was dhrunk as a coot.

'"Good mornin', Peg," I sez, whin he dhrew breath afther cursin' the Adj'tint-Gin'ral. "I've put on my best coat to see you, Peg Barney," sez I.

'"Thin take ut off agin," sez Peg Barney, latherin' away wid the boot. "Take ut off an' dance, ye lousy civilian!"

'Wid that he begins cursin' ould Dhrumshticks, being so full he clane misremimbers the Brigade-Major an' the Judge-Advokit-Gin'ral.

'"Do you not know me, Peg?" sez I, though me blood was hot in me wid being called a civilian.'

'An' him a decent married man!' wailed Dinah Shadd.

'"I do not," sez Peg, "but dhrunk or sober I'll tear the hide off your back wid a shovel whin I've stopped singin'."

'"Say you so, Peg Barney?" sez I. "'Tis clear as mud you've forgotten me. I'll assist your autobiography." Wid that I stretched[19] Peg Barney, boot an' all, an' wint into the camp. An awful sight ut was!

'"Where's the orf'cer in charge av the detachment?" sez I to Scrub Greene – the manest little wurrum that iver walked.

'"There's no orf'cer, ye ould cook," sez Scrub; "we're a bloomin' Republic."

'"Are you that?" sez I; "thin I'm O'Connell[20] the Dictator, an' by this you will larn to kape a civil tongue in your rag-box."

'Wid that I stretched Scrub Greene an' wint to the orf'cer's tint. 'Twas a new little bhoy – not wan I'd iver seen before. He was sittin' in his tint, purtendin' not to have ear av the racket.

'I saluted – but for the life av me I mint to shake hands whin I went in. 'Twas the sword hangin' on the tint-pole changed my will.

'"Can't I help, sorr?" sez I. "'Tis a strong man's job they've given you, an' you'll be wantin' help by sundown." He was a bhoy wid bowils, that child, an' a rale gintleman.

'"Sit down," sez he.

'"Not before my orf'cer," sez I; an' I tould him fwhat my service was.

'"I've heard av you," sez he. "You tuk the town av Lungtungpen nakid."[21]

'"Faith," thinks I, "that's Honour an' Glory"; for 'twas Lift'nint Brazenose did that job. "I'm wid ye, sorr," sez I, "if I'm av use. They shud niver ha' sent you down wid the draf'. Savin' your presince, sorr," I sez, "'tis only Lift'nint Hackerston in the Ould Rig'mint can manage a Home draf'."

'"I've niver had charge of men like this before," sez he, playin' wid the pen on the table; "an' I see by the Rig'lations –"

'"Shut your eye to the Rig'lations, sorr," I sez, "till the throoper's into blue wather.[22] By the Rig'lations you've got to tuck thim up for the night, or they'll be runnin' foul av my coolies an' makin' a shiverarium[23] half through the country. Can you trust your non-coms,[24] sorr?"

'"Yes," sez he.

'"Good," sez I; "there'll be throuble before the night. Are you marchin', sorr?"

'"To the next station," sez he.

'"Better still," sez I. "There'll be big throuble."

'"Can't be too hard on a Home draf'," sez he; "the great thing is to get thim in-ship."

'"Faith, you've larnt the half av your lesson, sorr," sez I, "but av you shtick to the Rig'lations you'll niver get thim in-ship at all, at all. Or there won't be a rag av kit betune thim whin you do."

''Twas a dear little orf'cer bhoy, an' by way av kapin' his heart up, I tould him fwhat I saw wanst in a draf' in Egypt.'

'What was that, Mulvaney?' said I.

'Sivin-an'-fifty men sittin' on the bank av a canal, laughin' at a poor little squidgereen[25] av an orf'cer that they'd made wade into the slush an' pitch the things out av the boats for their Lord High Mightinesses. That made me orf'cer bhoy woild wid indignation.

'"Soft an' aisy, sorr," sez I; "you've niver had your draf' in hand since you left cantonmints. Wait till the night, an' your work will be ready to you. Wid your permission, sorr, I will invistigate the camp, an' talk to my ould frinds. 'Tis no manner av use thryin' to shtop the divilmint *now*."

'Wid that I wint out into the camp an' inthrojuced mesilf to ivry man sober enough to remimber me. I was some wan in the ould days, an' the bhoys was glad to see me – all excipt Peg Barney wid a eye like a tomata five days in the bazar, an' a nose to match. They come round me an' shuk me, an' I tould thim I was in privit employ wid an income av me own, an' a drrrawin'-room fit to bate the Quane's; an' wid me lies an' me shtories an' nonsinse gin'rally, I kept 'em quiet in wan way an' another, knockin' roun' the camp. 'Twas *bad* even thin whin I was the Angil av Peace.

'I talked to me ould non-coms – *they* was sober – an' betune me an' thim we wore[26] the draf' over into their tints at the proper time. The little orf'cer bhoy he comes round, dacint an' civil-spoke as might be.

'"Rough quarters, men," sez he, "but you can't look to be as comfortable as in barricks. We must make the best av things. I've shut me eyes to a dale av dog's tricks to-day, an' now there must be no more av ut."

'"No more we will. Come an' have a dhrink, me son," sez Peg Barney, staggerin' where he stud. Me little orf'cer bhoy kep' his timper.

'"You're a sulky swine, you are," sez Peg Barney, an' at that the men in the tint began to laugh.

'I tould you me orf'cer bhoy had bowils. He cut Peg Barney as near as might be on the eye that I'd squshed whin we first met. Peg wint spinnin' across the tint.

'"Peg him out, sorr," sez I, in a whishper.

'"Peg him out!" sez me orf'cer bhoy, up loud, just as if 'twas battalion-p'rade an' he pickin' his wurruds from the Sargint.

'The non-coms tuk Peg Barney – a howlin' handful he was – an' in three minut's he was pegged out – chin down, tight-dhrawn – on his stummick, a tint-peg to each arrum an' leg, swearin' fit to turn a naygur white.

'I tuk a peg an' jammed ut into his ugly jaw. – "Bite on that, Peg Barney," I sez; "the night is settin' frosty, an' you'll be wantin' divarsion before the mornin'. But for the Rig'lations you'd be bitin' on a bullet now at the thriangles,[27] Peg Barney," sez I.

'All the draf' was out av their tints watchin' Barney bein' pegged.

'"'Tis agin' the Rig'lations! He strook him!" screeches out Scrub Greene, who was always a lawyer; an' some of the men tuk up the shoutin'.

'"Peg out that man!" sez me orf'cer bhoy, niver losin' his timper; an' the non-coms wint in and pegged out Scrub Greene by the side av Peg Barney.

'I cud see that the draf' was comin' roun'. The men stud not knowin' fwhat to do.

'"Get to your tints!" sez me orf'cer bhoy. "Sargint, put a sinthry over these two men."

'The men wint back into the tints like jackals,[28] an' the rest av the night there was no noise at all excipt the stip av the sinthry over the two, an' Scrub Greene blubberin' like a child. 'Twas a chilly night, an', faith, ut sobered Peg Barney.

'Just before Revelly,[29] me orf'cer bhoy comes out an' sez: "Loose those men an' send thim to their tints!" Scrub Greene wint away widout a word, but Peg Barney, stiff wid the cowld, stud like a sheep, thryin' to make his orf'cer ondhersthand he was sorry for playin' the goat.

'There was no tucker[30] in the draf' whin ut fell in for the march, an' divil a wurrud about "illegality" cud I hear.

'I wint to the ould Colour-Sargint and I sez: "Let me die in glory," sez I. "I've seen a man this day!"

'"A man he is," sez ould Hother; "the draf's as sick as a herrin'. They'll all go down to the sea like lambs. That bhoy has the bowils av a cantonmint av Gin'rals."

'"Amin," sez I, "an' good luck go wid him, wheriver he be, by land or by sea. Let me know how the draf' gets clear."

'An' do you know how they *did*? That bhoy, so I was tould by letter from Bombay, bully-damned 'em down to the docks, till they cudn't call their sowls their own. From the time they left me eye till they was 'tween decks, not wan av thim was more than dacintly dhrunk. An', by the Holy Articles av War, whin they wint aboard they cheered him till they cudn't spake, an' *that*, mark you, has not come about wid a draf' in the mim'ry av livin' man! You look to that little orf'cer bhoy. He has bowils. 'Tis not ivry child that wud chuck the Rig'lations to Flanders an' stretch Peg Barney on a wink from a brokin an' dilapidated ould carkiss like mesilf. I'd be proud to serve –'

'Terence, you're a civilian,' said Dinah Shadd warningly.

'So I am – so I am. Is ut like I wud forget ut? But he was a gran' bhoy all the same, an' I'm only a mud-tipper[31] wid a hod on my shoulthers. The whisky's in the heel av your hand, sorr. Wid your good lave we'll dhrink to the Ould Rig'mint – three fingers[32] – standin' up!'

And we drank.

{ The Solid Muldoon }

Did ye see John Malone, wid his shinin' brand-new hat?
Did ye see how he walked like a grand aristocrat?
There was flags an' banners wavin' high, an' dhress and shtyle were shown,
But the best av all the company was Misther John Malone.

John Malone.

There had been a royal dog-fight in the ravine at the back of the rifle-butts, between Learoyd's Jock and Ortheris's Blue Rot – both mongrel Rampur hounds,[1] chiefly ribs and teeth. It lasted for twenty happy, howling minutes, and then Blue Rot collapsed and Ortheris paid Learoyd three rupees, and we were all very thirsty. A dog-fight is a most heating entertainment, quite apart from the shouting, because Rampurs fight over a couple of acres of ground. Later, when the sound of belt-badges clicking against the necks of beer-bottles had died away, conversation drifted from dog- to man-fights of all kinds. Humans resemble red deer in some respects. Any talk of fighting seems to wake up a sort of imp in their breasts, and they bell one to the other, exactly like challenging bucks. This is noticeable even in men who consider themselves superior to Privates of the Line. It shows the Refining Influence of Civilization and the March of Progress.

Tale provoked tale, and each tale more beer. Even dreamy Learoyd's eyes began to brighten, and he unburdened himself of a long history in which a trip to Malham Cove,[2] a girl at Pateley Brigg,[3] a ganger, himself, and a pair of clogs were mixed in a drawling tangle.

'An' soa Ah coot's heead oppen from t' chin to t' hair, an' he was abed for t' matter o' a month,' concluded Learoyd pensively.

Mulvaney came out of a reverie – he was lying down – and flourished his heels in the air. 'You're a man, Learoyd,' said he critically, 'but you've only fought wid men, an' that's an ivry-day expayrience; but I've stud up to a ghost, an' that was *not* an ivry-day expayrience.'

'No?' said Ortheris, throwing a cork at him. 'You git up an' address the 'ouse – you an' yer expayriences. Is it a bigger one nor usual?'

''Twas the livin' truth!' answered Mulvaney, stretching out a huge arm and catching Ortheris by the collar. 'Now where are ye, me son? Will ye take the Wurrud av the Lorrd out av my mouth another time?' He shook him to emphasize the question.

'No, somethin' else, though,' said Ortheris, making a dash at Mulvaney's pipe, capturing it, and holding it at arm's length; 'I'll chuck it acrost the Ditch if you don't let me go!'

'Ye maraudhin' haythen! 'Tis the only cutty[4] I iver loved. Handle her tinder or I'll chuck *you* acrost the nullah.[5] If that poipe was bruk – Ah! Give her back to me, sorr!'

Ortheris had passed the treasure to my hand. It was an absolutely perfect clay, as shiny as the black ball at Pool. I took it reverently, but I was firm.

'Will you tell us about the ghost-fight if I do?' I said.

'Is ut the shtory that's throublin' you? Av coorse I will. I mint to all along. I was only gettin' at ut my own way, as Popp Doggle said whin they found him thryin' to ram a cartridge down the muzzle.[6] Orth'ris, fall away!'

He released the little Londoner, took back his pipe, filled it, and his eyes twinkled. He has the most eloquent eyes of any one that I know.

'Did I iver tell you,' he began, 'that I was wanst the divil av a man?'

'You did,' said Learoyd with a childish gravity that made Ortheris yell with laughter, for Mulvaney was always impressing upon us his great merits in the old days.

'Did I iver tell you,' Mulvaney continued calmly, 'that I was wanst more av a divil than I am now?'

'Mer – ria! You don't mean it?' said Ortheris.

'Whin I was Corp'ril[7] – I was rejuced aftherwards – but, as I say, *whin* I was Corp'ril, I was the divil av a man.'

He was silent for nearly a minute, while his mind rummaged among old memories and his eye glowed. He bit upon the pipe-stem and charged into his tale.

'Eyah! They was great times. I'm ould now. Me hide's wore off in patches; sinthry-go[8] has disconceited me, an' I'm married tu. But I've had my day – I've had my day, an' nothin' can take away the taste av that! Oh, my time past, whin I put me fut through ivry livin' wan av the Tin Commandmints betune Revelly and Lights Out, blew the froth off a pewter,[9] wiped me moustache wid the back av me hand, an' slept on ut all as quiet as a little child! But ut's over – ut's over, an' 'twill niver come back to me; not though I prayed for a week av Sundays. Was there *any* wan in the Ould Rig'mint to touch Corp'ril Terence Mulvaney whin that same was turned out for sedukshin? I niver met him. Ivry woman that was not a witch was worth the runnin' afther in those days, an' ivry man was my dearest frind or – I had stripped to him[10] an' we knew which was the betther av the tu.

'Whin I was Corp'ril I wud not ha' changed wid the Colonel – no, nor yet the Commandher-in-Chief. I wud be a Sargint. There was nothin' I wud not be! Mother av Hivin, look at me! Fwhat am I *now*?

'We was quartered in a big cantonmint – 'tis no manner av use namin' names, for ut might give the barricks disreputation – an' I was the Imperor av the Earth in me own mind, an' wan or tu wimmen thought the same. Small blame to thim. Afther we had lain there a year, Bragin, the Colour-Sargint av E Comp'ny, wint an' took a wife that was lady's maid to some big lady in the station. She's dead now, is Annie Bragin – died in child-bed at Kirpa Tal, or ut may ha' been Almorah[11] – sivin – nine years gone, an' Bragin he married agin. But she was a pretty woman whin Bragin inthrojuced her to cantonmint society. She had eyes like the brown av a buttherfly's wing whin the sun catches ut, an' a waist no thicker than me arrum, an' a little sof' button av a mouth I wud ha' gone through all Asia bristlin' wid bay'nits to get the kiss av. An' her hair was as long as the tail av the Colonel's charger – forgive me mentionin' that blundherin' baste in the same mouthful wid Annie Bragin – but 'twas all shpun gowld, an' time was whin a lock av ut was more than di'monds to me. There was niver pretty woman yet, an' I've had thruck wid a few, cud open the door to Annie Bragin.

''Twas in the Cath'lic Chapel I saw her first, me eye rollin' round as usual to see fwhat was to be seen. "You're too good for Bragin, me love," thinks I to mesilf, "but that's a mistake I can put straight, or me name is not Terence Mulvaney."

'Now take me wurrud for ut, you Orth'ris there an' Learoyd, an' kape out av the Married Quarters – as I did *not*. No good iver comes av ut, an' there's always the chance av your bein' found wid your face in the dirt, a long picket[12] in the back av your head, an' your hands playin' the fifes on the tread av another man's doorstep. 'Twas so we found O'Hara,[13] he that Rafferty killed six years gone, whin he wint to his death wid his hair oiled, whistlin' *Larry O'Rourke* betune his teeth. Kape out av the Married Quarters, I say, as I did not. 'Tis onwholesim, 'tis dangerous, an' 'tis ivrything else that's bad, but – O my sowl, 'tis swate while ut lasts!

'I was always hangin' about there whin I was off jooty an' Bragin wasn't, but niver a swate word beyon' ordinar' did I get from Annie Bragin. "'Tis the pervarsity av the sect," sez I to mesilf, an' gave me cap another cock on me head an' straightened me back – 'twas the back av a Dhrum-Major[14] in those days – an' wint off as tho' I did not care, wid all the wimmen in the Married Quarters laughin'. I was pershuaded – most bhoys *are*, I'm thinkin' – that no woman born av woman cud stand agin' me av I hild up me little finger. I had good cause for to think that way – till I met Annie Bragin.

'Time an' agin whin I was blandandherin' in the dusk a man wud go past me as quiet as a cat. "That's quare," thinks I, "for I am, or I shud be, the only man in these parts. Now what divilmint can Annie be up to?" Thin I called myself a blayguard for thinkin' such things; but I thought thim all the same. An' that, mark you, is the way av a man.

'Wan evenin' I said: "Mrs Bragin, manin' no disrespect to you, who *is* that Corp'ril man" – I had seen the shtripes though I cud niver get sight av his face – "*who* is that Corp'ril man that comes in always whin I'm goin' away?"

'"Mother av God!" sez she, turnin' as white as my belt;[15] "have *you* seen him too?"

'"Seen him!" sez I; "av coorse I have. Did ye wish me not to see him, for" – we were standin' talkin' in the dhark, outside the veranda av Bragin's quarters – "you'd betther tell me to shut me eyes. Onless I'm mistaken, he's come now."

'An', sure enough, the Corp'ril man was walkin' to us, hangin' his head down as though he was ashamed av himsilf.

'"Good night Mrs Bragin," sez I, very cool. "'Tis not for me to interfere wid your *a-moors*; but you might manage some things wid more dacincy. I'm off to Canteen," I sez.

'I turned on my heel an' wint away, swearin' I wud give that man a dhressin' that wud shtop him messin' about the Married Quarters for a month an' a week. I had not tuk ten paces before Annie Bragin was hangin' on to my arrum, an' I cud feel that she was shakin' all over.

'"Shtay wid me, Mister Mulvaney," sez she. "You're flesh and blood, at the least – are ye not?"

'"I'm *all* that," sez I, an' my anger wint in a flash. "Will I want to be asked twice, Annie?"

'Wid that I slipped my arrum round her waist, for, begad, I fancied she had surrindered at discretion, an' the honours av war were mine.

'"Fwhat nonsinse is this?" sez she, dhrawin' hersilf up on the tips av her dear little toes. "Wid the mother's milk not dhry on your impident mouth! Let go!" she sez.

'"Did ye not say just now that I was flesh and blood?" sez I. "I have not changed since," I sez; and I kep' my arrum where ut was.

'"Your arrums to yoursilf!" sez she, an' her eyes sparkild.

'"Sure, 'tis only human natur'," sez I; an' I kep' my arrum where ut was.

'"Natur' or no natur'," says she, "you take your arrum away or I'll tell Bragin, an' he'll alter the natur' av your head. Fwhat d'you take me for?" she sez.

'"A woman," sez I; "the prettiest in barricks."

'"A *wife*," sez she. "The straightest in cantonmints!"

'Wid that I dropped my arrum, fell back tu paces, an' saluted, for I saw that she mint fwhat she said.'

'Then you know something that some men would give a good deal to be certain of. How could you tell?' I demanded in the interests of Science.

'Watch the hand,' said Mulvaney. 'Av she shuts her hand tight, thumb down over the knuckle, take up your hat an' go. You'll only make a fool av yoursilf av you shtay. But av the hand lies opin on the lap, or av you see her thryin' to shut ut, an' she can't, – go on! She's not past reasonin' wid.

'Well, as I was sayin', I fell back, saluted, an' was goin' away.

'"Shtay wid me," she sez. "Look! He's comin' agin."

'She pointed to the veranda, an' by the Hoight av Impart'nince, the Corp'ril man was comin' out av Bragin's quarters.

'"He's done that these five evenin's past," sez Annie Bragin. "Oh, fwhat will I do!"

'"He'll not do ut agin," sez I, for I was fightin' mad.

'Kape away from a man that has been a thrifle crossed in love till the fever's died down. He rages like a brute baste.

'I wint up to the man in the veranda, manin', as sure as I sit, to knock the life out av him. He slipped into the open. "Fwhat are you doin' philandherin' about here, ye scum av the gutter?" sez I polite, to give him his warnin', for I wanted him ready.

'He niver lifted his head, but sez, all mournful an' melancolious, as if he thought I wud be sorry for him: "I can't find her," sez he.

'"My troth," sez I, "you've lived too long – you an' your seekin's an' findin's in a dacint married woman's quarters! Hould up your head, ye frozen thief av Genesis," sez I, "an' you'll find all you want an' more!"

'But he niver hild up, an' I let go from the shoulther to where the hair is short over the eyebrows.

'"That'll do your business," sez I, but it nearly did mine instid. I put me bodyweight behind the blow, but I hit nothing at all, an' near put me shoulther out. The Corp'ril man was not there, an' Annie Bragin, who had been watchin' from the veranda, throws up her heels, an' carries on like a cock whin his neck's wrung by the dhrummer-bhoy. I wint back to her, for a livin' woman, an' a woman like Annie Bragin, is more than a p'rade-groun' full av ghosts. I'd niver seen a woman faint before, an' I stud like a shtuck calf, askin' her whether she was dead, an' prayin' her for the love av me, an' the love av her husband, an' the love av the Virgin, to opin her blessed eyes agin, an' callin' mesilf all the names undher the canopy av Hivin for plaguin' her wid my miserable *a-moors* whin I ought to ha' stud betune her an' this Corp'ril man that had lost the number av his mess.

'I misremimber fwhat nonsinse I said, but I was not so far gone that I cud not hear a fut on the dirt outside. 'Twas Bragin comin' in, an' by the same token Annie was comin' to. I jumped to the far end av the veranda an' looked as if butther wudn't melt in my mouth.

But Mrs Quinn, the Quartermaster's wife that was, had tould Bragin about my hangin' round Annie.

'"I'm not plazed wid you, Mulvaney," sez Bragin, unbucklin' his sword, for he had been on jooty.

'"That's bad hearin'," I sez, an' I knew that me pickets were dhriven in. "What for, Sargint?" sez I.

'"Come outside," sez he, "an' I'll show you why."

'"I'm willin'," I sez; "but my shtripes are none so ould that I can afford to lose thim. Tell me now, *who* do I go out wid?" sez I.

'He was a quick man an' a just, an' saw fwhat I wud be afther. "Wid Mrs Bragin's husband," sez he. He might ha' known by me askin' that favour that I had done him no wrong.

'We wint to the back av the arsenal an' I stripped to him, an' for ten minut's 'twas all I cud do to prevent him killin' himsilf agin' my fistes. He was mad as a dumb dog – just frothin' wid rage; but he had no chanst wid me in reach, or learnin', or anything else.

'"Will ye hear reason?" sez I, whin his first wind was run out.

'"Not whoile I can see," sez he. Wid that I gave him both, one afther the other, smash through the low gyard that he'd been taught whin he was a bhoy, an' the eyebrow shut down on the cheek-bone like the wing av a sick crow.

'"Will you hear reason now, brave man?" sez I.

'"Not whoile I can speak," sez he, staggerin' up blind as a stump. I was loath to du ut, but I wint round an' swung into the jaw side-on an' shifted ut a half-pace to the lef'.

'"Will ye hear reason now?" sez I. "I can't keep my timper much longer, an' 'tis like I will hurt you."

'"Not whoile I can stand," he mumbles out av one corner av his mouth. So I closed an' threw him – blind, dumb, an' sick, an' jammed the jaw straight.

'"You're an ould fool, *Mister* Bragin," sez I.

'"You're a young thafe," sez he, "an' you've bruk my heart, you an' Annie betune you!"

'Thin he began cryin' like a child as he lay. I was sorry as I had niver been before. 'Tis an awful thing to see a strong man cry.

'"I'll swear on the Cross!" sez I.

'"I care for none av your oaths," sez he.

'"Come back to your quarters," sez I, "an' if you don't believe the livin', begad, you shall listen to the dead," I sez.

'I hoisted him an' tuk him back to his quarters. "Mrs Bragin," sez I, "here's a man that you can cure quicker than me."

'"You've shamed me before my wife," he whimpers.

'"Have I so?" sez I. "By the look on Mrs Bragin's face I think I'm for a dhressin'-down worse than I gave you."

'An' I was! Annie Bragin was woild wid indignation. There was not a name that a dacint woman cud use that was not given my way. I've had my Colonel walk roun' me like a cooper roun' a cask[16] for fifteen minut's in Ord'ly-Room, bekaze I wint into the Corner Shop[17] an unstrapped lewnatic; but all that I iver tuk from his tongue was ginger-pop to fwhat Annie tould me. An' that, mark you, is the way av a woman.

'Whin ut was done for want av breath, an' Annie was bendin' over her husband, I sez: "'Tis all thrue, an' I'm a blayguard an' you're an honust woman; but will you tell him av wan service that I did you?"

'As I finished speakin' the Corp'ril man came up to the veranda, and Annie Bragin shquealed. The moon was up, an' we cud see his face.

'"I can't find her," sez the Corp'ril man, an' wint out like the puff av a candle.

'"Saints stand betune us an' evil!" sez Bragin, crossin' himsilf; "that's Flahy av the Tyrone."[18]

'"Who was he?" I sez, "for he has given me a dale av fightin' this day."

'Bragin tould us that Flahy was a Corp'ril who lost his wife av cholera in those quarters three years gone, an' wint mad, an' *walked* afther they buried him, huntin' for her.

'"Well," sez I to Bragin, "he's been hookin' out av Purgathory to kape company wid Mrs Bragin ivry evenin' for the last fortnight. You may tell Mrs Quinn, wid my love, for I know that she's been talkin' to you, an' you've been listenin', that she ought to ondher-sthand the differ 'twixt a man an' a ghost. She's had three husbands," sez I, "an' *you*'ve got a wife too good for you. Instid av which you lave her to be boddered by ghosts an' – an' all manner av evil spirruts. I'll niver go talkin' in the way av politeness to a man's wife agin. Good night to you both," sez I; an' wid that I wint away, havin' fought wid woman, man, *an*' Divil all in the heart av an hour. By the same token I gave Father Victor wan rupee to say a mass for Flahy's soul, me havin' dishcommoded him by shtickin' my fist into his systim.'

'Your ideas of politeness seem rather large, Mulvaney,' I said.

'That's as you look at ut,' said Mulvaney calmly. 'Annie Bragin niver cared for me. For all that, I did not want to leave anythin' behin' me that Bragin cud take hould av to be angry wid her about – whin an honust wurrud cud ha' cleared all up. There's nothing like opin-spakin'. Orth'ris, ye scutt, let me put me eye to that bottle, for my throat's as dhry as whin I thought I wud get a kiss from Annie Bragin. An' that's fourteen years gone!

'Eyah! Cork's own city an' the blue sky above ut – an' the times that was – the times that was!'

With the Main Guard

Der jungere Uhlanen
Sit round mit open mouth
While Breitmann tell dem sdories
Of fightin' in the South;
Und gif dem moral lessons,
How before der battle pops,
Take a little prayer to Himmel
Und a goot long drink of Schnapps.
C. G. Leland.

'Mary, Mother av Mercy, fwhat the divil possist us to take an' kape this melancolious counthry? Answer me that, sorr.'

It was Mulvaney who was speaking. The time was one o'clock of a stifling June night, and the place was the main gate of Fort Amara,[1] most desolate and least desirable of all fortresses in India. What I was doing there at that hour is a question which only concerns M'Grath the Sergeant of the Guard, and the men on the gate.

'Slape,' said Mulvaney, 'is a shuparfluous necessity. This Gyard'll shtay lively till relieved.' He himself was stripped to the waist; Learoyd on the next bedstead was dripping from the skinful of water which Ortheris, clad only in white trousers, had just sluiced over his shoulders; and a fourth private was muttering uneasily as he dozed open-mouthed in the glare of the great guard-lantern. The heat under the bricked archway was terrifying.

'The worrst night that iver I remimber. Eyah! Is all Hell loose this tide?' said Mulvaney. A puff of burning wind lashed through the wicket-gate like a wave of the sea, and Ortheris swore.

'Are ye more heasy, Jock?' he said to Learoyd. 'Put yer 'ead between your legs. It'll go orf in a minute.'

'Ah doan't care. Ah would not care, but ma heart is plaayin' tivvy-tivvy[2] on ma ribs. Let ma die! Oh, leave ma die!' groaned the huge Yorkshireman, who was feeling the heat acutely, being of fleshy build.

The sleeper under the lantern roused for a moment and raised himself on his elbow. 'Die and be damned then!' he said. '*I*'m damned and I can't die!'

'Who's that?' I whispered, for the voice was new to me.

'Gentleman born,' said Mulvaney; 'Corp'ril wan year, Sargint nex'. Red-hot on his C'mission, but dhrinks like a fish. He'll be gone before the cowld weather's here. So!'

He slipped his boot, and with the naked toe just touched the trigger of his Martini.[3] Ortheris misunderstood the movement, and the next instant the Irishman's rifle was dashed aside, while Ortheris stood before him, his eyes blazing with reproof.

'You!' said Ortheris. 'My Gawd, *you*! If it was you, wot would *we* do?'

'Kape quiet, little man,' said Mulvaney, putting him aside, but very gently; ''tis not me, nor will ut be me whoile Dinah Shadd's here. I was but showin' somethin'.'

Learoyd, bowed on his bedstead, groaned, and the gentleman-ranker sighed in his sleep. Ortheris took Mulvaney's tendered pouch, and we three smoked gravely for a space while the dust-devils[4] danced on the glacis[5] and scoured the red-hot plain.

'Pop?' said Ortheris, wiping his forehead.

'Don't tantalise wid talkin' av dhrink, or I'll shtuff you into your own breech-block an' – fire you off!' grunted Mulvaney.

Ortheris chuckled, and from a niche in the veranda produced six bottles of gingerade.

'Where did ye get ut, ye Machiavel?'[6] said Mulvaney. ''Tis no bazar pop.'

''Ow do *I* know wot the orf'cers drink?' answered Ortheris. 'Arst the mess-man.'

'Ye'll have a Disthrict Coort-Martial settin' on ye yet, me son,' said Mulvaney, 'but' – he opened a bottle – 'I will not report ye this time. Fwhat's in the mess-kid is mint for the belly, as they say, 'specially whin that mate is dhrink. Here's luck! A bloody war or a – no, we've got the sickly season. War, thin!' – he waved the innocent 'pop' to the four quarters of heaven. 'Bloody war! North, East, South, an' West! Jock, ye quakin' hayrick, come an' dhrink.'

But Learoyd, half mad with the fear of death presaged in the swelling veins of his neck, was begging his Maker to strike him dead, and fighting for more air between his prayers. A second time Ortheris drenched the quivering body with water, and the giant revived.

'An' Ah divn't see thot a mon is i' fettle for gooin' on to live; an' Ah divn't see thot there is owt for t' livin' for. Hear now, lads! Ah'm tired – tired. There's nobbut watter i' ma bones. Leave mă die!'

The hollow of the arch gave back Learoyd's broken whisper in a bass boom. Mulvaney looked at me hopelessly, but I remembered how the madness of despair had once fallen upon Ortheris, that weary, weary afternoon on the banks of the Khemi River, and how it had been exorcised by the skilful magician Mulvaney.[7]

'Talk, Terence!' I said, 'or we shall have Learoyd slinging loose,[8] and he'll be worse than Ortheris was. Talk! He'll answer to your voice.'

Almost before Ortheris had deftly thrown all the rifles of the guard on Mulvaney's bedstead, the Irishman's voice was uplifted as that of one in the middle of a story, and, turning to me, he said: –

'In barricks or out av it, as *you* say, sorr, an Irish rig'mint is the divil an' more. 'Tis only fit for a young man wid eddicated fisteses. Oh, the crame av disrupshin is an Irish rig'mint, an' rippin', tearin', ragin' scattherers in the field av war! My first rig'mint was Irish – Faynians[9] an' rebils to the heart av their marrow was they, an' *so* they fought for the Widdy betther than most, bein' contrairy – Irish. They was the Black Tyrone. You've heard av thim, sorr?'

Heard of them! I knew the Black Tyrone for the choicest collection of unmitigated blackguards, dog-stealers, robbers of hen-roosts, assaulters of innocent citizens, and recklessly daring heroes in the Army List. Half Europe and half Asia has had cause to know the Black Tyrone – good luck be with their tattered Colours as Glory has ever been!

'They *was* hot pickils an' ginger! I cut a man's head tu deep wid me belt in the days av me youth, an', afther some circumstances which I will oblitherate, I came to the Ould Rig'mint, bearin' the character av a man wid hands an' feet. But, as I was goin' to tell you, I fell acrost the Black Tyrone agin wan day whin we wanted thim powerful bad. Orth'ris, me son, fwhat was the name av that place where they sint wan comp'ny av us an' wan av the Tyrone roun' a hill an' down agin, all for to tache the Paythans[10] something they'd niver learned before? Afther Ghuzni[11] 'twas.'

'Don't know what the bloomin' Paythans called it. We called it Silver's Theayter. You know that, sure!'

'Silver's Theatre[12] – so 'twas. A gut betwix' two hills, as black as a bucket, an' as thin as a gurl's waist. There was over-many Paythans for our convaynience in the gut, an' begad they called thimsilves a Reserve – bein' impident by natur'! Our Scotchies an' lashin's av Gurkys[13] was poundin' into some Paythan rig'mints, I think 'twas. Scotchies an' Gurkys are twins bekaze they're so onlike, an' they get dhrunk together whin God plazes. As I was sayin', they sint wan comp'ny av the Ould an' wan av the Tyrone to double up the hill an' clane out the Paythan Reserve. Orf'cers was scarce in thim days, fwhat wid dysint'ry an' not takin' care av thimsilves, an' we was sint out wid only wan orf'cer for the comp'ny; but he was a Man that had his feet beneath him an' all his teeth in their sockuts.'

'Who was he?' I asked.

'Captain O'Neil[14] – Old Crook – Cruik-na-bulleen – him that I tould ye that tale av whin he was in Burma.* Hah! He was a Man. The Tyrone tuk a little orf'cer bhoy, but divil a bit was he in command, as I'll dimonsthrate prisintly. We an' they came over the brow av the hill, wan on each side av the gut, an' there was that ondacint Reserve waitin' down below like rats in a pit.

'"Howld on, men," sez Crook, who tuk a mother's care av us always. "Rowl some rocks on thim by way av visitin'-kyards." We hadn't rowled more than twinty bowlders, an' the Paythans was beginnin' to swear tremenjus, whin the little orf'cer bhoy av the Tyrone shqueaks out acrost the valley: "Fwhat the divil an' all are you doin', shpoilin' the fun for my men? Do ye not see they'll stand?"

'"Faith, that's a rare pluckt wan!" sez Crook. "Niver mind the rocks, men. Come along down an' take tay wid thim!"

'"There's damned little sugar in ut!" sez my rear-rank man; but Crook heard.

'"Have ye not all got spoons?" he sez, laughin', an' down we wint as fast as we cud. Learoyd bein' sick at the Base, he, av coorse, was not there.'

* Now first of the foemen of Boh Da Thone
Was Captain O'Neil of the Black Tyrone.
The Ballad of Boh Da Thone.

'Thot's a lie!' said Learoyd, dragging his bedstead nearer. 'Ah gotten *thot* theer, an' you knaw it, Mulvaaney.' He threw up his arms, and from the right armpit ran, diagonally through the fell of his chest, a thin white line terminating near the fourth left rib.

'My mind's goin',' said Mulvaney, the unabashed. 'Ye were there. Fwhat was I thinkin' av? 'Twas another man, av coorse. Well, you'll remimber thin, Jock, how we an' the Tyrone met wid a bang at the bottom an' got jammed past all movin' among the Paythans?'

'Ow! It *was* a tight 'ole. I was squeezed till I thought I'd bloomin' well bust,' said Ortheris, rubbing his stomach meditatively.

''Twas no place for a little man, but *wan* little man' – Mulvaney put his hand on Ortheris's shoulder – 'saved the life av me. There we shtuck, for divil a bit did the Paythans flinch, an' divil a bit dare we; our business bein' to clear 'em out. An' the most exthryordinar' thing av all was that we an' they just rushed into each other's arrums, an' there was no firin' for a long time. Nothin' but knife an' bay'nit when we cud get our hands free: an' that was not often. We was breast-on to thim, an' the Tyrone was yelpin' behind av us in a way I didn't see the lean av at first. But I knew later, an' so did the Paythans.

'"Knee to knee!" sings out Crook, wid a laugh whin the rush av our comin' into the gut shtopped, an' he was huggin' a hairy great Paythan, neither bein' able to do anything to the other, tho' both was wishful.

'"Breast to breast!" he sez, as the Tyrone was pushin' us forward closer an' closer.

'"An' hand over back!" sez a Sargint that was behin'. I saw a sword lick out past Crook's ear, an' the Paythan was tuk in the apple av his throat like a pig at Dromeen Fair.[15]

'"Thank ye, Brother Inner Guard,"[16] sez Crook, cool as a cucumber widout salt. "I wanted that room." An' he wint forward by the thickness av a man's body, havin' turned the Paythan undher him. The man bit the heel off Crook's boot in his death-bite.

'"Push, men!" sez Crook. "Push, ye paper-backed beggars!" he sez. "Am *I* to pull ye through?" So we pushed, an' we kicked, an' we swung, an' we swore, an' the grass bein' slippery, our heels wudn't bite, an' God help the front-rank man that wint down that day!'

''Ave you ever bin in the Pit hentrance o' the Vic.[17] on a thick night?' interrupted Ortheris. 'It was worse nor that, for they was goin' one way, an' we wouldn't ave it. Leastaways, I 'adn't much to say.'

'Faith, me son, ye said ut, thin. I kep' this little man betune my knees as long as I cud, but he was pokin' roun' wid his bay'nit, blindin' an' stiffin' feroshus. The devil of a man is Orth'ris in a ruction – aren't ye?' said Mulvaney.

'Don't make game!' said the Cockney. 'I knowed I wasn't no good then, but I guv 'em compot from the lef' flank[18] when we opened out. No!' he said, bringing down his hand with a thump on the bedstead, 'a bay'nit ain't no good to a little man – might as well 'ave a bloomin' fishin'-rod! I 'ate a clawin', maulin' mess, but gimme a breech that's wore out a bit an' hamminition one year in store,[19] to let the powder kiss the bullet, an' put me somewheres where I ain't trod on by 'ulking swine like you, an' s'elp me Gawd, I could bowl you over five times outer seven at height 'undred. Would yer try, you lumberin' Hirishman?'

'No, ye wasp. I've seen ye do ut. I say there's nothin' better than the bay'nit, wid a long reach, a double twist av ye can, an' a slow recover.'

'Dom the bay'nit,' said Learoyd, who had been listening intently. 'Look a-here!' He picked up a rifle an inch below the foresight with an underhanded action, and used it exactly as a man would use a dagger.

'Sitha,' said he softly, 'thot's better than owt, for a mon can bash t' faace wi' thot, an', if he divn't, he can breeak t' forearm o' t' guaard. 'Tis nut i' t' books, though. Gie me t' butt.'

'Each does ut his own way, like makin' love,' said Mulvaney quietly; 'the butt or the bay'nit or the bullet accordin' to the natur' av the man. Well, as I was sayin', we shtuck there breathin' in each other's faces an' swearin' powerful; Orth'ris cursin' the mother that bore him bekaze he was not three inches taller.

'Prisintly he sez: "Duck, ye lump, an' I can get at a man over your shoulther!"

'"You'll blow me head off," I sez, throwin' my arrum clear; "go through under my arrumpit, ye bloodthirsty little scutt," sez I, "but don't shtick me or I'll wring your ears round."

'Fwhat was ut ye gave the Paythan man forninst me, him that cut at me whin I cudn't move hand or foot? Hot or cowld[20] was ut?'

'Cold,' said Ortheris, 'up an' under the rib-jints. 'E come down flat. Best for you 'e did.'

'Thrue, me son! This jam thing that I'm talkin' about lasted for five minut's good, an' thin we got our arrums clear an' wint in. I misremimber exactly fwhat I did, but I didn't want Dinah to be a widdy at the depôt.[21] Thin, afther some promishcuous hackin' we shtuck agin, an' the Tyrone behin' was callin' us dogs an' cowards an' all manner av names; we barrin' their way.

'"Fwhat ails the Tyrone?" thinks I. "They've the makin's av a most convanient fight here."

'A man behind me sez beseechful an' in a whisper: "Let me get at thim! For the love av Mary, give me room beside ye, ye tall man!"

'"An' who are you that's so anxious to be kilt?" sez I, widout turnin' my head, for the long knives was dancin' in front like the sun on Donegal Bay[22] whin ut's rough.

'"We've seen our dead," he sez, squeezin' into me; "our dead that was men two days gone! An' me that was his cousin by blood cud not bring Tim Coulan off! Let me get on," he sez, "let me get to thim or I'll run ye through the back!"

'"My troth," thinks I, "if the Tyrone have seen their dead, God help the Paythans this day!" An' thin I knew why the Tyrone was ragin' behind us as they was.

'I gave room to the man, an' he ran forward wid the Haymakers' Lift[23] on his bay'nit an' swung a Paythan clear off his feet by the belly-band av the brute, an' the iron bruk at the lockin'-ring.

'"Tim Coulan 'll slape aisy to-night," sez he wid a grin; an' the next minut' his head was in two halves and he wint down grinnin' by sections.

'The Tyrone was pushin' an' pushin' in, an' our men was swearin' at thim, an' Crook was workin' away in front av us all, his sword-arrum swingin' like a pump-handle an' his revolver spittin' like a cat. But the strange thing av ut was the quiet that lay upon. 'Twas like a fight in a drame – excipt for thim that was dead.

'Whin I gave room to the Irishman I was expinded an' forlorn in my inside. 'Tis a way I have, savin' your presince, sorr, in action. "Let me out, bhoys," sez I, backin' in among thim. "I'm goin' to be onwell!" Faith, they gave me room at the wurrud, though they wud not ha' given room for all Hell wid the chill off. When I got clear, I was, savin' your presince, sorr, outrajis sick bekaze I had dhrunk heavy that day.

'Well an' far out av harm was a Sargint av the Tyrone sittin' on the little orf'cer bhoy who had stopped Crook from rowlin' the rocks. Oh, he was a beautiful bhoy, an' the long black curses was slidin' out av his innocint mouth like mornin'-jew from a rose!

'"Fwhat have you got there?" sez I to the Sargint.

'"Wan av Her Majesty's bantams wid his spurs up," sez he. "He's goin' to Coort-Martial me."

'"Let me go!" sez the little orf'cer bhoy. "Let me go and command me men!" manin' thereby the Black Tyrone which was beyond any command – even av they had made the Divil Field-Orf'cer.

'"His father howlds my mother's cow-feed in Clonmel,"[24] sez the man that was sittin' on him. "Will I go back to *his* mother an' tell her that I've let him throw himsilf away? Lie still, ye little pinch of dynamite, an' Coort-Martial me aftherwards."

'"Good," sez I; "'tis the likes av him makes the likes av the Commandher-in-Chief, but we must presarve thim. Fwhat d'you want to do, sorr?" sez I, very politeful.

'"Kill the beggars – kill the beggars!" he shqueaks, his big blue eyes brimmin' wid tears.

'"An' how'll ye do that?" sez I. "You've shquibbed off your revolver like a child wid a cracker; you can make no play wid that fine large sword av yours; an' your hand's shakin' like an asp on a leaf.[25] Lie still and grow," sez I.

'"Get back to your comp'ny," sez he; "you're insolint!"

'"All in good time," sez I, "but I'll have a dhrink first."

'Just thin Crook comes up, blue an' white all over where he wasn't red.

'"Wather!" sez he; "I'm dead wid drouth! Oh, but it's a gran' day!"

'He dhrank half a skinful, and the rest he tilts into his chest, an' it fair hissed on the hairy hide av him. He sees the little orf'cer bhoy undher the Sargint.

'"Fwhat's yonder?" sez he.

'"Mutiny, sorr," sez the Sargint, an' the orf'cer bhoy begins pleadin' pitiful to Crook to be let go; but divil a bit wud Crook budge.

'"Kape him there," he sez; "'tis no child's work this day. By the same token," sez he, "I'll confishcate that iligant nickel-plated scent-sprinkler av yours, for my own has been vomitin' dishgraceful!"

'The fork av his hand was black wid the back-spit av the machine. So he tuk the orf'cer bhoy's revolver. Ye may look, sorr, but, by my faith, *there's a dale more done in the field than iver gets into Field Ordhers!*

'"Come on, Mulvaney," sez Crook; "is this a Coort-Martial?" The two av us wint back together into the mess an' the Paythans was still standin' up. They was not *too* impart'nint though, for the Tyrone was callin' wan to another to remimber Tim Coulan.

'Crook holted outside av the strife an' looked anxious, his eyes rowlin' roun'.

'"Fwhat is ut, sorr?" sez I; "can I get ye anything?"

'"Where's a bugler?" sez he.

'I wint into the crowd – our men was dhrawin' breath behin' the Tyrone, who was fightin' like sowls in tormint – an' prisintly I came acrost little Frehan, our bugler bhoy, pokin' roun' among the best wid a rifle an' bay'nit.

'"Is amusin' yoursilf fwhat you're paid for, ye limb?" sez I, catchin' him by the scruff. "Come out av that an' attind to your jooty," I sez; but the bhoy was not plazed.

'"I've got wan," sez he, grinnin', "big as you, Mulvaney, an' fair half as ugly. Let me go get another."

'I was dishplazed at the personability av that remark, so I tucks him under my arrum an' carries him to Crook, who was watchin' how the fight wint. Crook cuffs him till the bhoy cries, an' thin sez nothin' for a whoile.

'The Paythans began to flicker onaisy, an' our men roared. "Opin ordher! Double!"[26] sez Crook. "Blow, child, blow for the honour av the British Arrmy!"

'That bhoy blew like a typhoon, an' the Tyrone an' we opind out as the Paythans bruk, an' I saw that fwhat had gone before wud be kissin' an' huggin' to fwhat was to come. We'd dhruv thim into a broad part av the gut whin they gave, an' thin we opind out an' fair danced down the valley, dhrivin' thim before us. Oh, 'twas lovely, an' stiddy, too! There was the Sargints on the flanks av what was left av us, kapin' touch, an' the fire was runnin' from flank to flank, an' the Paythans was dhroppin'. We opind out wid the widenin' av the valley, an' whin the valley narrowed we closed agin like the shticks on a lady's fan, an' at the far ind av the gut where they thried to stand, we fair blew them off their feet, for we had expinded very little ammunition by reason av the knife-work.'

'*I* used thirty rounds goin' down that valley,' said Ortheris, 'an' it was gentleman's work. Might 'a' done it in a white 'andkerchief an' pink silk stockin's, that part. *Hi* was on in that piece.'

'You cud ha' heard the Tyrone yellin' a mile away,' said Mulvaney, 'an' 'twas all their Sargints cud do to get thim off. They was mad – mad – mad! Crook sits down in the quiet that fell whin we had gone down the valley, an' covers his face wid his hands. Prisintly we all came back agin accordin' to our natur's and disposishins, for they, mark you, show through the hide av a man in that hour.

'"Bhoys! bhoys!" sez Crook to himsilf. "I misdoubt we cud ha' engaged at long range an' saved betther men than me." He looked at our dead an' said no more.

'"Captain dear," sez a man av the Tyrone, comin' up wid his mouth bigger than iver his mother kissed ut, spittin' blood like a whale; "Captain dear," sez he, "if wan or two in the shtalls have been dishcommoded, the gallery have enjoyed the performinces av a Roshus."[27]

'Thin I knew that man for the Dublin dock-rat he was – wan av the bhoys that made the lessee av Silver's Theatre grey before his time wid tearin' out the bowils av the benches an' throwin' thim into the pit. So I passed the wurrud that I knew whin I was in the Tyrone an' we lay in Dublin. "I don't know who 'twas," I whishpers, "an' I don't care, but anyways I'll knock the face av you, Tim Kelly."

'"Eyah!" sez the man, "was you there too? We'll call ut Silver's Theatre." Half the Tyrone, knowin' the ould place, tuk ut up: so we called ut Silver's Theatre.

'The little orf'cer bhoy av the Tyrone was thremblin' an' cryin'. He had no heart for the Coort-Martials that he talked so big upon. "Ye'll do well later," sez Crook, very quiet, "for not bein' allowed to kill yoursilf for amusemint."

'"I'm a dishgraced man!" sez the little orf'cer bhoy.

'"Put me undher arrest, sorr, if you will, but, by my sowl, I'd do ut agin sooner than face your mother wid you dead," sez the Sargint that had sat on his head, standin' to attenshin an' salutin'. But the young wan only cried as tho' his little heart was breakin'.

'Thin another man av the Tyrone came up, wid the fog av fightin' on him.'

'The what, Mulvaney?'

'Fog av fightin'. You know, sorr, that, like makin' love, ut takes each man diff'rint. Now, I can't help bein' powerful sick whin I'm in action. Orth'ris, here, niver stops swearin' from ind to ind, an' the only time that Learoyd opins his mouth to sing is whin he is messin' wid other people's heads; for he's a dhirty fighter is Jock. Recruities sometime cry, an' sometime they don't know fwhat they do, an' sometime they are all for cuttin' throats an' such-like dhirtiness; but some men get heavy-dead-dhrunk on the fightin'. This man was. He was staggerin', an' his eyes were half shut, an' we cud hear him dhraw breath twinty yards away. He sees the little orf'cer bhoy, an' comes up, talkin' thick an' drowsy to himsilf. "Blood the young whelp!" he sez; "Blood the young whelp"; an' wid that he threw up his arrums, shpun roun', an' dropped at our feet, dead as a Paythan, an' there was niver sign or scratch on him. They said 'twas his heart was rotten, but oh, 'twas a quare thing to see!

'Thin we wint to bury our dead, for we wud not lave thim to the Paythans, an' in movin' among the haythen we nearly lost that little orf'cer bhoy. He was for givin' wan divil wather and layin' him aisy against a rock. "Be careful, sorr," sez I; "a wounded Paythan's worse than a live wan." My troth, before the words was out av me mouth, the man on the ground fires at the orf'cer bhoy lanin' over him, an' I saw the helmit fly. I dropped the butt on the face av the man an' tuk his pistol. The little orf'cer bhoy turned very white, for the hair av half his head was singed away.

'"I tould you so, sorr!" sez I; an', afther that, whin he wanted to help a Paythan I stud wid the muzzle contagious to the ear. They dared not do anythin' but curse. The Tyrone was growlin' like dogs over a bone that has been taken away too soon, for they had seen their dead an' they wanted to kill ivry sowl on the ground. Crook tould thim that he'd blow the hide off any man that misconducted himsilf; but, seeing that ut was the first time the Tyrone had iver seen their dead, I do not wondher they was on the sharp. 'Tis a shameful sight! Whin I first saw ut I wud niver ha' given quarter to any man north of the Khyber – no, nor woman either, for the wimmen used to come out afther dhark – Auggrh!

'Well, evenshually we buried our dead an' tuk away our wounded, an' come over the brow av the hills to see the Scotchies an' the Gurkys takin' tay with the Paythans in bucketsfuls. We were a gang av dissolute ruffians, for the blood had caked the dust, an' the sweat had cut the cake, an' our bay'nits was hangin' like butchers' steels[28] betune our legs, an' most av us was marked one way or another.

'A Staff Orf'cer man, clane as a new rifle, rides up an' sez: "What damned scarecrows are you?"

'"A comp'ny av Her Majesty's Black Tyrone an' wan av the Ould Rig'mint," sez Crook very quiet, givin' our visitors the flure as 'twas.

'"Oh!" sez the Staff Orf'cer. "Did you dislodge that Reserve?"

'"No!" sez Crook, an' the Tyrone laughed.

'"Thin fwhat the divil have ye done?"

'"Disthroyed ut," sez Crook, an' he took us on, but not before Toomey that was in the Tyrone sez aloud, his voice somewhere in his stummick: "Fwhat in the name av misfortune does this parrit widout a tail mane by shtoppin' the road av his betthers?"

'The Staff Orf'cer wint blue, an' Toomey makes him pink by changin' to the voice av a minowdherin' woman an' sayin': "Come an' kiss me, Major dear, for me husband's at the wars an' I'm all alone at the depôt."

'The Staff Orf'cer wint away, an' I cud see Crook's shoulthers shakin'.

'His Corp'ril checks Toomey. "Lave me alone," sez Toomey, widout a wink. "I was his batman before he was married an' he knows fwhat I mane, av you don't. There's nothin' like livin' in the hoight av society." D'you remimber that, Orth'ris?'

'Yuss. Toomey, 'e died in 'orspital, next week it was, 'cause I bought 'arf his kit; an' I remember after that –'

'GUARRD, TURN OUT!'

The Relief had come; it was four o'clock. 'I'll catch a kyart for you, sorr,' said Mulvaney, diving hastily into his accoutrements. 'Come up to the top av the Fort an' we'll pershue our invistigations into M'Grath's shtable.' The relieved guard strolled round the main bastion on its way to the swimming-bath, and Learoyd grew almost talkative. Ortheris looked into the Fort Ditch and across the plain. 'Ho! it's weary waitin' for Ma-ary!' he hummed; 'but I'd like to kill some more bloomin' Paythans before my time's up. War! Bloody war! North, East, South, and West.'

'Amen,' said Learoyd slowly.

'Fwhat's here?' said Mulvaney, checking at a blur of white by the foot of the old sentry-box. He stooped and touched it. 'It's Norah – Norah M'Taggart! Why, Nonie darlin', fwhat are ye doin' out av your mother's bed at this time?'

The two-year-old child of Sergeant M'Taggart must have wandered for a breath of cool air to the very verge of the parapet of the Fort Ditch. Her tiny nightshift was gathered into a wisp round her neck and she moaned in her sleep. 'See there!' said Mulvaney; 'poor lamb! Look at the heat-rash on the innocint shkin av her. 'Tis hard – crool hard even for us. Fwhat must it be for these? Wake up, Nonie, your mother will be woild about you. Begad, the child might ha' fallen into the Ditch!'

He picked her up in the growing light, and set her on his shoulder, and her fair curls touched the grizzled stubble of his temples. Ortheris and Learoyd followed snapping their fingers, while Norah smiled at them a sleepy smile. Then carolled Mulvaney, clear as a lark, dancing the baby on his arm: –

> 'If any young man should marry you,
>   Say nothin' about the joke;
> That iver ye slep' in a sinthry-box,
>   Wrapped up in a soldier's cloak.'[29]

'Though, on my sowl, Nonie,' he said gravely, 'there was not much cloak about you. Niver mind, you won't dhress like this ten years to come. Kiss your frinds an' run along to your mother.'

Nonie, set down close to the Married Quarters, nodded with the quiet obedience of the soldier's child, but, ere she pattered off over the flagged path, held up her lips to be kissed by the Three Musketeers.[30] Ortheris wiped his mouth with the back of his hand and swore sentimentally! Learoyd turned pink; and the two walked away together. The Yorkshireman lifted up his voice and gave in thunder the chorus of *The Sentry-Box*, while Ortheris piped at his side.

'Bin to a bloomin' sing-song, you two?' said the Artilleryman, who was taking his cartridge down to the Morning Gun.[31] 'You're over merry for these dashed days.'

> 'I bid ye take care o' the brat, said he,
> For it comes of a noble race,'

Learoyd bellowed. The voices died out in the swimming-bath.

'Oh, Terence!' I said, dropping into Mulvaney's speech, when we were alone, 'it's you that have the Tongue!'

He looked at me wearily; his eyes were sunk in his head, and his face was drawn and white. 'Eyah!' said he; 'I've blandandhered thim through the night somehow, but can thim that helps others help thimsilves? Answer me that, sorr!'

And over the bastions of Fort Amara broke the pitiless day.

In the Matter of a Private

Hurrah! hurrah! a soldier's life for me!
Shout, boys, shout! for it makes you jolly and free.
The Ramrod Corps.

People who have seen say that one of the quaintest spectacles of human frailty is an outbreak of hysterics in a girls' school. It starts without warning, generally on a hot afternoon, among the elder pupils. A girl giggles till the giggle gets beyond control. Then she throws up her head, and cries, '*Honk, honk, honk*,' like a wild goose, and tears mix with the laughter. If the mistress be wise, she will rap out something severe at this point to check matters. If she be tender-hearted, and send for a drink of water, the chances are largely in favour of another girl laughing at the afflicted one and herself collapsing. Thus the trouble spreads, and may end in half of what answers to the Lower Sixth of a boys' school rocking and whooping together. Given a week of warm weather, two stately promenades per diem,[1] a heavy mutton and rice meal in the middle of the day, a certain amount of nagging from the teachers, and a few other things, some amazing effects develop. At least, this is what folk say who have had experience.

Now, the Mother Superior of a Convent and the Colonel of a British Infantry Regiment would be justly shocked at any comparison being made between their respective charges. But it is a fact that, under certain circumstances, Thomas in bulk[2] can be worked up into dithering, rippling hysteria. He does not weep, but he shows his trouble unmistakably, and the consequences get into the newspapers, and all the good people who hardly know a Martini from a Snider[3] say: 'Take away the brute's ammunition!'

Thomas isn't a brute, and his business, which is to look after the virtuous people, demands that he shall have his ammunition to his hand. He doesn't wear silk stockings, and he really ought to be supplied with a new Adjective to help him to express his opinions;

but, for all that, he is a great man. If you call him 'the heroic defender of the national honour' one day, and 'a brutal and licentious soldiery'[4] the next, you naturally bewilder him, and he looks upon you with suspicion. There is nobody to speak for Thomas except people who have theories to work off on him; and nobody understands Thomas except Thomas, and he does not always know what is the matter with himself.

That is the prologue. This is the story: –

Corporal Slane was engaged to be married to Miss Jhansi M'Kenna, whose history is well known in the Regiment and elsewhere.[5] He had his Colonel's permission, and, being popular with the men, every arrangement had been made to give the wedding what Private Ortheris called 'eeklar'.[6] It fell in the heart of the hot weather, and, after the wedding, Slane was going up to the Hills with the bride. None the less, Slane's grievance was that the affair would be only a hired-carriage wedding, and he felt that the 'eeklar' of that was meagre. Miss M'Kenna did not care so much. The Sergeant's wife was helping her to make her wedding-dress, and she was very busy. Slane was, just then, the only moderately contented man in barracks. All the rest were more or less miserable.

And they had so much to make them happy, too. All their work was over at eight in the morning,[7] and for the rest of the day they could lie on their backs and smoke Canteen-plug and swear at the punkah-coolies.[8] They enjoyed a fine, full flesh meal in the middle of the day, and then threw themselves down on their cots and sweated and slept till it was cool enough to go out with their 'towny', whose vocabulary contained less than six hundred words, and the Adjective, and whose views on every conceivable question they had heard many times before.

There was the Canteen, of course, and there was the Temperance Room[9] with the second-hand papers in it; but a man of any profession cannot read for eight hours a day in a temperature of 96° or 98° in the shade, running up sometimes to 103° at midnight. Very few men, even though they get a pannikin of flat, stale, muddy beer and hide it under their cots, can continue drinking for six hours a day. One man tried, but he died, and nearly the whole Regiment went to his funeral because it gave them something to do. It was too early for the excitement of fever or cholera. The men could only wait and wait and wait, and watch the shadow of the barrack creeping across the blinding white dust. That was a gay life.

They lounged about cantonments – it was too hot for any sort of game, and almost too hot for vice – and fuddled themselves in the evening, and filled themselves to distension with the healthy nitrogenous food provided for them, and the more they stoked the less exercise they took and the more explosive they grew. Then tempers began to wear away, and men fell a-brooding over insults real or imaginary, for they had nothing else to think of. The tone of the repartees changed, and instead of saying light-heartedly, 'I'll knock your silly face in,' men grew laboriously polite and hinted that the cantonments were not big enough for themselves and their enemy, and that there would be more space for one of the two in another Place.

It may have been the Devil who arranged the thing, but the fact of the case is that Losson had for a long time been worrying Simmons in an aimless way. It gave him occupation. The two had their cots side by side, and would sometimes spend a long afternoon swearing at each other; but Simmons was afraid of Losson and dared not challenge him to a fight. He thought over the words in the hot still nights, and half the hate he felt towards Losson he vented on the wretched punkah-coolie.

Losson bought a parrot in the bazar, and put it into a little cage, and lowered the cage into the cool darkness of a well, and sat on the well-curb, shouting bad language down to the parrot. He taught it to say: 'Simmons, *ye so-oor*,'[10] which means swine, and several other things entirely unfit for publication. He was a big gross man, and he shook like a jelly when the parrot had the sentence correctly. Simmons, however, shook with rage, for all the room was laughing at him – the parrot was such a disreputable puff of green feathers and it looked so human when it chattered. Losson used to sit, swinging his fat legs, on the side of the cot, and ask the parrot what it thought of Simmons. The parrot would answer: 'Simmons, *ye so-oor*.' 'Good boy,' Losson used to say, scratching the parrot's head; 'ye 'ear that, Sim?' And Simmons used to turn over on his stomach and make answer: 'I 'ear. Take 'eed *you* don't 'ear something one of these days.'

In the restless nights, after he had been asleep all day, fits of blind rage came upon Simmons and held him till he trembled all over, while he thought in how many different ways he would slay Losson. Sometimes he would picture himself trampling the life out of the man with heavy ammunition-boots, and at others smashing in his face with the butt, and at others jumping on his shoulders and dragging the head back till the neckbone cracked. Then his mouth would feel hot and fevered, and he would reach out for another sup of the beer in the pannikin.

But the fancy that came to him most frequently and stayed with him longest was one connected with the great roll of fat under Losson's right ear. He noticed it first on a moonlight night, and thereafter it was always before his eyes. It was a fascinating roll of fat. A man could get his hand upon it and tear away one side of the neck; or he could place the muzzle of a rifle on it and blow away all the head in a flash. Losson had no right to be sleek and contented and well-to-do, when he, Simmons, was the butt of the room. Some day, perhaps, he would show those who laughed at the 'Simmons, ye *so-oor*' joke, that he was as good as the rest, and held a man's life in the crook of his forefinger. When Losson snored, Simmons hated him more bitterly than ever. Why should Losson be able to sleep when Simmons had to stay awake hour after hour, tossing and turning on the tapes,[11] with the dull liver pain gnawing into his right side and his head throbbing and aching after Canteen? He thought over this for many many nights, and the world became unprofitable to him.[12] He even blunted his naturally fine appetite with beer and tobacco; and all the while the parrot talked at and made a mock of him.

The heat continued and the tempers wore away more quickly than before. A Sergeant's wife died of heat-apoplexy in the night, and the rumour ran abroad that it was cholera. Men rejoiced openly, hoping that it would spread and send them into camp. But that was a false alarm.

It was late on a Tuesday evening, and the men were waiting in the deep double verandas for 'Last Post',[13] when Simmons went to the box at the foot of his bed, took out his pipe, and slammed the lid down with a bang that echoed through the deserted barrack like the crack of a rifle. Ordinarily speaking, the men would have taken no notice; but their nerves were fretted to fiddle-strings. They jumped up, and three or four clattered into the barrack-room only to find Simmons kneeling by his box.

'Ow! It's you, is it?' they said and laughed foolishly. 'We thought 'twas –'

Simmons rose slowly. If the accident had so shaken his fellows, what would not the reality do?

'You thought it was – did you? And what makes you think?' he said, lashing himself into madness as he went on. 'To Hell with your thinking, ye dirty spies.'

'Simmons, ye *so-oor*,' chuckled the parrot in the veranda sleepily, recognizing a well-known voice. Now that was absolutely all.

The tension snapped. Simmons fell back on the arm-rack deliberately, – the men were at the far end of the room, – and took out his rifle and packet of ammunition. 'Don't go playing the goat, Sim!' said Losson. 'Put it down'; but there was a quaver in his voice. Another man stooped, slipped his boot and hurled it at Simmons's head. The prompt answer was a shot which, fired at random, found its billet in Losson's throat. Losson fell forward without a word, and the others scattered.

'You thought it was!' yelled Simmons. 'You're drivin' me to it! I tell you you're drivin' me to it! Get up, Losson, an' don't lie shammin' there – you an' your blasted parrit that druv me to it!'

But there was an unaffected reality about Losson's pose that showed Simmons what he had done. The men were still clamouring in the veranda. Simmons appropriated two more packets of ammunition and ran into the moonlight, muttering: 'I'll make a night of it. Thirty roun's, an' the last for myself. Take you that, you dorgs!'

He dropped on one knee and fired into the brown of the men on the veranda, but the bullet flew high, and landed in the brickwork with a vicious *phwit* that made some of the younger ones turn pale. It is, as musketry theorists observe, one thing to fire and another to be fired at.

Then the instinct of the chase flared up. The news spread from barrack to barrack, and the men doubled out intent on the capture of Simmons, the wild beast, who was heading for the Cavalry parade-ground, stopping now and again to send back a shot and a curse in the direction of his pursuers.

'I'll learn you to spy on me!' he shouted; 'I'll learn you to give me dorg's names! Come on, the 'ole lot o' you! Colonel John Anthony Deever, C.B.!'[14] – he turned towards the Infantry Mess[15] and shook his rifle – 'you think yourself the devil of a man – but I tell you that if you put your ugly old carcass outside o' that door, I'll make you the poorest-lookin' man in the Army. Come out, Colonel John Anthony Deever, C.B.! Come out and see me practise on the rainge. I'm the crack shot of the 'ole bloomin' battalion.' In proof of which statement Simmons fired at the lighted windows of the Mess-house.

'Private Simmons, E Comp'ny, on the Cavalry p'rade-ground, sir, with thirty rounds,' said a sergeant breathlessly to the Colonel. 'Shootin' right and lef', sir. Shot Private Losson. What's to be done, sir?'

Colonel John Anthony Deever, C.B., sallied out, only to be saluted by a spurt of dust at his feet.

'Pull up!' said the Second-in-Command; 'I don't want my step in that way, Colonel. He's as dangerous as a mad dog.'

'Shoot him like one, then,' said the Colonel bitterly, 'if he won't take his chance. *My* Regiment, too! If it had been the Towheads[16] I could have understood.'

Private Simmons had occupied a strong position near a well on the edge of the parade-ground, and was defying the Regiment to come on. The Regiment was not anxious to comply, for there is small honour in being shot by a fellow-private. Only Corporal Slane, rifle in hand, threw himself down on the ground, and wormed his way towards the well.

'Don't shoot,' said he to the men round him; 'like as not you'll 'it me. I'll catch the beggar livin'.'

Simmons ceased shouting for a while, and the noise of trap-wheels could be heard across the plain. Major Oldyne, Commanding the Horse Battery,[17] was coming back from a dinner in the Civil Lines; was driving after his usual custom – that is to say, as fast as the horse could go.

'A orf'cer! A bloomin' spangled[18] orf'cer!' shrieked Simmons; 'I'll make a scarecrow of that orf'cer!' The trap stopped.

'What's this?' demanded the Major of Gunners. 'You there, drop your rifle.'

'Why, it's Jerry Blazes! I ain't got no quarrel with you, Jerry Blazes. Pass, frien', an' all's well!'[19]

But Jerry Blazes had not the faintest intention of passing a dangerous murderer. He was, as his adoring Battery swore long and fervently, without knowledge of fear, and they were surely the best judges, for Jerry Blazes, it was notorious, had done his possible to kill a man each time the Battery went out.

He walked towards Simmons, with the intention of rushing him, and knocking him down.

'Don't make me do it, sir,' said Simmons; 'I ain't got nothing agin' you. Ah! you would?' – the Major broke into a run – 'Take that then!'

The Major dropped with a bullet through his shoulder, and Simmons stood over him. He had lost the satisfaction of killing Losson in the desired way; but here was a helpless body to his hand. Should he slip in another cartridge, and blow off the head, or with the butt smash in the white face? He stopped to consider, and a cry went up from the far side of the parade-ground: 'He's killed Jerry Blazes!' But in the shelter of the well-pillars Simmons was safe, except when he stepped out to fire. 'I'll blow yer 'andsome 'ead off, Jerry Blazes,' said Simmons reflectively. 'Six an' three is nine an' one is ten, an' that leaves me another nineteen, an' one for myself.' He tugged at the string of the second packet of ammunition. Corporal Slane crawled out of the shadow of a bank into the moonlight.

'I see you!' said Simmons. 'Come a bit furder on an' I'll do for you.'

'I'm comin',' said Corporal Slane briefly. 'You've done a bad day's work, Sim. Come out 'ere an' come back with me.'

'Come to —' laughed Simmons, sending a cartridge home with his thumb. 'Not before I've settled you an' Jerry Blazes.'

The Corporal was lying at full length in the dust of the parade-ground, a rifle under him. Some of the less cautious men in the distance shouted: 'Shoot 'im! Shoot 'im, Slane!'

'You move 'and or foot, Slane,' said Simmons, 'an' I'll kick Jerry Blazes' 'ead in, and shoot you after.'

'I ain't movin',' said the Corporal, raising his head; 'you daren't 'it a man on 'is legs. Let go o' Jerry Blazes an' come out o' that with your fistes. Come an' 'it me. You daren't, you bloomin' dog-shooter!'

'I dare.'

'You lie, you man-sticker. You sneakin' Sheeny[20] butcher, you lie. See there!' Slane kicked the rifle away, and stood up at the peril of his life. 'Come on, now!'

The temptation was more than Simmons could resist, for the Corporal in his white clothes offered a perfect mark.

'Don't misname me,' shouted Simmons, firing as he spoke. The shot missed, and the shooter, blind with rage, threw his rifle down and rushed at Slane from the protection of the well. Within striking distance, he kicked savagely at Slane's stomach, but the weedy Corporal knew something of Simmons's weakness, and knew, too, the deadly guard for that kick. Bowing forward and drawing up his right leg till the heel of the right foot was set some three inches above the inside of the left knee-cap, he met the blow standing on one leg – exactly as Gonds[21] stand when they meditate – and ready for the fall that would follow. There was an oath, the Corporal fell over to his own left as shinbone met shinbone, and the private collapsed, his right leg broken an inch above the ankle.

'Pity you don't know that guard, Sim,' said Slane, spitting out the dust as he rose. Then raising his voice – 'Come an' take him orf. I've bruk 'is leg.' This was not strictly true, for the private had accomplished his own downfall, since it is the special merit of that leg-guard that the harder the kick the greater the kicker's discomfiture.

Slane walked to Jerry Blazes and hung over him with ostentatious anxiety, while Simmons, weeping with pain, was carried away. ''Ope you ain't 'urt badly, sir,' said Slane. The Major had fainted, and there was an ugly, ragged hole through the top of his arm. Slane knelt down and murmured: 'S'elp me, I believe 'e's dead. Well, if that ain't my bloomin' luck all over!'

But the Major was destined to lead his Battery afield for many a long day with unshaken nerve. He was removed, and nursed and petted into convalescence, while the Battery discussed the wisdom of capturing Simmons, and blowing him from a gun. They idolized their Major, and his reappearance on parade brought about a scene nowhere provided for in the Army Regulations.

Great, too, was the glory that fell to Slane's share. The Gunners would have made him drunk thrice a day for at least a fortnight. Even the Colonel of his own Regiment complimented him upon his coolness, and the local paper called him a hero. These things did not puff him up. When the Major offered him money and thanks, the virtuous Corporal took the one and put aside the other. But he had a request to make and prefaced it with many a 'Beg y' pardon, sir'. Could the Major see his way to letting the Slane–M'Kenna wedding be adorned by the presence of four Battery horses to pull a hired barouche? The Major could, and so could the Battery. Excessively so. It was a gorgeous wedding.

'Wot did I do it for?' said Corporal Slane. 'For the 'orses o' course. Jhansi ain't a beauty to look at, but I wasn't goin' to 'ave a hired turn-out. Jerry Blazes? If I 'adn't 'a' wanted something, Sim might ha' blowed Jerry Blazes' bloomin' 'ead into Hirish stew for aught I'd 'a' cared.'

And they hanged Private Simmons – hanged him as high as Haman[22] in hollow square[23] of the Regiment; and the Colonel said it was Drink; and the Chaplain was sure it was the Devil; and Simmons fancied it was both, but he didn't know, and only hoped his fate would be a warning to his companions; and half-a-dozen 'intelligent publicists' wrote six beautiful leading articles on 'The Prevalence of Crime in the Army'.

But not a soul thought of comparing the 'bloody-minded Simmons' to the squawking, gasping schoolgirl with which this story opens.

Black Jack

To the wake av Tim O'Hara
  Came company,
All St Patrick's Alley
  Was there to see.
    Robert Buchanan.

As the Three Musketeers share their silver, tobacco, and liquor together, as they protect each other in barracks or camp, and as they rejoice together over the joy of one, so do they divide their sorrows. When Ortheris's irrepressible tongue has brought him into cells for a season, or Learoyd has run amok through his kit and accoutrements, or Mulvaney has indulged in strong waters, and under their influence reproved his Commanding Officer, you can see the trouble in the faces of the untouched two. And the rest of the Regiment know that comment or jest is unsafe. Generally the three avoid Orderly-Room and the Corner Shop[1] that follows, leaving both to the young bloods who have not sown their wild oats; but there are occasions –

For instance, Ortheris was sitting on the drawbridge of the main gate of Fort Amara, with his hands in his pockets and his pipe, bowl down, in his mouth. Learoyd was lying at full length on the turf of the glacis, kicking his heels in the air, and I came round the corner and asked for Mulvaney.

Ortheris spat into the Ditch and shook his head. 'No good seein' 'im now,' said Ortheris; ''e's a bloomin' camel. Listen.'

I heard on the flags of the veranda opposite to the cells, which are close to the Guard-Room, a measured step that I could have identified out of the tramp of an army. There were twenty paces *crescendo*, a pause, and then twenty *diminuendo.*[2]

'That's 'im,' said Ortheris; 'my Gawd, that's 'im! All for a bloomin' button you could see your face in an' a bit o' lip that a bloomin' Harkangel would 'a' guv back.'

Mulvaney was doing pack-drill – was compelled, that is to say, to walk up and down for certain hours[3] in full marching order, with rifle, bayonet, ammunition, knapsack, and overcoat. And his offence was being dirty on parade! I nearly fell into the Fort Ditch with astonishment and wrath, for Mulvaney is the smartest man that ever mounted guard, and would as soon think of turning out uncleanly as of dispensing with his trousers.

'Who was the Sergeant that checked him?' I asked.

'Mullins, o' course,' said Ortheris. 'There ain't no other man would whip 'im on the peg so. But Mullins ain't a man. 'E's a dirty little pig-scraper, that's wot 'e is.'

'What did Mulvaney say? He's not the make of man to take that quietly.'

'Say! Bin better for 'im if 'e'd shut 'is mouth. Lord, 'ow we laughed! " Sargint," 'e sez, "ye say I'm dirty. Well," sez 'e, "when your wife lets you blow your own nose for yourself, perhaps you'll know wot dirt is. You're himperfec'ly eddicated, Sargint," sez 'e, an' then we fell in. But after p'rade, 'e was up an' Mullins was swearin' 'imself black in the face at Ord'ly-Room that Mulvaney 'ad called 'im a swine an' Lord knows wot all. You know Mullins. 'E'll 'ave 'is 'ead broke in one o' these days. 'E's too big a bloomin' liar for ord'nary consumption. "Three hours' can an' kit," sez the Colonel; "not for bein' dirty on p'rade, but for 'avin' said somethin' to Mullins, tho' I do not believe," sez 'e, "you said wot 'e said you said." An' Mulvaney fell away sayin' nothin'. You know 'e never speaks to the Colonel for fear o' gettin' 'imself fresh copped.'

Mullins, a very young and very much married Sergeant, whose manners were partly the result of innate depravity and partly of imperfectly digested Board School,[4] came over the bridge, and most rudely asked Ortheris what he was doing.

'Me?' said Ortheris. 'Ow! I'm waiting for my C'mission.[5] Seed it comin' along yit?'

Mullins turned purple and passed on. There was the sound of a gentle chuckle from the glacis where Learoyd lay.

''E expects to get his C'mission some day,' explained Ortheris. 'Gawd 'elp the Mess that 'ave to put their 'ands into the same kiddy[6] as 'im! Wot time d'you make it, sir? Fower! Mulvaney'll be out in 'arf an hour. You don't want to buy a dorg, sir, do you? A pup you can trust – 'arf Rampur[7] by the Colonel's grey'ound.'

'Ortheris,' I answered sternly, for I knew what was in his mind, 'do you mean to say that –'

'I didn't mean to arx money o' you, any'ow,' said Ortheris. 'I'd 'a' sold you the dorg good an' cheap, but – but – I know Mulvaney'll want somethin' after we've walked 'im orf, an' I ain't got nothin', nor 'e 'asn't neither. I'd sooner sell you the dorg, sir. 'Strewth I would!'

A shadow fell on the drawbridge, and Ortheris began to rise into the air, lifted by a huge hand upon his collar.

'Onnything but t' braass,' said Learoyd quietly, as he held the Londoner over the Ditch. 'Onnything but t' braass, Orth'ris, ma son! Ah've got one rupee eight annas ma own.' He showed two coins, and replaced Ortheris on the drawbridge rail.

'Very good,' I said; 'where are you going to?'

'Goin' to walk 'im orf w'en 'e comes out – two miles or three or fower,' said Ortheris.

The footsteps within ceased. I heard the dull thud of a knapsack falling on a bedstead, followed by the rattle of arms. Ten minutes later, Mulvaney, faultlessly dressed, his lips tight and his face as black as a thunderstorm, stalked into the sunshine on the drawbridge. Learoyd and Ortheris sprang from my side and closed in upon him, both leaning towards him as horses lean upon the pole. In an instant they had disappeared down the sunken road to the cantonments, and I was left alone. Mulvaney had not seen fit to recognize me; so I knew that his trouble must be heavy upon him.

I climbed one of the bastions and watched the figures of the Three Musketeers grow smaller and smaller across the plain. They were walking as fast as they could put foot to the ground, and their heads were bowed. They fetched a great compass round the parade-ground, skirted the Cavalry lines, and vanished in the belt of trees that fringes the low land by the river.

I followed slowly, and sighted them – dusty, sweating, but still keeping up their long, swinging tramp – on the river bank. They crashed through the Forest Reserve, headed towards the Bridge of Boats,[8] and presently established themselves on the bow of one of the pontoons. I rode cautiously till I saw three puffs of white smoke rise and die out in the clear evening air, and knew that peace had come again. At the bridge-head they waved me forward with gestures of welcome.

'Tie up your 'orse,' shouted Ortheris, 'an' come on, sir. We're all goin' 'ome in this 'ere bloomin' boat.'

From the bridge-head to the Forest Officer's bungalow is but a step. The mess-man[9] was there, and would see that a man held my horse. Did the Sahib require aught else – a peg, or beer? Ritchie Sahib had left half-a-dozen bottles of the latter, but since the Sahib was a friend of Ritchie Sahib, and he, the mess-man, was a poor man –

I gave my order quietly, and returned to the bridge. Mulvaney had taken off his boots, and was dabbling his toes in the water; Learoyd was lying on his back on the pontoon; and Ortheris was pretending to row with a big bamboo.

'I'm an ould fool,' said Mulvaney reflectively, 'dhraggin' you two out here bekaze I was undher the Black Dog[10] – sulkin' like a child. Me that was sodgerin' when Mullins, an' be damned to him, was shquealin' on a counterpin for five shillin' a week[11] – an' that not paid! Bhoys, I've tuk you five miles out av natural pivarsity. Phew!'

'Wot's the odds[12] as long as you're 'appy?' said Ortheris, applying himself afresh to the bamboo. 'As well 'ere as anywhere else.'

Learoyd held up a rupee and an eight-anna bit, and shook his head sorrowfully. 'Five miles from t' Canteen, all along o' Mulvaaney's blaasted pride.'

'I know ut,' said Mulvaney penitently. 'Why will ye come wid me? An' yet I wud be mortial sorry av ye did not – any time – though I am ould enough to know betther. But I will do penance. I will take a dhrink av wather.'

Ortheris squeaked shrilly. The butler of the Forest bungalow was standing near the railings with a basket, uncertain how to clamber down to the pontoon.

'Might 'a' know'd you'd 'a' got liquor out o' bloomin' desert, sir,' said Ortheris gracefully to me. Then to the mess-man: 'Easy with them there bottles. They're worth their weight in gold. Jock, ye long-armed beggar, get out o' that an' hike 'em down.'

Learoyd had the basket on the pontoon in an instant, and the Three Musketeers gathered round it with dry lips. They drank my health in due and ancient form, and thereafter tobacco tasted sweeter than ever. They absorbed all the beer, and disposed themselves in picturesque attitudes to admire the setting sun – no man speaking for a while.

Mulvaney's head dropped upon his chest, and we thought that he was asleep.

'What on earth did you come so far for?' I whispered to Ortheris.

'To walk 'im orf, o' course. When 'e's been checked we allus walks 'im orf. 'E ain't fit to be spoke to those times – nor 'e ain't fit to leave alone neither. So we takes 'im till 'e is.'

Mulvaney raised his head, and stared straight into the sunset. 'I had my rifle,' said he dreamily, 'an' I had my bay'nit, an' Mullins came round the corner, an' he looked in my face an' grinned dishpiteful. "*You* can't blow your own nose," sez he. Now, I cannot tell fwhat Mullins's expayrience may ha' been, but, Mother av God, he was nearer to his death that minut' than I have iver been to mine – and that's less than the thicknuss av a hair!'

'Yes,' said Ortheris calmly, 'you'd look fine with all your buttons took orf, an' the Band in front o' you, walkin' roun' slow time. We're both front-rank men, me an' Jock, when the Rig'ment's in 'ollow square. Bloomin' fine you'd look. "The Lord giveth an' the Lord taketh awai,[13] – Heasy with that there drop! – Blessed be the naime o' the Lord."' He gulped in a quaint and suggestive fashion.

'Mullins! What's Mullins?' said Learoyd slowly. 'Ah'd taake a coomp'ny o' Mullinses – ma hand behind me. Sitha, Mulvaaney, don't be a fool.'

'*You* were not checked for fwhat you did not do, an' made a mock av afther. 'Twas for less than that the Tyrone wud ha' sent O'Hara to Hell, instid av lettin' him go by his own choosin', whin Rafferty[14] shot him,' retorted Mulvaney.

'And who stopped the Tyrone from doing it?' I asked.

'This ould fool who's sorry he did not shtick that pig Mullins.' His head dropped again. When he raised it he shivered and put his hands on the shoulders of his two companions.

'Ye've walked the Divil out av me, bhoys,' said he.

Ortheris shot out the red-hot dottle of his pipe on the back of the hairy fist. 'They say 'Ell's 'otter than that,' said he, as Mulvaney swore aloud. 'You be warned so. Look yonder!' – he pointed across the river to a ruined temple – 'Me an' you an' '*im*' – he indicated me by a jerk of his head – 'was there one day when Hi made a bloomin' show o' myself. You an' 'im stopped me doin' such – an' Hi was on'y wishful for to desert.[15] You are makin' a bigger bloomin' show o' yourself now.'

'Don't mind him, Mulvaney,' I said; 'Dinah Shadd won't let you hang yourself yet awhile, and you don't intend to try it either. Let's hear about the Tyrone and O'Hara. Rafferty shot him for fooling with his wife. What happened before that?'

'There's no fool like an ould fool. Ye know ye can do anythin' wid me whin I'm talkin'. Did I say I wud like to cut Mullins's liver out? I deny the imputashin, for fear that Orth'ris here wud report me – Ah! You wud tip me into the river, wud you? Set quiet, little man. Anyways, Mullins is not worth the throuble av an extry p'rade, an' I will trate him wid outrajis contimpt. The Tyrone an' O'Hara! O'Hara an' the Tyrone, begad! Ould days are hard to bring back into the mouth, but they're always inside the head.'

Followed a long pause.

'O'Hara was a Divil. Though I saved him, for the honour av the Rig'mint, from his death that time, I say it now. He was a Divil – a long, bould, black-haired Divil.'

'Which way?' asked Ortheris.

'Wimmen.'

'Then I know another.'

'Not more than in reason, if you mane me, ye warped walkin'-shtick. I have been young, an' for why shud I not have tuk what I cud? Did I iver, whin I was Corp'ril, use the rise av my rank – wan step an' that taken away, more's the sorrow an' the fault av me! – to prosecute nefarious inthrigues, as O'Hara did? Did I, whin I was Corp'ril, lay my spite upon a man an' make his life a dog's life from day to day? Did I lie, as O'Hara lied, till the young wans in the Tyrone turned white wid the fear av the Judgment av God killin' thim all in a lump, as ut killed the woman at Devizes?[16] I did not! I have sinned my sins an' I have made my confesshin, an' Father Victor knows the worst av me. O'Hara was tuk, before he cud spake, on Rafferty's door-stip, an' no man knows the worst av him. But this much I know!

'The Tyrone was recruited any fashion in the ould days. A draf' from Connemara – a draf' from Portsmouth – a draf' from Kerry, an' that was a blazin' bad draf' – here, there, and ivrywhere – but the large av thim was Irish – Black Irish. Now there are Irish an' Irish. The good are good as the best, but the bad are wurrse than the wurrst. 'Tis this way. They clog together in pieces as fast as thieves, an' no wan knows fwhat they will do till wan turns informer an' the gang is bruk. But ut begins agin, a day later, meetin' in holes an' corners an' swearin' bloody oaths an' shtickin' a man in the back an' runnin' away, an' thin waitin' for the blood-money on the reward papers – to see if ut's worth enough. Those are the Black Irish, an' 'tis they that bring dishgrace upon the name av Ireland, an' thim I wud kill – as I nearly killed wan wanst.

'But to reshume. My room – 'twas before I was married – was wid twelve av the scum av the earth – the pickin's av the gutther – mane men that wud neither laugh nor talk nor yet get dhrunk as a man shud. They thried some av their dog's thricks on me, but I dhrew a line round my cot, an' the man that thransgressed ut wint into hospital for three days good.

'O'Hara had put his spite on the room – he was my Colour-Sargint – an' nothing cud we do to plaze him. I was younger than I am now, an' I tuk fwhat I got in the way av dhressing-down and punishmint-dhrill wid me tongue in me cheek. But it was diff'rint wid the others, an' why I cannot say, excipt that some men are borrun mane an' go to dhirty murther where a fist is more than enough. Afther a whoile, they changed their chune to me an' was desp'rit frien'ly – all twelve av thim cursin' O'Hara in chorus.

'"Eyah!" sez I, "O'Hara's a divil and I'm not for denyin' ut, but is he the only man in the wurruld? Let him go. He'll get tired av findin' our kit foul an' our 'coutrements onproperly kep'."

'"We will *not* let him go," sez they.

'"Thin take him," sez I, "an' a dashed poor yield you will get for your throuble."

'"Is he not misconductin' himsilf wid Slimmy's wife?" sez another.

'"She's common to the Rig'mint," sez I. "Fwhat has made ye this partic'lar on a suddint?"

'"Has he not put his spite on the roomful av us? Can we do anythin' that he will not check us for?" sez another.

'"That's thrue," sez I.

'"Will ye not help us to do aught," sez another – "a big bould man like you?"

'"I will break his head upon his shoulthers av he puts hand on me," sez I. "I will give him the lie av he says that I'm dhirty, an' I wud not mind duckin' him in the Artillery troughs[17] if ut was not that I'm thryin' for me shtripes."

'"Is that all ye will do?" sez another. "Have ye no more spunk than that, ye blood-dhrawn calf?"'[18]

'"Blood-dhrawn I may be," says I, gettin' back to my cot an' makin' my line round ut; "but ye know that the man who comes acrost this mark will be more blood-dhrawn than me. No man gives me the name in my mouth," I sez. "Ondhersthand, I will have no part wid you in anythin' ye do, nor will I raise my fist to my shuperior. Is any wan comin' on?" sez I.

'They made no move, tho' I gave thim full time, but stud growlin' an' snarlin' together at wan ind av the room. I tuk up my cap and wint out to Canteen, thinkin' no little av mesilf, an' there I grew most ondacintly dhrunk in my legs. My head was all reasonable.

'"Houligan," I sez to a man in E Comp'ny that was by way av bein' a frind av mine; "I'm overtuk from the belt down. Do you give me the touch av your shoulther to presarve me formashin[19] an' march me acrost the ground into the high grass. I'll sleep ut off there," sez I; an' Houligan – he's dead now, but good he was whoile he lasted – walked wid me, givin' me the touch whin I wint wide, ontil we came to the high grass, an', my faith, sky an' earth was fair rowlin' undher me. I made for where the grass was thickust, an' there I slep' off my liquor wid an aisy conscience. I did not desire to come on the books too frequint; my characther havin' been shpotless for the good half av a year.

'Whin I roused, the dhrink was dyin' out in me, an' I felt as though a she-cat had littered in me mouth. I had not learned to hould my liquor wid comfort in thim days. 'Tis little betther I am now. "I will get Houligan to pour a bucket over my head," thinks I, an' I wud ha' risen, but I heard some wan say: "Mulvaney can take the blame av ut for the backslidin' hound he is."

'"Oho!" sez I, an' me head ringing like a guard-room gong:[20] "fwhat is the blame that this young man must take to oblige Tim Vulmea?" For 'twas Tim Vulmea that shpoke.

'I turned on me belly an' crawled through the grass, a bit at a time, to where the spache came from. There was the twelve av my room sittin' down in a little patch, the dhry grass wavin' above their heads an' the sin av black murther in their hearts. I put the stuff aside to get clear view.

'"Fwhat's that?" sez wan man, jumpin' up.

'"A dog," says Vulmea. "You're a nice hand to this job! As I said, Mulvaney will take the blame – av ut comes to a pinch."

'"'Tis harrd to swear a man's life away," sez a young wan.

'"Thank ye for that," thinks I. "Now, fwhat the divil are you paragins conthrivin' agin' me?"

'"'Tis as aisy as dhrinkin' your quart," sez Vulmea. "At sivin or thereon, O'Hara will come acrost to the Married Quarters, goin' to call on Slimmy's wife, the swine! Wan av us 'll pass the wurrud to the room an' we shtart the divil an' all av a shine – laughin' an' crackin' on an' t'rowin' our boots about. Thin O'Hara will come to give us the ordher to be quiet, the more by token bekaze the room lamp will be knocked over in the larkin'. He will take the straight road to the ind door where there's the lamp in the veranda, an' that'll bring him clear agin' the light as he shtands. He will not be able to look into the dhark. Wan av us will loose off, an' a close shot ut will be, an' shame to the man that misses. 'Twill be Mulvaney's rifle, she that is at the head av the rack – there's no mishtakin' that long-shtocked, cross-eyed bitch even in the dhark."

'The thief misnamed my ould firin'-piece out av jealousy – I was pershuaded av that – an' ut made me more angry than all.

'But Vulmea goes on: "O'Hara will dhrop, an' by the time the light's lit agin, there'll be some six av us on the chest av Mulvaney, cryin' murther an' rape. Mulvaney's cot is near the ind door, an' the shmokin' rifle will be lyin' undher him whin we've knocked him over. We know, an' all the Rig'mint knows, that Mulvaney has given O'Hara more lip than any man av us. Will there be any doubt at the Coort-Martial? Wud twelve honust sodger-bhoys swear away the life av a dear, quiet, swate-timpered man such as is Mulvaney – wid his line av pipe-clay roun' his cot, threatenin' us wid murther av we overshtepped ut, as we can truthful testify?"

'"Mary, Mother av Mercy!" thinks I to mesilf; "ut is this to have an unruly mimber[21] an' fistes fit to use! The hounds!"

'The big dhrops ran down my face, for I was wake wid the liquor an' had not the full av my wits about me. I laid sthill an' heard thim workin' thimsilves up to swear me life away by tellin' tales av ivry time I had put my mark on wan or another; an', my faith, they was few that was not so dishtinguished. 'Twas all in the way av fair fight, though, for niver did I raise my hand excipt whin they had provoked me to ut.

'"'Tis all well," sez wan av thim, "but who's to do this shootin'?"

'"Fwhat matther?" sez Vulmea. "'Tis Mulvaney will do that – at the Coort-Martial."

'"He will so," sez the man, "but whose hand is put to the thrigger – *in the room*?"

'"Who'll do ut?" sez Vulmea, lookin' round, but divil a man answered. They began to dishpute till Kiss, that was always playin' Shpoil Five,[22] sez: "Thry the kyards!" Wid that he opind his tunic an' tuk out the greasy palammers,[23] an' they all fell in wid the notion.

'"Deal on!" sez Vulmea, wid a big rattlin' oath, "an' the Black Curse av Shielygh come to the man that will not do his jooty as the kyards say. Amin!"

'"Black Jack is the masther," sez Kiss, dealin'. Black Jack, sorr, I shud expaytiate to you, is the Ace av Shpades which from time immimorial has been intimately connect wid battle, murther, an' suddin death.

'*Wanst* Kiss dealt, an' there was no sign, but the men was whoite wid the workin's av their sowls. *Twice* Kiss dealt, an' there was a grey shine on their cheeks like the mess av an egg.[24] *Three* times Kiss dealt, an' they was blue. "Have ye not lost him?" sez Vulmea, wipin' the sweat on him; "let's ha' done quick!" "Quick ut is," sez Kiss, throwin' him the kyard; an' ut fell face up on his knee – Black Jack!

'Thin they all cackled wid laughin'. "Jooty thrippence,"[25] sez wan av thim, "an' damned cheap at that price!" But I cud see they all dhrew a little away from Vulmea an' lef' him sittin' playin' wid the kyard. Vulmea sez no wurrud for a whoile but licked his lips – cat-ways. Thin he threw up his head an' made the men swear by ivry oath known to stand by him not alone in the room but at the Coort-Martial that was to set on *me*! He tould off five av the biggest to stretch me on my cot whin the shot was fired, an' another man he tould off to put out the light, an' yet another to load my rifle. He wud not do that himsilf; an' that was quare, for 'twas but a little thing considherin'.

'Thin they swore over agin that they wud not bethray wan

another, an' crep' out av the grass in diff'rint ways, two by two. A mercy ut was that they did not come on me. I was sick wid fear in the pit av me stummick – sick, sick, sick! Afther they was all gone, I wint back to Canteen an' called for a quart to put a thought in me. Vulmea was there, dhrinkin' heavy, an' politeful to me beyond reason. "Fwhat will I do? – fwhat will I do?" thinks I to mesilf whin Vulmea wint away.

'Prisintly the Arm'rer-Sargint comes in stiffin' an' crackin' on, not plazed wid any wan, bekaze the Martini-Henry bein' new to the Rig'mint[26] in those days we used to play the mischief wid her arrangemints. 'Twas a long time before I cud get out av the way av thryin' to pull back the backsight an' turnin' her over afther firin' – as if she was a Snider.[27]

'"Fwhat tailor-men do they give me to work wid?" sez the Arm'rer-Sargint. "Here's Hogan, his nose flat as a table, laid by for a week, an' ivry Comp'ny sendin' their arrums in knocked to small shivreens."

'"Fwhat's wrong wid Hogan, Sargint?" sez I.

'"Wrong!" sez the Arm'rer-Sargint; "I showed him, as though I had been his mother, the way av shtrippin' a 'Tini, an' he shtrup her clane an' aisy. I tould him to put her to agin an' fire a blank into the blow-pit to show how the dhirt hung on the groovin'.[28] He did that, but he did not put in the pin av the fallin'-block,[29] an' av coorse whin he fired he was strook by the block jumpin' clear. Well for him 'twas but a blank – a full charge wud ha' cut his eye out."

'I looked a thrifle wiser than a boiled sheep's head. "How's that, Sargint?" sez I.

'"This way, ye blundherin' man, an' don't you be doin' ut," sez he. Wid that he shows me a Waster action – the breech av her all cut away to show the inside – an' so plazed he was to grumble that he dimonsthrated fwhat Hogan had done twice over. "An' that comes av not knowin' the wepping you're provided wid," sez he.

'"Thank ye, Sargint," sez I; "I will come to you agin for further informashin."

'"Ye will not," sez he. "Kape your clanin'-rod away from the breech-pin or you will get into throuble."

'I wint outside an' I cud ha' danced wid delight for the grandeur av ut. "They will load my rifle, good luck to thim, whoile I'm away," thinks I, and back I wint to the Canteen to give thim their clear chanst.

'The Canteen was fillin' wid men at the ind av the day. I made feign to be far gone in dhrink, an', wan by wan, all my roomful came in wid Vulmea. I wint away, walkin' thick an' heavy, but not so thick an' heavy that any wan cud ha' tuk me. Sure an' thrue, there was a kyartridge gone from my pouch an' lyin' snug in my rifle. I was hot wid rage agin' thim all, and I worried the bullet out wid me teeth as fast as I cud, the room bein' empty. Then I tuk my boot an' the clanin'-rod and knocked out the pin av the fallin'-block. Oh, 'twas music whin that pin rowled on the flure! I put ut into my pouch an' shtuck a dab av dhirt on the holes in the plate, puttin' the fallin'-block back. "That'll do your business, Vulmea," sez I, lyin' aisy on me cot. "Come an' sit on me chest, the whole room av you, an' I will take you to me bosom for the biggest divils that iver cheated halter." I wud have no mercy on Vulmea. His eye or his life – little I cared!

'At dusk they came back, the twelve av thim, an' they had all been dhrinkin'. I was shammin' sleep on the cot. Wan man wint outside in the veranda. Whin he whishtled they began to rage roun' the room an' carry on tremenjus. But I niver want to hear men laugh as they did – skylarkin' too! 'Twas like mad jackals.

'"Shtop that blasted noise!" sez O'Hara in the dark, an' pop goes the room lamp. I cud hear O'Hara runnin' up an' the rattlin' av my rifle in the rack an' the men breathin' heavy as they stud roun' my cot. I cud see O'Hara in the light av the veranda lamp, an' thin I heard the crack av my rifle. She cried loud, poor darlint, bein' mishandled. Next minut' five men were houldin' me down. "Go aisy," I sez; "fwhat's ut all about?"

'Thin Vulmea, on the flure, raised a howl you cud hear from wan ind av cantonmints to the other. "I'm dead, I'm butchered, I'm blind!" sez he. "Saints have mercy on my sinful sowl! Sind for Father Constant! Oh, sind for Father Constant an' let me go clane!" By that I knew he was not so dead as I cud ha' wished.

'O'Hara picks up the lamp in the veranda wid a hand as stiddy as a rest. "Fwhat damned dog's thrick is this av yours?" sez he, and turns the light on Tim Vulmea that was shwimmin' in blood from top to toe. The fallin'-block had sprung free behin' a full charge av powther – good care I tuk to bite down the brass afther takin' out the bullet, that there might be somethin' to give ut full worth – an' had cut Tim from the lip to the corner av the right eye, lavin' the eyelid in tatthers, an' so up an' along by the forehead to the hair. 'Twas more av a rakin' plough, if you will ondhersthand, than a clane cut; an' niver did I see a man bleed as Vulmea did. The dhrink an' the stew that he was in pumped the blood strong. The minut' the men sittin' on my chest heard O'Hara spakin' they scatthered each wan to his cot, an' cried out very politeful: "Fwhat is ut, Sargint?"

'"Fwhat is ut!" sez O'Hara, shakin' Tim. "Well an' good do you know fwhat ut is, ye skulkin' ditch-lurkin' dogs! Get a *dooli*,[30] an' take this whimperin' scutt away. There will be more heard av ut than any av you will care for."

'Vulmea sat up rockin' his head in his hand an' moanin' for Father Constant.

'"Be done!" sez O'Hara, dhraggin' him up by the hair. "You're none so dead that you cannot go fifteen years for thryin' to shoot me."

'"I did not," sez Vulmea; "I was shootin' mesilf."

'"That's quare," sez O'Hara, "for the front av my jackut is black wid your powther." He tuk up the rifle that was still warm an' began to laugh. "I'll make your life Hell to you," sez he, "for attempted murther an' kapin' your rifle onproperly. You'll be hanged first an' thin put undher stoppages for four fifteen.[31] The rifle's done for," sez he.

'"Why, 'tis *my* rifle!" sez I, comin' up to look. "Vulmea, ye divil, fwhat were you doin' wid her – answer me that?'

'"Lave me alone," sez Vulmea; "I'm dyin'!"

'"I'll wait till you're betther," sez I, "an' thin we two will talk ut out umbrageous."

'O'Hara pitched Tim into the *dooli*, none too tinder, but all the bhoys kep' by their cots, which was not the sign av innocint men. I was huntin' ivrywhere for my fallin'-block, but not findin' ut at all. I niver found ut.

'"*Now* fwhat will I do?" sez O'Hara, swinging the veranda light in his hand an' lookin' down the room. I had hate and contimpt av O'Hara an' I have now, dead tho' he is, but for all that will I say he was a brave man. He is baskin' in Purgathory this tide, but I wish he cud hear that, whin he stud lookin' down the room an' the bhoys shivered before the eye av him, I knew him for a brave man an' I liked him *so*.

'"Fwhat will I do?" sez O'Hara agin, an' we heard the voice av a woman low an' sof' in the veranda. 'Twas Slimmy's wife, come over at the shot, sittin' on wan av the benches an' scarce able to walk.

'"O Denny! – Denny, dear," sez she, "have they kilt you?"

'O'Hara looked down the room agin an' showed his teeth to the gum. Thin he spat on the flure.

'"You're not worth ut," sez he. "Light that lamp, ye dogs," an' wid that he turned away, an' I saw him walkin' off wid Slimmy's wife; she thryin' to wipe off the powther-black on the front av his jackut wid her handkerchief. "A brave man you are," thinks I – "a brave man an' a bad woman."

'No wan said a wurrud for a time. They was all ashamed, past spache.

'"Fwhat d'you think he will do?" sez wan av thim at last. "He knows we're all in ut."

'"Are we so?" sez I from my cot. "The man that sez that to me will be hurt. I do not know," sez I, "fwhat ondherhand divilmint you have conthrived, but by fwhat I've seen I know that you cannot commit murther wid another man's rifle – such shakin' cowards you are. I'm goin' to slape," I sez, "an' you can blow my head off whoile I lay." I did not slape, though, for a long time. Can ye wonder?

'Next morn the news was through all the Rig'mint, an' there was nothin' that the men did not tell. O'Hara reports, fair an' aisy, that Vulmea was come to grief through tamperin' wid his rifle in barricks, all for to show the mechanism. An', by my sowl, he had the impart'nince to say that he was on the shpot at the time an' cud certify that ut was an accidint! You might ha' knocked my roomful down wid a straw whin they heard that. 'Twas lucky for thim that the bhoys were always thryin' to find out how the new rifle was made, an' a lot av thim had come up for aisin' the pull[32] by shtickin' bits av grass an' such in the part av the lock that showed near the thrigger. The first issues of the 'Tinis was not covered in, an' I mesilf have aised the pull av mine time an' agin. A light pull is ten points on the range to me.

'"I will not have this foolishness!" sez the Colonel. "I will twist the tail off Vulmea!" sez he; but whin he saw him, all tied up an' groanin' in hospital, he changed his will. "Make him an early convalescint," sez he to the Doctor, an' Vulmea was made so for a warnin'. His big bloody bandages an' face puckered up to wan side did more to kape the bhoys from messin' wid the insides av their rifles than any punishmint.

'O'Hara gave no reason for fwhat he'd said, an' all my roomful were too glad to ask, tho' he put his spite upon thim more wearin' than before. Wan day, howiver, he tuk me apart very polite, for he cud be that at his choosin'.

'"You're a good sodger, tho' you're a damned insolint man," sez he.

'"Fair wurruds, Sargint," sez I, "or I may be insolint agin."

'"'Tis not like you," sez he, "to lave your rifle in the rack widout the breech-pin, for widout the breech-pin she was whin Vulmea fired. I shud ha' found the break av ut in the eyes av the holes, else," he sez.

'"Sargint," sez I, "fwhat wud your life ha' been worth av the breech-pin had been in place, for, on my sowl, my life wud be worth just as much to me av I tould you whether ut was or was not? Be thankful the bullet was not there," I sez.

'"That's thrue," sez he, pulling his moustache; "but I do not believe that you, for all your lip, were in that business."

'"Sargint," sez I, "I cud hammer the life out av a man in ten minut's wid my fistes if that man dishplazed me; for I am a good sodger, an' I will be threated as such, an' whoile my fistes are my own they're strong enough for all the work I have to do. *They* do not fly back towards me!" sez I, lookin' him betune the eyes.

'"You're a good man," sez he, lookin' me betune the eyes – an' oh, he was a gran'-built man to see! – "you're a good man," he sez, "an' I cud wish, for the pure frolic av ut, that I was not a Sargint, or that you were not a Privit; an' you will think me no coward whin I say this thing."

'"I do not," sez I. "I saw you whin Vulmea mishandled the rifle. But, Sargint," I sez, "take the wurrud from me now, spakin' as man to man wid the shtripes off, tho' 'tis little right I have to talk, me bein' fwhat I am by natur'. This time ye tuk no harm, an' next time ye may not, but, in the ind, so sure as Slimmy's wife came into the veranda, so sure will ye take harm – an' bad harm. Have thought, Sargint," sez I. "Is ut worth ut?"

'"Ye're a bould man," sez he, breathin' harrd. "A very bould man. But I am a bould man tu. Do you go your ways, Privit Mulvaney, an' I will go mine."

'We had no further spache thin or afther, but, wan by another, he drafted the twelve av my room out into other rooms an' got thim spread among the Comp'nies, for they was not a good breed to live together, an' the Comp'ny Orf'cers saw ut. They wud ha' shot me in the night av they had known fwhat I knew; but that they did not.

'An', in the ind, as I said, O'Hara met his death from Rafferty for foolin' wid his wife. He wint his own way too well – Eyah, too well! Shtraight to that affair, widout turnin' to the right or to the lef', he wint, an' may the Lord have mercy on his sowl. Amin!'

''Ear! 'ear!' said Ortheris, pointing the moral with a wave of his pipe. 'An' this is 'im 'oo would be a bloomin' Vulmea all for the sake of Mullins an' a bloomin' button! Mullins never went after a woman in his life. Mrs Mullins, she saw 'im one day –'

'Ortheris,' I said hastily, for the romances of Private Ortheris are all too daring for publication, 'look at the sun. It's a quarter past six!'

'Oh, Lord! Three-quarters of an hour for five an' a 'arf miles! We'll 'ave to run like Jimmy O.'

The Three Musketeers clambered on to the bridge, and departed hastily in the direction of the cantonment road. When I overtook them I offered them two stirrups and a tail, which they accepted enthusiastically. Ortheris held the tail, and in this manner we trotted steadily through the shadows by an unfrequented road.

At the turn into the cantonments we heard carriage wheels. It was the Colonel's barouche, and in it sat the Colonel's wife and daughter. I caught a suppressed chuckle, and my beast sprang forward with a lighter step.

The Three Musketeers had vanished into the night.

IN BLACK AND WHITE

IN BLACK AND WHITE
BY RUDYARD KIPLING
A.H. WHEELER & Co's
No. 3
ONE RUPEE
INDIAN RAILWAY LIBRARY
LAHORE

Contents

The Dedication

To My Most Deare Father,

When I was in your House and we went abroade together, in the outskirtes of the Citie, among the Gentoo Wrestlours, you had poynted me how in all Empryzes he gooing forth flang backe alwaies a Word to hym that had instruct hym in his Crafte to the better Sneckynge of a Victorie or at the leaste the auoidance of anie greate Defeate: And presentlie each man wolde run to his *Vstad* (which is as we shoulde say *Master*) and geat such as he deserued of Admoneshment Reprouf and Council, concernynge the Gripp, the Houlde, Cross-buttock and Fall, and then lay to afreshe.

In lyke maner I, drawynge back a lytel, from this my Rabble and Encompasment of Labour, have runn asyde to you who were euer my *Vstad* and Speake as it were in your priuie Eare [yet that others may knowe] that if I have here done aught of Faire Craft and Reverentiall it is come from your hande as trewly [but by i. Degree remouen] as though it had been the coperture of thys Booke that you haue made for me in loue. How may I here tell of that Tender Diligence which in my wauerynge and inconstante viages was in all tymes about me to showe the Passions and Occasions, Shifts, Humours, and Sports that in due proporcion combinate haue bred that Rare and Terrible Mystery the which, for lacke of a more compleat Vnderstandinge, the Worlde has cauled Man: aswel the maner in which you shoulde goo about to pourtraie the same, a lytel at a tyme in Feare and Decencie. By what hand, when I wolde have dabbled a Greene and unused Pen in all Earthe Heauen and Hell, bicause of the pitiful Confidence of Youthe, was I bounde in and restrict to wayte tyl I coulde in some sort discerne from the Shadowe, that is not by any peynes to be toucht, the small Kernel and Substance that mighte conforme to the sclenderness of my Capacitie. All thys and other Council (that, though I dyd then not followe, Tyme hath since sadlie prouen trewe) is my unpayable Debt to you (most deare Father) and for marke I have set asyde for you, if you will take it, thys my thirde

Booke. The more thys and no other sense it is of common knowledge that Men do rather esteem a Pebble gathered under the Burnynge Lyne (or anie place that they haue gone farr to travel in) then the Paue-way of theyr owne Citie, though that may be the better wrought. Your Charitie and the large Tenderness that I haue nowhere founde sense I haue gone from your House shall look upon it fauorably and ouerpass the Blemyshes, Spottes, Foul Crafte, and Maculations that do as throughly marke it as anie Toil of Me. None the less it is sett presomptuously before that Wilde Beaste the Publick which, though when aparte and one by one examined is but compost of such meere Men and Women as you in theyr outwarde form peynt and I would fayne peynt in theyr inward workynges, yet in totalitie, is a Great and thanklesse God (like unto *Dagon*) upon whose Altars a man must offer of his Beste alone or the Priestes (which they caul *Reuiewers*) pack hym emptie awai. If I faile in thys Seruyce you shall take me asyde and giue me more Instruction, which is but the olde Counsel unreguarded and agayne made playne: As our *Vstads* take hym whose Nose is rubben in the dyrte and speak in hys Eare. But thys I knowe, that if I fail or if I geat my Wage from the God aforesayd; and thus dance perpetually before that Altar till he be wearyed, the Wisdom that made in my Vse, when I was neere to listen, and the Sweep and Swing temperate of the Pen that, when I was afarr, gaue me alwaies and untyryng the most delectable Tillage of that Wisdom shall neuer be lackynge to me in Lyfe.

And though I am more rich herein then the richest, my present Pouertie can but make return in thys lytel Booke which your owne Toil has nobilitated beyon the deseruynge of the Writer your Son.

Introduction
by Kadir Baksh, Khitmatgar

HEAVENBORN,

Through your favour this is a book written by my *Sahib*. I know that he wrote it because it was his custom to write far into the night; I greatly desiring to go to my house. But there was no order: therefore it was my fate to sit without the door until the work was accomplished. Then came I and made shut all the papers in the office box, and these papers, by the peculiar operation of Time and owing to the skilful manner in which I picked them up from the floor, became such a book as you now see. God alone knows what is written therein, for I am a poor man, and the *Sahib* is my father and my mother, and I have no concern with his writings until he has left his table and gone to bed.

Nabi Baksh, the clerk, says that it is a book about the black men – common people. This is a manifest lie, for by what road can my *Sahib* have acquired knowledge of the common people? Have I not, for several years, been perpetually with the *Sahib*: and throughout that time have I not stood between him and the other servants who would persecute him with complaints or vex him with idle tales about my work? Did I not smite Dunnoo, the groom, only yesterday in the matter of the badness of the harness composition which I had procured? I am the head of the *Sahib*'s household and hold his purse. Without me he does not know where are his rupees or his clean collars. So great is my power over the *Sahib* and the love that he bears to me! Have *I* ever told the *Sahib* about the customs of servants or black men? Am I a fool? I have said 'very good talk' upon all occasions. I have cut always smooth his wristbands with scissors, and timely warned him of the passing away of his tobacco that he might not be left smokeless upon a Sunday. More than this I have not done. The *Sahib* cannot go out to dinner lacking my aid. How then should he know aught that I did not tell him? Certainly Nabi Baksh is a liar.

None the less this is a book, and the *Sahib* wrote it, for his name is in it and it is not his washing-book. Now, such is the wisdom of the *Sahib-log* that, upon opening this thing, they will instantly discover the purport. Yet I would of their favour beg them to observe how correct is the order of the pages, which I have counted, from the first to the last. Thus, One is followed by Two and Two by Three, and so forward to the end of the book. Even as I picked the pages one by one with great trouble from the floor, when the *Sahib* had gone to bed, so have they been placed: and there is not a fault in the whole account. And this is *my* work. It was a great burden, but I accomplished it; and if the *Sahib* gains reputation by that which he has written – and God knows what he is always writing about – I, Kadir Baksh, his servant, also have a claim to honour.

Dray Wara Yow Dee

For jealousy is the rage of a man: therefore he will not spare in the day of vengeance. – *Proverbs* vi.34.

Almonds and raisins, Sahib? Grapes from Kabul?[1] Or a pony of the rarest if the Sahib will only come with me. He is thirteen-three,[2] Sahib, plays polo, goes in a cart, carries a lady and – Holy Kurshed and the Blessed Imams,[3] it is the Sahib himself! My heart is made fat and my eye glad. May you never be tired! As is cold water in the Tirah,[4] so is the sight of a friend in a far place. And what do *you* in this accursed land? South of Delhi, Sahib, you know the saying – 'Rats are the men and trulls the women.' It was an order? Ahoo! An order is an order till one is strong enough to disobey. O my brother, O my friend, we have met in an auspicious hour! Is all well in the heart and the body and the house? In a lucky day have we two come together again.

I am to go with you? Your favour is great. Will there be picket-room[5] in the compound? I have three horses and the bundles and the horse-boy. Moreover, remember that the police here hold me a horse-thief. What do these Lowland bastards know of horse-thieves? Do you remember that time in Peshawur when Kamal hammered on the gates of Jumrud[6] – mountebank that he was – and lifted the Colonel's horses all in one night? Kamal is dead now, but his nephew has taken up the matter, and there will be more horses a-missing if the Khyber Levies do not look to it.

The Peace of God and the favour of His Prophet[7] be upon this house and all that is in it! Shafiz Ullah, rope the mottled mare under the tree and draw water. The horses can stand in the sun, but double the felts[8] over the loins. Nay, my friend, do not trouble to look them over. They are to sell to the Officer-fools who know so many things of the horse. The mare is heavy in foal; the grey is a devil unlicked; and the dun – but you know the trick of the peg. When they are sold I go back to Pubbi,[9] or, it may be, the Valley of Peshawur.

O friend of my heart, it is good to see you again. I have been bowing and lying all day to the Officer-Sahibs in respect to those horses; and my mouth is dry for straight talk. *Auggrh!* Before a meal tobacco is good. Do not join me, for we are not in our own country. Sit in the veranda and I will spread my cloth here. But first I will drink. *In the name of God returning thanks, thrice!* This is sweet water, indeed – sweet as the water of Sheoran when it comes from the snows.

They are all well and pleased in the North – Khoda Baksh and the others. Yar Khan has come down with the horses from Kurdistan[10] – six-and-thirty head only, and a full half pack-ponies – and has said openly in the Kashmir Serai[11] that you English should send guns and blow the Amir[12] into Hell. There are *fifteen* tolls[13] now on the Kabul road; and at Dakka,[14] when he thought he was clear, Yar Khan was stripped of all his Balkh[15] stallions by the Governor! This is a great injustice, and Yar Khan is hot with rage. And of the others: Mahbub Ali[16] is still at Pubbi, writing God knows what. Tugluq Khan is in jail for the business of the Kohat[17] Police Post. Faiz Beg came down from Ismail-ki-Dhera[18] with a Bokhariot[19] belt for thee, my brother, at the closing of the year, but none knew whither thou hadst gone: there was no news left behind. The Cousins have taken a new run near Pakpattan[20] to breed mules for the Government carts, and there is a story in the Bazar of a priest. Oho! Such a salt tale! Listen –

Sahib, why do you ask that? My clothes are fouled because of the dust on the road. My eyes are sad because of the glare of the sun. My feet are swollen because I have washed them in bitter water, and my cheeks are hollow because the food here is bad. Fire burn your money! What do I want with it? I am rich. I thought you were my friend. But you are like the others – a Sahib. Is a man sad? Give him money, say the Sahibs. Is he dishonoured? Give him money, say the Sahibs. Hath he a wrong upon his head? Give him money, say the Sahibs. Such are the Sahibs, and such art thou – even thou.

Nay, do not look at the feet of the dun. Pity it is that I ever taught you to know the legs of a horse. Footsore? Be it so. What of that? The roads are hard. And the mare footsore? She bears a double burden,[21] Sahib.

And now, I pray you, give me permission to depart. Great favour and honour has the Sahib done me, and graciously has he shown his belief that the horses are stolen. Will it please him to send me to the Thana?[22] To call a sweeper and have me led away by one of these lizard-men? I am the Sahib's friend. I have drunk water in the shadow of his house, and he has blackened my face.[23] Remains there anything more to do? Will the Sahib give me eight annas to make smooth the injury and – complete the insult –?

Forgive me, my brother. I knew not – I know not now – what I say. Yes, I lied to you! I will put dust on my head – and I am an Afridi![24] The horses have been marched footsore from the Valley to this place, and my eyes are dim, and my body aches for the want of sleep, and my heart is dried up with sorrow and shame. But as it was my shame, so by God the Dispenser of Justice – by Allah-al-Mumît![25] – it shall be my own revenge!

We have spoken together with naked hearts before this, and our hands have dipped into the same dish, and thou hast been to me as a brother. Therefore I pay thee back with lies and ingratitude – as a Pathan. Listen now! When the grief of the soul is too heavy for endurance it may be a little eased by speech; and, moreover, the mind of a true man is as a well, and the pebble of confession dropped therein sinks and is no more seen. From the Valley have I come on foot, league by league, with a fire in my chest like the fire of the Pit. And why? Hast thou, then, so quickly forgotten our customs, among this folk who sell their wives and their daughters for silver? Come back with me to the North and be among men once more. Come back, when this matter is accomplished and I call for thee! The bloom of the peach-orchards is upon all the Valley, and *here* is only dust and a great stink. There is a pleasant wind among the mulberry trees, and the streams are bright with snow-water,[26] and the caravans go up and the caravans go down, and a hundred fires sparkle in the gut of the Pass, and tent-peg answers hammer-nose, and pack-horse squeals to pack-horse across the drift-smoke of the evening. It is good in the North now. Come back with me. Let us return to our own people! Come!

Whence is my sorrow? Does a man tear out his heart and make fritters thereof over a slow fire for aught other than a woman? Do not laugh, friend of mine, for your time will also be. A woman of the

Abazai[27] was she, and I took her to wife to staunch the feud between our village and the men of Ghor.[28] 'I am no longer young? The lime has touched my beard? True. I had no need of the wedding? Nay, but I loved her. What saith Rahman?[29] 'Into whose heart Love enters, there is Folly *and naught else*. By a glance of the eye she hath blinded thee; and by the eyelids and the fringe of the eyelids taken thee into the captivity without ransom, *and naught else*.' Dost thou remember that song at the sheep-roasting in the Pindi camp among the Uzbegs[30] of the Amir?

The Abazai are dogs and their women the servants of sin. There was a lover of her own people, but of that her father told me naught. My friend, curse for me in your prayers, as I curse at each praying from the Fakr to the Isha,[31] the name of Daoud Shah, Abazai, whose head is still upon his neck, whose hands are still upon his wrists, who has done me dishonour, who has made my name a laughing-stock among the women of Little Malikand.[32]

I went into Hindustan at the end of two months – to Cherat.[33] I was gone twelve days only; but I had said that I would be fifteen days absent. This I did to try her, for it is written: 'Trust not the incapable.'[34] Coming up the gorge alone in the falling of the light, I heard the voice of a man singing at the door of my house; and it was the voice of Daoud Shah, and the song that he sang was '*Dray wara yow dee*' – 'All three are one.' It was as though a heel-rope[35] had been slipped round my heart and all the Devils were drawing it tight past endurance. I crept silently up the hill-road, but the fuse of my matchlock was wetted with the rain, and I could not slay Daoud Shah from afar. Moreover, it was in my mind to kill the woman also. Thus he sang, sitting outside my house, and, anon, the woman opened the door, and I came nearer, crawling on my belly among the rocks. I had only my knife to my hand. But a stone slipped under my foot, and the two looked down the hillside, and he, leaving his matchlock, fled from my anger, because he was afraid for the life that was in him. But the woman moved not till I stood in front of her, crying: 'O woman, what is this that thou hast done?' And she, void of fear, though she knew my thought, laughed, saying: 'It is a little thing. I loved him, and *thou* art a dog and cattle-thief coming by night. Strike!' And I, being still blinded by her beauty, for, O my friend, the women of the Abazai are very fair, said: 'Hast thou no fear?' And she answered: 'None – but only the fear that I do not die.' Then said I: 'Have no fear.' And she bowed her head, and I smote it off at the neck-bone so that it leaped between my feet. Thereafter the rage of our people came upon me, and I hacked off the breasts, that the men of Little Malikand might know the crime, and cast the body into the watercourse that flows to the Kabul River.[36] *Dray wara yow dee! Dray wara yow dee!* The body without the head, the soul without light, and my own darkling heart – all three are one – all three are one!

That night, making no halt, I went to Ghor and demanded news of Daoud Shah. Men said: 'He is gone to Pubbi for horses. What wouldst thou of him? There is peace between the villages.' I made answer: 'Ay! The peace of treachery and the love that the Devil Atala bore to Gurel.'[37] So I fired thrice into the tower-gate and laughed and went my way.

In those hours, brother and friend of my heart's heart, the moon and the stars were as blood above me, and in my mouth was the taste of dry earth. Also, I broke no bread, and my drink was the rain of the valley of Ghor upon my face.

At Pubbi I found Mahbub Ali, the writer, sitting upon his charpoy,[38] and gave up my arms according to your Law. But I was not grieved, for it was in my heart that I should kill Daoud Shah with my bare hands thus – as a man strips a bunch of raisins. Mahbub Ali said: 'Daoud Shah has even now gone hot-foot to Peshawur, and he will pick up his horses upon the road to Delhi, for it is said that the Bombay Tramway Company[39] are buying horses there by the truckload; eight horses to the truck.' And that was a true saying.

Then I saw that the hunting would be no little thing, for the man was gone into your borders to save himself against my wrath. And shall he save himself so? Am I not alive? Though he run northward to the Dora[40] and the snow, or southerly to the Black Water,[41] I will follow him, as a lover follows the footsteps of his mistress, and coming upon him I will take him tenderly – Aho! so tenderly! – in my arms, saying: 'Well hast thou done and well shalt thou be repaid.' And out of that embrace Daoud Shah shall not go forth with the breath in his nostrils. *Auggrh!* Where is the pitcher? I am as thirsty as a mother mare in the first month.

Your Law! What is your Law to me? When the horses fight on the runs do they regard the boundary pillars; or do the kites of Ali Musjid[42] forbear because the carrion lies under the shadow of the Ghor Kuttri?[43] The matter began across the Border. It shall finish where God pleases. Here; in my own country; or in Hell. All three are one.

Listen now, sharer of the sorrow of my heart, and I will tell of the hunting. I followed to Peshawur from Pubbi, and I went to and fro about the streets of Peshawur like a houseless dog, seeking for my enemy. Once I thought that I saw him washing his mouth in the conduit in the big square, but when I came up he was gone. It may be that it was he, and, seeing my face, he had fled.

A girl of the bazar said that he would go to Nowshera.[44] I said: 'O heart's heart, does Daoud Shah visit thee?' And she said: 'Even so.' I said: 'I would fain see him, for we be friends parted for two years. Hide me, I pray, here in the shadow of the window-shutter, and I will wait for his coming.' And the girl said: 'O Pathan, look into my eyes!' And I turned, leaning upon her breast, and looked into her eyes, swearing that I spoke the very Truth of God. But she answered: 'Never friend waited friend with such eyes. Lie to God and the Prophet, but to a woman ye cannot lie. Get hence! There shall no harm befall Daoud Shah by cause of me.'

I would have strangled that girl but for the fear of your Police; and thus the hunting would have come to naught. Therefore I only laughed and departed, and she leaned over the window-bar in the night and mocked me down the street. Her name is Jamun. When I have made my account with the man I will return to Peshawur and – her lovers shall desire her no more for her beauty's sake. She shall not be *Jamun*, but *Ak*,[45] the cripple among trees. Ho! ho! *Ak* shall she be!

At Peshawur I bought the horses and grapes, and the almonds and dried fruits, that the reason of my wanderings might be open to the Government, and that there might be no hindrance upon the road. But when I came to Nowshera he was gone; and I knew not where to go. I stayed one day at Nowshera, and in the night a Voice spoke in my ears as I slept among the horses. All night it flew round my head and would not cease from whispering. I was upon my belly, sleeping as the Devils sleep, and it may have been that the Voice was the voice of a Devil. It said: 'Go south, and thou shalt come upon Daoud Shah.' Listen, my brother and chiefest among friends – listen! Is the tale a long one? Think how it was long to me. I have trodden every league of the road from Pubbi to this place; and from Nowshera my guide was only the Voice and the lust of vengeance.

To the Uttock[46] I went, but that was no hindrance to me. Ho! ho! A man may turn the word twice, even in his trouble. The Uttock was no *uttock* [obstacle] to me; and I heard the Voice above the noise of the waters beating on the big rock, saying: 'Go to the right.' So I went to Pindigheb,[47] and in those days my sleep was taken from me utterly, and the head of the woman of the Abazai was before me night and day, even as it had fallen between my feet. *Dray wara yow dee! Dray wara yow dee!* Fire, ashes, and my couch, all three are one – all three are one!

Now I was far from the winter path of the dealers who had gone to Sialkot,[48] and so south by the rail and the Big Road[49] to the line of cantonments; but there was a Sahib in camp at Pindigheb who bought from me a white mare at a good price, and told me that one Daoud Shah had passed to Shahpur[50] with horses. Then I saw that the warning of the Voice was true, and made swift to come to the Salt Hills.[51] The Jhelum[52] was in flood, but I could not wait, and, in the crossing, a bay stallion was washed down and drowned. Herein was God hard to me – not in respect of the beast, of that I had no care – but in this snatching. While I was upon the right bank urging the horses into the water, Daoud Shah was upon the left; for – *Alghias! Alghias!* – the hoofs of my mare scattered the hot ashes of his fires when we came up the hither bank in the light of morning. But he had fled. His feet were made swift by the terror of Death. And I went south from Shahpur as the kite flies. I dared not turn aside lest I should miss my vengeance – which is my right. From Shahpur I skirted by the Jhelum, for I thought that he would avoid the Desert of the Rechna.[53] But, presently, at Sahiwal,[54] I turned away upon the road to Jhang, Samundri, and Gugera,[55] till, upon a night, the mottled mare breasted the fence of the rail that runs to Montgomery.[56] And that place was Okara, and the head of the woman of the Abazai lay upon the sand between my feet.

Thence I went to Fazilka,[57] and they said that I was mad to bring starved horses there. The Voice was with me, and I was *not* mad, but only wearied, because I could not find Daoud Shah. It was written that I should not find him at Rania nor Bahadurgarh,[58] and I came into Delhi from the west, and there also I found him not. My friend, I have seen many strange things in my wanderings. I have seen the Devils rioting across the Rechna as the stallions riot in spring. I have heard the *Djinns*[59] calling to each other from holes in the sand, and I have seen them pass before my face. There are no Devils, say the Sahibs? They are very wise, but they do not know all things about Devils or – horses. Ho! ho! I say to you who are laughing at my misery, that I have seen the Devils at high noon whooping and leaping on the shoals of the Chenab. And was I afraid? My brother, when the desire of a man is set upon one thing alone, he fears neither God nor Man nor Devil. If my vengeance failed, I would splinter the Gates of Paradise with the butt of my gun, or I would cut my way into Hell with my knife, and I would call upon Those who Govern there for the body of Daoud Shah. What love so deep as hate?

Do not speak. I know the thought in your heart. Is the white of this eye clouded? How does the blood beat at the wrist? There is no madness in my flesh, but only the vehemence of the desire that has eaten me up. Listen!

South of Delhi I knew not the country at all. Therefore I cannot say where I went, but I passed through many cities. I knew only that it was laid upon me to go south. When the horses could march no more, I threw myself upon the earth and waited till the day. There was no sleep with me in that journeying; and that was a heavy burden. Dost thou know, brother of mine, the evil of wakefulness that cannot break – when the bones are sore for lack of sleep, and the skin of the temples twitches with weariness, and yet – there is no sleep – there is no sleep? *Dray wara yow dee! Dray wara yow dee!* The eye of the Sun, the eye of the Moon, and my own unrestful eyes – all three are one – all three are one!

There was a city the name whereof I have forgotten, and there the Voice called all night. That was ten days ago. It has cheated me afresh.

I have come hither from a place called Hamirpur,[60] and, behold, it is my Fate that I should meet with thee to my comfort, and the increase of friendship. This is a good omen. By the joy of looking upon thy face the weariness has gone from my feet, and the sorrow of my so long travel is forgotten. Also my heart is peaceful; for I know that the end is near.

It may be that I shall find Daoud Shah in this city going northward, since a Hillman will ever head back to his Hills when the spring warns. And shall he see those hills of our country? Surely I shall overtake him! Surely my vengeance is safe! Surely God hath him in the hollow of His hand against my claiming! There shall no harm befall Daoud Shah till I come; for I would fain kill him quick and whole with the life sticking firm in his body. A pomegranate is sweetest when the cloves break away unwilling from the rind. Let it be in the daytime, that I may see his face, and my delight may be crowned.

And when I have accomplished the matter and my Honour is made clean, I shall return thanks unto God, the Holder of the Scales of the Law, and I shall sleep. From the night, through the day, and into the night again I shall sleep; and no dream shall trouble me.

And now, O my brother, the tale is all told. *Ahi! Ahi! Alghias! Ahi!*

The Judgment of Dungara

See the pale martyr with his shirt on fire.

– *Printer's Error.*

They tell the tale even now among the groves of the Berbulda Hills,[1] and for corroboration point to the roofless and windowless Mission-house. The great God Dungara, the God of Things as They Are, Most Terrible, One-eyed, Bearing the Red Elephant Tusk, did it all; and he who refuses to believe in Dungara will assuredly be smitten by the Madness of Yat – the madness that fell upon the sons and the daughters of the Buria Kol[2] when they turned aside from Dungara and put on clothes. So says Athon Dazé, who is High Priest of the shrine and Warden of the Red Elephant Tusk. But if you ask the Assistant Collector and Agent in Charge of the Buria Kol, he will laugh – not because he bears any malice against missions, but because he himself saw the vengeance of Dungara executed upon the spiritual children of the Reverend Justus Krenk, Pastor of the Tübingen[3] Mission, and upon Lotte, his virtuous wife.

Yet if ever a man merited good treatment of the Gods it was the Reverend Justus, one time of Heidelberg,[4] who, on the faith of a call, went into the wilderness and took the blonde, blue-eyed Lotte with him. 'We will these Heathen now by idolatrous practices so darkened better make,' said Justus in the early days of his career. 'Yes,' he added with conviction, 'they shall good be and shall with their hands to work learn. For all good Christians must work.' And upon a stipend more modest even than that of an English lay-reader, Justus Krenk kept house beyond Kamala and the gorge of Malair, beyond the Berbulda River close to the foot of the blue hill of Panth on whose summit stands the Temple of Dungara – in the heart of the country of the Buria Kol – the naked, good-tempered, timid, shameless, lazy Buria Kol.

Do you know what life at a Mission outpost means? Try to imagine a loneliness exceeding that of the smallest station to which

Government has ever sent you – isolation that weighs upon the waking eyelids and drives you by force headlong into the labours of the day. There is no post, there is no one of your own colour to speak to, there are no roads: there is, indeed, food to keep you alive, but it is not pleasant to eat; and whatever of good or beauty or interest there is in your life, must come from yourself and the grace that may be planted in you.

In the morning, with a patter of soft feet, the converts, the doubtful, and the open scoffers troop up to the veranda. You must be infinitely kind and patient, and, above all, clear-sighted, for you deal with the simplicity of childhood, the experience of man, and the subtlety of the savage. Your congregation have a hundred material wants to be considered; and it is for you, as you believe in your personal responsibility to your Maker, to pick out of the clamouring crowd any grain of spirituality that may lie therein. If to the cure of souls you add that of bodies, your task will be all the more difficult, for the sick and the maimed will profess any and every creed for the sake of healing, and will laugh at you because you are simple enough to believe them.

As the day wears and the impetus of the morning dies away, there will come upon you an overwhelming sense of the uselessness of your toil. This must be striven against, and the only spur in your side will be the belief that you are playing against the Devil for the living soul. It is a great, a joyous belief. But he who can hold it unwavering for four-and-twenty consecutive hours must be blessed with an abundantly strong physique and equable nerve.

Ask the grey heads of the Bannockburn[5] Medical Crusade what manner of life their preachers lead; speak to the Racine[6] Gospel Agency, those lean Americans whose boast is that they go where no Englishman dare follow; get a Pastor of the Tübingen Mission to talk of his experiences – if you can. You will be referred to the printed reports, but these contain no mention of the men who have lost youth and health, all that a man may lose except faith, in the wilds; of English maidens who have gone forth and died in the fever-stricken jungle of the Panth Hills, knowing from the first that death was almost a certainty. Few Pastors will tell you of these things any more than they will speak of that young David of St Bees,[7] who, set apart for the Lord's work, broke down in the utter desolation, and returned half distraught to the Head Mission, crying, 'There is no God, but I have walked with the Devil!'

The reports are silent here, because heroism, failure, doubt, despair, and self-abnegation on the part of a mere cultured white man are things of no weight as compared to the saving of one half-human soul from a fantastic faith in wood-spirits, goblins of the rock, and river-fiends.

And Gallio, the Assistant Collector of the countryside, 'cared for none of these things'. He had been long in the District, and the Buria Kol loved him and brought him offerings of speared fish, orchids from the dim moist heart of the forests, and as much game as he could eat. In return, he gave them quinine, and with Athon Dazé, the High Priest, controlled their simple policies.

'When you have been some years in the country,' said Gallio at the Krenks' table, 'you get to find one creed as good as another. I'll give you all the assistance in my power, of course, but don't hurt my Buria Kol. They are a good people and they trust me.'

'I will them the Word of the Lord teach,' said Justus, his round face beaming with enthusiasm, 'and I will assuredly to their prejudices no wrong hastily without thinking make. But, O my friend, this in the mind impartiality-of-creed-judgment-belooking is very bad.'

'Heigh-ho!' said Gallio. 'I have their bodies and the District to see to, but you can try what you can do for their souls. Only don't behave as your predecessor did, or I'm afraid that I can't guarantee your life.'

'And that?' said Lotte sturdily, handing him a cup of tea.

'He went up to the Temple of Dungara – to be sure, he was new to the country – and began hammering old Dungara over the head with an umbrella; so the Buria Kol turned out and hammered *him* rather savagely. I was in the District, and he sent a runner to me with a note saying: "Persecuted for the Lord's sake. Send wing of regiment." The nearest troops were about two hundred miles off, but I guessed what he had been doing. I rode to Panth and talked to old Athon Dazé like a father, telling him that a man of his wisdom ought to have known that the Sahib had sunstroke and was mad. You never saw a people more sorry in your life. Athon Dazé apologized, sent wood and milk and fowls and all sorts of things; and

I gave five rupees to the shrine and told Macnamara that he had been injudicious. He said that I had bowed down in the House of Rimmon;[8] but if he had only just gone over the brow of the hill and insulted Palin Deo, the idol of the Suria Kol, he would have been impaled on a charred bamboo long before I could have done anything, and then I should have had to hang some of the poor brutes. Be gentle with them, Padre – but I don't think you'll do much.'

'Not I,' said Justus, 'but my Master. We will with the little children begin. Many of them will be sick – that is so. After the children the mothers; and then the men. But I would greatly prefer that you in internal sympathies with us were.'

Gallio departed to risk his life in mending the rotten bamboo bridges of his people, in killing a too persistent tiger here or there, in sleeping out in the reeking jungle, or in tracking the Suria Kol raiders who had taken a few heads from their brethren of the Buria clan. He was a knock-kneed, shambling young man, naturally devoid of creed or reverence, with a longing for absolute power which his undesirable District gratified.

'No one wants my post,' he used to say grimly, 'and my Collector only pokes his nose in when he's quite certain that there is no fever. I'm monarch of all I survey,[9] and Athon Dazé is my viceroy.'

Because Gallio prided himself on his supreme disregard of human life – though he never extended the theory beyond his own – he naturally rode forty miles to the Mission with a tiny brown girl-baby on his saddle-bow.

'Here is something for you, Padre,' said he. 'The Kols leave their surplus children to die. Don't see why they shouldn't, but you may rear this one. I picked it up beyond the Berbulda forks. I've a notion that the mother has been following me through the woods ever since.'

'It is the first of the fold,' said Justus, and Lotte caught up the screaming morsel to her bosom and hushed it craftily; while, as a wolf hangs in the field, Matui who had borne it, and in accordance with the law of her tribe had exposed it to die, panted weary and footsore in the bamboo-brake, watching the house with hungry mother-eyes. What would the omnipotent Assistant Collector do? Would the little man in the black coat eat her daughter alive, as Athon Dazé said was the custom of all men in black coats?

Matui waited among the bamboos through the long night; and, in the morning, there came forth a fair white woman, the like of whom Matui had never seen, and in her arms was Matui's daughter clad in spotless raiment. Lotte knew little of the tongue of the Buria Kol, but when mother calls to mother, speech is easy to follow. By the hands stretched timidly to the hem of her gown, by the passionate gutturals and the longing eyes, Lotte understood with whom she had to deal. So Matui took her child again – would be a servant, even a slave, to this wonderful white woman, for her own tribe would recognize her no more. And Lotte wept with her exhaustively, after the German fashion, which includes much blowing of the nose.

'First the Child, then the Mother, and last the Man, and to the Glory of God all,' said Justus the Hopeful. And the man came, with a bow and arrows, very angry indeed, for there was no one to cook for him.

But the tale of the Mission is a long one, and I have no space to show how Justus, forgetful of his injudicious predecessor, grievously smote Moto, the husband of Matui, for his brutality; how Moto was startled, but being released from the fear of instant death, took heart and became the faithful ally and first convert of Justus; how the little gathering grew, to the huge disgust of Athon Dazé; how the Priest of the God of Things as They Are argued subtilely with the Priest of the God of Things as They Should Be, and was worsted; how the dues of the Temple of Dungara fell away in fowls and fish and honeycomb; how Lotte lightened the Curse of Eve[10] among the women, and how Justus did his best to introduce the Curse of Adam;[11] how the Buria Kol rebelled at this, saying that their God was an idle God, and how Justus partially overcame their scruples against work, and taught them that the black earth was rich in other produce than pig-nuts only.

All these things belong to the history of many months, and throughout those months the white-haired Athon Dazé meditated revenge for the tribal neglect of Dungara. With savage cunning he feigned friendship towards Justus, even hinting at his own conversion; but to the congregation of Dungara he said darkly: 'They of the Padre's flock have put on clothes and worship a busy God. Therefore Dungara will afflict them grievously till they throw themselves, howling, into the waters of the Berbulda.' At night the Red Elephant Tusk boomed and groaned among the hills, and the faithful waked and said: 'The God of Things as They Are matures revenge against the backsliders. Be merciful, Dungara, to us Thy children, and give us all their crops!'

Late in the cold weather the Collector and his wife came into the Buria Kol country. 'Go and look at Krenk's Mission,' said Gallio. 'He is doing good work in his own way, and I think he'd be pleased if you opened the bamboo chapel that he has managed to run up. At any rate you'll see a civilized Buria Kol.'

Great was the stir in the Mission. 'Now he and the gracious lady will that we have done good work with their own eyes see, and – yes – we will him our converts in all their by their own hands constructed new clothes exhibit. It will a great day be – for the Lord always,' said Justus; and Lotte said 'Amen.'

Justus had, in his quiet way, felt jealous of the Basel[12] Weaving Mission, his own converts being unhandy; but Athon Dazé had latterly induced some of them to hackle[13] the glossy silky fibres of a plant that grew plenteously on the Panth Hills. It yielded a cloth white and smooth almost as the *tappa* of the South Seas,[14] and that day the converts were to wear for the first time clothes made therefrom. Justus was proud of his work.

'They shall in white clothes clothed to meet the Collector and his well-born lady come down, singing "*Now thank we all our God*".[15] Then he will the Chapel open, and – yes – even Gallio to believe will begin. Stand so, my children, two by two, and – Lotte, why do they thus themselves bescratch? It is not seemly to wriggle, Nala, my child. The Collector will be here and be pained.'

The Collector, his wife, and Gallio climbed the hill to the Mission-station. The converts were drawn up in two lines, a shining band nearly forty strong. 'Hah!' said the Collector, whose acquisitive bent of mind led him to believe that he had fostered the institution from the first. 'Advancing, I see, by leaps and bounds.'

Never was truer word spoken! The Mission was advancing exactly as he had said – at first by little hops and shuffles of shamefaced uneasiness, but soon by the leaps of fly-stung horses and the bounds of maddened kangaroos. From the hill of Panth the Red Elephant Tusk delivered a dry and anguished blare. The ranks of the converts wavered, broke, and scattered with yells and shrieks of pain, while Justus and Lotte stood horror-stricken.

'It is the Judgment of Dungara!' shouted a voice. 'I burn! I burn! To the river or we die!'

The mob wheeled and headed for the rocks that overhung the Berbulda, writhing, stamping, twisting, and shedding its garments as it ran, pursued by the thunder of the trumpet of Dungara. Justus and Lotte fled to the Collector almost in tears.

'I cannot understand! Yesterday,' panted Justus, 'they had the Ten Commandments. – What is this? Praise the Lord, all good spirits by land and by sea! Nala! Oh, shame!'

With a bound and a scream there alighted on the rocks above their heads, Nala, once the pride of the Mission, a maiden of fourteen summers, good, docile, and virtuous – now naked as the dawn and spitting like a wild-cat.

'Was it for this?' she raved, hurling her petticoat at Justus; 'was it for this I left my people and Dungara – for the fires of your Bad Place? Blind ape, little earth-worm, dried fish that you are, you said that I should never burn! O Dungara, I burn now! I burn now! Have mercy, God of Things as They Are!'

She turned and flung herself into the Berbulda, and the trumpet of Dungara bellowed jubilantly. The last of the converts of the Tübingen Mission had put a quarter of a mile of rapid river between herself and her teachers.

'Yesterday,' gulped Justus, 'she taught in the school A, B, C, D. – Oh! It is the work of Satan!'

But Gallio was curiously regarding the maiden's petticoat where it had fallen at his feet. He felt its texture, drew back his shirt-sleeve beyond the deep tan of his wrist and pressed a fold of the cloth against the flesh. A blotch of angry red rose on the white skin.

'Ah!' said Gallio calmly, 'I thought so.'

'What is it?' said Justus.

'I should call it the Shirt of Nessus,[16] but – where did you get the fibre of this cloth from?'

'Athon Dazé,' said Justus. 'He showed the boys how it should manufactured be.'

'The old fox! Do you know that he has given you the Nilgiri Nettle[17] – scorpion – *Girardenia heterophylla*[18] – to work up. No wonder they squirmed! Why, it stings even when they make bridge-ropes of it unless it's soaked for six weeks. The cunning brute! It would take about half an hour to burn through their thick hides, and then – !'

Gallio burst into laughter, but Lotte was weeping in the arms of the Collector's wife, and Justus had covered his face with his hands.

'*Girardenia heterophylla!*' repeated Gallio. 'Krenk, why *didn't* you tell me? I could have saved you this. Woven fire! Anybody but a naked Kol would have known it, and, if I'm a judge of their ways, you'll never get them back.'

He looked across the river to where the converts were still wallowing and wailing in the shallows, and the laughter died out of his eyes, for he saw that the Tübingen Mission to the Buria Kol was dead.

Never again, though they hung mournfully round the deserted school for three months, could Lotte or Justus coax back even the most promising of their flock. No! The end of conversion was the fire of the Bad Place – fire that ran through the limbs and gnawed into the bones. Who dare a second time tempt the anger of Dungara? Let the little man and his wife go elsewhere. The Buria Kol would have none of them. An unofficial message to Athon Dazé that if a hair of their heads were touched, Athon Dazé and the priests of Dungara would be hanged by Gallio at the temple shrine, protected Justus and Lotte from the stumpy poisoned arrows of the Buria Kol, but neither fish nor fowl, honeycomb, salt, nor young pig were brought to their doors any more. And, alas! man cannot live by grace alone[19] if meat be wanting.

'Let us go, mine wife,' said Justus; 'there is no good here, and the Lord has willed that some other man shall the work take – in good time – in His own good time. We will away go, and I will – yes – some botany bestudy.'

If any one is anxious to convert the Buria Kol afresh, there lies at least the core of a Mission-house under the hill of Panth. But the chapel and school have long since fallen back into jungle.

At Howli Thana

His own shoe, his own head. – *Native Proverb*.

As a messenger, if the heart of the Presence[1] be moved to so great favour. And on six rupees. Yes, Sahib, for I have three little, little children whose stomachs are always empty, and corn is now but forty pounds to the rupee. I will make so clever a messenger that you shall all day long be pleased with me, and, at the end of the year, shall bestow a turban. I know all the roads of the station and many other things. Aha, Sahib! I am clever. Give me service. I was aforetime in the Police. A bad character? Now without doubt an enemy has told this tale. Never was I a scamp. I am a man of clean heart, and all my words are true. They knew this when I was in the Police. They said: 'Afzal Khan is a true speaker in whose words men may trust.' I am a Delhi Pathan, Sahib. All Delhi Pathans are good men. You have seen Delhi? Yes, it is true that there be many scamps among the Delhi Pathans. How wise is the Sahib! Nothing is hid from his eyes, and he will make me his messenger, and I will take all his notes secretly and without ostentation. Nay, Sahib, God is my witness that I meant no evil. I have long desired to serve under a true Sahib – a virtuous Sahib. Many young Sahibs are as devils unchained. With these Sahibs I would take no service – not though all the stomachs of my little children were crying for bread.

Why am I not still in the Police? I will speak true talk. An evil came to the Thana – to Ram Baksh, the Havildar,[2] and Maula Baksh, and Juggut Ram, and Bhim Singh, and Suruj Bul. Ram Baksh is in the jail for a space, and so also is Maula Baksh.

It was at the Thana of Howli, on the road that leads to Gokral-Seetarun wherein are many dacoits.[3] We were all brave men – Rustums.[4] Wherefore we were sent to that Thana, which was eight miles from the next Thana. All day and all night we watched for dacoits. Why does the Sahib laugh? Nay, I will make a confession. The dacoits were too clever, and, seeing this, we made no further trouble. It was in the hot weather. What can a man do in the hot days? Is the Sahib who is so strong – is *he*, even, vigorous in that hour? We made an arrangement with the dacoits for the sake of peace. That was the work of the Havildar, who was fat. Ho! ho! Sahib, he is now getting thin in the jail among the carpets. The Havildar said: 'Give us no trouble, and we will give you no trouble. At the end of the reaping send us a man to lead before the judge, a man of infirm mind against whom the trumped-up case will break down. Thus we shall save our honour.' To this talk the dacoits agreed, and we had no trouble at the Thana, and could eat melons in peace, sitting upon our charpoys all day long. Sweet as sugar-cane are the melons of Howli!

Now there was an Assistant Commissioner – a Stunt Sahib,[5] in that district, called Yunkum Sahib. Aha! He was hard – hard even as is the Sahib who, without doubt, will give me the shadow of his protection. Many eyes had Yunkum Sahib, and moved quickly through his District. Men called him The Tiger of Gokral-Seetarun,[6] because he would arrive unannounced and make his kill, and, before sunset, would be giving trouble to the Tehsildars[7] thirty miles away. No one knew the comings or the goings of Yunkum Sahib. He had no camp, and when his horse was weary he rode upon a devil-carriage. I do not know its name, but the Sahib sat in the midst of three silver wheels that made no creaking, and drave them with his legs, prancing like a bean-fed horse – thus. A shadow of a hawk upon the fields was not more without noise than the devil-carriage of Yunkum Sahib. It was here: it was there: it was gone:[8] and the rapport[9] was made, and there was trouble. Ask the Tehsildar of Rohestri how the hen-stealings came to be known, Sahib.

It fell upon a night that we of the Thana slept according to custom upon our charpoys, having eaten the evening meal and drunk tobacco. When we awoke in the morning, behold, of our six rifles not one remained! Also, the big Police-book that was in the Havildar's charge was gone. Seeing these things, we were very much afraid, thinking on our parts that the dacoits, regardless of honour, had come by night, and put us to shame. Then said Ram Baksh, the Havildar: 'Be silent! The business is an evil business, but it may yet go well. Let us make the case complete. Bring a kid and my tulwar.[10] See you not *now*, O fools? A kick for a horse, but for a man a word is enough.'

We of the Thana, perceiving quickly what was in the mind of the Havildar, and greatly fearing that the service would be lost, made haste to take the kid into the inner room, and attended to the words of the Havildar. 'Twenty dacoits came,' said the Havildar, and we, taking his words, repeated after him according to custom. 'There was a great fight,' said the Havildar, 'and of us no man escaped unhurt. The bars of the window were broken. Suruj Bul, see thou to that; and, O men, put speed into your work, for a runner must go with the news to The Tiger of Gokral-Seetarun.' Thereon, Suruj Bul, leaning with his shoulder, brake in the bars of the window, and I, beating her with a whip, made the Havildar's mare skip among the melon-beds till they were much trodden with hoof-prints.

These things being made, I returned to the Thana, and the goat was slain, and certain portions of the walls were blackened with fire, and each man dipped his clothes a little into the blood of the goat. Know, O Sahib, that a wound made by man upon his own body can, by those skilled, be easily discerned from a wound wrought by another man. Therefore, the Havildar, taking his tulwar, smote one of us lightly on the forearm in the fat, and another on the leg, and a third on the back of the hand. Thus dealt he with all of us till the blood came; and Suruj Bul, more eager than the others, took out much hair. O Sahib, never was so perfect an arrangement. Yea, even I would have sworn that the Thana had been treated as we said. There was smoke and breaking and blood and trampled earth.

'Ride now, Maula Baksh,' said the Havildar, 'to the house of the Stunt Sahib, and carry the news of the dacoity. Do you also, O Afzal Khan, run there, and take heed that you are mired with sweat and dust on your incoming. The blood will be dry on the clothes. I will stay and send a straight rapport to the Dipty Sahib,[11] and we will catch certain that ye know of, villagers, so that all may be ready against the Dipty Sahib's arrival.'

Thus Maula Baksh rode, and I ran hanging on the stirrup, and together we came in an evil plight before The Tiger of Gokral-Seetarun in the Rohestri tehsil.[12] Our tale was long and correct, Sahib, for we gave even the names of the dacoits and the issue of the fight, and besought him to come. But The Tiger made no sign, and only smiled after the manner of Sahibs when they have a wickedness in their hearts. 'Swear ye to the rapport?' said he, and we said: 'Thy servants swear. The blood of the fight is but newly dry upon us. Judge thou if it be the blood of the servants of the Presence, or not.' And he said: 'I see. Ye have done well.' But he did not call for his horse or his devil-carriage, and scour the land as was his custom. He said: 'Rest now and eat bread, for ye be wearied men. I will wait the coming of the Dipty Sahib.'

Now it is the order that the Havildar of the Thana should send a straight rapport of all dacoities to the Dipty Sahib. At noon came he, a fat man and an old, and overbearing withal, but we of the Thana had no fear of his anger, dreading more the silences of The Tiger of Gokral-Seetarun. With him came Ram Baksh, the Havildar, and the others, guarding ten men of the village of Howli – all men evil affected towards the Police of the Sirkar.[13] As prisoners they came, the irons upon their hands, crying for mercy – Imam Baksh, the farmer, who had denied his wife to the Havildar, and others, ill-conditioned rascals against whom we of the Thana bore spite. It was well done, and the Havildar was proud. But the Dipty Sahib was angry with the Stunt Sahib for lack of zeal, and said 'Dam-Dam' after the custom of the English people, and extolled the Havildar. Yunkum Sahib lay still in his long chair. 'Have the men sworn?' said Yunkum Sahib. 'Ay, and captured ten evildoers,' said the Dipty Sahib. 'There be more abroad in *your* charge. Take horse – ride, and go in the name of the Sirkar!' 'Truly there be more evildoers abroad,' said Yunkum Sahib, 'but there is no need of a horse. Come all men with me.'

I saw the mark of a string on the temples of Imam Baksh. Does the Presence know the torture of the Cold Draw?[14] I saw also the face of The Tiger of Gokral-Seetarun, the evil smile was upon it, and I stood back ready for what might befall. Well it was, Sahib, that I did this thing. Yunkum Sahib unlocked the door of his bathroom, and smiled anew. Within lay the six rifles and the big Police-book of the Thana of Howli! He had come by night in the devil-carriage that is noiseless as a ghoul,[15] and, moving among us asleep, had taken away both the guns and the book! Twice had he come to the Thana, taking each time three rifles. The liver of the Havildar was turned to water, and he fell scrabbling in the dirt about the boots of Yunkum Sahib, crying: 'Have mercy!'

And I? Sahib, I am a Delhi Pathan, and a young man with little children. The Havildar's mare was in the compound. I ran to her and rode. The black wrath of the Sirkar was behind me, and I knew not whither to go. Till she dropped and died I rode the red mare; and by the blessing of God, Who is without doubt on the side of all just men, I escaped. But the Havildar and the rest are now in jail.

I am a scamp? It is as the Presence pleases. God will make the Presence a Lord, and give him a rich Memsahib as fair as a Peri[16] to wife, and many strong sons, if he makes me his orderly. The Mercy of Heaven be upon the Sahib! Yes, I will only go to the Bazar and bring my children to these so-palace-like quarters, and then – the Presence is my Father and my Mother, and I, Afzal Khan, am his slave.

Ohé, *Sirdar-ji*![17] I also am of the household of the Sahib.

Gemini

> Great is the justice of the White Man – greater the power of a lie. – *Native Proverb.*

This is your English Justice, Protector of the Poor. Look at my back and loins which are beaten with sticks – heavy sticks! I am a poor man, and there is no justice in Courts.

There were two of us, and we were born of one birth, but I swear to you that I was born the first, and Ram Dass is the younger by three full breaths. The astrologer said so, and it is written in my horoscope – the horoscope of Durga Dass.[1]

But we were alike – I and my brother, who is a beast without honour – so alike that none knew, together or apart, which was Durga Dass. I am a Mahajun of Pali in Marwar,[2] and an honest man. This is true talk. When we were men, we left our father's house in Pali, and went to the Punjab, where all the people are mud-heads and sons of asses. We took shop together in Isser Jang – I and my brother – near the big well where the Governor's camp draws water. But Ram Dass, who is without truth, made quarrel with me, and we were divided. He took his books, and his pots, and his Mark,[3] and became a *bunnia* – a money-lender – in the long street of Isser Jang, near the gateway of the road that goes to Montgomery.[4] It was not my fault that we pulled each other's turban. I am a Mahajun of Pali, and I *always* speak true talk. Ram Dass was the thief and the liar.[5]

Now no man, not even the little children, could at one glance see which was Ram Dass and which was Durga Dass. But all the people of Isser Jang – may they die without sons! – said that we were thieves. They used much bad talk, but I took money on their bedsteads and their cooking-pots, and the standing crop and the calf unborn, from the well in the big square to the gate of the Montgomery road. They were fools, these people – unfit to cut the toe-nails of a Marwari from Pali. I lent money to them all. A little, very little only – here a pice and there a pice.[6] God is my witness that I am a poor man! The money is all with Ram Dass – may his sons turn Christian, and his daughter be a burning fire and a shame in the house from generation to generation! May she die unwed, and be the mother of a multitude of bastards! Let the light go out in the house of Ram Dass, my brother. This I pray daily twice – with offerings and charms.

Thus the trouble began. We divided the town of Isser Jang between us – I and my brother. There was a landholder beyond the gates, living but one short mile out, on the road that leads to Montgomery, and his name was Mohammed Shah, son of a Nawab.[7] He was a great devil and drank wine.[8] So long as there were women in his house, and wine and money for the marriage-feasts, he was merry and wiped his mouth. Ram Dass lent him the money, a lakh[9] or half a lakh – how do I know? – and so long as the money was lent, the landholder cared not what he signed.

The people of Isser Jang were my portion, and the landholder and the out-town[10] were the portion of Ram Dass; for so we had arranged. I was the poor man, for the people of Isser Jang were without wealth. I did what I could, but Ram Dass had only to wait without the door of the landholder's garden-court, and to lend him the money, taking the bonds from the hand of the steward.

In the autumn of the year after the lending, Ram Dass said to the landholder: 'Pay me my money,' but the landholder gave him abuse. But Ram Dass went into the Courts with the papers and the bonds – all correct – and took out decrees against the landholder; and the name of the Government was across the stamps of the decrees. Ram Dass took field by field, and mango-tree by mango-tree, and well by well; putting in his own men – debtors of the out-town of Isser Jang – to cultivate the crops. So he crept up across the land, for he had the papers, and the name of the Government was across the stamps, till his men held the crops for him on all sides of the big white house of the landholder. It was well done; but when the landholder saw these things he was very angry and cursed Ram Dass after the manner of the Mohammedans.

And thus the landholder was angry, but Ram Dass laughed and claimed more fields, as was written upon the bonds. This was in the month of Phagun.[11] I took my horse and went out to speak to the man who makes lac-bangles[12] upon the road that leads to Montgomery, because he owed me a debt. There was in front of me, upon his horse, my brother Ram Dass. And when he saw me he turned aside into the high crops, because there was hatred between us. And I went forward till I came to the orange-bushes by the landholder's house. The bats were flying, and the evening smoke was low down upon the land. Here met me four men – swashbucklers and Mohammedans – with their faces bound up, laying hold of my horse's bridle and crying out: 'This is Ram Dass! Beat!' Me they beat with their staves – heavy staves bound about with wire at the end, such weapons as those swine of Punjabis use – till, having cried for mercy, I fell down senseless. But these shameless ones still beat me, saying: 'O Ram Dass, this is your interest – well-weighed and counted into your hand, Ram Dass.' I cried aloud that I was not Ram Dass, but Durga Dass, his brother, yet they only beat me the more, and when I could make no more outcry they left me. But I saw their faces. There was Elahi Baksh who runs by the side of the landholder's white horse, and Nur Ali the keeper of the door, and Wajib Ali the very strong cook, and Abdul Latif the messenger – all of the household of the landholder. These things I can swear on the Cow's Tail[13] if need be, but – *Ahi! Ahi!* – they have been already sworn, and I am a poor man whose honour is lost.

When these four had gone away laughing, my brother Ram Dass came out of the crops and mourned over me as one dead. But I opened my eyes, and prayed him to get me water. When I had drunk, he carried me on his back, and by byways brought me into the town of Isser Jang. My heart was turned to Ram Dass, my brother, in that hour because of his kindness, and I lost my enmity.

But a snake is a snake till it is dead; and a liar is a liar till the Judgment of the Gods takes hold of his heel. I was wrong in that I trusted my brother – the son of my mother.

When we had come to his house and I was a little restored, I told him my tale, and he said: 'Without doubt, it is me whom they would have beaten. But the Law Courts are open, and there is the Justice of the Sirkar[14] above all; and to the Law Courts do thou go when this sickness is overpast.'

Now when we two had left Pali in the old years, there fell a famine that ran from Jeysulmir to Gurgaon and touched Gogunda[15] in the south. At that time the sister of my father came away and lived with us in Isser Jang; for a man must above all see that his folk do not die of want. When the quarrel between us twain came about, the sister of my father – a lean she-dog without teeth – said that Ram Dass had the right, and went with him. Into her hands – because she knew medicines and many cures – Ram Dass, my brother, put me faint with the beating, and much bruised even to the pouring of blood from the mouth. When I had two days' sickness the fever came upon me; and I set aside the fever to the account written in my mind against the landholder.

The Punjabis of Isser Jang are all the sons of Belial[16] and a she-ass, but they are very good witnesses, bearing testimony unshakenly whatever the pleaders may say. I would purchase witnesses by the score, and each man should give evidence, not only against Nur Ali, Wajib Ali, Abdul Latif, and Elahi Baksh, but against the landholder, saying that he upon his white horse had called his men to beat me; and, further, that they had robbed me of two hundred rupees. For the latter testimony, I would remit a little of the debt of the man who sold the lac-bangles, and he should say that he had put the money into my hands, and had seen the robbery from afar, but, being afraid, had run away. This plan I told to my brother Ram Dass; and he said that the arrangement was good, and bade me take comfort and make swift work to be abroad again. My heart was opened to my brother in my sickness, and I told him the names of those whom I would call as witnesses – all men in my debt, but of that the Magistrate Sahib could have no knowledge, nor the landholder. The fever stayed with me, and after the fever I was taken with colic and gripings very terrible. In that day I thought that my end was at hand, but I know now that she who gave me the medicines, the sister of my father – a widow with a widow's heart – had brought about my second sickness. Ram Dass, my brother, said that my house was shut and locked, and brought me the big door-key and my books, together with all the moneys that were in my house – even the money that was buried under the floor; for I was in great fear lest thieves should break in and dig. I speak true talk; there was but very little money in my house. Perhaps ten rupees – perhaps twenty. How can I tell? God is my witness that I am a poor man.

One night, when I had told Ram Dass all that was in my heart of the lawsuit that I would bring against the landholder, and Ram Dass had said that he had made the arrangements with the witnesses, giving me their names written, I was taken with a new great sickness, and they put me on the bed. When I was a little recovered – I cannot tell how many days afterwards – I made inquiry for Ram Dass, and the sister of my father said that he had gone to Montgomery upon a lawsuit. I took medicine and slept very heavily without waking. When my eyes were opened there was a great stillness in the house of Ram Dass, and none answered when I called – not even the sister of my father. This filled me with fear, for I knew not what had happened.

Taking a stick in my hand, I went out slowly, till I came to the great square by the well, and my heart was hot in me against the landholder because of the pain of every step I took.

I called for Jowar Singh, the carpenter, whose name was first upon the list of those who should bear evidence against the landholder, saying: 'Are all things ready, and do you know what should be said?'

Jowar Singh answered: 'What is this, and whence do you come, Durga Dass?'

I said: 'From my bed, where I have so long lain sick because of the landholder. Where is Ram Dass, my brother, who was to have made the arrangement for the witnesses? Surely you and yours know these things!'

Then Jowar Singh said: 'What has this to do with us, O Liar? I have borne witness and I have been paid, and the landholder has, by the order of the Court, paid both the five hundred rupees that he robbed from Ram Dass and yet other five hundred because of the great injury he did to your brother.'

The well and the jujube-tree[17] above it and the square of Isser Jang became dark in my eyes, but I leaned on my stick and said: 'Nay! This is child's talk and senseless. It was I who suffered at the hands of the landholder, and I am come to make ready the case. Where is my brother Ram Dass?'

But Jowar Singh shook his head, and a woman cried: 'What lie is here? What quarrel had the landholder with you, *bunnia*? It is only a shameless one and one without faith who profits by his brother's smarts. Have these *bunnias* no bowels?'

I cried again, saying: 'By the Cow – by the Oath of the Cow, by the Temple of the Blue-throated Mahadeo,[18] I and I only was beaten – beaten to the death! Let your talk be straight, O people of Isser Jang, and I will pay for the witnesses.' And I tottered where I stood, for the sickness and the pain of the beating were heavy upon me.

Then Ram Narain, who has his carpet spread under the jujube-tree by the well, and writes all letters for the men of the town, came up and said: 'To-day is the one-and-fortieth day since the beating, and since these six days the case has been judged in the Court, and the Assistant Commissioner Sahib has given it for your brother Ram Dass, allowing the robbery, to which, too, I bore witness, and all things else as the witnesses said. There were many witnesses, and twice Ram Dass became senseless in the Court because of his wounds, and the Stunt Sahib – the *baba*[19] Stunt Sahib – gave him a chair before all the pleaders. Why do you howl, Durga Dass? These things fell as I have said. Was it not so?'

And Jowar Singh said: 'That is truth. I was there, and there was a red cushion in the chair.'

And Ram Narain said: 'Great shame has come upon the landholder because of this judgment, and, fearing his anger, Ram Dass and all his house have gone back to Pali. Ram Dass told us that you also had gone first, the enmity being healed between you, to open a shop in Pali. Indeed, it were well for you that you go even now, for the landholder has sworn that if he catch any one of your house, he will hang him by the heels from the well-beam, and, swinging him to and fro, will beat him with staves till the blood runs from his ears. What I have said in respect to the case is true, as these men here can testify – even to the five hundred rupees.'

I said: 'Was it five hundred?' And Kirpa Ram, the Jat,[20] said: 'Five hundred; for I bore witness also.'

And I groaned, for it had been in my heart to have said two hundred only.

Then a new fear came upon me and my bowels turned to water, and, running swiftly to the house of Ram Dass, I sought for my books and my money in the great wooden chest under my bedstead. There remained nothing – not even a cowrie's value.[21] All had been taken by the devil who said he was my brother. I went to my own house also and opened the boards of the shutters; but there also was nothing save the rats among the grain-baskets. In that hour my senses left me, and, tearing my clothes, I ran to the well-place, crying out for the Justice of the English on my brother Ram Dass, and, in my madness, telling all that the books were lost. When men saw that I would have jumped down the well they believed the truth of my talk, more especially because upon my back and bosom were still the marks of the staves of the landholder.

Jowar Singh the carpenter withstood me, and turning me in his hands – for he is a very strong man – showed the scars upon my body, and bowed down with laughter upon the well-curb. He cried aloud so that all heard him, from the well-square to the Caravanserai[22] of the Pilgrims: 'Oho! The jackals have quarrelled, and the grey one has been caught in the trap. In truth, this man has been grievously beaten, and his brother has taken the money which the Court decreed! Oh, *bunnia*, this shall be told for years against you! The jackals have quarrelled, and, moreover, the books are burned. O people indebted to Durga Dass – and I know that ye be many – the books are burned!'

Then all Isser Jang took up the cry that the books were burned – *Ahi! Ahi!* that in my folly I had let that escape my mouth – and they laughed throughout the city. They gave me the abuse of the Punjabi, which is a terrible abuse and very hot; pelting me also with sticks and cow-dung till I fell down and cried for mercy.

Ram Narain, the letter-writer, bade the people cease, for fear that the news should get into Montgomery, and the Policemen might come down to inquire. He said, using many bad words: 'This much mercy will I do to you, Durga Dass, though there was no mercy in your dealings with my sister's son over the matter of the dun heifer. Has any man a pony on which he sets no store, that this fellow may escape? If the landholder hears that one of the twain (and God knows whether he beat one or both, but this man is certainly beaten) be in the city, there will be a murder done, and then will come the Police, making inquisition into each man's house and eating the sweet-seller's stuff all day long.'

Kirpa Ram, the Jat, said: 'I have a pony very sick. But with beating he can be made to walk for two miles. If he dies, the hide-sellers will have the body.'

Then Chumbo, the hide-seller, said: 'I will pay three annas for the body, and will walk by this man's side till such time as the pony dies. If it be more than two miles, I will pay two annas only.'

Kirpa Ram said: 'Be it so.' Men brought out the pony, and I asked leave to draw a little water from the well, because I was dried up with fear.

Then Ram Narain said: 'Here be four annas. God has brought you very low, Durga Dass, and I would not send you away empty, even though the matter of my sister's son's dun heifer be an open sore between us. It is a long way to your own country. Go, and if it be so willed, live; but, above all, do not take the pony's bridle, for that is mine.'

And I went out of Isser Jang amid the laughing of the huge-thighed Jats, and the hide-seller walked by my side waiting for the pony to fall dead. In one mile it died, and being full of fear of the landholder, I ran till I could run no more, and came to this place.

But I swear by the Cow, I swear by all things whereon Hindus and Mohammedans, and even the Sahibs swear, that I, and not my brother, was beaten by the landholder. But the case is shut, and the doors of the Law Courts are shut, and God knows where the *baba* Stunt Sahib – the mother's milk is not dry upon his hairless lip – is gone. *Ahi! Ahi!* I have no witnesses, and the scars will heal, and I am a poor man. But, on my Father's Soul, on the oath of a Mahajun from Pali, I, and not my brother, I was beaten by the landholder!

What can I do? The Justice of the English is as a great river. Having gone forward, it does not return. Howbeit, do you, Sahib, take a pen and write clearly what I have said, that the Dipty Sahib may see, and reprove the Stunt Sahib, who is a colt yet unlicked by the mare, so young is he. I, and not my brother, was beaten, and he is gone to the west – I do not know where.

But, above all things, write – so that the Sahibs may read, and his disgrace be accomplished – that Ram Dass, my brother, son of Purun Dass, Mahajun of Pali, is a swine and a night-thief, a taker of life, an eater of flesh, a jackal-spawn without beauty, or faith, or cleanliness, or honour!

place, and when, after six years, the Company changed all the allotments to prevent the miners from acquiring proprietary rights, Janki Meah represented, with tears in his eyes, that were his holding shifted he would never be able to find his way to the new one. 'My horse only knows that place,' pleaded Janki Meah, and so he was allowed to keep his land.

On the strength of this concession and his accumulated oil-savings, Janki Meah took a second wife – a girl of the Jolaha main stock of the Meahs, and singularly beautiful. Janki Meah could not see her beauty; wherefore he took her on trust, and forbade her to go down the pit. He had not worked for thirty years in the dark without knowing that the pit was no place for pretty women. He loaded her with ornaments – not brass or pewter, but real silver ones – and she rewarded him by flirting outrageously with Kundoo of Number Seven gallery gang. Kundoo was really the head of the gang, but Janki Meah insisted upon all the work being entered in his own name, and chose the men that he worked with. Custom – stronger even than the Jimahari Company – dictated that Janki, by right of his years, should manage these things, and should, also, work despite his blindness. In Indian mines, where they cut into the solid coal with the pick and clear it out from floor to ceiling, he could come to no great harm. At Home, where they undercut the coal and bring it down in crashing avalanches from the roof, he would never have been allowed to set foot in a pit. He was not a popular man because of his oil-savings; but all the gangs admitted that Janki knew all the *khads*, or workings, that had ever been sunk or worked since the Jimahari Company first started operations on the Tarachunda fields.

Pretty little Unda only knew that her old husband was a fool who could be managed. She took no interest in the colliery except in so far as it swallowed up Kundoo five days out of the seven, and covered him with coal-dust. Kundoo was a great workman, and did his best not to get drunk, because, when he had saved forty rupees, Unda was to steal everything that she could find in Janki's house and run with Kundoo to a land where there were no mines, and every one kept three fat bullocks and a milch-buffalo. While this scheme ripened it was his custom to drop in upon Janki and worry him about the oil-savings. Unda sat in a corner and nodded approval. On the night when Kundoo had quoted that objectionable proverb about weavers, Janki grew angry.

'Listen, you pig,' said he. 'Blind I am, and old I am, but, before ever you were born, I was grey among the coal. Even in the days when the Twenty-Two *khad* was unsunk, and there were not two thousand men here, I was known to have all knowledge of the pits. What *khad* is there that I do not know, from the bottom of the shaft to the end of the last drive? Is it the Baromba *khad*, the oldest, or the Twenty-Two where Tibu's gallery runs up to Number Five?'

'Hear the old fool talk!' said Kundoo, nodding to Unda. 'No gallery of Twenty-Two will cut into Five before the end of the Rains. We have a month's solid coal before us. The Babuji[2] says so.'

'Babuji! Pigji! Dogji! What do these fat slugs from Calcutta know? He draws and draws and draws, and talks and talks and talks, and his maps are all wrong. I, Janki, know that this is so. When a man has been shut up in the dark for thirty years God gives him knowledge. The old gallery that Tibu's gang made is not six feet from Number Five.'

'Without doubt God gives the blind knowledge,' said Kundoo, with a look at Unda. 'Let it be as you say. I, for my part, do not know where lies the gallery of Tibu's gang, but *I* am not a withered monkey who needs oil to grease his joints with.'

Kundoo swung out of the hut laughing, and Unda giggled. Janki turned his sightless eyes towards his wife and swore. 'I have land, and I have sold a great deal of lamp-oil,' mused Janki, 'but I was a fool to marry this child.'

A week later the Rains set in with a vengeance, and the gangs paddled about in coal-slush at the pit-banks. Then the big mine-pumps were made ready, and the Manager of the Colliery ploughed through the wet towards the Tarachunda River swelling between its soppy banks. 'Lord send that this beastly beck doesn't misbehave,' said the Manager piously, and he went to take counsel with his Assistant about the pumps.

But the Tarachunda misbehaved very much indeed. After a fall of three inches of rain in an hour it was obliged to do something. It topped its bank and joined the flood-water that was hemmed between two low hills just where the embankment of the Colliery main line crossed. When a large part of a rain-fed river, and a few acres of flood-water, make a dead set for a nine-foot culvert, the culvert may spout its finest, but the water cannot *all* get out. The Manager pranced upon one leg with excitement, and his language was improper.

He had reason to swear, because he knew that one inch of water on land meant a pressure of one hundred tons to the acre; and here was about five feet of water forming, behind the railway embankment, over the shallower workings of Twenty-Two. You must understand that, in a coal-mine, the coal nearest the surface is worked first from the central shaft. That is to say, the miners may clear out the stuff to within ten, twenty, or thirty feet of the surface, and, when all is worked out, leave only a skin of earth upheld by some few pillars of coal. In a deep mine, where they know that they have any amount of material at hand, men prefer to get all their mineral out at one shaft, rather than make a number of little holes to tap the comparatively unimportant surface-coal.

And the Manager watched the flood.

The culvert spouted a nine-foot gush; but the water still formed, and word was sent to clear the men out of Twenty-Two. The cages came up crammed and crammed again with the men nearest the pit's-eye, as they call the place where you can see daylight from the bottom of the main shaft. All away and away up the long black galleries the flare-lamps were winking and dancing like so many fireflies, and the men and the women waited for the clanking, rattling, thundering cages to come down and fly up again. But the out-workings were very far off, and word could not be passed quickly, though the heads of the gangs and the Assistant shouted and swore and tramped and stumbled. The Manager kept one eye on the great troubled pool behind the embankment, and prayed that the culvert would give way and let the water through in time. With the other eye he watched the cages come up and saw the headman counting the roll of the gangs. With all his heart and soul he swore at the winder who controlled the iron drum that wound up the wire rope on which hung the cages.

In a little time there was a down-draw in the water behind the embankment – a sucking whirlpool, all yellow and yeasty. The water had smashed through the skin of the earth and was pouring into the old shallow workings of Twenty-Two.

Deep down below, a rush of black water caught the last gang

waiting for the cage, and as they clambered in, the whirl was about their waists. The cage reached the pit-bank, and the Manager called the roll. The gangs were all safe except Gang Janki, Gang Mogul, and Gang Rahim, eighteen men, with perhaps ten basket-women who loaded the coal into the little iron carriages that ran on the tramways of the main galleries. These gangs were in the out-workings, three-quarters of a mile away, on the extreme fringe of the mine. Once more the cage went down, but with only two Englishmen in it, and dropped into a swirling, roaring current that had almost touched the roof of some of the lower side-galleries. One of the wooden balks with which they had propped the old workings shot past on the current, just missing the cage.

'If we don't want our ribs knocked out, we'd better go,' said the Manager. 'We can't even save the Company's props.'

The cage drew out of the water with a splash, and a few minutes later it was officially reported that there was at least ten feet of water in the pit's-eye. Now ten feet of water there meant that all other places in the mine were flooded except such galleries as were more than ten feet above the level of the bottom of the shaft. The deep workings would be full, the main galleries would be full, but in the high workings reached by inclines from the main roads there would be a certain amount of air cut off, so to speak, by the water and squeezed up by it. The little science-primers explain how water behaves when you pour it down test-tubes. The flooding of Twenty-Two was an illustration on a large scale.

'By the Holy Grove, what has happened to the air?' It was a Sonthal gangman of Gang Mogul in Number Nine gallery, and he was driving a six-foot way through the coal. Then there was a rush from the other galleries, and Gang Janki and Gang Rahim stumbled up with their basket-women.

'Water has come in the mine,' they said, 'and there is no way of getting out.'

'I went down,' said Janki – 'down the slope of my gallery, and I felt the water.'

'There has been no water in the cutting in our time,' clamoured the women. 'Why cannot we go away?'

'Be silent!' said Janki. 'Long ago, when my father was here, water came to Ten – no, Eleven – cutting, and there was great trouble. Let us get away to where the air is better.'

The three gangs and the basket-women left Number Nine gallery and went farther up Number Sixteen. At one turn of the road they could see the pitchy black water lapping on the coal. It had touched the roof of a gallery that they knew well – a gallery where they used to smoke their pipes and manage their flirtations. Seeing this, they called aloud upon their Gods, and the Mehas,[3] who are thrice bastard Mohammedans, strove to recollect the name of the Prophet. They came to a great open square whence nearly all the coal had been extracted. It was the end of the out-workings, and the end of the mine.

Far away down the gallery a small pumping-engine, used for keeping dry a deep working and fed with steam from above, was throbbing faithfully. They heard it cease.

'They have cut off the steam,' said Kundoo hopefully. 'They have given the order to use all the steam for the pit-bank pumps. They will clear out the water.'

'If the water has reached the smoking-gallery,' said Janki, 'all the Company's pumps can do nothing for three days.'

'It is very hot,' moaned Jasoda, the Meah basket-woman. 'There is a very bad air here because of the lamps.'

'Put them out,' said Janki. 'Why do you want lamps?' The lamps were put out, and the company sat still in the utter dark. Somebody rose quietly and began walking over the coals. It was Janki, who was touching the walls with his hands. 'Where is the ledge?' he murmured to himself.

'Sit, sit!' said Kundoo. 'If we die, we die. The air is very bad.'

But Janki still stumbled and crept and tapped with his pick upon the walls. The women rose to their feet.

'Stay all where you are. Without the lamps you cannot see, and I – I am always seeing,' said Janki. Then he paused, and called out: 'O you who have been in the cutting more than ten years, what is the name of this open place? I am an old man and I have forgotten.'

'Bullia's Room,' answered the Sonthal who had complained of the vileness of the air.

'Again,' said Janki.

'Bullia's Room.'

'Then I have found it,' said Janki. 'The name only had slipped my memory. Tibu's gang's gallery is here.'

'A lie,' said Kundoo. 'There have been no galleries in this place since my day.'

'Three paces was the depth of the ledge,' muttered Janki without heeding – 'and – oh, my poor bones! – I have found it! It is here, up this ledge. Come all you, one by one, to the place of my voice, and I will count you.'

There was a rush in the dark, and Janki felt the first man's face hit his knees as the Sonthal scrambled up the ledge.

'Who?' cried Janki.

'I, Sunua Manji.'

'Sit you down,' said Janki. 'Who next?'

One by one the women and the men crawled up the ledge which ran along one side of 'Bullia's Room'. Degraded Mohammedan, pig-eating Musahr, and wild Sonthal, Janki ran his hand over them all.

'Now follow after,' said he, 'catching hold of my heel, and the women catching the men's clothes.' He did not ask whether the men had brought their picks with them. A miner, black or white, does not drop his pick. One by one, Janki leading, they crept into the old gallery – a six-foot way with a scant four feet from thill[4] to roof.

'The air is better here,' said Jasoda. They could hear her heart beating in thick, sick bumps.

'Slowly, slowly,' said Janki. 'I am an old man, and I forget many things. This is Tibu's gallery, but where are the four bricks where they used to put their hookah fire on when the Sahibs never saw? Slowly, slowly, O you people behind.'

They heard his hands disturbing the small coal on the floor of the gallery and then a dull sound. 'This is one unbaked brick, and this is another and another. Kundoo is a young man – let him come forward. Put a knee upon this brick and strike here. When Tibu's gang were at dinner on the last day before the good coal ended, they heard the men of Five on the other side, and Five worked *their* gallery two Sundays later – or it may have been one. Strike there, Kundoo, but give me room to go back.'

Kundoo, doubting, drove the pick, but the first soft crush of the coal was a call to him. He was fighting for his life and for Unda – pretty little Unda with rings on all her toes – for Unda and the forty rupees. The women sang the Song of the Pick – the terrible, slow, swinging melody with the muttered chorus that repeats the sliding of the loosened coal, and, to each cadence, Kundoo smote in the black dark. When he could do no more, Sunua Manji took the pick, and struck for his life and his wife, and his village beyond the blue hills over the Tarachunda River. An hour the men worked, and then the women cleared away the coal.

'It is farther than I thought,' said Janki. 'The air is very bad; but strike, Kundoo, strike hard.'

For the fifth time Kundoo took up the pick as the Sonthal crawled back. The song had scarcely recommenced when it was broken by a yell from Kundoo that echoed down the gallery: '*Par hua! Par hua!* We are through, we are through!' The imprisoned air in the mine shot through the opening, and the women at the far end of the gallery heard the water rush through the pillars of 'Bullia's Room' and roar against the ledge. Having fulfilled the law under which it worked, it rose no farther. The women screamed and pressed forward. 'The water has come – we shall be killed! Let us go.'

Kundoo crawled through the gap and found himself in a propped gallery by the simple process of hitting his head against a beam.

'Do I know the pits or do I not?' chuckled Janki. 'This is the Number Five; go you out slowly, giving me your names. Ho, Rahim! count your gang! Now let us go forward, each catching hold of the other as before.'

They formed line in the darkness and Janki led them – for a pitman in a strange pit is only one degree less liable to err than an ordinary mortal underground for the first time. At last they saw a flare-lamp, and Gangs Janki, Mogul, and Rahim of Twenty-Two stumbled dazed into the glare of the draught-furnace at the bottom of Five: Janki feeling his way and the rest behind.

'Water has come into Twenty-Two. God knows where are the others. I have brought these men from Tibu's gallery in our cutting, making connection through the north side of the gallery. Take us to the cage,' said Janki Meah.

At the pit-bank of Twenty-Two some thousand people clamoured and wept and shouted. One hundred men – one thousand men – had been drowned in the cutting. They would all go to their homes tomorrow.

Where were their men? Little Unda, her clothes drenched with the rain, stood at the pit-mouth calling down the shaft for Kundoo. They had swung the cages clear of the mouth, and her only answer was the murmur of the flood in the pit's-eye two hundred and sixty feet below.

'Look after that woman! She'll chuck herself down the shaft in a minute,' shouted the Manager.

But he need not have troubled; Unda was afraid of death. She wanted Kundoo. The Assistant was watching the flood and seeing how far he could wade into it. There was a lull in the water, and the whirlpool had slackened. The mine was full, and the people at the pit-bank howled.

'My faith, we shall be lucky if we have five hundred hands on the place to-morrow!' said the Manager. 'There's some chance yet of running a temporary dam across that water. Shove in anything – tubs and bullock-carts if you haven't enough bricks. Make them work *now* if they never worked before. Hi! you gangers! make them work.'

Little by little the crowd was broken into detachments, and pushed towards the water with promises of overtime. The dam-making began, and when it was fairly under way, the Manager thought that the hour had come for the pumps. There was no fresh inrush into the mine. The tall, red, iron-clamped pump-beam rose and fell, and the pumps snored and guttered and shrieked as the first water poured out of the pipe.

'We must run her all to-night,' said the Manager wearily, 'but there's no hope for the poor devils down below. Look here, Gur Sahai, if you are proud of your engines, show me what they can do now.'

Gur Sahai grinned and nodded, with his right hand upon the lever and an oil-can in his left. He could do no more than he was doing, but he could keep that up till the dawn. Were the Company's pumps to be beaten by the vagaries of that troublesome Tarachunda River? Never, never! And the pumps sobbed and panted: 'Never, never!' The Manager sat in the shelter of the pit-bank roofing, trying to dry himself by the pump-boiler fire, and, in the dreary dusk, he saw the crowds on the dam scatter and fly.

'That's the end,' he groaned. ''Twill take us six weeks to persuade 'em that we haven't tried to drown their mates on purpose. Oh for a decent, rational Geordie!'[5]

But the flight had no panic in it. Men had run over from Five with astounding news, and the foremen could not hold their gangs together. Presently, surrounded by a clamorous crew, Gangs Rahim, Mogul, and Janki, and ten basket-women, walked up to report themselves, and pretty little Unda stole away to Janki's hut to prepare his evening meal.

'Alone I found the way,' explained Janki Meah, 'and now will the Company give me pension?'

The simple pit-folk shouted and leaped and went back to the dam, reassured in their old belief that, whatever happened, so great was the power of the Company whose salt they ate, none of them could be killed. But Gur Sahai only bared his white teeth, and kept his hand upon the lever and proved his pumps to the uttermost.

'I say,' said the Assistant to the Manager, a week later, 'do you recollect *Germinal*?'[6]

'Yes. Queer thing. I thought of it in the cage when that balk went by. Why?'

'Oh, this business seems to be *Germinal* upside-down. Janki was in my veranda all this morning, telling me that Kundoo had eloped with his wife – Unda or Anda, I think her name was.'

'Hillo! And those were the cattle you risked your life for to clear out of Twenty-Two!'

'No – I was thinking of the Company's props, not the Company's men.'

'Sounds better to say so *now*; but I don't believe you, old fellow.'

In Flood Time

Tweed said tae Till:
'What gars ye rin sae still?'
Till said tae Tweed:
'Though ye rin wi' speed
An' I rin slaw –
Yet where ye droon ae man
I droon twa.'

There is no getting over the river to-night, Sahib. They say that a bullock-cart has been washed down already, and the *ekka*[1] that went over a half-hour before you came has not yet reached the far side. Is the Sahib in haste? I will drive the ford-elephant[2] in to show him. Ohé, mahout[3] there in the shed! Bring out Ram Pershad, and if he will face the current, good. An elephant never lies, Sahib, and Ram Pershad is separated from his friend Kala Nag.[4] He, too, wishes to cross to the far side. Well done! Well done! my King! Go half-way across, *mahoutji*, and see what the river says. Well done, Ram Pershad! Pearl among elephants, go into the river! Hit him on the head, fool! Was the goad made only to scratch thine own fat back with, bastard? Strike! strike! What are the boulders to thee, Ram Pershad, my Rustum, my mountain of strength? Go in! Go in!

No, Sahib! It is useless. You can hear him trumpet. He is telling Kala Nag that he cannot come over. See! He has swung round and is shaking his head. He is no fool. He knows what the Barhwi means when it is angry. Aha! Indeed, thou art no fool, my child! Salaam, Ram Pershad, Bahadur![5] Take him under the trees, mahout, and see that he gets his spices. Well done, thou chiefest among tuskers! Salaam to the Sirkar and go to sleep.

What is to be done? The Sahib must wait till the river goes down. It will shrink to-morrow morning, if God pleases, or the day after at the latest! Now why does the Sahib get so angry? I am his servant. Before God, *I* did not create this stream! What can I do? My hut and all that is therein is at the service of the Sahib, and it is beginning to rain. Come away, my Lord. How will the river go down for your throwing abuse at it? In the old days the English people were not thus. The fire-carriage[6] has made them soft. In the old days, when they drave behind horses by day or by night, they said naught if a river barred the way, or a carriage sat down in the mud. It was the will of God – not like a fire-carriage which goes and goes and goes, and would go though all the devils in the land hung on to its tail. The fire-carriage hath spoiled the English people. After all, what is a day lost, or, for that matter, what are two days? Is the Sahib going to his own wedding, that he is so mad with haste? Ho! ho! ho! I am an old man and see few Sahibs. Forgive me if I have forgotten the respect that is due to them. The Sahib is not angry?

His own wedding! Ho! ho! ho! The mind of an old man is like the *numah*-tree. Fruit, bud, blossom, and the dead leaves of all the years of the past flourish together. Old and new and that which is gone out of remembrance, all three are there! Sit on the bedstead, Sahib, and drink milk. Or – would the Sahib in truth care to drink my tobacco?[7] It is good. It is the tobacco of Nuklao.[8] My son, who is in service there, sends it to me. Drink, then, Sahib, if you know how to handle the tube. The Sahib takes it like a Mussulman. Wah![9] Wah! Where did he learn that? His own wedding! Ho! ho! ho! The Sahib says that there is no wedding in the matter at all. Now *is* it likely that the Sahib would speak true talk to me who am only a black man? Small wonder, then, that he is in haste. Thirty years have I beaten the gong at this ford, but never have I seen a Sahib in such haste. Thirty years, Sahib! That is a very long time. Thirty years ago this ford was on the track of the *bunjaras*,[10] and I have seen two thousand pack-bullocks cross in one night. Now the rail has come, and the fire-carriage says *buz-buz-buz*, and a hundred lakhs of maunds[11] slide across that big bridge. It is very wonderful; but the ford is lonely now that there are no *bunjaras* to camp under the trees.

Nay, do not trouble to look at the sky without. It will rain till the dawn. Listen! The boulders are talking to-night in the bed of the river. Hear them! They would be husking your bones, Sahib, had you tried to cross. See, I will shut the door and no rain can enter.

Wahi![12] *Ahi! Ugh!* Thirty years on the banks of the ford. An old man am I and – where is the oil for the lamp?

Your pardon, but, because of my years, I sleep no sounder than a dog; and you moved to the door. Look then, Sahib. Look and listen. A full half *koss*[13] from bank to bank is the stream now – you can see it under the stars – and there are ten feet of water therein. It will not shrink because of the anger in your eyes, and it will not be quiet on account of your curses. Which is louder, Sahib – your voice or the voice of the river? Call to it – perhaps it will be ashamed. Lie down and sleep afresh, Sahib. I know the anger of the Barhwi when there has fallen rain in the foot-hills. I swam the flood, once, on a night tenfold worse than this, and by the Favour of God I was released from Death when I had come to the very gates thereof.

May I tell the tale? Very good talk. I will fill the pipe anew.

Thirty years ago it was, when I was a young man and had but newly come to the ford. I was strong then, and the *bunjaras* had no doubt when I said: 'This ford is clear.' I have toiled all night up to my shoulder-blades in running water amid a hundred bullocks mad with fear, and have brought them across losing not a hoof. When all was done I fetched the shivering men, and they gave me for reward the pick of their cattle – the bell-bullock[14] of the drove. So great was the honour in which I was held! But to-day, when the rain falls and the river rises, I creep into my hut and whimper like a dog. My strength is gone from me. I am an old man and the fire-carriage has made the ford desolate. They were wont to call me the Strong One of the Barhwi.

Behold my face, Sahib – it is the face of a monkey. And my arm – it is the arm of an old woman. I swear to you, Sahib, that a woman has loved this face and has rested in the hollow of this arm. Twenty years ago, Sahib. Believe me, this was true talk – twenty years ago.

Come to the door and look across. Can you see a thin fire very far away down the stream? That is the temple-fire, in the shrine of Hanuman,[15] of the village of Pateera. North, under the big star, is the village itself, but it is hidden by a bend of the river. Is that far to swim, Sahib? Would you take off your clothes and adventure? Yet I swam to Pateera – not once, but many times; and there are *muggers*[16] in the river too.

Love knows no caste; else why should I, a Mussulman and the son of a Mussulman, have sought a Hindu woman – a widow of the Hindus – the sister of the headman of Pateera? But it was even so. They of the headman's household came on a pilgrimage to Muttra[17] when She was but newly a bride. Silver tyres were upon the wheels of the bullock-cart, and silken curtains hid the woman. Sahib, I made no haste in their conveyance, for the wind parted the curtains and I saw Her. When they returned from pilgrimage the boy that was Her husband had died, and I saw Her again in the bullock-cart. By God, these Hindus are fools! What was it to me whether She was Hindu or Jain[18] – scavenger, leper, or whole? I would have married Her and made Her a home by the ford. The Seventh of the Nine Bars[19] says that a man may not marry one of the idolaters? Is that truth? Both Shiahs and Sunnis[20] say that a Mussulman may not marry one of the idolaters? Is the Sahib a priest, then, that he knows so much? I will tell him something that he does not know. There is neither Shiah nor Sunni, forbidden nor idolater, in Love; and the Nine Bars are but nine little faggots that the flame of Love utterly burns away. In truth, I would have taken Her; but what could I do? The headman would have sent his men to break my head with staves. I am not – I was not – afraid of any five men; but against half a village who can prevail?

Therefore it was my custom, these things having been arranged between us twain, to go by night to the village of Pateera, and there we met among the crops, no man knowing aught of the matter. Behold, now! I was wont to cross here, skirting the jungle to the river bend where the railway bridge is, and thence across the elbow of land to Pateera. The light of the shrine was my guide when the nights were dark. That jungle near the river is very full of snakes – little *karaits*[21] that sleep on the sand – and moreover, Her brothers would have slain me had they found me in the crops. But none knew – none knew save She and I; and the blown sand of the river-bed covered the track of my feet. In the hot months it was an easy thing to pass from the ford to Pateera, and in the first Rains, when the river rose slowly, it was an easy thing also. I set the strength of my body against the strength of the stream, and nightly I ate in my hut here and drank at Pateera yonder. She had said that one Hirnam Singh, a thief, had sought Her, and he was of a village up the river but on the same bank. All Sikhs are dogs, and they have refused in their folly that good gift of God – tobacco.[22] I was ready to destroy Hirnam Singh that ever he had come nigh Her; and the more because he had sworn to Her that She had a lover, and that he would lie in wait and give the name to the headman unless She went away with him. What curs are these Sikhs!

After that news I swam always with a little sharp knife in my belt, and evil would it have been for a man had he stayed me. I knew not the face of Hirnam Singh, but I would have killed any who came between me and Her.

Upon a night in the beginning of the Rains I was minded to go across to Pateera, albeit the river was angry. Now the nature of the Barhwi is this, Sahib. In twenty breaths it comes down from the Hills a wall three feet high, and I have seen it, between the lighting of a fire and the cooking of a cake, grow from a runnel to a sister of the Jumna.

When I left this bank there was a shoal a half-mile down, and I made shift to fetch it and draw breath there ere going forward; for I felt the hands of the river heavy upon my heels. Yet what will a young man not do for Love's sake? There was but little light from the stars, and midway to the shoal a branch of the stinking deodar tree brushed my mouth as I swam. That was a sign of heavy rain in the foot-hills and beyond, for the deodar is a strong tree, not easily shaken from the hillsides. I made haste, the river aiding me, but ere I had touched the shoal, the pulse of the stream beat, as it were, within me and around, and, behold, the shoal was gone and I rode high on the crest of a wave that ran from bank to bank. Has the Sahib ever been cast into much water that fights and will not let a man use his limbs? To me, my head upon the water, it seemed as though there were naught but water to the world's end, and the river drave me with its driftwood. A man is a very little thing in the belly of a flood. And *this* flood, though I knew it not, was the Great Flood about which men talk still. My liver was dissolved and I lay like a log upon my back in the fear of Death. There were living things in the water, crying and howling grievously – beasts of the forest and cattle, and once the voice of a man asking for help. But the rain came and lashed the water white, and I heard no more save the roar of the boulders below and the roar of the rain above. Thus I was whirled down-stream, wrestling for the breath in me. It is very hard to die when one is young. Can the Sahib, standing here, see the railway bridge? Look, there are the lights of the mail-train going to Peshawur! The bridge is now twenty feet above the river, but upon that night the water was roaring against the lattice-work,[23] and against the lattice came I feet first. But much driftwood was piled there and upon the piers, and I took no great hurt. Only the river pressed me as a strong man presses a weaker. Scarcely could I take hold of the lattice-work and crawl to the upper boom. Sahib, the water was foaming across the rails a foot deep! Judge therefore what manner of flood it must have been. I could not hear. I could not see. I could but lie on the boom and pant for breath.

After a while the rain ceased and there came out in the sky certain new-washed stars, and by their light I saw that there was no end to the black water as far as the eye could travel, and the water had risen upon the rails. There were dead beasts in the driftwood on the piers, and others caught by the neck in the lattice-work, and others not yet drowned who strove to find a foothold on the lattice-work – buffaloes and kine, and wild pig, and deer one or two, and snakes and jackals past all counting. Their bodies were black upon the left side of the bridge, but the smaller of them were forced through the lattice-work and whirled down-stream.

Thereafter the stars died and the rain came down afresh and the river rose yet more, and I felt the bridge begin to stir under me as a man stirs in his sleep ere he wakes. But I was not afraid, Sahib. I swear to you that I was not afraid, though I had no power in my limbs. I knew that I should not die till I had seen Her once more. But I was very cold, and I felt that the bridge must go.

There was a trembling in the water, such a trembling as goes before the coming of a great wave, and the bridge lifted its flank to the rush of that coming so that the right lattice dipped under water and the left rose clear. On my beard, Sahib, I am speaking God's truth! As a Mirzapore stone-boat[24] careens[25] to the wind, so the Barhwi Bridge turned. Thus and in no other manner.

I slid from the boom into deep water, and behind me came the wave of the wrath of the river. I heard its voice and the scream of the middle part of the bridge as it moved from the piers and sank, and I knew no more till I rose in the middle of the great flood. I put forth my hand to swim, and lo! it fell upon the knotted hair[26] of the head of a man. He was dead, for no one but I, the Strong One of Barhwi, could have lived in that race. He had been dead full two days, for he rode high, wallowing, and was an aid to me. I laughed then, knowing for a surety that I should yet see Her and take no harm; and I twisted my fingers in the hair of the man, for I was far spent, and together we went down the stream – he the dead and I the living. Lacking that help I should have sunk: the cold was in my marrow, and my flesh was ribbed and sodden on my bones. But *he* had no fear who had known the uttermost of the power of the river; and I let him go where he chose. At last we came into the power of a side-current that set to the right bank, and I strove with my feet to draw with it. But the dead man swung heavily in the whirl, and I feared that some branch had struck him and that he would sink. The tops of the tamarisks brushed my knees, so I knew we were come into flood-water above the crops, and, after, I let down my legs and felt bottom – the ridge of a field – and, after, the dead man stayed upon a knoll under a fig-tree, and I drew my body from the water rejoicing.

Does the Sahib know whither the backwash of the flood had borne me? To the knoll which is the eastern boundary-mark of the village of Pateera! No other place. I drew the dead man up on the grass for the service that he had done me, and also because I knew not whether I should need him again. Then I went, crying thrice like a jackal, to the appointed place, which was near the byre of the headman's house. But my Love was already there, weeping. She feared that the flood had swept my hut at the Barhwi Ford. When I came softly through the ankle-deep water, She thought it was a ghost and would have fled, but I put my arms round Her, and – I was no ghost in those days, though I am an old man now. Ho! ho! Dried corn, in truth. Maize without juice.[27] Ho! ho!*

I told Her the story of the breaking of the Barhwi Bridge, and She said that I was greater than mortal man, for none may cross the Barhwi in full flood, and I had seen what never man had seen before. Hand in hand we went to the knoll where the dead lay, and I

* I grieve to say that the Warden of the Barhwi Ford is responsible here for two very bad puns in the vernacular. – *R.K.*

showed Her by what help I had made the ford. She looked also upon the body under the stars, for the latter end of the night was clear, and hid Her face in Her hands, crying: 'It is the body of Hirnam Singh!' I said: 'The swine is of more use dead than living, my Beloved,' and She said: 'Surely, for he has saved the dearest life in the world to my love. None the less, he cannot stay here, for that would bring shame upon me.' The body was not a gunshot from Her door.

Then said I, rolling the body with my hands: 'God hath judged between us, Hirnam Singh, that thy blood might not be upon my head. Now, whether I have done thee a wrong in keeping thee from the burning-ghat,[28] do thou and the crows settle together.' So I cast him adrift into the flood-water, and he was drawn out to the open, ever wagging his thick black beard like a priest under the pulpit-board. And I saw no more of Hirnam Singh.

Before the breaking of the day we two parted, and I moved towards such of the jungle as was not flooded. With the full light I saw what I had done in the darkness, and the bones of my body were loosened in my flesh, for there ran two *koss* of raging water between the village of Pateera and the trees of the far bank, and, in the middle, the piers of the Barhwi Bridge showed like broken teeth in the jaw of an old man. Nor was there any life upon the waters – neither birds nor boats, but only an army of drowned things – bullocks and horses and men – and the river was redder than blood from the clay of the foot-hills. Never had I seen such a flood – never since that year have I seen the like – and, O Sahib, no man living had done what I had done. There was no return for me that day. Not for all the lands of the headman would I venture a second time without the shield of darkness that cloaks danger. I went a *koss* up the river to the house of a blacksmith, saying that the flood had swept me from my hut, and they gave me food. Seven days I stayed with the blacksmith, till a boat came and I returned to my house. There was no trace of wall, or roof, or floor – naught but a patch of slimy mud. Judge, therefore, Sahib, how far the river must have risen.

It was written that I should not die either in my house, or in the heart of the Barhwi, or under the wreck of the Barhwi Bridge, for God sent down Hirnam Singh two days dead, though I know not how the man died, to be my buoy and support. Hirnam Singh has been in Hell these twenty years, and the thought of that night must be the flower of his torment.

Listen, Sahib! The river has changed its voice. It is going to sleep before the dawn, to which there is yet one hour. With the light it will come down afresh. How do I know? Have I been here thirty years without knowing the voice of the river as a father knows the voice of his son? Every moment it is talking less angrily. I swear that there will be no danger for one hour or, perhaps, two. I cannot answer for the morning. Be quick, Sahib! I will call Ram Pershad, and he will not turn back this time. Is the paulin tightly corded upon all the baggage? Ohé, mahout with a mud head, the elephant for the Sahib, and tell them on the far side that there will be no crossing after daylight.

Money? Nay, Sahib. I am not of that kind. No, not even to give sweetmeats to the baby-folk. My house, look you, is empty, and I am an old man.

Dutt, Ram Pershad! *Dutt! Dutt! Dutt!*[29] Good luck go with you, Sahib.

The Sending of Dana Da

When the Devil rides on your chest remember the low-caste man. – *Native Proverb*.

Once upon a time, some people in India made a new Heaven and a new Earth out of broken teacups, a missing brooch or two, and a hair-brush.[1] These were hidden under bushes, or stuffed into holes in the hillside, and an entire Civil Service of subordinate Gods used to find or mend them again; and every one said: 'There are more things in Heaven and Earth than are dreamt of in our philosophy.'[2] Several other things happened also, but the Religion never seemed to get much beyond its first manifestations; though it added an air-line postal service[3] and orchestral effects in order to keep abreast of the times and choke off competition.

This Religion was too elastic for ordinary use. It stretched itself and embraced pieces of everything[4] that the medicine-men of all ages have manufactured. It approved of and stole from Freemasonry;[5] looted the Latter-day Rosicrucians[6] of half their pet words; took any fragments of Egyptian philosophy that it found in the *Encyclopædia Britannica*; annexed as many of the Vedas[7] as had been translated into French or English, and talked of all the rest; built in the German versions of what is left of the Zend Avesta;[8] encouraged White, Grey, and Black Magic, including spiritualism, palmistry, fortune-telling by cards, hot chestnuts, double-kernelled nuts, and tallow droppings; would have adopted Voodoo and Obeah[9] had it known anything about them, and showed itself, in every way, one of the most accommodating arrangements that had ever been invented since the birth of the Sea.

When it was in thorough working order, with all the machinery, down to the subscriptions, complete, Dana Da came from nowhere, with nothing in his hands, and wrote a chapter in its history which has hitherto been unpublished. He said that his first name was Dana, and his second was Da. Now, setting aside Dana[10] of the *New*

York Sun, Dana is a Bhil name, and Da fits no native of India unless you accept the Bengali Dé as the original spelling. Da is Lap or Finnish; and Dana Da was neither Finn, Chin, Bhil, Bengali, Lap, Nair, Gond,[11] Romany, Magh, Bokhariot, Kurd, Armenian, Levantine,[12] Jew, Persian, Punjabi, Madrasi, Parsee,[13] nor anything else known to ethnologists. He was simply Dana Da, and declined to give further information. For the sake of brevity and as roughly indicating his origin, he was called 'The Native'. He might have been the original Old Man of the Mountains,[14] who is said to be the only authorized Head of the Tea-cup Creed. Some people said that he was; but Dana Da used to smile and deny any connection with the cult, explaining that he was an 'Independent Experimenter'.

As I have said, he came from nowhere, with his hands behind his back, and studied the Creed for three weeks, sitting at the feet of those best competent to explain its mysteries. Then he laughed aloud and went away, but the laugh might have been either of devotion or derision.

When he returned he was without money, but his pride was unabated. He declared that he knew more about the Things in Heaven and Earth than those who taught him, and for this contumacy was abandoned altogether.

His next appearance in public life was at a big cantonment in Upper India, and he was then telling fortunes with the help of three leaden dice, a very dirty old cloth, and a little tin box of opium pills. He told better fortunes when he was allowed half a bottle of whisky; but the things which he invented on the opium were quite worth the money. He was in reduced circumstances. Among other people's he told the fortune of an Englishman who had once been interested in the Simla Creed, but who, later on, had married and forgotten all his old knowledge in the study of babies and things. The Englishman allowed Dana Da to tell a fortune for charity's sake, and gave him five rupees, a dinner, and some old clothes. When he had eaten, Dana Da professed gratitude, and asked if there were anything he could do for his host – in the esoteric line.[15]

'Is there any one that you love?' said Dana Da. The Englishman loved his wife, but had no desire to drag her name into the conversation. He therefore shook his head.

'Is there any one that you hate?' said Dana Da. The Englishman said that there were several men whom he hated deeply.

'Very good,' said Dana Da, upon whom the whisky and the opium were beginning to tell. 'Only give me their names, and I will despatch a Sending to them and kill them.'

Now a Sending is a horrible arrangement, first invented, they say, in Iceland. It is a Thing sent by a wizard, and may take any form, but, most generally, wanders about the land in the shape of a little purple cloud till it finds the Sendee, and him it kills by changing into the form of a horse, or a cat, or a man without a face. It is not strictly a native patent, though *chamars*[16] of the skin and hide castes can, if irritated, despatch a Sending which sits on the breast of their enemy by night and nearly kills him. Very few natives care to irritate *chamars* for this reason.

'Let me despatch a Sending,' said Dana Da. 'I am nearly dead now with want, and drink, and opium; but I should like to kill a man before I die. I can send a Sending anywhere you choose, and in any form except in the shape of a man.'

The Englishman had no friends that he wished to kill, but partly to soothe Dana Da, whose eyes were rolling, and partly to see what would be done, he asked whether a modified Sending could not be arranged for – such a Sending as should make a man's life a burden to him, and yet do him no harm. If this were possible, he notified his willingness to give Dana Da ten rupees for the job.

'I am not what I was once,' said Dana Da, 'and I must take the money because I am poor. To what Englishman shall I send it?'

'Send a Sending to Lone Sahib,' said the Englishman, naming a man who had been most bitter in rebuking him for his apostasy from the Tea-cup Creed. Dana Da laughed and nodded.

'I could have chosen no better man myself,' said he. 'I will see that he finds the Sending about his path and about his bed.'

He lay down on the hearth-rug, turned up the whites of his eyes, shivered all over, and began to snort. This was Magic, or Opium, or the Sending, or all three. When he opened his eyes he vowed that the Sending had started upon the war-path, and was at that moment flying up to the town where Lone Sahib lived.

'Give me my ten rupees,' said Dana Da wearily, 'and write a letter to Lone Sahib, telling him, and all who believe with him, that you and a friend are using a power greater than theirs. They will see that you are speaking the truth.'

He departed unsteadily, with the promise of some more rupees if anything came of the Sending.

The Englishman sent a letter to Lone Sahib, couched in what he remembered of the terminology of the Creed. He wrote: 'I also, in the days of what you held to be my backsliding, have obtained Enlightenment, and with Enlightenment has come Power.' Then he grew so deeply mysterious that the recipient of the letter could make neither head nor tail of it, and was proportionately impressed; for he fancied that his friend had become a 'fifth-rounder'.[17] When a man is a 'fifth-rounder' he can do more than Slade and Houdin[18] combined.

Lone Sahib read the letter in five different fashions, and was beginning a sixth interpretation when his bearer dashed in with the news that there was a cat on the bed. Now if there was one thing that Lone Sahib hated more than another, it was a cat. He scolded the bearer for not turning it out of the house. The bearer said that he was afraid. All the doors of the bedroom had been shut throughout the morning, and no *real* cat could possibly have entered the room. He would prefer not to meddle with the creature.

Lone Sahib entered the room gingerly, and there, on the pillow of his bed, sprawled and whimpered a wee white kitten; not a jump-some, frisky little beast, but a slug-like crawler with its eyes barely opened and its paws lacking strength or direction – a kitten that ought to have been in a basket with its mamma. Lone Sahib caught it by the scruff of its neck, handed it over to the sweeper to be drowned, and fined the bearer four annas.

That evening, as he was reading in his room, he fancied that he saw something moving about on the hearth-rug, outside the circle of light from his reading-lamp. When the thing began to myowl he realized that it was a kitten – a wee white kitten, nearly blind and very miserable. He was seriously angry, and spoke bitterly to his bearer, who said that there was no kitten in the room when he brought in the lamp, and *real* kittens of tender age generally had mother-cats in attendance.

'If the Presence will go out into the veranda and listen,' said the bearer, 'he will hear no cats. How, therefore, can the kitten on the bed and the kitten on the hearth-rug be real kittens?'

Lone Sahib went out to listen, and the bearer followed him, but there was no sound of any one mewing for her children. He returned to his room, having hurled the kitten down the hillside, and wrote out the incidents of the day for the benefit of his co-religionists. Those people were so absolutely free from superstition that they ascribed anything a little out of the common to Agencies. As it was their business to know all about the Agencies, they were on terms of almost indecent familiarity with Manifestations of every kind. Their letters dropped from the ceiling – unstamped – and Spirits used to squatter up and down their staircases all night; but they had never come into contact with kittens. Lone Sahib wrote out the facts, noting the hour and the minute, as every Psychical Observer is bound to do, and appending the Englishman's letter, because it was the most mysterious document and might have had a bearing upon anything in this world or the next. An outsider would have translated all the tangle thus: 'Look out! You laughed at me once, and now I am going to make you sit up.'

Lone Sahib's co-religionists found that meaning in it; but their translation was refined and full of four-syllable words. They held a sederunt,[19] and were filled with tremulous joy, for, in spite of their familiarity with all the other worlds and cycles, they had a very human awe of things sent from Ghostland. They met in Lone Sahib's room in shrouded and sepulchral gloom, and their conclave was broken up by a clinking among the photo-frames on the mantelpiece. A wee white kitten, nearly blind, was looping and writhing itself between the clock and the candlesticks. That stopped all investigations or doubtings. Here was the Manifestation in the flesh. It was, so far as could be seen, devoid of purpose, but it was a Manifestation of undoubted authenticity.

They drafted a Round Robin to the Englishman, the backslider of old days, adjuring him in the interests of the Creed to explain whether there was any connection between the embodiment of some Egyptian God or other (I have forgotten the name) and his communication. They called the kitten Ra, or Thoth, or Tum,[20] or something; and when Lone Sahib confessed that the first one had, at his most misguided instance, been drowned by the sweeper, they said consolingly that in his next life he would be a 'bounder', and not even a 'rounder' of the lowest grade. These words may not be quite correct, but they accurately express the sense of the house.

When the Englishman received the Round Robin – it came by post – he was startled and bewildered. He sent into the bazar for Dana Da, who read the letter and laughed. 'That is my Sending,' said he. 'I told you I would work well. Now give me another ten rupees.'

'But what in the world is this gibberish about Egyptian Gods?' asked the Englishman.

'Cats,' said Dana Da with a hiccough, for he had discovered the Englishman's whisky-bottle. 'Cats, and cats, and cats! Never was such a Sending. A hundred of cats. Now give me ten more rupees and write as I dictate.'

Dana Da's letter was a curiosity. It bore the Englishman's signature, and hinted at cats – at a Sending of Cats. The mere words on paper were creepy and uncanny to behold.

'What have you done, though?' said the Englishman. 'I am as much in the dark as ever. Do you mean to say that you can actually send this absurd Sending you talk about?'

'Judge for yourself,' said Dana Da. 'What does that letter mean? In a little time they will all be at my feet and yours, and I – oh, glory! – will be drugged or drunk all day long.'

Dana Da knew his people.

When a man who hates cats wakes up in the morning and finds a little squirming kitten on his breast, or puts his hand into his ulster-pocket and finds a little half-dead kitten where his gloves should be, or opens his trunk and finds a vile kitten among his dress-shirts, or goes for a long ride with his mackintosh strapped on his saddle-bow and shakes a little squawling kitten from its folds when he opens it, or goes out to dinner and finds a little blind kitten under his chair, or stays at home and finds a writhing kitten under the quilt, or wriggling among his boots, or hanging, head downwards, in his tobacco-jar, or being mangled by his terrier in the veranda, – when such a man finds one kitten, neither more nor less, once a day in a place where no kitten rightly could or should be, he is naturally upset. When he dare not murder his daily trove because he believes it to be a Manifestation, an Emissary, an Embodiment, and half-a-dozen other things all out of the regular course of nature, he is more than upset. He is actually distressed. Some of Lone Sahib's co-religionists thought that he was a highly-favoured individual; but many said that if he had treated the first kitten with proper respect – as suited a Thoth-Ra-Tum-Sennacherib[21] Embodiment – all this trouble would have been averted. They compared him to the Ancient Mariner,[22] but none the less they were proud of him and proud of the Englishman who had sent the Manifestation. They did not call it a Sending because Icelandic magic was not in their programme.

After sixteen kittens, that is to say, after one fortnight, for there were three kittens on the first day to impress the fact of the Sending, the whole camp was uplifted by a letter – it came flying through a window – from the Old Man of the Mountains – the Head of all the Creed – explaining the Manifestation in the most beautiful language and soaking up all the credit of it for himself. The Englishman, said the letter, was not there at all. He was a backslider without Power or Asceticism, who could not even raise a table by force of volition, much less project an army of kittens through space. The entire arrangement, said the letter, was strictly orthodox, worked and sanctioned by the highest Authorities within the pale of the Creed. There was great joy at this, for some of the weaker brethren, seeing that an outsider who had been working on independent lines could create kittens, whereas their own rulers had never gone beyond crockery – and broken at best – were showing a desire to break line on their own trail. In fact, there was the promise of a schism. A second Round Robin was drafted to the Englishman, beginning: 'O Scoffer,' and ending with a selection of curses from the Rites of Mizraim and Memphis,[23] and the Commination of Jugana, who was a 'fifth-rounder' upon whose name an upstart 'third-rounder' once traded. A papal excommunication is a *billet-doux* compared with the Commination of Jugana. The Englishman had been proved, under the hand and seal of the Old Man of the Mountains, to have appropriated Virtue and pretended to have Power which, in reality, belonged only to the Supreme Head. Naturally the Round Robin did not spare him.

He handed the letter to Dana Da to translate into decent English. The effect on Dana Da was curious. At first he was furiously angry, and then he laughed for five minutes.

'I had thought,' he said, 'that they would have come to me. In another week I would have shown that I sent the Sending, and they would have discrowned the Old Man of the Mountains who has sent this Sending of mine. Do you do nothing. The time has come for me to act. Write as I dictate, and I will put them to shame. But give me ten more rupees.'

At Dana Da's dictation the Englishman wrote nothing less than a formal challenge to the Old Man of the Mountains. It wound up: 'And if this Manifestation be from your hand, then let it go forward; but if it be from my hand, I will that the Sending shall cease in two days' time. On that day there shall be twelve kittens and thenceforward none at all. The people shall judge between us.' This was signed by Dana Da, who added pentacles and pentagrams, and a *crux ansata*, and half-a-dozen *swastikas*, and a Triple Tau[24] to his name, just to show that he was all he laid claim to be.

The challenge was read out to the gentlemen and ladies, and they remembered then that Dana Da had laughed at them some years ago. It was officially announced that the Old Man of the Mountains would treat the matter with contempt; Dana Da being an Independent Investigator without a single 'round' at the back of him. But this did not soothe his people. They wanted to see a fight. They were very human for all their spirituality. Lone Sahib, who was really being worn out with kittens, submitted meekly to his fate. He felt that he was being 'kittened to prove the power of Dana Da',[25] as the poet says.

When the stated day dawned the shower of kittens began. Some were white and some were tabby, and all were about the same loathsome age. Three were on his hearth-rug, three in his bathroom, and the other six turned up at intervals among the visitors who came to see the prophecy break down. Never was a more satisfactory Sending. On the next day there were no kittens, and the next day and all the other days were kittenless and quiet. The people murmured and looked to the Old Man of the Mountains for an explanation. A letter, written on a palm-leaf, dropped from the ceiling, but every one except Lone Sahib felt that letters were not what the occasion demanded. There should have been cats, there should have been cats, – full-grown ones. The letter proved conclusively that there had been a hitch in the Psychic Current which, colliding with a Dual Identity, had interfered with the Percipient Activity all along the main line. The kittens were still going on, but owing to some failure in the Developing Fluid,[26] they were not materialized. The failure in the Developing Fluid,[26] they were not materialized. The air was thick with letters for a few days afterwards. Unseen hands played Glück and Beethoven on finger-bowls and clock-shades; but all men felt that Psychic Life was a mockery without materialized kittens. Even Lone Sahib shouted with the majority on this head. Dana Da's letters were very insulting, and if he had then offered to lead a new departure, there is no knowing what might not have happened.

But Dana Da was dying of whisky and opium in the Englishman's godown, and had small heart for honours.

'They have been put to shame,' said he. 'Never was such a Sending. It has killed me.'

'Nonsense!' said the Englishman. 'You are going to die, Dana Da, and that sort of stuff must be left behind. I'll admit that you have made some queer things come about. Tell me honestly, now, how was it done?'

'Give me ten more rupees,' said Dana Da faintly, 'and if I die before I spend them, bury them with me.' The silver was counted out while Dana Da was fighting with Death. His hand closed upon the money and he smiled a grim smile.

'Bend low,' he whispered. The Englishman bent.

'*Bunnia* – Mission-school – expelled – *box-wallah* [peddler] – Ceylon pearl-merchant – all mine English education – out-casted, and made up name Dana Da – England with American thought-reading man and – and – you gave me ten rupees several times – I gave the Sahib's bearer two-eight a month for cats – little, little cats. I wrote – and he put them about – very clever man. Very few kittens now in the bazar. Ask Lone Sahib's sweeper's wife.'

So saying, Dana Da gasped and passed away into a land where, if all be true, there are no materializations and the making of new creeds is discouraged.

But consider the gorgeous simplicity of it all!

On the City Wall

Then she let them down by a cord through the window; for her house was upon the town wall, and she dwelt upon the wall. – *Joshua* ii.15.

Lalun[1] is a member of the most ancient profession in the world. Lilith[2] was her very-great-grandmamma, and that was before the days of Eve, as every one knows. In the West, people say rude things about Lalun's profession, and write lectures about it, and distribute the lectures to young persons in order that Morality may be preserved. In the East, where the profession is hereditary, descending from mother to daughter, nobody writes lectures or takes any notice; and that is a distinct proof of the inability of the East to manage its own affairs.

Lalun's real husband, for even ladies of Lalun's profession in the East must have husbands, was a big jujube-tree. Her Mamma, who had married a fig-tree, spent ten thousand rupees on Lalun's wedding, which was blessed by forty-seven clergymen of Mamma's Church, and distributed five thousand rupees in charity to the poor. And that was the custom of the land. The advantages of having a jujube-tree for a husband are obvious. You cannot hurt his feelings, and he looks imposing.

Lalun's husband stood on the plain outside the City walls, and Lalun's house was upon the east wall facing the river.[3] If you fell from the broad window-seat you dropped thirty feet sheer into the City Ditch. But if you stayed where you should and looked forth, you saw all the cattle of the City being driven down to water, the students of the Government College playing cricket, the high grass and trees that fringed the river-bank, the great sand-bars that ribbed the river, the red tombs of dead Emperors[4] beyond the river, and very far away through the blue heat-haze a glint of the snows of the Himalayas.

Wali Dad used to lie in the window-seat for hours at a time

watching this view. He was a young Mohammedan who was suffering acutely from education of the English variety and knew it. His father had sent him to a Mission-school to get wisdom, and Wali Dad had absorbed more than ever his father or the Missionaries intended he should. When his father died, Wali Dad was independent and spent two years experimenting with the creeds of the Earth and reading books that are of no use to anybody.

After he had made an unsuccessful attempt to enter the Roman Catholic Church and the Presbyterian fold at the same time (the Missionaries found him out and called him names; but they did not understand his trouble), he discovered Lalun on the City wall and became the most constant of her few admirers. He possessed a head that English artists at home would rave over and paint amid impossible surroundings – a face that female novelists would use with delight through nine hundred pages. In reality he was only a clean-bred young Mohammedan, with pencilled eyebrows, small-cut nostrils, little feet and hands, and a very tired look in his eyes. By virtue of his twenty-two years he had grown a neat black beard which he stroked with pride and kept delicately scented. His life seemed to be divided between borrowing books from me and making love to Lalun in the window-seat. He composed songs about her, and some of the songs are sung to this day in the City from the Street of the Mutton-Butchers to the Copper-Smiths' ward.

One song, the prettiest of all, says that the beauty of Lalun was so great that it troubled the hearts of the British Government and caused them to lose their peace of mind. That is the way the song is sung in the streets; but, if you examine it carefully and know the key to the explanation, you will find that there are three puns in it – on 'beauty', 'heart', and 'peace of mind', – so that it runs: 'By the subtlety of Lalun the administration of the Government was troubled and it lost such-and-such a man.' When Wali Dad sings that song his eyes glow like hot coals, and Lalun leans back among the cushions and throws bunches of jasmine-buds at Wali Dad.

But first it is necessary to explain something about the Supreme Government which is above all and below all and behind all. Gentlemen come from England, spend a few weeks in India, walk round this great Sphinx of the Plains, and write books upon its ways and its works, denouncing or praising it as their own ignorance prompts. Consequently all the world knows how the Supreme Government conducts itself. But no one, not even the Supreme Government, knows everything about the administration of the Empire. Year by year England sends out fresh drafts for the first fighting-line, which is officially called the Indian Civil Service. These die, or kill themselves by overwork, or are worried to death, or broken in health and hope in order that the land may be protected from death and sickness, famine and war, and may eventually become capable of standing alone. It will never stand alone, but the idea is a pretty one, and men are willing to die for it, and yearly the work of pushing and coaxing and scolding and petting the country into good living goes forward. If an advance be made all credit is given to the native, while the Englishmen stand back and wipe their foreheads. If a failure occurs the Englishmen step forward and take the blame. Overmuch tenderness of this kind has bred a strong belief among many natives that the native is capable of administering the country, and many devout Englishmen believe this also, because the theory is stated in beautiful English with all the latest political colours.

There are other men who, though uneducated, see visions and dream dreams, and they, too, hope to administer the country in their own way – that is to say, with a garnish of Red Sauce.[5] Such men must exist among two hundred million people, and, if they are not attended to, may cause trouble and even break the great idol called *Pax Britannica*, which, as the newspapers say, lives between Peshawur and Cape Comorin.[6] Were the Day of Doom to dawn tomorrow, you would find the Supreme Government 'taking measures to allay popular excitement', and putting guards upon the graveyards that the Dead might troop forth orderly. The youngest Civilian would arrest Gabriel on his own responsibility if the Archangel could not produce a Deputy-Commissioner's permission to 'make music or other noises' as the licence says.

Whence it is easy to see that mere men of the flesh who would create a tumult must fare badly at the hands of the Supreme Government. And they do. There is no outward sign of excitement; there is no confusion; there is no knowledge. When due and sufficient reasons have been given, weighed and approved, the machinery moves forward, and the dreamer of dreams and the seer of visions is gone from his friends and following. He enjoys the hospitality of Government; there is no restriction upon his movements within certain limits; but he must not confer any more with his brother dreamers. Once in every six months the Supreme Government assures itself that he is well and takes formal acknowledgement of his existence. No one protests against his detention, because the few people who know about it are in deadly fear of seeming to know him; and never a single newspaper 'takes up his case' or organizes demonstrations on his behalf, because the newspapers of India have got behind that lying proverb which says the Pen is mightier than the Sword, and can walk delicately.

So now you know as much as you ought about Wali Dad, the educational mixture, and the Supreme Government.

Lalun has not yet been described. She would need, so Wali Dad says, a thousand pens of gold, and ink scented with musk. She has been variously compared to the Moon, the Dil Sagar Lake, a spotted quail, a gazelle, the Sun on the Desert of Kutch, the Dawn, the Stars, and the young bamboo. These comparisons imply that she is beautiful exceedingly according to the native standards, which are practically the same as those of the West. Her eyes are black and her hair is black, and her eyebrows are black as leeches; her mouth is tiny and says witty things; her hands are tiny and have saved much money; her feet are tiny and have trodden on the naked hearts of many men. But, as Wali Dad sings: 'Lalun *is* Lalun, and when you have said that, you have only come to the Beginnings of Knowledge.'

The little house on the City wall was just big enough to hold Lalun, and her maid, and a pussy-cat with a silver collar. A big pink-and-blue cut-glass chandelier hung from the ceiling of the reception room. A petty Nawab had given Lalun the horror, and she kept it for politeness' sake. The floor of the room was of polished chunam,[7] white as curds. A latticed window of carved wood was set in one wall; there was a profusion of squabby pluffy cushions and fat carpets everywhere, and Lalun's silver hookah, studded with turquoises, had a special little carpet all to its shining self. Wali Dad was nearly as permanent a fixture as the chandelier. As I have said, he lay in the window-seat and meditated on Life and Death and Lalun – 'specially Lalun. The feet of the young men of the City tended to her doorways and then – retired, for Lalun was a particular maiden, slow of speech, reserved of mind, and not in the least inclined to orgies which were nearly certain to end in strife. 'If I am of no value, I am unworthy of this honour,' said Lalun. 'If I am of value, they are unworthy of Me.' And that was a crooked sentence.

In the long hot nights of latter April and May all the City seemed to assemble in Lalun's little white room to smoke and to talk. Shiahs of the grimmest and most uncompromising persuasion; Sufis[8] who had lost all belief in the Prophet and retained but little in God; wandering Hindu priests passing southward on their way to the Central India fairs and other affairs; Pundits[9] in black gowns, with spectacles on their noses and undigested wisdom in their insides; bearded headmen of the wards; Sikhs with all the details of the latest ecclesiastical scandal in the Golden Temple;[10] red-eyed priests from beyond the Border, looking like trapped wolves and talking like ravens; M.A.'s of the University, very superior and very voluble – all these people and more also you might find in the white room. Wali Dad lay in the window-seat and listened to the talk.

'It is Lalun's *salon*,' said Wali Dad to me, 'and it is electic – is not that the word? Outside of a Freemasons' Lodge I have never seen such gatherings. *There* I dined once with a Jew[11] – a Yahoudi!' He spat into the City Ditch with apologies for allowing national feelings to overcome him. 'Though I have lost every belief in the world,' said he, 'and try to be proud of my losing, I cannot help hating a Jew. Lalun admits no Jews here.'

'But what in the world do all these men do?' I asked.

'The curse of our country,' said Wali Dad. 'They talk. It is like the Athenians – always hearing and telling some new thing.[12] Ask the Pearl and she will show you how much she knows of the news of the City and the Province. Lalun knows everything.'

'Lalun,' I said at random – she was talking to a gentleman of the Kurd persuasion who had come in from God-knows-where – 'when does the 175th Regiment go to Agra?'

'It does not go at all,' said Lalun, without turning her head. 'They have ordered the 118th to go in its stead. That Regiment goes to Lucknow in three months, unless they give a fresh order.'

'That is so,' said Wali Dad, without a shade of doubt. 'Can you, with your telegrams and your newspapers, do better? Always hearing and telling some new thing,' he went on. 'My friend, has your God ever smitten a European nation for gossiping in the bazars? India has gossiped for centuries – always standing in the bazars until the soldiers go by. Therefore – you are here to-day instead of starving in your own country, and I am not a Mohammedan – I am a Product – a Demnition Product.[13] *That* also I owe to you and yours: that I cannot make an end to my sentence without quoting from your authors.' He pulled at the hookah and mourned, half feelingly, half in earnest, for the shattered hopes of his youth. Wali Dad was always mourning over something or other – the country of which he despaired, or the creed in which he had lost faith, or the life of the English which he could by no means understand.

Lalun never mourned. She played little songs on the *sitar*, and to hear her sing, 'O Peacock, cry again', was always a fresh pleasure. She knew all the songs that have ever been sung, from the war-songs of the South, that make the old men angry with the young men and the young men angry with the State, to the love-songs of the North, where the swords whinny-whicker like angry kites in the pauses between the kisses, and the Passes fill with armed men, and the Lover is torn from his Beloved and cries *Ai! Ai! Ai!* evermore. She knew how to make up tobacco for the pipe so that it smelt like the Gates of Paradise and wafted you gently through them. She could embroider strange things in gold and silver, and dance softly with the moonlight when it came in at the window. Also she knew the hearts of men, and the heart of the City, and whose wives were faithful and whose untrue, and more of the secrets of the Government Offices than are good to be set down in this place. Nasiban, her maid, said that her jewelry was worth ten thousand pounds, and that, some night, a thief would enter and murder her for its possession; but Lalun said that all the City would tear that thief limb from limb, and that he, whoever he was, knew it.

So she took her *sitar* and sat in the window-seat, and sang a song of old days that had been sung by a girl of her profession in an armed camp on the eve of a great battle – the day before the Fords of the Jumna ran red and Sivaji[14] fled fifty miles to Delhi with a Toorkh stallion at his horse's tail and another Lalun on his saddle-bow. It was what men call a Mahratta *laonee*,[15] and it said: –

Their warrior forces Chimnajee
  Before the Peishwa led,
The Children of the Sun and Fire
  Behind him turned and fled.

And the chorus said:–

With them there fought who rides so free
  With sword and turban red,
The warrior-youth who earns his fee
  At peril of his head.

'At peril of his head,' said Wali Dad in English to me. 'Thanks to your Government, all our heads are protected, and with the educational facilities at my command' – his eyes twinkled wickedly – 'I might be a distinguished member of the local administration. Perhaps, in time, I might even be a member of a Legislative Council.'

'Don't speak English,' said Lalun, bending over her *sitar* afresh. The chorus went out from the City wall to the blackened wall of Fort Amara[16] which dominates the City. No man knows the precise extent of Fort Amara. Three kings built it hundreds of years ago, and they say that there are miles of underground rooms beneath its walls. It is peopled with many ghosts, a detachment of Garrison Artillery, and a Company of Infantry. In its prime it held ten thousand men and filled its ditches with corpses.

'At peril of his head,' sang Lalun again and again.

A head moved on one of the ramparts – the grey head of an old man – and a voice, rough as shark-skin on a sword-hilt, sent back the last line of the chorus and broke into a song that I could not understand, though Lalun and Wali Dad listened intently.

'What is it?' I asked. 'Who is it?'

'A consistent man,' said Wali Dad. 'He fought you in '46, when he was a warrior-youth; refought you in '57, and he tried to fight you in '71,[17] but you had learned the trick of blowing men from guns too well. Now he is old; but he would still fight if he could.'

'Is he a Wahabi,[18] then? Why should he answer to a Mahratta *laonee* if he be Wahabi – or Sikh?' said I.

'I do not know,' said Wali Dad. 'He has lost, perhaps, his religion. Perhaps he wishes to be a King. Perhaps he *is* a King. I do not know his name.'

'That is a lie, Wali Dad. If you know his career you must know his name.'

'That is quite true. I belong to a nation of liars. I would rather not tell you his name. Think for yourself.'

Lalun finished her song, pointed to the Fort, and said simply: 'Khem Singh.'

'Hm,' said Wali Dad. 'If the Pearl chooses to tell you, the Pearl is a fool.'

I translated to Lalun, who laughed. 'I choose to tell what I choose to tell. They kept Khem Singh in Burma,'[19] said she. 'They kept him there for many years until his mind was changed in him. So great was the kindness of the Government. Finding this, they sent him back to his own country that he might look upon it before he died. He is an old man, but when he looks upon this his country his memory will come. Moreover, there be many who remember him.'

'He is an Interesting Survival,' said Wali Dad, pulling at the pipe. 'He returns to a country now full of educational and political reform, but, as the Pearl says, there are many who remember him. He was once a great man. There will never be any more great men in India. They will all, when they are boys, go whoring after strange gods, and they will become citizens – "fellow-citizens" – "illustrious fellow-citizens". What is it that the native papers call them?'

Wali Dad seemed to be in a very bad temper. Lalun looked out of the window and smiled into the dust-haze. I went away thinking about Khem Singh, who had once made history with a thousand followers, and would have been a princeling but for the power of the Supreme Government aforesaid.

The Senior Captain Commanding Fort Amara was away on leave, but the Subaltern, his Deputy, had drifted down to the Club, where I found him and inquired of him whether it was really true that a political prisoner had been added to the attractions of the Fort. The Subaltern explained at great length, for this was the first time that he had held command of the Fort, and his glory lay heavy upon him.

'Yes,' said he, 'a man was sent in to me about a week ago from down the line – a thorough gentleman, whoever he is. Of course I did all I could for him. He had his two servants and some silver cooking-pots, and he looked for all the world like a native officer. I called him Subadar Sahib. Just as well to be on the safe side, y'know. "Look here, Subadar Sahib," I said, "you're handed over to my authority, and I'm supposed to guard you. Now I don't want to make your life hard, but you must make things easy for me. All the Fort is at your disposal, from the flagstaff to the dry Ditch, and I shall be happy to entertain you in any way I can, but you mustn't take advantage of it. Give me your word that you won't try to escape, Subadar Sahib, and I'll give you my word that you shall have no heavy guard put over you." I thought the best way of getting at him was by going at him straight, y'know; and it was, by Jove! The old man gave me his word, and moved about the Fort as contented as a sick crow. He's a rummy chap – always asking to be told where he is and what the buildings about him are. I had to sign a slip of blue paper when he turned up, acknowledging receipt of his body and all that, and I'm responsible, y'know, that he doesn't get away. Queer thing, though, looking after a Johnnie old enough to be your grandfather, isn't it? Come to the Fort one of these days and see him.'

For reasons which will appear, I never went to the Fort while Khem Singh was then within its walls. I knew him only as a grey head seen from Lalun's window – a grey head and a harsh voice. But natives told me that, day by day, as he looked upon the fair lands round Amara, his memory came back to him and, with it, the old hatred against the Government that had been nearly effaced in far-off Burma. So he raged up and down the West face of the Fort from morning till noon and from evening till the night, devising vain things in his heart, and croaking war-songs when Lalun sang on the City wall. As he grew more acquainted with the Subaltern he unburdened his old heart of some of the passions that had withered it. 'Sahib,' he used to say, tapping his stick against the parapet, 'when I was a young man I was one of twenty thousand horsemen who came out of the City and rode round the plain here. Sahib, I was the leader of a hundred, then of a thousand, then of five thousand, and now!' – he pointed to his two servants. 'But from the beginning to to-day I would cut the throats of all the Sahibs in the land if I could. Hold me fast, Sahib, lest I get away and return to those who would follow me. I forgot them when I was in Burma, but now that I am in my own country again, I remember everything.'

'Do you remember that you have given me your Honour not to make your tendance a hard matter?' said the Subaltern.

'Yes, to you, only to you, Sahib,' said Khem Singh. 'To you because you are of a pleasant countenance. If my turn comes again, Sahib, I will not hang you nor cut your throat.'

'Thank you,' said the Subaltern gravely, as he looked along the line of guns that could pound the City to powder in half an hour. 'Let us go into our own quarters, Khem Singh. Come and talk with me after dinner.'

Khem Singh would sit on his own cushion at the Subaltern's feet, drinking heavy, scented aniseed brandy in great gulps, and telling strange stories of Fort Amara, which had been a palace in the old days, of Begums and Ranees tortured to death – in the very vaulted chamber that now served as a mess-room; would tell stories of Sobraon[20] that made the Subaltern's cheeks flush and tingle with pride of race, and of the Kuka[21] rising from which so much was expected and the foreknowledge of which was shared by a hundred thousand souls. But he never told tales of '57 because, as he said, he was the Subaltern's guest, and '57 is a year that no man, Black or White, cares to speak of. Once only, when the aniseed brandy had slightly affected his head, he said: 'Sahib, speaking now of a matter which lay between Sobraon and the affair of the Kukas, it was ever a wonder to us that you stayed your hand at all, and that, having stayed it, you did not make the land one prison. Now I hear from without that you do great honour to all men of our country and by your own hands are destroying the Terror of your Name which is your strong rock and defence. This is a foolish thing. Will oil and water mix? Now in '57 –'

'I was not born then, Subadar Sahib,' said the Subaltern, and Khem Singh reeled to his quarters.

The Subaltern would tell me of these conversations at the Club, and my desire to see Khem Singh increased. But Wali Dad, sitting in the window-seat of the house on the City wall, said that it would be a cruel thing to do, and Lalun pretended that I preferred the society of a grizzled old Sikh to hers.

'Here is tobacco, here is talk, here are many friends and all the news of the City, and, above all, here is myself. I will tell you stories and sing you songs, and Wali Dad will talk his English nonsense in your ears. Is that worse than watching the caged animal yonder? Go to-morrow then, if you must, but to-day such-and-such an one will be here, and he will speak of wonderful things.'

It happened that To-morrow never came, and the warm heat of the latter Rains gave place to the chill of early October almost before I was aware of the flight of the year. The Captain Commanding the Fort returned from leave and took over charge of Khem Singh according to the laws of seniority. The Captain was not a nice man. He called all natives 'niggers', which, besides being extrème bad form, shows gross ignorance.

'What's the use of telling off two Tommies to watch that old nigger?' said he.

'I fancy it soothes his vanity,' said the Subaltern. 'The men are ordered to keep well out of his way, but he takes them as a tribute to his importance, poor old chap.'

'I won't have Line men taken off regular guards in this way. Put on a couple of Native Infantry.'

'Sikhs?' said the Subaltern, lifting his eyebrows.

'Sikhs, Pathans, Dogras – they're all alike, these black people,' and the Captain talked to Khem Singh in a manner which hurt that old gentleman's feelings. Fifteen years before, when he had been caught for the second time, every one looked upon him as a sort of tiger. He liked being regarded in this light. But he forgot that the world goes forward in fifteen years, and many Subalterns are promoted to Captaincies.

'The Captain-pig is in charge of the Fort?' said Khem Singh to his native guard every morning. And the native guard said: 'Yes, Subadar Sahib,' in deference to his age and his air of distinction; but they did not know who he was.

In those days the gathering in Lalun's little white room was always large and talked more than before.

'The Greeks,' said Wali Dad, who had been borrowing my books, 'the inhabitants of the city of Athens, where they were always hearing and telling some new thing, rigorously secluded their women – who were fools. Hence the glorious institution of the heterodox women[22] – is it not? – who were amusing and *not* fools. All the Greek philosophers delighted in their company. Tell me, my friend, how it goes now in Greece and the other places upon the Continent of Europe. Are your women-folk also fools?'

'Wali Dad,' I said, 'you never speak to us about your women-folk and we never speak about ours to you. That is the bar between us.'

'Yes,' said Wali Dad, 'it is curious to think that our common meeting-place should be here, in the house of a common – how do you call *her*?' He pointed with the pipe-mouth to Lalun.

'Lalun is nothing but Lalun,' I said, and that was perfectly true. 'But if you took your place in the world, Wali Dad, and gave up dreaming dreams –'

'I might wear an English coat and trousers. I might be a leading Mohammedan pleader. I might be received even at the Commissioner's tennis-parties where the English stand on one side and the natives on the other, in order to promote social intercourse throughout the Empire. Heart's Heart,' said he to Lalun quickly, 'the Sahib says that I ought to quit you.'

'The Sahib is always talking stupid talk,' returned Lalun with a laugh. 'In this house I am a Queen and thou art a King. The Sahib' – she put her arms above her head and thought for a moment – 'the Sahib shall be our Vizier – thine and mine, Wali Dad – because he has said that thou shouldst leave me.'

Wali Dad laughed immoderately, and I laughed too. 'Be it so,' said he. 'My friend, are you willing to take this lucrative Government appointment? Lalun, what shall his pay be?'

But Lalun began to sing, and for the rest of the time there was no hope of getting a sensible answer from her or Wali Dad. When the one stopped, the other began to quote Persian poetry with a triple pun in every other line. Some of it was not strictly proper, but it was all very funny, and it only came to an end when a fat person in black, with gold pince-nez, sent up his name to Lalun, and Wali Dad dragged me into the twinkling night to walk in a big rose-garden and talk heresies about Religion and Governments and a man's career in life.

The Mohurrum,[23] the great mourning-festival of the Mohammedans, was close at hand, and the things that Wali Dad said about religious fanaticism would have secured his expulsion from the loosest-thinking Muslim sect. There were the rose-bushes round us, the stars above us, and from every quarter of the City came the boom of the big Mohurrum drums. You must know that the City is divided in fairly equal proportions between the Hindus and the Mussulmans, and where both creeds belong to the fighting races, a big religious festival gives ample chance for trouble. When they can – that is to say, when the authorities are weak enough to allow it – the Hindus do their best to arrange some minor feast-day of their own in time to clash with the period of general mourning for the martyrs Hasan and Hussain, the heroes of the Mohurrum. Gilt and painted paper representations of their tombs are borne with shouting and wailing, music, torches, and yells, through the principal thoroughfares of the City; which fakements are called *tazias*. Their passage is rigorously laid down beforehand by the Police, and detachments of Police accompany each *tazia*, lest the Hindus should throw bricks at it and the peace of the Queen and the heads of Her loyal subjects should thereby be broken. Mohurrum time in a 'fighting' town means anxiety to all the officials, because, if a riot breaks out, the officials and not the rioters are held responsible. The former must foresee everything, and while not making their precautions ridiculously elaborate, must see that they are at least adequate.

'Listen to the drums!' said Wali Dad. 'That is the heart of the people – empty and making much noise. How, think you, will the Mohurrum go this year? *I* think that there will be trouble.'

He turned down a side-street and left me alone with the stars and a sleepy Police patrol. Then I went to bed and dreamed that Wali Dad had sacked the City and I was made Vizier, with Lalun's silver pipe for mark of office.

All day the Mohurrum drums beat in the City, and all day deputations of tearful Hindu gentlemen besieged the Deputy-Commissioner with assurances that they would be murdered ere next dawning by the Mohammedans. 'Which,' said the Deputy-Commissioner, in confidence to the Head of Police, 'is a pretty fair indication that the Hindus are going to make 'emselves unpleasant. I think we can arrange a little surprise for them. I have given the heads of both Creeds fair warning. If they choose to disregard it, so much the worse for them.'

There was a large gathering in Lalun's house that night, but of men that I had never seen before, if I except the fat gentleman in black with the gold pince-nez. Wali Dad lay in the window-seat, more bitterly scornful of his Faith and its manifestations than I had ever known him. Lalun's maid was very busy cutting up and mixing tobacco for the guests. We could hear the thunder of the drums as the processions accompanying each *tazia* marched to the central gathering-place in the plain outside the City, preparatory to their triumphant re-entry and circuit within the walls. All the streets seemed ablaze with torches, and only Fort Amara was black and silent.

When the noise of the drums ceased, no one in the white room spoke for a time. 'The first *tazia* has moved off,' said Wali Dad, looking to the plain.

'That is very early,' said the man with the pince-nez. 'It is only half-past eight.' The company rose and departed.

'Some of them were men from Ladakh,'[24] said Lalun, when the last had gone. 'They brought me brick-tea[25] such as the Russians sell, and a tea-urn from Peshawur. Show me, now, how the English Memsahibs make tea.'

The brick-tea was abominable. When it was finished Wali Dad suggested going into the streets. 'I am nearly sure that there will be trouble to-night,' he said. 'All the City thinks so, and *Vox Populi* is *Vox Dei*,[26] as the Babus say. Now I tell you that at the corner of the Padshahi Gate[27] you will find my horse all this night if you want to go about and to see things. It is a most disgraceful exhibition. Where is the pleasure of saying "*Ya Hasan! Ya Hussain!*" twenty thousand times in a night?'

All the processions – there were two-and-twenty of them – were now well within the City walls. The drums were beating afresh, the crowd were howling '*Ya Hasan! Ya Hussain!*' and beating their breasts, the brass bands were playing their loudest, and at every corner where space allowed, Mohammedan preachers were telling the lamentable story of the death of the Martyrs. It was impossible to move except with the crowd, for the streets were not more than twenty feet wide. In the Hindu quarters the shutters of all the shops were up and cross-barred. As the first *tazia*, a gorgeous erection, ten feet high, was borne aloft on the shoulders of a score of stout men into the semi-darkness of the Gully of the Horsemen, a brickbat crashed through its talc and tinsel sides.

'Into thy hands, O Lord!'[28] murmured Wali Dad profanely, as a yell went up from behind, and a native officer of Police jammed his horse through the crowd. Another brickbat followed, and the *tazia* staggered and swayed where it had stopped.

'Go on! In the name of the Sirkar,[29] go forward!' shouted the Policeman, but there was an ugly cracking and splintering of shutters, and the crowd halted, with oaths and growlings, before the house whence the brickbat had been thrown.

Then, without any warning, broke the storm – not only in the Gully of the Horsemen, but in half-a-dozen other places. The *tazias* rocked like ships at sea, the long pole-torches dipped and rose round them while the men shouted: 'The Hindus are dishonouring the *tazias*! Strike! strike! Into their temples for the Faith!' The six or eight Policemen with each *tazia* drew their batons, and struck as long as they could in the hope of forcing the mob forward, but they were overpowered, and as contingents of Hindus poured into the streets, the fight became general. Half a mile away where the *tazias* were yet untouched the drums and the shrieks of '*Ya Hasan! Ya Hussain!*' continued, but not for long. The priests at the corners of the streets knocked the legs from the bedsteads that supported their pulpits and smote for the Faith, while stones fell from the silent houses upon friend and foe, and the packed streets bellowed: '*Din! Din! Din!*' A *tazia* caught fire, and was dropped for a flaming barrier between Hindu and Mussulman at the corner of the Gully. Then the crowd surged forward, and Wali Dad drew me close to the stone pillar of a well.

'It was intended from the beginning!' he shouted in my ear, with more heat than blank unbelief should be guilty of. 'The bricks were carried up to the houses beforehand. These swine of Hindus! We shall be killing kine in their temples to-night!'

Tazia after *tazia*, some burning, others torn to pieces, hurried past us and the mob with them, howling, shrieking, and striking at the house doors in their flight. At last we saw the reason of the rush. Hugonin, the Assistant District Superintendent of Police, a boy of twenty, had got together thirty constables and was forcing the crowd through the streets. His old grey Police-horse showed no sign of uneasiness as it was spurred breast-on into the crowd, and the long dog-whip with which he had armed himself was never still.

'They know we haven't enough Police to hold 'em,' he cried as he passed me, mopping a cut on his face. 'They *know* we haven't! Aren't any of the men from the Club[30] coming down to help? Get on, you sons of burnt fathers!' The dog-whip cracked across the writhing backs, and the constables smote afresh with baton and gun-butt. With these passed the lights and the shouting, and Wali Dad began to swear under his breath. From Fort Amara shot up a single rocket; then two side by side. It was the signal for troops.

Petitt, the Deputy-Commissioner, covered with dust and sweat, but calm and gently smiling, cantered up the clean-swept street in rear of the main body of the rioters. 'No one killed yet,' he shouted. 'I'll keep 'em on the run till dawn! Don't let 'em halt, Hugonin! Trot 'em about till the troops come.'

The science of the defence lay solely in keeping the mob on the move. If they had breathing-space they would halt and fire a house, and then the work of restoring order would be more difficult, to say the least of it. Flames have the same effect on a crowd as blood has on a wild beast.

Word had reached the Club, and men in evening-dress were beginning to show themselves and lend a hand in heading off and breaking up the shouting masses with stirrup-leathers, whips, or chance-found staves. They were not very often attacked, for the rioters had sense enough to know that the death of a European would not mean one hanging but many, and possibly the appearance of the thrice-dreaded Artillery. The clamour in the City redoubled. The Hindus had descended into the streets in real earnest and ere long the mob returned. It was a strange sight. There were no *tazias* – only their riven platforms – and there were no Police. Here and there a City dignitary, Hindu or Mohammedan, was vainly imploring his co-religionists to keep quiet and behave themselves – advice for which his white beard was pulled. Then a native officer of Police, unhorsed but still using his spurs with effect, would be borne along, warning all the crowd of the danger of insulting the Government. Everywhere men struck aimlessly with sticks, grasping each other by the throat, howling and foaming with rage, or beat with their bare hands on the doors of the houses.

'It is a lucky thing that they are fighting with natural weapons,' I said to Wali Dad, 'else we should have half the City killed.'

I turned as I spoke and looked at his face. His nostrils were distended, his eyes were fixed, and he was smiting himself softly on the breast. The crowd poured by with renewed riot – a gang of Mussulmans hard pressed by some hundred Hindu fanatics. Wali

Dad left my side with an oath, and shouting: '*Ya Hasan! Ya Hussain!*' plunged into the thick of the fight, where I lost sight of him.

I fled by a side alley to the Padshahi Gate, where I found Wali Dad's horse, and thence rode to the Fort. Once outside the City wall, the tumult sank to a dull roar, very impressive under the stars and reflecting great credit on the fifty thousand angry able-bodied men who were making it. The troops who, at the Deputy-Commissioner's instance, had been ordered to rendezvous quietly near the Fort, showed no signs of being impressed. Two companies of Native Infantry, a squadron of Native Cavalry, and a company of British Infantry were kicking their heels in the shadow of the East face, waiting for orders to march in. I am sorry to say that they were all pleased, unholily pleased, at the chance of what they called 'a little fun'. The senior officers, to be sure, grumbled at having been kept out of bed, and the English troops pretended to be sulky, but there was joy in the hearts of all the subalterns, and whispers ran up and down the line: 'No ball-cartridge – what a beastly shame!' 'D'you think the beggars will really stand up to us?' 'Hope I shall meet my money-lender there. I owe him more than I can afford.' 'Oh, they won't let us even unsheath swords.' 'Hurrah! Up goes the fourth rocket. Fall in, there!'

The Garrison Artillery, who to the last cherished a wild hope that they might be allowed to bombard the City at a hundred yards' range, lined the parapet above the East gateway and cheered themselves hoarse as the British Infantry doubled along the road to the Main Gate of the City. The Cavalry cantered on to the Padshahi Gate, and the Native Infantry marched slowly to the Gate of the Butchers. The surprise was intended to be of a distinctly unpleasant nature, and to come on top of the defeat of the Police, who had been just able to keep the Mohammedans from firing the houses of a few leading Hindus. The bulk of the riot lay in the north and north-west wards. The east and south-east were by this time dark and silent, and I rode hastily to Lalun's house, for I wished to tell her to send some one in search of Wali Dad. The house was unlighted, but the door was open, and I climbed upstairs in the darkness. One small lamp in the white room showed Lalun and her maid leaning half out of the window, breathing heavily and evidently pulling at something that refused to come.

'Thou art late – very late,' gasped Lalun without turning her head. 'Help us now, O Fool, if thou hast not spent thy strength howling among the *tazias*. Pull! Nasiban and I can do no more! O Sahib, is it you? The Hindus have been hunting an old Mohammedan round the Ditch with clubs. If they find him again they will kill him. Help us to pull him up.'

I put my hands to the long red silk waist-cloth that was hanging out of the window, and we three pulled and pulled with all the strength at our command. There was something very heavy at the end, and it swore in an unknown tongue as it kicked against the City wall.

'Pull, oh, pull!' said Lalun at the last. A pair of brown hands grasped the window-sill and a venerable Mohammedan tumbled upon the floor, very much out of breath. His jaws were tied up, his turban had fallen over one eye, and he was dusty and angry.

Lalun hid her face in her hands for an instant and said something about Wali Dad that I could not catch.

Then, to my extreme gratification, she threw her arms round my neck and murmured pretty things. I was in no haste to stop her; and Nasiban, being a handmaiden of tact, turned to the big jewel-chest that stands in the corner of the white room and rummaged among the contents. The Mohammedan sat on the floor and glared.

'One service more, Sahib, since thou hast come so opportunely,' said Lalun. 'Wilt thou' – it is very nice to be thou-ed by Lalun – 'take this old man across the City – the troops are everywhere, and they might hurt him, for he is old – to the Kumharsen Gate?[31] There I think he may find a carriage to take him to his house. He is a friend of mine, and thou art – more than a friend – therefore I ask this.'

Nasiban bent over the old man, tucked something into his belt, and I raised him up and led him into the streets. In crossing from the east to the west of the City there was no chance of avoiding the troops and the crowd. Long before I reached the Gully of the Horsemen I heard the shouts of the British Infantry crying cheerily: '*Hutt*, ye beggars! *Hutt*, ye devils! Get along! Go forward, there!' Then followed the ringing of rifle-butts and shrieks of pain. The troops were banging the bare toes of the mob with their gun-butts – for not a bayonet had been fixed. My companion mumbled and jabbered as we walked on until we were carried back by the crowd and had to force our way to the troops. I caught him by the wrist and felt a bangle there – the iron bangle of the Sikhs – but I had no suspicions, for Lalun had only ten minutes before put her arms round me. Thrice we were carried back by the crowd, and when we made our way past the British Infantry it was to meet the Sikh Cavalry driving another mob before them with the butts of their lances.

'What are these dogs?' said the old man.

'Sikhs of the Cavalry, Father,' I said, and we edged our way up the line of horses two abreast and found the Deputy-Commissioner, his helmet smashed on his head, surrounded by a knot of men who had come down from the Club as amateur constables and had helped the Police mightily.

'We'll keep 'em on the run till dawn,' said Petitt. 'Who's your villainous friend?'

I had only time to say: 'The Protection of the Sirkar!' when a fresh crowd flying before the Native Infantry carried us a hundred yards nearer to the Kumharsen Gate, and Petitt was swept away like a shadow.

'I do not know – I cannot see – this is all new to me!' moaned my companion. 'How many troops are there in the City?'

'Perhaps five hundred,' I said.

'A lakh of men beaten by five hundred – and Sikhs among them! Surely, surely, I am an old man, but – the Kumharsen Gate is new. Who pulled down the stone lions? Where is the conduit? Sahib, I am a very old man, and, alas, I – I cannot stand.' He dropped in the shadow of the Kumharsen Gate where there was no disturbance. A fat gentleman wearing gold pince-nez came out of the darkness.

'You are most kind to bring my old friend,' he said suavely. 'He is a landholder of Akala. He should not be in a big City when there is religious excitement. But I have a carriage here. You are quite truly kind. Will you help me to put him into the carriage? It is very late.'

We bundled the old man into a hired victoria that stood close to the gate, and I turned back to the house on the City wall. The troops were driving the people to and fro, while the Police shouted, 'To your houses! Get to your houses!' and the dog-whip of the Assistant District Superintendent cracked remorselessly. Terror-stricken *bunnias*[32] clung to the stirrups of the Cavalry, crying that their houses had been robbed (which was a lie), and the burly Sikh horsemen patted them on the shoulder and bade them return to those houses lest a worse thing should happen. Parties of five or six British soldiers, joining arms, swept down the side-gullies, their rifles on their backs, stamping, with shouting and song, upon the toes of Hindu and Mussulman. Never was religious enthusiasm more systematically squashed; and never were poor breakers of the peace more utterly weary and footsore. They were routed out of holes and corners, from behind well-pillars and byres, and bidden to go to their houses. If they had no houses to go to, so much the worse for their toes.

On returning to Lalun's door I stumbled over a man at the threshold. He was sobbing hysterically and his arms flapped like the wings of a goose. It was Wali Dad, Agnostic and Unbeliever, shoeless, turbanless, and frothing at the mouth, the flesh on his chest bruised and bleeding from the vehemence with which he had smitten himself. A broken torch-handle lay by his side, and his quivering lips murmured, '*Ya Hasan! Ya Hussain!*' as I stooped over him. I pushed him a few steps up the staircase, threw a pebble at Lalun's City window and hurried home.

Most of the streets were very still, and the cold wind that comes before the dawn whistled down them. In the centre of the Square of the Mosque a man was bending over a corpse. The skull had been smashed in by gun-butt or bamboo-stave.

'It is expedient that one man should die for the people,' said Petitt grimly, raising the shapeless head. 'These brutes were beginning to show their teeth too much.'

And from afar we could hear the soldiers singing 'Two Lovely Black Eyes'[33] as they drove the remnant of the rioters within doors.

Of course you can guess what happened? I was not so clever. When the news went abroad that Khem Singh had escaped from the Fort, I did not, since I was then living this story, not writing it, connect myself, or Lalun, or the fat gentleman of the gold pince-nez, with his disappearance. Nor did it strike me that Wali Dad was the man who should have convoyed him across the City, or that Lalun's arms round my neck were put there to hide the money that Nasiban gave to Khem Singh, and that Lalun had used me and my white face as even a better safeguard than Wali Dad who proved himself so untrustworthy. All that I knew at the time was that, when Fort Amara was taken up with the riots, Khem Singh profited by the confusion to get away, and that his two Sikh guards also escaped.

But later on I received full enlightenment; and so did Khem Singh. He fled to those who knew him in the old days, but many of them were dead and more were changed, and all knew something of the Wrath of the Government. He went to the young men, but the glamour of his name had passed away, and they were entering native regiments or Government offices, and Khem Singh could give them neither pension, decorations, nor influence – nothing but a glorious death with their back to the mouth of a gun. He wrote letters and made promises, and the letters fell into bad hands, and a wholly insignificant subordinate officer of Police tracked them down and gained promotion thereby. Moreover, Khem Singh was old, and aniseed brandy was scarce, and he had left his silver cooking-pots in Fort Amara with his nice warm bedding, and the gentleman with the gold pince-nez was told by Those who had employed him that Khem Singh as a popular leader was not worth the money paid.

'Great is the mercy of these fools of English!' said Khem Singh when the situation was put before him. 'I will go back to Fort Amara of my own free will and gain honour. Give me good clothes to return in.'

So, at his own time, Khem Singh knocked at the wicket-gate of the Fort and walked to the Captain and the Subaltern, who were nearly grey-headed on account of correspondence that daily arrived from Simla marked 'Private'.

'I have come back, Captain Sahib,' said Khem Singh. 'Put no more guards over me. It is no good out yonder.'

A week later I saw him for the first time to my knowledge, and he made as though there were an understanding between us.

'It was well done, Sahib,' said he, 'and greatly I admired your astuteness in thus boldly facing the troops when I, whom they would have doubtless torn to pieces, was with you. Now there is a man in Fort Ooltagarh whom a bold man could with ease help to escape. This is the position of the Fort as I draw it on the sand –'

But I was thinking how I had become Lalun's Vizier after all.

Notes

These notes are particularly indebted to two publications of the Kipling Society: Roger Lancelyn Green and Alec Mason (eds.), *The Reader's Guide to Kipling's Works*, Vol. I (privately printed, 1961) and *The Kipling Journal*. In addition, reference has been made to the following: Charles Carrington, *Rudyard Kipling: His Life and Work* (London: Macmillan, 1955; Penguin Books, 1970); Rudyard Kipling, *Plain Tales from the Hills* (London: Macmillan, 1890; Penguin Books, 1987); Rudyard Kipling, *Life's Handicap* (London: Macmillan, 1891; Penguin Books, 1987); Rudyard Kipling, *The Jungle Books* (London: Macmillan, 1894; Penguin Books, 1987); Rudyard Kipling, *The Day's Work* (London: Macmillan, 1898; Penguin Books, 1988); Rudyard Kipling, *Kim* (London: Macmillan, 1901; Penguin Books, 1989); Rudyard Kipling, *Something of Myself* (London: Macmillan, 1936; Penguin Books, 1987); Thomas Pinney (ed.), *Kipling's India: Uncollected Sketches 1884–88* (London: Macmillan, 1986).

SOLDIERS THREE

The God from the Machine

First printed in *The Week's News*, 7 January 1888.

1. *The Inexpressibles:* apparently another name for the 'Ould Regiment' (see p. 31).
2. *a seven-pounder:* a light, wheeled field-piece, firing a 7lb shell.
3. *Private Mulvaney:* for an account of the three soldiers, see 'The Incarnation of Krishna Mulvaney', *Life's Handicap*. Mulvaney has been identified with Corporal MacNamara of the 5th Foot, whom Kipling met at Mian Mir in May 1885. (See *The Kipling Journal*, XI, 188 (December 1973), p. 2; but see also Appendix B.) From 1770 to 1857, over half the soldiers in the East India Company's 'European Regiments' were Irish; after 1857, seven out of the ten numbered battalions were Irish.

4. *Ord'ly-Room:* the court of the commanding officer, where charges brought against the men of his regiment are investigated and sentence passed.
5. *C.B.:* 'Confined to Barracks' as a punishment.
6. *the Fort Ditch:* forts were protected by ditches, even when they were inside the city walls. Lahore's fort had such a protective ditch.
7. *whip* me *on the peg:* punish me.
8. *thracked:* tracked (Kipling's representation of an Irish accent).
9. *fifteen years ago:* the time of narration is around 1885; this would date the incident narrated to about 1870.
10. *the Rig'mint:* he was then in 'The Tyrones' (see Appendix B).
11. *dhrill:* drill (instruction or participation in parade-ground exercises).
12. *Gosport:* town across the harbour from Portsmouth, used for Militia training.
13. *combs to be cut:* 'someone needs taking down a peg'. ('To cut someone's comb' means to lower someone's self-conceit.)
14. *menowdherin', and minandherin', an' blandandherin':* (Hiberno-English) menowdher (cf. French *minauder*), to put on affected expressions; blandandher (cf. Irish *blanndar*, dissimulation, flattery), to tempt by blandishment, to cajole. (See also pp. 40, 57 and 59.)
15. *like a Comm'ssariat bullock:* frightened. (The Commissariat is responsible for providing the Army with food and other supplies.)
16. *stamp wid their boots:* instead of clapping (to show approval).
17. *Aggra:* Agra, historic Mogul capital on the Jumna (see map, p. vii).
18. Sweethearts*:* a play by W.S. Gilbert, first performed at the Prince of Wales Theatre, London, on 7 November 1874. Since amateur performances date from 1878, this clashes with the chronology suggested in note 9 above.
19. *Spread Broom:* in fact, the hero of the play is called 'Spreadbarrow'. (Either Kipling or Mulvaney has misremembered.)
20. *death:* very keen, very strong.
21. ayah: from Portuguese *aia* (governess), the word exists in most Indian languages to mean either a lady's maid (as here) or a children's nurse or nanny.

22. *sootherin':* (Hiberno-English) cajoling or flattering.
23. *the theory av the flight:* Mulvaney puns on flight/trajectory and flight/elopement.
24. *Musk'thry:* each company and troop in the regiment went through an annual course of musketry under the regimental instructor. In addition to drill and practice, this involved the teaching of theory. The theory of musketry dates from the Franco-Prussian War: trajectories obviously became more important as rifles became capable of longer-range shooting.
25. Couples: perhaps Slingsby Lawrence's *A Cosy Couple* (first performed at the Lyceum in 1854).
26. *easin' the flag:* stealing the flag.
27. *Arrmy List:* monthly publication, issued by the War Office, containing the names of all the commissioned officers of the Army.
28. *the Gaff:* (slang) a public place of entertainment; a music-hall or theatre; (military slang) an entertainment arranged for soldiers.
29. *rampin':* standing on its hind legs.
30. *through Athlone:* allusion unidentified. Athlone is a district in Co. Westmeath, Ireland.
31. *Jezebel:* see 1 Kings 16.31–21.25 and 2 Kings 9.7–37.
32. Bote acchy: (Hind. *bahut achch'ha*) very good.
33. pechy: (Hind. *pichhe*) later.
34. baito: (Hind.) sit, sit down.
35. sart: (Hind. *sath*) with me.
36. Hitherao: (Hind. *Idharo*) come here.
37. sais: (Hind. *syce*) a groom.
38. dekkoed: from imperative of Hind. *deckna*, to look, used here to mean 'seen'; marrow: (Hind.) beat; sumjao: imperative of Hind. *samjhana*, to cause to know, used here to mean 'recognize'.
39. *a caution:* something out of the common, wonderful or surprising.
40. bukshish: (Hind. *bakhshish*) a tip.
41. Hutt: (Hind.) go away, get away.
42. gharri: (Hind. *gari*) cart or carriage.
43. tikka: from Hind. *thika* (hire, fare, fixed price), an adjective applied to any person or thing engaged by the job; hence *thika gari*, hired carriage, abbreviated as here.

44. owin' *an'* fere-owin': coming and going.
45. mut-walla: (Hind. *muthwalla*) drunk, intoxicated.
46. *cantonmints:* cantonments, military stations in India, usually built on the plan of a standing camp.
47. *scutt:* term of contempt (variant of 'scout').
48. *blazin' copped:* very drunk when caught.

Private Learoyd's Story

First published in *The Week's News*, 14 July 1888. The epigraph is taken from the Jatakas. For more about the Jatakas, see P.L. Caracciolo, 'Buddhist Teaching Stories and their Influence on Conrad, Wells and Kipling', *The Conradian*, XI.1 (May 1986), 24–34. For Learoyd's home life in Yorkshire as a young miner, his wooing of a Methodist minister's daughter, and his enlistment at her death, see 'On Greenhow Hill', *Life's Handicap*.

1. pipal: (Hind.) the *Ficus religiosa*, one of the great fig-trees of India.
2. *Houdin pullets:* French breed of poultry.
3. *neat-handed dog-stealers:* in *Something of Myself*, Kipling recalls his friendship with the 31st East Surrey Regiment in Lahore, whom he describes as 'a London-recruited confederacy of skilful dog-stealers' (Penguin Books, p. 65). Ortheris, in 'The Madness of Private Ortheris', describes himself as a 'dog-stealin' Tommy' (*Plain Tales from the Hills*, Penguin Books, p. 243). There is perhaps also an allusion to 'neat-handed Phyllis' of Milton's 'L'Allegro'.
4. *niche:* below the well-wheel and between its supports.
5. *tykes:* dogs.
6. '*little stuff*' bird-shop: see 'The Madness of Private Ortheris', where Ortheris expresses regret that he had not 'married that gal' and sold 'little stuffed birds' in a shop in Hammersmith High Street (Penguin Books, p. 243).
7. *a Central India line:* see 'The Big Drunk Draf'' (pp. 28–36 below). Mulvaney is compared with Ulysses as traveller, trickster and perhaps also as married man.
8. *Hewrasian:* Kipling's representation of the Cockney pronunciation of 'Eurasian' (a person of mixed European and Asian descent).

9. *Cantonment Magistrate:* the official responsible for the administration of the cantonment.
10. *one o' t' Ten Commandments:* in fact, the Tenth Commandment. See Deuteronomy 5.7–21.
11. *addled his brass i' jute:* made his money in sacking.
12. *t' Widdy:* the Widow (i.e. Queen Victoria). Prince Albert died in 1861, and Victoria spent the next ten years in gloomy seclusion.
13. *a-tewin':* (dialect) 'to tew' means 'to bustle'.
14. *dry swimmin'-bath:* a tank.
15. *pariah dogs: paraiyar* (Tamil) was the name of a low caste in Southern India; in English parlance, 'pariah' was used to mean a social outcast. Learoyd is referring to the common, ownerless dog of India.
16. *agaate:* (Northern dialect) 'agoing', in motion.
17. *swagger-cane:* a short stick carried by soldiers when walking out. See the cover of the Indian Railway Library edition of *Soldiers Three* (p. 5).
18. *sheep's eyes:* looks of admiration and wistfulness.
19. *Munsoorie Pahar:* the Himalayan hill-station of Mussoorie in Uttar Pradesh (*pahar* (Hind.), hill). (For both Mussoorie and Rawalpindi, see map, p. vii.)
20. *Canteen plug:* a stick of compressed tobacco (to be sliced up for smoking) supplied by the Army canteen.
21. *t' Andamning Islands:* the Andaman Islands, a group of islands in the Bay of Bengal used as a penal settlement during the Raj. In Arthur Conan Doyle's *The Sign of Four*, Jonathan Small's narrative describes his time as a convict on one of the Andaman Islands, 'digging and ditching and yam-planting' in 'a dreary, fever-stricken place'.
22. *Hamilton's:* a jeweller's in Simla.
23. *Sitha:* (archaic/dialect) 'See thou'.
24. *duff:* (Northern dialect) dough.
25. *bad cess to him:* (Hiberno-English) may evil befall him.
26. *ringstraked:* having bands of colour around the body (cf. Genesis 31.8–12).
27. *Royal Academies:* the Royal Academy, Piccadilly. Learoyd's 'animal painting' is a punning allusion to paintings of animals as a pictorial genre.

28. *Howrah:* the main station in Calcutta.
29. *melted:* (slang) 'blew', spent.
30. *Father Victor:* he is described in *Kim* as 'the Roman Catholic Chaplain of the Irish contingent' (Penguin Books, 1989, p. 133), and he arranges for Kim's education at St Xavier's in Partibus, Lucknow. He is briefly referred to in 'The Solid Muldoon' and 'Black Jack'.
31. *Pindi:* Rawalpindi.

The Big Drunk Draf'

First published in *The Week's News*, 24 March 1888. The epigraph is taken from the poem 'Trooping'. Chronologically, this is the last of the stories about Mulvaney.

1. Serapis: one of the three Government transports. The others were the *Jumna* and the *Crocodile.*
2. *time-expired:* non-commissioned officers and men signed on for a fixed period of service.
3. *eighty-five rupees a month:* compare the Simla dinner in *The Story of the Gadsbys*, which is 'carefully calculated to scale of Rs. 6000 per mensem'.
4. *Sahib:* title by which British men (and Europeans generally) were addressed throughout India.
5. sisham: (Hind. *sisu*, *sisun* and *shisham*) one of the most useful timber trees in India, used for furniture, construction-work, boat- and carriage-building. See Kipling's 'A Week in Lahore', *Civil and Military Gazette*, 7 May 1884; reprinted in Thomas Pinney (ed.), *Kipling's India: Uncollected Sketches 1884–1888*, pp. 32–6.
6. *a fresh peg:* another drink. In India at this time, it would probably be a brandy and soda.
7. *grey garron:* a small horse, bred in Ireland or Scotland.
8. *bahadherin':* from *bahadur* (Hind.), hero, champion; 'playing the bahadur', acting as boss.
9. *hoppers:* earth-carriers.
10. *jildiest:* from *jildi* (Hind.), fast; 'fastest'.
11. *powtherin':* (Hiberno-English) hurrying, rushing.
12. *the Blue Lights:* the Army Temperance Association. 1887 was the year of Queen Victoria's Golden Jubilee.

13. *Phoebus Apollonius:* the Greek god, Phoebus Apollo, who is usually represented naked. The story of Horker Kelley has not been told.
14. *Articles av War:* with the Mutiny Act, the Articles of War formed the code of laws which governed the British Army.
15. *a Solomon:* Solomon, as King of Israel, was famous for his wisdom and judgment. See 1 Kings 3.5–28.
16. *a Kibbereen horse-fair:* unidentified. Skibbereen is a market-town in Cork.
17. *copped:* drunk.
18. *an Orange Lodge:* named after William of Orange (William III), the Protestant opposer of James II in the Glorious Revolution of 1689, Orange Lodges were formed among northern Ireland Protestants to uphold the Protestant succession. The first regular lodges were founded in 1795, although the system existed earlier.
19. *stretched:* knocked down.
20. *O'Connell:* presumably an allusion to Daniel O'Connell 'the Liberator' (1775–1847). An outstanding speaker at the Irish bar and M.P. from 1828, O'Connell formed the Catholic Association as a national movement and campaigned successfully for the removal of Catholic disabilities.
21. *Lungtungpen nakid:* see 'The Taking of Lungtungpen' in *Plain Tales from the Hills.* The name suggests Burma, although it is not in fact a Burmese place-name.
22. *the throoper's into blue wather:* 'the troopship is in the open sea'.
23. *shiverarium:* (nonce-word) panic.
24. *non-coms:* non-commissioned officers (corporals and sergeants).
25. *squidgereen:* from 'squidger' (Cockney: 'sparrow') and the diminutive '-een'.
26. *wore:* from 'to wear' (used of sheep), i.e. 'to conduct gradually (into an enclosure)'.
27. *the thriangles:* a framework upon which men were tied, arms outstretched and legs apart, for flogging. Biting 'on a bullet' would be to avoid crying out with pain.
28. *like jackals:* i.e. with tails between their legs.
29. *Revelly:* reveille, the morning signal given to soldiers (usually by drum or bugle) to waken them and get them up.

30. *tucker:* apparently a back-formation from the Americanism 'tuckered out'.
31. *a mud-tipper:* a navvy.
32. *three fingers:* the breadth of a finger used as a measure of alcohol.

The Solid Muldoon

First published in *The Week's News*, 9 June 1888. The title appears to be taken from a Minstrel song, 'Muldoon, the Solid Man', written by Edward Harrigan. Harrigan was also part-author of 'The Mulligan Guards', the regimental march of the 'Mavericks' (see *Kim*, Chapter 5). The epigraph is from 'John Malone' by Robert Buchanan (1841–1901), who also supplied the epigraph to 'Black Jack'.

1. *Rampur hounds:* dogs like coarse greyhounds but with a heavier head.
2. *Malham Cove:* in the Yorkshire Dales, near the village of Malham.
3. *Pateley Brigg:* Pateley Bridge, a town in the Nidd valley in the West Riding of Yorkshire.
4. *cutty:* a short clay pipe.
5. *nullah:* (Hind. *nala*) a watercourse; here, the Ditch.
6. *down the muzzle:* i.e. confusing a breech-loader (using cartridges) with the earlier muzzle-loader.
7. *whin I was a Corp'ril:* before his marriage to Dinah Shadd. See 'The Courting of Dinah Shadd' in *Life's Handicap*.
8. *sinthry-go:* sentry-duty.
9. *a pewter:* a beer-tankard; i.e. to have a drink.
10. *stripped to him:* in order to fight him.
11. *Almorah:* Almore is the name of a district in the foothills near Rampur and of a hill-station near Ranikhet. Kirpa Tal is unidentified. Mulvaney's pursuit of Annie Bragin is mentioned again in 'The Courting of Dinah Shadd'.
12. *a long picket:* the elongated rifle-bullet fired by the Martini-Henri.
13. *O'Hara:* O'Hara and his relations with married women feature in 'Black Jack'.
14. *a Dhrum-Major:* a non-commissioned officer in charge of the drummers.

15. *as white as my belt:* Mulvaney's belt was pipe-clayed white.
16. *a cooper roun' a cask:* to fix the hoops to the staves, the cask is stood on end and the cooper walks round it hammering.
17. *the Corner Shop:* the cells.
18. *the Tyrone:* Mulvaney was with the Tyrones after the change-over to the Martini in 1874/75 (see 'Black Jack'); Flahy must have joined the Tyrones later – or Mulvaney would have recognized him. On the other hand, this story takes place before Mulvaney's marriage to Dinah Shadd and his reduction to the ranks, which must have been in the early 1870s. His marriage to Dinah Shadd seems to have taken place six or seven years after he joined the Army ('The Courting of Dinah Shadd'), while in 'The Incarnation of Krishna Mulvaney' there is a reference to 'his little son, dead many years ago' (*Life's Handicap*, Penguin Books, p. 51). See Appendix B: Mulvaney's Career.

With the Main Guard

First published in *The Week's News*, 4 August 1888. The epigraph is taken from 'Breitman in Bivouac' by Charles Leland (1824–1903). See Ann M. Weygandt, *Kipling's Reading and Its Influence on His Poetry*, for Kipling's other references to Leland; and *The Kipling Journal*, 123 (October 1957), p. 10. The Uhlanen were originally Polish light cavalry armed with a lance. Carrington has sought to identify the battle at 'Silver's Theatre' with the defeat of a British column at Maiwand, near Kandahar, on 27 July 1880 (*The Kipling Journal*, 132 (December 1959), pp. 13–16); F.E. Stafford, on the other hand, describes Kipling's account as 'not only militarily incomprehensible, but farcical', instancing in particular the decision to abandon a dominating position in order to engage in hand-to-hand fighting in a nullah (*The Kipling Journal*, 216 (December 1980), p. 27).

1. *Fort Amara:* in 'On the City Wall', Fort Amara is very clearly Fort Lahore. See p. 159; also *The Kipling Journal*, 39 (September 1936), where the frontispiece is an illustration of the main gate.
2. *tivvy-tivvy:* cf. Bengali *dhiv-dhiv*, an onomatopoeic term for the throbbing of the heart.

3. *Martini:* the Martini-Henri rifle, issued in India in 1875.
4. *dust-devils:* a sand-storm.
5. *glacis:* an artificial slope of earth in front of works, designed to provide a clear field of fire against attacking forces.
6. *Machiavel:* Niccolò Machiavelli, secretary to the Republic of Florence from 1490 to 1512 and author of *The Prince*, a treatise on statecraft, came to represent the type of the amoral schemer.
7. *Mulvaney:* see 'The Madness of Private Ortheris' in *Plain Tales from the Hills*.
8. *slinging loose:* acting recklessly.
9. *Faynians:* Fenians, members of an organization, originally founded among the Irish of North America, dedicated to Irish independence. See 'The Mutiny of the Mavericks', *Life's Handicap*, written October 1889, which begins with information about the Fenians given by the spy Le Caron to the Parnell Commission.
10. *Paythans:* Pathans; the name given during the Raj to the Afghans, especially those permanently settled in India or dwelling in the borderland on the Punjab frontier.
11. *Ghuzni:* Ghazni, a small town on the Kabul–Kandahar road. Mulvaney is probably referring to the battle at Ahmed Khel on 19 April 1880 during the Second Afghan War: the British left Kandahar on 30 March and reached Ghazni on 22 April. He refers to both Ahmed Khel and Maiwand in 'The Three Musketeers' (*Plain Tales from the Hills*, Penguin Books, p. 89).
12. *Silver's Theatre:* Dublin had three patent theatres (the Gaiety, the Queen's and the Theatre Royal); Silver's Theatre is presumably a Dublin music-hall. See the reference to 'the Dublin dock-rat' and 'the lessee av Silver's Theatre' (p. 55). See also Mulvaney's more detailed account of Silver and his theatre in 'The Courting of Dinah Shadd', *Life's Handicap* (Penguin Books, 1987, p. 61).
13. *Scotchies . . . Gurkys:* the 72nd and 92nd Highlanders and the 2nd and 5th Gurkhas took part in this campaign. The 92nd Highlanders and the 2nd Gurkhas captured guns together on the Baba Wali Kotal; the 72nd Highlanders and the 5th Gurkhas exchanged presents after the campaign to commemorate it.

14. *Captain O'Neil:* also mentioned in Kipling's 'Ballad of Boh da Thone', an episode which took place after the Afghan War. In the ballad, he is described as an officer of the Black Tyrone, whereas here he is an officer in the Ould Regiment.
15. *Dromeen Fair:* this might refer to either Dromin in Louth, thirty-five miles north of Dublin, or Dromin near Limerick.
16. *Brother Inner Guard:* the title of the man on the door of the Lodge during Masonic ceremonies. Kipling's account of the hand-to-hand fighting up to this point is covertly underpinned by the Five Points of Fellowship of the initiation ceremony into Freemasonry: 'hand to hand', 'foot to foot', 'knee to knee', 'breast to breast' and 'hand over back'.
17. *the Vic.:* the Victoria Music-Hall on the Waterloo Bridge Road, London (which subsequently became the 'Old Vic').
18. *compot from the lef' flank:* presumably the obsolete sense of compot ('reckoning') rather than the more recent compote ('fruit salad') to describe the effect of Ortheris's rifle-fire. For 'opened out', see note 26 below.
19. *one year in store:* not applicable to the propellants of the Mulvaney period. The first year would make no difference to cordite, which takes a longer period to deteriorate.
20. *Hot or cowld:* fire-arm or cold steel.
21. *the depôt:* regimental headquarters.
22. *Donegal Bay:* on the north-west coast of Ireland.
23. *Haymakers' Lift:* a short-arm grip for tossing a heavy pitchfork of hay high on to a wagon.
24. *Clonmel:* county-town on the River Suir in the south of Ireland. The true motive for the Sergeant's behaviour is suggested in 'Love o' Women' in *Many Inventions.*
25. *an asp on a leaf:* presumably the aspen leaf (the 'trembling poplar') is intended.
26. *Opin ordher! Double!:* 'open order' means leaving gaps between soldiers of six feet in files (front to rear) and twelve feet in ranks (side to side). 'Double' indicates at double the usual marching pace. The command has been given because of the widening of the valley, but it also signals the re-assertion of military discipline after the 'fog of fighting'.
27. *a Roshus:* Quintus Roscius Gallus (*c.*126–62 B.C.), the Roman

actor, who was praised for his grace and elegance on stage and became the type of the great actor.

28. *butchers' steels:* the steel rods used by butchers to sharpen their knives, usually worn hanging from a belt.
29. *a soldier's cloak:* from a popular ballad 'The Sentry Box' (see bottom of p. 58).
30. *the Three Musketeers:* an allusion to the famous romance by Alexandre Dumas. Kipling had borrowed the title for the story 'The Three Musketeers', *Civil and Military Gazette*, 11 March 1887 (collected in *Plain Tales from the Hills*), in which he had introduced his three soldiers.
31. *the Morning Gun:* the gun fired to announce daybreak.

In the Matter of a Private

First published in *The Week's News*, 14 April 1888. This is a sequel to 'The Daughter of the Regiment' in *Plain Tales from the Hills*. It should also be compared with 'The Madness of Private Ortheris' in the same volume for its representation of the intolerable strain of the soldiers' lives. If the epigraph is by Kipling, the poem has not been collected.

1. *per diem:* (Latin) per day, each day.
2. *Thomas in bulk:* Thomas Atkins, the name given to a fictitious soldier on sample documents (War Office Circular, 31 August 1815; War Office Circular, 30 June 1830; King's Regulations, 1837); immortalized by Kipling as the typical British foot-soldier. The Indian Railway Library editions of *Soldiers Three* were dedicated to 'that very strong man, T. Atkins, Private of the Line'.
3. *a Martini from a Snider:* Jacob Snider converted the muzzle-loading Enfield into a breech-loader; the Snider with its hinged block was replaced by the Martini-Henry, which combined Martini's 'falling-block' breech mechanism with Henry's rifled barrel. See also 'Black Jack', note 29, below.
4. *'a brutal and licentious soldiery':* in a 1783 debate on India, Edmund Burke referred to 'a rapacious and licentious soldiery'; in 1796 Thomas Erskine improved the phrase to 'the uncontrolled licentiousness of a brutal and insolent soldiery'. The

phrase reappears in 'The Courting of Dinah Shadd', *Life's Handicap*.

5. *and elsewhere:* see 'The Daughter of the Regiment', *Plain Tales from the Hills*.
6. '*eeklar*'*:* i.e. éclat: distinction.
7. *eight in the morning:* F.E. Stafford has objected to this depiction of the life of the British Army in India: 'no military unit in India or anywhere else would function like this' (*The Kipling Journal*, XLVII, p. 28). There would be training, guards, fatigues, exercise, and arms and equipment to clean.
8. *punkah-coolies:* servants who operated the ceiling fans.
9. *Temperance Room:* later called the Reading Room. The existence of a Temperance Room reflects Lord Roberts's attempt to reduce the consumption of beer in the Army.
10. so-oor: pig. According to Kipling's father, 'Suar is universally considered the vilest word in all the copious abuse vocabulary of the country' (*Beast and Man in India*, London, 1891).
11. *on the tapes:* tapes of the charpoy (the bed). The wooden frame of the charpoy is criss-crossed by cotton tapes.
12. *unprofitable to him:* cf. *Hamlet*, I.ii.133–4: 'How weary, stale, flat, and unprofitable/Seem to me all the uses of this world!'. Significantly, these lines occur in the soliloquy in which Hamlet contemplates 'self-slaughter'.
13. *Last Post:* the bugle-call that gives notice of the hour of retiring (also used at funerals).
14. *C.B.:* Companion of the Order of the Bath.
15. *the Infantry Mess:* presumably the Officers' Mess is intended.
16. *the Towheads:* i.e. some other regiment (the nickname conceals their identity).
17. *Horse Battery:* a division of artillery in which the gunners are carried on horseback.
18. *spangled:* wearing medals and/or gold lace.
19. *all's well:* part of the exchange used by a soldier on guard.
20. *Sheeny:* (derogatory term) Jewish.
21. *Gonds:* a tribal people of Central India.
22. *as high as Haman:* literally 50 cubits high (see Esther 7.9–10), but this is merely a way of saying 'well and truly hanged'.

23. *hollow square:* the troops are drawn up in square formation with an open space in the centre and with the men facing inwards.

Black Jack

First published in *Soldiers Three*, Indian Railway Library, 1888. The epigraph is taken from 'The Wake of Tim O'Hara', *London Poems* (1866), by Robert Buchanan. In the three editions published in the Indian Railway Library, this story began with the following paragraph, which was omitted from the first English edition onwards:

> There is a writer called Mr Robert Louis Stevenson, who makes most delicate inlay-work in black and white, and files out to the fraction of a hair. He has written a story about a Suicide Club, wherein men gambled for Death because other amusements did not bite sufficiently. My friend Private Mulvaney knows nothing about Mr Stevenson, but he once assisted informally at a meeting of almost such a club as that gentleman has described; and his words are true.

Kipling was perhaps familiar with the case of Private George Flaxman, who was executed at Lucknow in front of the battalion on 10 January 1887 for the murder of a Lance-Sergeant: Flaxman and two other soldiers had dealt out a pack of cards and the one who received the ace of spades had to commit the murder.

1. *Corner Shop:* the cells.
2. crescendo . . . diminuendo*:* (*Latin*) 'growing . . . diminishing'.
3. *for certain hours:* compare Hamlet's father's ghost, which was 'doomed for a certain term to walk the night' (*Hamlet, I. v. 10*].
4. *Board School:* the free public education school of the time.
5. *my C'mission:* promotion to the position of officer.
6. *kiddy:* box or tub for mess stores.
7. *'arf Rampur:* its mother was a Rampur hound. (See 'The Solid Muldoon', note 1.)
8. *Bridge of Boats:* a bridge built from military pontoons.
9. *mess-man:* Roger Lancelyn Green observes that it is 'not clear why there should be a mess-man, if it was available for the public a khansamah would be expected and a chowkidar (a steward and watchman)'.
10. *the Black Dog:* melancholy, depression.

11. *five shillin' a week:* maintenance from the putative father (i.e. Mulvaney implies that Mullins was illegitimate).
12. *Wot's the odds:* this is presumably a music-hall comedian's catch-phrase. It seems to have originated in the 1850s: see *Punch*, 25 September 1852, where the answer is 'Ten to one in your favour'. It occurs in Du Maurier's *Trilby* (1894) and also in *Stalky & Co.* ('In Ambush').
13. *'The Lord . . . taketh awai':* Job 1.21, used in the Burial Service.
14. *O'Hara . . . Rafferty:* see 'The Solid Muldoon'.
15. *to desert:* see 'The Madness of Private Ortheris', *Plain Tales from the Hills.*
16. *the woman at Devizes:* Devizes is a market-town in Wiltshire. The incident occurred in 1753: a woman who had committed perjury fell down dead. A memorial was erected to point the moral.
17. *Artillery troughs:* to water the horses that pull the guns.
18. *blood-dhrawn calf:* a calf drained of blood to make veal of a pale colour.
19. *presarve me formashin:* keep me straight.
20. *guard-room gong:* alarm for the guard to turn out.
21. *an unruly mimber:* the tongue. This is a common misquotation from James 3.5 and 8: 'The tongue is a little member . . . it is an unruly evil.'
22. *Shpoil Five:* card-game, 'Spoil Five'.
23. *palammers:* playing-cards.
24. *the mess av an egg:* the uncooked white of an egg.
25. *Jooty thrippence:* duty of threepence per pack remained until the 1960 Budget; a stamp for this amount is apparently stuck on the ace of spades.
26. *new to the Rig'mint:* the Martini-Henry was adopted by the Army from 1871, but it was not on general issue in India until 1874–5. It was replaced in 1888 by the Lee-Metford rifle, with its box-magazine for cartridges, which in turn gave way to an improved version, the Lee-Enfield.
27. *a Snider:* the Snider did not eject; it had to be turned upside down for the cartridge to fall out. (See also 'In the Matter of a Private', note 3 above.)
28. *dhirt hung on the groovin'*: i.e. the rifling was full of greasy powder.

29. *the pin av the fallin'-block:* the Martini-Henry replaced the hinged block of the Snider with a falling-block mechanism, which drove the fire-pin or piston into the percussion cap at the base of the cartridge. The falling-block was housed in the receiver, a strong steel frame enclosing the action and connecting the rifle barrel to the butt. The rear of the block pivoted on a pin, but, with the pin removed, the block could not have been dislodged, since the extractor, the trigger-guard plate and the cocking-piece would have prevented it from moving forwards. For a full and detailed explanation, see M.C. Jones, 'Gun Lore', *The Kipling Journal*, LVII, 225 (March 1983), 39–41. Jones concludes that 'Kipling was unfamiliar with the workings of the Martini-Henry' (p.40), because it is unlikely, if not impossible, for the falling-block to spring out of a Martini-Henry in the way this story requires.
30. dooli: (Hind. *doli*) a cot suspended by the four corners from a bamboo pole and carried by two or four men as a stretcher.
31. *four fifteen:* 4 rupees 15 annas.
32. *aisin' the pull*: making the trigger responsive to lighter pressure.

IN BLACK AND WHITE

Dray Wara Yow Dee

First published in *The Week's News*, 28 April 1888. The title is Pushtu for 'All three are one'. Kipling's account of the Sultan Serai and the horse-dealer Afzul, published under the title 'A Week in Lahore' in the *Civil and Military Gazette*, 19 January 1886 (reprinted in *Kipling's India*, pp. 141–6), appears to have contributed not only to the depiction of Mahbub Ali in *Kim* but also to the narrator of this story.

1. *Kabul:* capital of Afghanistan.
2. *thirteen-three:* thirteen and three-quarter hands; about four feet seven inches at the shoulder.
3. *Holy Kurshed and the Blessed Imams:* Khurshid, the last Dabuyid prince, reigned in Tabaristan from 740 to 761 A.D. Imam ('leader') is the title given to patriarchs or priests in Islam.

Originally the Imam was the Prophet himself or, in his absence, someone authorized by him. After his death, the title was given to his successors (the caliphs) or their delegates. It is the title given to the heads of the four orthodox sects, but also to the ordinary functionary of the mosque who leads the congregation in daily prayers.

4. *the Tirah:* mountain area west of Peshawur (see map, p. vii).
5. *picket-room:* a room to picket horses.
6. *Jumrud:* a fort about eleven miles west of Peshawur, on the road to the Khyber Pass.
7. *His Prophet:* Mohammed (570–632), the founder of Islam.
8. *double the felts:* to prevent the horses from taking cold.
9. *Pubbi:* between Peshawur and Nowshera.
10. *Kurdistan:* mountainous area between Iran, Turkey, Iraq and Armenia.
11. *Kashmir Serai:* Kipling's name for the Sultan Serai, a meeting-place for pilgrims and caravans, a 'huge open square over against the railway station, surrounded with arched cloisters' (*Kim*, Penguin Books, p. 65), in the northern part of Lahore. For a photograph, see *The Kipling Journal*, LVII, 227 (September 1983), p. 44.
12. *the Amir:* Abdur Rahman, the Amir of Kabul, the ruler of Afghanistan. See 'To Meet the Ameer', *Civil and Military Gazette*, 7 and 8 April 1885 (reprinted in *Kipling's India*, pp. 95–104).
13. fifteen *tolls:* barriers where tax is levied. In his account of the Sultan Serai ('A Week in Lahore'), Kipling lists seven tolls from Kabul to Dakka and the price levied per horse.
14. *Dakka:* a town in Afghanistan not far from the Khyber Pass.
15. *Balkh:* a town 200 miles north of Kabul on the northern frontier of Afghanistan (see map, p. vii).
16. *Mahbub Ali:* the name of the famous horse-dealer in *Kim*.
17. *Kohat:* a district and town in the North-West Frontier Province to the south of Peshawur.
18. *Ismail-ki-Dhera:* perhaps another way of saying Dhera Ismail Khan, a town on the River Indus in the North-West Frontier Province, due west of Lahore.
19. *Bokhariot:* made in Bokhara, a Russian district north of Afghanistan.

20. *Pakpattan:* a town in the Montgomery district to the south of the Punjab.
21. *a double burden:* i.e. in foal.
22. *the Thana:* (Hind.) the police-post.
23. *blackened my face:* insulted me.
24. *Afridi:* the frontier people who live in the Kharber Valley or the Bazar and Bara Valleys, south-west of Peshawur.
25. *Allah-al-Mumit:* one of the ninety-nine names of God; significantly, this means 'The Killer', not 'The Dispenser of Justice'.
26. *snow-water:* i.e. from melted snow.
27. *the Abazai:* a border people, occupying territory to the north of Peshawur.
28. *Ghor:* mountainous country, now included in Afghanistan, between the Helmand Valley and Herat.
29. *Rahman:* another of the ninety-nine names of God ('The Merciful').
30. *the Uzbegs:* a Turkish people; Kipling records his own encounter with the Amir's Uzbeg lancers in 'To Meet the Ameer', *Civil and Military Gazette*, 7 April 1885 (reprinted in *Kipling's India*, pp. 95–7).
31. *from the Fakr to the Isha:* the Isha is the Night Prayer; 'Fakr' is perhaps a mistake for 'al-Fajr' ('The Daybreak'), Surah LXXXIX of the Qur'an.
32. *Little Malikand:* about forty miles north of Peshawur.
33. *Cherat:* a town about twenty-five miles south-east of Peshawur.
34. *Trust not the incapable:* perhaps Surah XI.116 ('Lean not on the evil-doers') or Surah XLV.17 ('Follow not the wishes of those who are devoid of knowledge').
35. *a heel-rope:* a rope with which horses' legs are fastened to prevent them kicking.
36. *the Kabul River:* flows easterly from Kabul to north of Peshawur.
37. *the Devil Atala . . . Gurel:* unidentified.
38. *charpoy:* (Hind. *charpai*) the common, lightweight Indian wooden bedstead.
39. *the Bombay Tramway Company:* Afzul, Kipling's informant in the Sultan Serai, told him that he had two regular customers, the Calcutta and Bombay Tramway Companies: 'The Calcutta

Tramway Company buys perhaps three hundred horses in the year ... The Bombay Tramway Company also took a good many not long ago' ('A Week in Lahore').

40. *the Dora:* a pass in Badakshan, about 150 miles north of Peshawur.
41. *the Black Water:* the sea (at Bombay or some other port).
42. *Ali Musjid:* half-way up the Khyber Pass, ten miles from Jumrud.
43. *Ghor Kuttri:* a building in Peshawur.
44. *Nowshera:* cantonment town, Mirpur district, South-West Kashmir; twenty-five miles east of Peshawur.
45. Jamun ... Ak*:* the *jamun* is a fine-looking fruit-tree, common in many parts of India, whose bitter-sweet fruit resembles the black grape, except that it has a stone like the damson. The *ak*, known outside of north India as the *madar*, is a rather ugly bush.
46. *the Uttock:* district in Punjab where the Kabul River joins the Indus.
47. *Pindigheb:* town in Uttock district, forty miles south of the town of Uttock.
48. *Sialkot:* a district and town about seventy-five miles to the north of Lahore.
49. *the Big Road:* the Grand Trunk Road, which runs from the Khyber Pass to Calcutta.
50. *Shahpur:* district and town about 100 miles west of Sialkot.
51. *the Salt Hills:* the range runs from Rawalpindi south-east across the Indus.
52. *Jhelum:* one of the five great rivers of the Punjab.
53. *the Desert of the Rechna:* the Rechna Doab is an alluvial area between the Rivers Chenab and Ravi in the Punjab.
54. *Sahiwal:* town on the River Jhelum in the Sech Doab, 120 miles west of Lahore.
55. *Jhang, Samundri, and Gugera:* Jhang is on the River Chenab near the junction with the Jhelum; Samundri is thirty miles south of Lyallpur; Gugera is near the River Ravi, twenty miles north-north-west of Montgomery.
56. *Montgomery:* town and district in the centre of the Bart Doab, ninety miles south-west of Lahore.

57. *Fazilka:* town on the River Sutlej, eighty miles south of Lahore.
58. *Rania . . . Bahadurgarh:* Rania is in the Punjab, about sixty-five miles south of Bhatinda; Bahadurgarh is also in the Punjab, about twenty miles west of Delhi.
59. Djinns*:* the devils of Islam.
60. *Hamirpur:* town on the River Jumna, south of Lucknow. The latter part of the journey has been heading generally southeastwards, and the encounter with the Sahib, which is the occasion for the dramatic monologue, is signalled as taking place 'south of Delhi' in the 'lowlands'. Allahabad would be a possible location. (*The Week's News* was, after all, published in Allahabad.)

The Judgment of Dungara

First published in *The Week's News*, 28 July 1888, under the title 'The Peculiar Embarrassment of Justus Krenk'. The epigraph is a misprint of a line from Alexander Smith's *A Life Drama* (1853): 'Like a pale martyr in his shirt of fire'. Smith was one of the poets Kipling read at Westward Ho! (see 'The Last Term', in *Stalky & Co.*).

1. *the Berbulda Hills:* the names of non-European places, peoples and gods in this story seem to be invented: they suggest either a Burmese or an Indian setting.
2. *the Buria Kol:* there is an Indian people called the Kols; *kula* is Sanskrit for caste or tribe; in Burmese, *kula* signifies a native of India.
3. *Tübingen:* a town in Württemberg Hohenzollern, Germany, famous for its university.
4. *Heidelberg:* another famous German university town.
5. *Bannockburn:* town in Stirlingshire, Scotland, best known as the site of Robert the Bruce's victory over the English.
6. *Racine:* not Jean Racine (1639–99), the French dramatist and poet, whose early libertine life was followed by twenty years among the Jansenists of Port Royal; but rather the town of Racine in Wisconsin.
7. *David of St Bees:* unidentified.
8. *the House of Rimmon:* see 2 Kings 5.18.
9. *monarch of all I survey:* from Cowper's poem 'Alexander Selkirk'.

10. *the Curse of Eve:* child-bearing (Genesis 3.16: 'in sorrow thou shalt bring forth children').
11. *the Curse of Adam:* work (Genesis 3.23: 'to till the ground').
12. *Basel:* the seat of the chief missionary society in Switzerland.
13. *to hackle:* to dress (flax or hemp) with a hackle (steel flax-comb), so that the fibres are split, straightened and combed out ready for spinning.
14. *the* tappa *of the South Seas:* see Herman Melville's *Typee* (1846) – especially Chapter XIX, 'Process of Making Tappa' – for a full description of 'the beautiful white tappa generally worn on the Marquesan islands'.
15. Now thank we all our God: translated from the German of M. Rinkart, *Hymns Ancient and Modern*, no. 379.
16. *the Shirt of Nessus:* to save his wife, Deianira, from attempted rape, Hercules shot the centaur Nessus with a poisoned arrow. Nessus took his revenge by giving Deianira his tunic, stained with poisoned blood, telling her it had the power to reclaim an errant husband. When Hercules was unfaithful to her, Deianira sent him the garment, which caused Hercules' death.
17. *Nilgiri Nettle: Nilagiri* (Sanskrit) means 'blue mountain'. It is the name of one of the mythical mountain ranges of Puranic cosmography; it is also the name given to several ranges of hills in Orissa and south India.
18. Girardenia heterophylla: nettles belonging to the genus *Urtica*.
19. *by grace alone:* a play on Jesus's words, 'Man shall not live by bread alone' (Matthew 4.4, alluding to Deuteronomy 8.3).

At Howli Thana

First published in *The Week's News*, 31 March 1888. The Thana is the police station. According to Kipling's *The Naulakha*, Howli is a small town in eastern Rajputana, but Howli and Gokral-Seetarun may both be fictitious.

1. *the Presence:* cf. Arabic *huzur* (literally 'the presence'), a form of humble address.
2. *Havildar:* (Hind.) policeman ranking as a sergeant.
3. *dacoits:* (Hind.) robbers who operate in armed gangs.

4. *Rustums:* Rustum is a Persian hero. He is perhaps best known in England through Arnold's poem 'Sohrab and Rustum'.
5. *Stunt:* corruption of 'Assistant'; Kipling annotated this 'an assistant Commissioner' in his copy of the second Indian edition (now in the Henry W. and Albert A. Berg Collection of the New York Public Library).
6. *Gokral-Seetarun:* in 'The Incarnation of Krishna Mulvaney', the Maharanee of Gokral-Seetarun is described as coming from 'the Central Indian States' (*Life's Handicap*, Penguin Books, p. 50).
7. *Tehsildars:* District Officials; Kipling annotates this 'heads of villages'.
8. *It was here . . . gone: Hamlet*, I.i.142–4.
9. *rapport:* report.
10. *tulwar:* (Hind. *talwar*) a sabre or curved sword.
11. *Dipty Sahib:* i.e. Deputy Collector in charge of a sub-district.
12. *tehsil:* sub-district.
13. *the Sirkar:* (from Persian *sarkar*, 'head of affairs') the State or Government.
14. *the Cold Draw:* a form of torture involving a stick and string tourniquet around the head; hence the 'mark of a string on the temples of Imam Baksh'.
15. *a ghoul:* (Arabic *ghul*) a man-eating demon.
16. *a Peri:* (Persian *pari*, 'the winged one') in Persian mythology, a being of a superhuman race; subsequently used for good djinn and female djinn; later used to mean a woman of great beauty and grace. (See the tale of 'Prince Ahmed and the Peri Banou' in *The Arabian Nights.*)
17. Sirdar-ji*: Sirdar* (Persian *sardar*) a military leader or chief; *ji* is an honorific affix.

Gemini

First published in *The Week's News*, 14 January 1888. Gemini means 'The Twins'.

1. *Ram . . . Durga Dass:* Ram is named after the hero of the Hindu epic the *Ramayana*, a great and just king who is also an avatar (a human incarnation) of the god Vishnu; Durga is one of the names of the Hindu mother-goddess.

2. *a Mahajun . . . Marwar:* a Mahajun (literally 'a great person') is a banker or merchant; Marwar is in Jodhpur.
3. *Mark:* trade sign.
4. *Montgomery:* town and district in the centre of the Bart Doab, ninety miles south-west of Lahore.
5. *the liar:* Durga Dass's assertions about himself and his brother bear some resemblance to Codlin's assertions about himself and Short in Dickens's *The Old Curiosity Shop:* 'Codlin's the friend, not Short. Short's very well as far as he goes, but the real friend is Codlin' (Penguin Books, 1972, p. 207).
6. *a pice:* (Hind. *paisa*) a small copper coin worth a quarter of an anna; i.e. a very small amount of money.
7. *a Nawab:* an Indian ruler.
8. *drank wine:* this is forbidden for a Moslem.
9. *lakh:* (Hind.) 100,000; used here to mean 100,000 rupees.
10. *out-town:* area situated outside the town boundary.
11. *Phagun:* the eleventh month; Kipling annotates this as 'March'.
12. *lac-bangles:* glass bangles for wrists or ankles.
13. *on the Cow's Tail:* the cow is a sacred animal for Hindus, but the oath is Kipling's invention.
14. *the Sirkar:* the Government of India.
15. *Jeysulmir . . . Gurgaon . . . Gogunda:* Jeyselmir is in Rajputana (see map, p. vii); Gurgaon is fifty miles south of Delhi; Gogunda is fifteen miles north of Udaipur.
16. *Belial:* the Spirit of Evil (see Deuteronomy 13.13).
17. *the jujube-tree:* this name is given to at least two species of Zisyphus, a small fruit-bearing tree. Here it is probably *Zisyphus vulgaris*, which is found both wild and cultivated in the Punjab.
18. *Mahadeo:* Shiva, who, in later Hindu mythology, forms a triad with Brahma and Vishnu to represent the three aspects of the Supreme: Brahma the creator, Vishnu the preserver and Shiva the destroyer. He is 'blue-throated' because of the venom of the snake Basuki: when the gods and demons sought to acquire immortality, they tried to use Basuki to bring nectar up from the bottom of the divine sea; Basuki poisoned the sea with his venom, but Shiva drank the poison to clear the water again. See the 'old, old song about the great God Shiv' in 'Toomai of the Elephants', *The Jungle Book* (Penguin Books, p. 142).

19. baba: applied in Anglo-Indian families to children; hence, here, 'young, inexperienced'.
20. *the Jat:* a member of the caste that includes farmers and small-holders.
21. *a cowrie's value:* the cowrie is a small white shell which was used extensively as money in parts of South Asia and Africa. In the late eighteenth century, the exchange rate in Bengal was 5,120 cowries to the rupee.
22. *Caravanserai:* (Persian *karwansarai*) a caravan is a convoy of travellers, and a *serai* is a building for the accommodation of travellers and their pack-animals, consisting of an enclosed yard with chambers round it.

At Twenty-Two

First published in *The Week's News*, 18 February 1888. 'Twenty-Two' is the name of a shaft in a coal-mine. Kipling had seen a coal-mine at Giridh in Bihar, but all the place-names in the story seem to be invented.

1. Sonthal: properly *Santal.* The Santals are a non-Aryan people, settled in the hilly country to the west of the Hooghly River and to the south of Bhagalpur in a district called the Santal Parganas.
2. *Babuji:* Babu (Hind.) is a term of respect. From the extensive employment as clerks in English offices of the class to which the term was applied as a title, 'babu' came to signify 'an Indian clerk who writes English'.
3. *Mehas:* Bangladeshi Moslems, i.e. Bengalis who had converted to Islam.
4. *thill:* Northumberland/Durham miners' term for the thin stratum of fire-clay, etc. that usually underlies a coal-seam; hence the floor or bottom of a seam of coal.
5. *Geordie:* a person from Newcastle.
6. Germinal: a novel by Émile Zola.

In Flood Time

First published in *The Week's News*, 11 August 1888. The epigraph is taken from an old Scottish poem, 'Two Rivers': the Tweed is the border river between England and Scotland; the Till is a tributary that enters the Tweed near Berwick.

1. ekka: (Hind.) light one-horse carriage; Kipling annotates this as 'pony cart'.
2. *ford-elephant:* women and children travelling on foot would be carried across the river on the elephant's back.
3. *mahout:* (Hind. *maha-wat*, 'great in measure') elephant-driver.
4. *Ram Pershad . . . Kala Nag:* for Ram, see 'Gemini', note 1, above; Kala Nag ('Black Snake') is the name given to the elephant hero of 'Toomai of the Elephants' in *The Jungle Book*, and the name of one of the elephants mentioned in J.L. Kipling's *Beast and Man in India* (London, 1891), p. 241.
5. *Bahadur:* (Hind.) hero, champion.
6. *fire-carriage:* the railway.
7. *drink my tobacco:* because the smoke is drawn through water in a hookah (to cool it). Hence the reference to knowing 'how to handle the tube': the mouthpiece on the end of the tube is not put into the mouth, but held between the ring and little finger of the clenched fist, with the thumb and first finger held against the mouth. (See also p. 113.)
8. *Nuklao:* Lucknow.
9. *Wah!:* exclamation of admiration.
10. bunjaras: a nomadic people, who work as carters and entertainers; Kipling's annotation reads 'gypsies'.
11. *a hundred lakhs of maunds:* a hundred lakhs is ten million; a maund is a measure of weight, equivalent to about 80 lbs; therefore a total of around 350,000 tons.
12. Wahi!: exclamation of discomfort.
13. koss: a measurement of distance which varied in different parts of India from one and a quarter to two and a half miles; in Bengal, it is the equivalent of about a mile and a quarter. Kipling annotated this as 'a league'.
14. *bell-bullock:* the herd-leader.
15. *Hanuman:* the Monkey God of Hinduism. He helped Rama to conquer Sri Lanka and to vanquish the demon Ravana.
16. muggers: (Hind. *magar*) crocodiles.

17. *Muttra:* (Matthra) on the River Jumna, thirty miles north-west of Agra; as the birthplace of Krishna, it is one of the seven most sacred Hindu cities.
18. *Jain:* Vaddhamana, better known as Mahavira (the great hero), founder of the Jain religion, was a contemporary of Gautama Buddha. His teaching grew out of the active philosophical speculation and religious inquiry that prevailed in the Gangetic plain during the fifth and sixth centuries B.C.
19. *the Nine Bars:* these include consanguinity and affinity.
20. *Shiahs and Sunnis:* this is the major religious division of Islam. Shi'as (Arabic, 'sect' or 'followers') hold that the Imamate and Caliphate belong hereditarily to the family of Mahommed. They therefore reject the first three Caliphs of the Sunnis as usurpers, and venerate Ali, the Sunnis' fourth Caliph, the cousin and son-in-law of the Prophet, as the first legitimate successor, indeed as the pre-ordained successor. They regard the Caliphate as divinely appointed, and believe that the only authoritative source of doctrine is the Imam. Sunnis (Arabic, 'the people of the Path') believe that the Caliphate was to go by majority vote, but that the Caliph has no interpretative functions and cannot define dogma: they give equal authority to the Koran and to the Sunna, the traditional sayings and decisions of the Prophet, as sources of religious and legal doctrines.
21. karaits*:* the *karait* is a very venomous snake, sometimes known as the 'Bootlace Snake'.
22. *Sikhs . . . tobacco:* founded by guru Nanak (1469–1539) as a monotheistic, quietist and ascetic religion, Sikhism, under persecution from Jahangir (1569–1627), became a militant and political power. Govind Singh (1675–1708), the tenth guru, among other rules, prohibited the use of tobacco.
23. *the lattice-work:* above the level of the railway line.
24. *a Mirzapore stone-boat:* Mirzapore, on the right bank of the Ganges, about thirty miles upstream from Benares, was well known for its sandstone quarries.
25. *careens:* leans over, tilts.
26. *the knotted hair:* long hair worn in a top-knot under the turban, one of the 'Five Ks' established by Govind Singh, identifies the man as a Sikh.

27. *Dried corn . . . without juice:* presumably the Punjabi saying: '*Daaney mook gaie ney. Bootey sook gaie ney*'.
28. *the burning-ghat:* open-air, riverside site for Hindu cremations.
29. Dutt!: 'Kneel!'.

The Sending of Dana Da

First published in *The Week's News*, 11 February 1888. The 'Religion' the story satirizes is clearly Theosophy. In *Something of Myself*, Kipling recorded:

> At one time our little world was full of the aftermaths of Theosophy as taught by Madame Blavatsky to her devotees. My Father knew the lady and, with her, would discuss wholly secular subjects; she being, he told me, one of the most interesting and unscrupulous impostors he had ever met . . . I was not so fortunate, but came across queer, bewildered, old people, who lived in an atmosphere of 'manifestations' running about their houses. But the earliest days of Theosophy devastated the *Pioneer*, whose editor became a devout believer . . . (Penguin Books, 1987, p. 67)

Helena Petrovna Blavatsky (1831–91) founded the Theosophical Society in New York in 1875 with Colonel H.S. Olcott. They came to India in 1879 and set up the Society's headquarters in Adyar near Madras. They visited A.P. Sinnett, the editor of the *Pioneer*, in Allahabad in December 1879 and in Simla in 1880 and 1881. Their visit led to the founding of the Simla Eclectic Theosophical Society and to various 'occult' happenings, to which Kipling alludes in this story. In 1884, Richard Hodgson of the Society for Psychical Research investigated these 'phenomena' and produced a critical report; A.P. Sinnett's reply to Hodgson, *The Occult World Phenomena and the Society for Psychical Research* (London: George Redway, 1886) contains an account of various 'occult' happenings in Simla. Kipling came to work under Sinnett on the *Pioneer* in 1887, and *The Week's News* was subsequently developed as the *Pioneer*'s weekly supplement. For a sympathetic account of Madame Blavatsky, see Sinnett's *Incidents in the Life of Madame Blavatsky* (London: George Redway, 1886); for a hostile account, see J.N. Maskelyne, *The Fraud of Modern 'Theosophy' Exposed* (London: George Routledge & Sons, 1912).

1. *teacups . . . a hair-brush:* Kipling alludes to 'occult' events that took place during Madame Blavatsky's stay at Simla in 1880: the finding of a cup and saucer under the ground at a designated place in the Sinnetts' garden; the discovery of Mrs Hume's lost brooch in a flower-bed; the mending of broken china.
2. Cf. *Hamlet*, I.v.166–7.
3. *postal service:* Kipling alludes to the 'astral letters' that Madame Blavatsky claimed to receive from 'the Mahatmas'. Hodgson, in his report to the Society for Psychical Research, noted that the letters were projected by means of spring contrivances through cracks in the ceiling. Maskelyne asserts that Blavatsky 'invented the precipitation letter dodge': 'They prepared the ceilings of the rooms so that letters would come floating down when required; they prepared a cabinet from which letters to the Mahatmas would disappear and in which replies would arrive . . . broken china placed in it would be miraculously mended' (*The Fraud of Modern 'Theosophy' Exposed*, pp. 37, 50). (The first regular international air-line postal service did not begin until 1919; the first experiments with airmail services were as late as 1911.)
4. *pieces of everything:* in the Preface to *The Secret Doctrine* (London: The Theosophical Publishing Co., 1888), Madame Blavatsky notes that 'the teachings . . . contained in these volumes, belong neither to the Hindu, the Zoroastrian, the Chaldean, nor the Egyptian religion, neither to Buddhism, Islam, Judaism nor Christianity exclusively. The Secret Doctrine is the essence of all these' (I, xviii). She subsequently refers to both the Freemasons (I, xxxvi) and the Rosicrucians (I, 19).
5. *Freemasonry:* a secret society, organized in 'lodges', with an elaborate system of symbolic ritual. Kipling himself became a Freemason on 5 April 1886. See *Something of Myself*, Penguin Books, p. 64.
6. *Rosicrucians:* the Society of Rosicrucians was reputedly founded in 1484 by Christian Rosenkreuz, who, it was claimed, had discovered 'the secret wisdom of the East' on a pilgrimage; it is first evidenced in publications of 1614.
7. *the Vedas:* the Vedas, the ancient, sacred books of Hinduism, in the strict sense consist of three parts – the *Samhitas*, the

Brahmanas, and the *Upanishads*. Generally, however, the term 'Vedas' is used to refer to the *Samhitas* alone, which consists of a collection of hymns in praise of gods (the *Rigveda*), a collection of melodies connected with the hymns (the *Sama Veda*), a collection of sacrificial formulae (the *Yajur-veda*), and a collection of magical formulae (the *Atharvaveda*). Blavatsky included part of the *Rigveda* in *The Secret Doctrine*, where it appears as an extract from 'The Book of Dzyan'.

8. *Zend Avesta:* the sacred books of Zoroastrianism. According to Parsee tradition, there were originally twenty-one books, most of which were burned by Alexander the Great in his conquest of Persia; what is left is known as the Zend-Avesta. This is divided into two parts: the Avesta, which contains the Vendidad (a compilation of religious laws and mythical tales), the Visperad (a collection of litanies for the sacrifice), and the Yasna (a collection of litanies and hymns); and the Khorda (or small) Avesta, which contains short prayers for particular moments of the day, month and year.
9. *Voodoo and Obeah:* kinds of sorcery, of African origin, found in the West Indies and Haiti. Sinnett, in his *Incidents in the Life of Madame Blavatsky*, observed that 'the principal interest' of Blavatsky's 1851 visit to New Orleans 'centred in the Voodoos' (p. 63).
10. *Dana:* Charles Anderson Dana (1819–97). He became part-proprietor of the *New York Sun* in 1867 and editor in 1868. Coincidentally, Dana was to become involved in the history of the Theosophical Society: on 20 July 1890, the *New York Sun* published an article attacking Madame Blavatsky and the Theosophical Society; two years later (26 September 1892), it published an editorial retraction and a reply by William Q. Judge.
11. *Chin, Bhil . . . Nair, Gond:* the Chin are inhabitants of part of Burma; the Bhil, inhabitants of the north-western Deccan; the Nair are from Malabar on the south-west coast of India; the Gond are a hill-people from Central India.
12. *Levantine:* from the countries bordering the eastern Mediterranean.
13. *Parsee:* a descendant of the Zoroastrian Persians who fled to India during the seventh and eighth centuries.

14. *Old Man of the Mountains:* Kipling's version of 'the great Mahatmas, Monya and Koot Hoomi' in the Himalayas, with whom Madame Blavatsky claimed to be in psychic communication.
15. *the esoteric line:* the Theosophical Society professed to expound the esoteric tradition of Buddhism. In *Incidents in the Life of Madame Blavatsky*, Sinnett refers to 'the Esoteric Doctrine or great "Wisdom Religion" of the East' (p. 185), and Madame Blavatsky's aim of communicating some of its ideas to the world at large.
16. chamars: the caste of leather-sellers and shoemakers.
17. *a 'fifth-rounder':* In *Esoteric Buddhism* (London: Trubner & Co., 1883), Sinnett explained: 'Man . . . is evolved in a series of rounds . . . and seven of these rounds have to be accomplished before the destinies of our system are worked out' (p. 47). The present round was the fourth, but it was possible for an exceptional individual to be ahead of their contemporaries – indeed, 'Buddha was a sixth round man' (p. 119). The same ideas are repeated in Blavatsky's *The Secret Doctrine*: 'Gautama Buddha, it was held, was a Sixth-Rounder, Plato and some other great philosophers and minds, Fifth-Rounders' (I.161).
18. *Slade and Houdin:* Henry Slade was an American medium. An associate of Madame Blavatsky and Colonel Olcott, he specialized in slate-writing, partial materializations, and telekinetic phenomena (including levitation and musical instruments 'played by invisible hands'). Robert Houdin (1805–71) was a famous French conjuror. In *Incidents in the Life of Madame Blavatsky*, Sinnett quotes the judgment of 'a Russian gentleman' that, if all the 'phenomena' were 'but jugglery', 'then we have in Madame Blavatsky a woman who beats all the Boscos and Robert Houdins of the century' (p. 161).
19. *sederunt:* (Latin) the sitting of an important body (now chiefly ecclesiastical).
20. *Ra, or Thoth, or Tum:* in Egyptian mythology, Ra was the sun-god; Thoth, his son, was an ibis-headed god; Tum (more usually, Atem or Atum) was the creator-god. (The cat-headed goddess was Bast.)
21. *Sennacherib:* King of Assyria (705–681 B.C.). See 2 Chronicles 32, and Byron's poem 'The Destruction of Sennacherib'.

22. *Ancient Mariner:* see Coleridge's poem 'The Rime of the Ancient Mariner': by killing the albatross, the mariner brings a curse upon his ship and shipmates.
23. *Mizraim and Memphis:* Mizraim is the biblical name for Egypt (Genesis 10.6); Memphis the ancient capital of Egypt; Mizraim and Memphis signify Upper and Lower Egypt. Compare *Something of Myself* (Penguin Books, p. 40), where the reference is probably to Hosea 9.6: 'Egypt shall gather them up, Memphis shall bury them'.
24. *pentacles . . . Triple Tau:* a pentacle is a hexagram made from two intersecting triangles; a pentagram is a five-pointed star (used as a magic symbol); the *crux ansata* (Latin, 'cross with a handle') is the Egyptian cross (the ankh); the swastika (Sanskrit, 'good fortune') is an ancient Indian symbol; the Triple Tau is a sacred symbol. All figure in the 'Proem' to *The Secret Doctrine* (I.5); and the *crux ansata* (II.545–9) and the swastika and tau (II.556–62) are subsequently discussed at some length.
25. '*kittened . . . Dana Da*': perhaps a parody of Byron's 'butchered to make a Roman holiday' (*Childe Harold*, iv.141).
26. *Psychic Current . . . Developing Fluid:* this parody of the language of spiritualism slips from an electrical image by means of a railway metaphor to the language of photographic developing.

On the City Wall

First published in *In Black and White* (Indian Railway Library, Number 3). Kipling had already written an account of communal fighting occasioned by the Mohurrum festival in Lahore in his two-part article, 'The City of Two Creeds', *Civil and Military Gazette*, 19 and 22 October 1885.

1. *Lalun:* see Charles Ames, 'Lalun, the Beragun', *The Kipling Journal*, 114 (July 1955) for Kipling's debt to Mirza Moorad Alleebeg's *Lalun the Bergun* (Bhaunagar: State Press, 1879; reprinted Bombay: Union Press, 2 vols., 1884). *Lalun the Bergun* contains a detailed account of the flight of Mohadji Rao Sindhia, the great Mahratta leader, after his defeat at the Battle of Pannipat (7 January 1761) – see Kipling's ballad, 'With Scindia to Delhi'; see also 'To be Filed for Reference', *Plain Tales from the Hills*, Penguin Books, p. 276.

2. *Lilith:* Adam's first wife. (See D.G. Rossetti's poem 'Eden Bower'.)
3. *the river:* if the story is set in Lahore, the *west* wall faces the River Ravi, and the prostitutes' quarters (near the Taksali Gate) were in the north-west of the city.
4. *tombs of dead Emperors:* perhaps the tomb of Jahangir across the River Ravi at Shahdara.
5. *Red Sauce:* i.e. blood.
6. *Cape Comorin:* at the southern tip of India. Kipling uses the same phrase in a pseudonymous 'Letter to the Editor', *Civil and Military Gazette*, 21 June 1884 (*Kipling's India*, p. 43).
7. *chunam:* a cement made from shell lime and sand.
8. *Sufis:* Islamic mystics. As early as al-Ghazali (d.1111), Neo-platonist ideas and vocabulary had entered into Sufi thought (though subordinated to a Koranic structure), but the system of Ibn al-Arabi of Murcia (d.1240), which had a great influence on later leaders of the Sufi movement, was clearly monist and pantheistic.
9. *Pundits:* (Sanskrit *pandita*) learned men.
10. *the Golden Temple:* the Golden Temple of Amritsar, the Sikh religious centre.
11. *a Jew:* Kipling's own Lodge at Lahore included Moslem, Sikh, Hindu and Jewish members (*Something of Myself*, Penguin Books, p. 64).
12. *some new thing:* see Acts 17.21.
13. *a Demnition Product:* Wali Dad alludes to Mr Mantalini in *Nicholas Nickleby*, who regularly uses 'demnition' as an adjective.
14. *Sivaji:* Sivaji (1627–1680) was the founder of Mahratta power. His name is used here to refer to his descendant Mohadji Rao Sindhia. The 'great battle' is the Battle of Pannipat, which broke the power of the Mahratta Confederacy, and the other 'Lalun' is Lalun the Bergun (see note 1 above).
15. laonee*:* this is based on a *laonee* by Mirza Moorad Alleebeg. The *laonee* is a ballad, which maintains a particular rhythm throughout and repeats its first line (with slight variations). Chimnajee was the father of the Commander-in-Chief of the Mahrattas at Pannipat; the Peishwa was a hereditary Mahratta minister.

16. *Fort Amara:* here clearly Fort Lahore. It was enlarged and repaired by Akbar (1542–1605), the third Mughul Emperor; added to by Shah Jahan (1592–1666), Aurangzeb (1618–1707) and Runjit Singh (1780–1839). In *Something of Myself*, Kipling describes it as 'a mausoleum of ghosts' (Penguin Books, p. 58).
17. *'46 . . . '57 . . . '71:* '46 alludes to the First Sikh War, which began on 11 December 1845, when the Sikh Army crossed the River Sutlej, and ended in February 1846 with a British victory; '57 refers to the Indian Mutiny of 1857–9, otherwise known as the First War of Indian Independence, which began as a mutiny among Indian elements of the East India Company armed forces combined with uprisings among the Marathis; '71 perhaps alludes to the Kuka uprising of 1872 (see p. 162).
18. *Wahabi:* the name used by Europeans for members of the Hanbali school of Sunni Islam, as revived by Muhammed ibn Abd al-Wahhab (1708–92). The revivalist campaign began in Central Arabia around 1744; the movement grew into an important political power (until 1818); it has continued to be a profound religious force. Wahabi doctrine was introduced into India by Saiyid Ahmed (1786–1831), who established a centre in Patna: in 1824, he led an army in a *jihad* (holy war) against the Sikh cities of the Punjab; subsequently the *jihad* was extended to the British and to Hindus.
19. *Burma:* cf. the fate of Bahadur Shah II, the King of Delhi. After his trial in 1859 for his part in the Mutiny, he was condemned by the British to be transported for life to Rangoon.
20. *Sobraon:* the Battle of Sabraon, which took place on 10 February 1846, was a British victory. It was the last of four battles in the Sutlej campaign of the First Sikh War (1845–6).
21. *Kuka:* the Kuka Khel Afridis, who lived in Jamrud and Rajgal.
22. *heterodox women:* presumably courtesans (like Pericles' mistress, Aspasia).
23. *Mohurrum:* a ten-day period of mourning for the two Imams, Hasan and Hussain, the grandsons of the Prophet. (In India Sunnis and Shias both take part in these observances.)
24. *Ladakh:* in the north of Kashmir.
25. *brick-tea:* tea sold as a slab rather than in leaf form.
26. Vox Populi . . . Vox Dei*:* (Latin) 'The voice of the people is the voice of God'.

27. *Padshahi Gate:* ('King's Gate') in the north-west corner of Lahore.
28. *'Into thy hands . . .':* Luke 23.46.
29. *the Sirkar:* the Government.
30. *the Club:* presumably the Punjab Club on the Mall. In *Something of Myself*, Kipling describes it as 'the centre' of his world in Lahore, a place where 'bachelors, for the most part, gathered to eat meals of no merit among men whose merit they knew well' (Penguin Books, p. 58).
31. *Kumharsen Gate:* 'Gate of the Potters'.
32. bunnias*:* shopkeepers.
33. *'Two Lovely Black Eyes':* a music-hall song of the 1880s, written by Charles Coborn (1852–1946).

Appendix A:
Soldiers Three *and Associated Stories*

GROUP 1. Three stories which first appeared in *The Civil and Military Gazette* – 'The Three Musketeers' (March 1887); 'The Taking of Lungtungpen' (April 1887); 'The Daughter of the Regiment' (May 1887) – together with 'The Madness of Private Ortheris', which was collected with them in *Plain Tales from the Hills* (Calcutta: A.H. Wheeler & Co., 1888).

GROUP 2. Six stories which first appeared in *The Week's News* – 'The God from the Machine' (January 1888), 'The Big Drunk Draf'' (March 1888), 'In the Matter of a Private' (April 1888), 'The Solid Muldoon' (June 1888), 'Private Learoyd's Story' (July 1888), 'With the Main Guard' (August 1888) – together with 'Black Jack', which was collected with them in *Soldiers Three* (Calcutta: A.H. Wheeler & Co., 1888).

GROUP 3. Three stories which first appeared in *Macmillan's Magazine* – 'The Incarnation of Krishna Mulvaney' (December 1889), 'The Courting of Dinah Shadd' (March 1890), 'On Greenhow Hill' (August 1890) – and were collected in *Life's Handicap* (London: Macmillan, 1891).

GROUP 4. Two stories which were published in *Macmillan's Magazine* – 'His Private Honour' (October 1891) and 'My Lord the Elephant' (January 1893) – together with 'Love-o'-Women', which was collected with them in *Many Inventions* (London: Macmillan, 1893). ('My Lord the Elephant' was first published in *The Civil and Military Gazette*, December 1892.)

GROUP 5. 'Garm – A Hostage', which first appeared in the *Saturday Evening Post* (December 1899) and was collected in *Actions and Reactions* (London: Macmillan, 1909).

Appendix B: Mulvaney's Career

The first Mulvaney story, 'The Three Musketeers', was written shortly before Kipling left Lahore for Allahabad in 1887. Many of the stories are located in or near Lahore, involving a regiment stationed at the Mian Mir cantonment or a detachment at 'Fort Amara'. The East Lancashire regiment were at Mian Mir from 1880 to 1885, and some of its members had fought at the battle of Ahmed Khel in 1880. Kipling also knew members of the 5th Northumberland Fusiliers (who were stationed at Mian Mir from 1886 to 1888) and the 31st East Surrey Regiment (whom he met at Allahabad in 1888). The 'Black Tyrone' owes something to the 18th Royal Irish Regiment, whom Kipling came in contact with at Simla, but the 'three musketeers' and their regiments are clearly composites. Mulvaney, Ortheris and Learoyd serve in Afghanistan, Burma and on the North-West Frontier, but no British line regiment served in all three campaigns. 'The Taking of Lungtungpen', as Charles Carrington has noted, was derived from a news item in *The Civil and Military Gazette* (1 January 1887) about an incident involving soldiers of the Queen's (Royal West Surrey) Regiment, while Mulvaney and Ortheris are perhaps indebted to Sergeant Kearney and Sergeant-major Schofield, the two veterans employed successively as 'school sergeants' at Westward Ho!. Kearney, an Irishman, delighted in talking about the Sikh Wars of the 1840s; Schofield, like Ortheris, was a Londoner (he appears as 'Foxy' in *Stalky & Co.*).

Mulvaney 'had served with various regiments from Bermuda to Halifax' ('The Incarnation of Krishna Mulvaney'), but only two are named – the 'Ould' Regiment and the 'Black Tyrone'. His transfer from one to the other coincides with the introduction of the Martini-Henry rifle as general issue in India (i.e. 1874–5). A rough chronology of his career would place his birth in Leinster in the late 1840s; his recruitment into the Tyrones in the 1860s; and his transfer to the 'Ould' Regiment in the mid 1870s. He fought at the Battle of Ahmed Khel in the Second Afghan War in 1880, served in Upper Burma against King Thebaw during 1885–6, told his stories to the narrator during 1885–7, and left the Army on pension around 1888 to work as a civilian on the Indian Railways ('The Big Drunk Draf''). He married Dinah Shadd during the 1870s.

READ MORE IN PENGUIN

In every corner of the world, on every subject under the sun, Penguin represents quality and variety – the very best in publishing today.

For complete information about books available from Penguin – including Puffins, Penguin Classics and Arkana – and how to order them, write to us at the appropriate address below. Please note that for copyright reasons the selection of books varies from country to country.

In the United Kingdom: Please write to *Dept. JC, Penguin Books Ltd, FREEPOST, West Drayton, Middlesex UB7 OBR*

If you have any difficulty in obtaining a title, please send your order with the correct money, plus ten per cent for postage and packaging, to *PO Box No. 11, West Drayton, Middlesex UB7 OBR*

In the United States: Please write to *Penguin USA Inc., 375 Hudson Street, New York, NY 10014*

In Canada: Please write to *Penguin Books Canada Ltd, 10 Alcorn Avenue, Suite 300, Toronto, Ontario M4V 3B2*

In Australia: Please write to *Penguin Books Australia Ltd, 487 Maroondah Highway, Ringwood, Victoria 3134*

In New Zealand: Please write to *Penguin Books (NZ) Ltd,182–190 Wairau Road, Private Bag, Takapuna, Auckland 9*

In India: Please write to *Penguin Books India Pvt Ltd, 706 Eros Apartments, 56 Nehru Place, New Delhi 110 019*

In the Netherlands: Please write to *Penguin Books Netherlands B.V., Keizersgracht 231 NL–1016 DV Amsterdam*

In Germany: Please write to *Penguin Books Deutschland GmbH, Friedrichstrasse 10–12, W–6000 Frankfurt/Main 1*

In Spain: Please write to *Penguin Books S. A., C. San Bernardo 117–6° E–28015 Madrid*

In Italy: Please write to *Penguin Italia s.r.l., Via Felice Casati 20, I–20124 Milano*

In France: Please write to *Penguin France S. A., 17 rue Lejeune, F–31000 Toulouse*

In Japan: Please write to *Penguin Books Japan, Ishikiribashi Building, 2–5–4, Suido, Tokyo 112*

In Greece: Please write to *Penguin Hellas Ltd, Dimocritou 3, GR–106 71 Athens*

In South Africa: Please write to *Longman Penguin Southern Africa (Pty) Ltd, Private Bag X08, Bertsham 2013*

READ MORE IN PENGUIN

Penguin Twentieth-Century Classics offer a selection of the finest works of literature published this century. Spanning the globe from Argentina to America, from France to India, the masters of prose and poetry are represented by the Penguin.

If you would like a catalogue of the Twentieth-Century Classics library, please write to:

Penguin Marketing, 27 Wrights Lane, London W8 5TZ

(Available while stocks last)

READ MORE IN PENGUIN

A CHOICE OF TWENTIETH - CENTURY CLASSICS

The Sea of Fertility Yukio Mishima

'Mishima's thrilling storytelling is unique; there is nothing like it. His flashing style is perfect for his dark motives and there are times when his words are so splendid, and his concepts so tragic, that reading him becomes a profound experience' – Ronald Blythe in the *Sunday Times*

Nineteen Eighty-Four George Orwell

'It is a volley against the authoritarian in every personality, a polemic against every orthodoxy, an anarchistic blast against every unquestioning conformist ... *Nineteen Eighty-Four* is a great novel and a great tract because of the clarity of its call, and it will endure because its message is a permanent one: erroneous thought is the stuff of freedom' – Ben Pimlott

The Outsider Albert Camus

Meursault leads an apparently unremarkable bachelor life in Algiers, until his involvement in a violent incident calls into question the fundamental values of society. 'Few French writers of this century have been more versatile or more influential than Camus ... No one in his lifetime wrote better prose than he, no one better blended conviction and grace of style' – *The Times*

Mittee Daphne Rooke

Daphne Rooke is one of South Africa's finest post-war novelists and *Mittee*, set in nineteenth-century Transvaal, remains her masterpiece. Juxtaposing violence and sexuality, the novel is a searing indictment of the alienation created by the excesses of Afrikaaner nationalism.

The Home and the World Rabindranath Tagore

Rabindranath Tagore's powerful novel, set on a Bengali noble's estate in 1908, is both a love story and a novel of political awakening. 'It has the complexity and tragic dimensions of Tagore's own time, and ours' – Anita Desai

READ MORE IN PENGUIN

A CHOICE OF TWENTIETH -CENTURY CLASSICS

The Grand Babylon Hotel Arnold Bennett

Focusing on Theodore Racksole's discovery of the world inside the luxury hotel he purchased on a whim, Arnold Bennett's witty and grandiose serial records the mysterious comings and goings of the eccentric aristocrats, stealthy conspirators and great nobles who grace the corridors of the Grand Babylon.

Mrs Dalloway Virginia Woolf

Into *Mrs Dalloway* Virginia Woolf poured all her passionate sense of how other people live, remember and love as well as hate, and in prose of astonishing beauty she struggled to catch, impression by impression and minute by minute, the feel of life itself.

The Counterfeiters André Gide

'It's only after our death that we shall really be able to hear'. From puberty through adolescence to death, *The Counterfeiters* is a rare encyclopedia of human disorder, weakness and despair.

The Great Wall of China and Other Short Works Franz Kafka

This volume contains the major short works left by Kafka, including *Blumfeld*, *An Elderly Bachelor*, *The Great Wall of China* and *Investigations of a Dog*, together with *The Collected Aphorisms* and *He: Aphorisms from the 1920 Diary*.

The Guide R. K. Narayan

'There is something almost Irish in the humour, buzz and blarney of Narayan's world which seems continents removed from the anguished India of most fiction, and the rope trick of irony, fun and feeling is beautifully adroit' – *Observer*

The Fight Norman Mailer

In 1975, at the World Heavyweight Boxing Championship in Kinshasa, Zaïre, an ageing Muhammad Ali met George Foreman in the ring. Mesmeric and profound, *The Fight* covers the tense weeks of preparation and the fight itself.

READ MORE IN PENGUIN

A CHOICE OF TWENTIETH - CENTURY CLASSICS

Despair Vladimir Nabokov

'*Despair* is about murder and madness but in artistic terms it is a work of rapture – jolting, hilarious and incredibly racy' – Martin Amis in *The Times*. 'One of Mr Nabokov's finest, most challenging and provocative novels' – *The New York Times*

Remembrance of Things Past (3 volumes) Marcel Proust

'What an extraordinary world it is, the universe that Proust created! Like all great novels, *A la Recherche* has changed and enlarged our vision of the "real" world in which we live' – Peter Quennell

Victory Joseph Conrad

Marked by a violent and tragic conclusion, *Victory* is both a tale of rescue and adventure and a perceptive study of a complex relationship and of the power of love.

Travels With My Aunt Graham Greene

Henry Pulling, a retired bank manager, meets his septuagenarian Aunt Augusta for the first time in over fifty years at what he supposes to be his mother's funeral. Soon after, she persuades Henry to abandon Southwood, his dahlias and the Major next door to travel her way – Brighton, Paris, Istanbul, Paraguay …

Chance Acquaintances and **Julie de Carneilhan** Colette

'She said what no man could have said, and she spoke of sensations and feelings as nobody had spoken of them before, for none of the great women of letters who had preceded her had lived in an age of such great freedom of expression' – André Maurois

Letters and Journals Katherine Mansfield

'She has the rare talent of being able to address herself intimately to anyone … The particularity and vividness of the writing is an extension of the particularity and vividness of the personality, and it is everywhere present' – C. K. Stead

READ MORE IN PENGUIN

A CHOICE OF TWENTIETH - CENTURY CLASSICS

Between the Acts Virginia Woolf

'Her posthumous novel ... suggests several new directions ... Its weave of past and present, quotidian reality and imminent catastrophe, the thin line between civilization and barbarism, its erotic overtones and continual humour make a powerful and prophetic statement' – *The Times*

Gentlemen Prefer Blondes Anita Loos

Gentlemen Prefer Blondes had its first acclaimed appearance in *Harpers Bazaar* and was later made famous on stage and screen. In this brilliant satire of the Jazz Age Anita Loos has created the funniest Bad Blonde in American literature.

The Living and the Dead Patrick White

To hesitate on the edge of life or to plunge in and risk change – this is the dilemma explored in *The Living and the Dead*. 'Scene after scene is worked out with an exactness and subtlety which no second-string novelist can scent, far less nail to paper' – *Time*. 'He is, in the finest sense, a world novelist' – *Guardian*

Go Tell It on the Mountain James Baldwin

'*Mountain* is the book I had to write if I was ever going to write anything else. I had to deal with what hurt me most. I had to deal with my father' – James Baldwin. 'Passionately eloquent' – *The Times*

Memories of a Catholic Girlhood Mary McCarthy

Blending memories and family myths, Mary McCarthy takes us back to the twenties, when she was orphaned in a world of relations as colourful, potent and mysterious as the Catholic religion. 'Superb ... so heartbreaking that in comparison Jane Eyre seems to have got off lightly' – Anita Brookner